"S   : the

w   A in

"   ed!"

"]   how
Nic   o take

"   na,

En   e's
                                                     TER!"

04871240

Nicky Wells

Sophie's Encore

Part 3 in the Rock Star Romance Trilogy

Her rock star is waiting in the wings, but will he get a second chance?

Sapphire Star Publishing
www.sapphirestarpublishing.com
First Sapphire Star Publishing trade paperback edition, September 2013

The characters and events in this book are fictitious. Names, characters, places, and plots are a product of the author's imagination. Any similarity to real persons, living or dead, is coincidental and not intended by the author.

ISBN-13: 978-1-938404-65-8

Cover design: Nicky Wells and Chad Lichtenhan

Cover image: Singer in the darkness © Dmytro Konstantynov

Author photograph by Deborah Smith

www.sapphirestarpublishing.com/nickywells

Dedication

For Richard.
You planted the idea but you never got the chance to see the results.

PART ONE:
New Beginnings

Chapter One

"So how is Dan?"

"Dan?" My best friend's unexpected departure from our lively debate about suitable baby names momentarily blindsided me.

"Yes, Dan. You know, rock star extraordinaire, lead singer of mega-rock band Tuscq, erstwhile boyfriend, now godfather to your children. *Dan.*" Rachel's voice was sweetness and innocence but her meaning was clear. I played dumb, as I always did.

"How should I know? I suppose he's off recording or something. I haven't seen him for a while."

Rachel raised her eyebrows at me and grinned. She turned onto her side, gently supporting her bump with her left hand, and with her other hand she fumbled under the sofa to retrieve a pair of men's socks. I nearly choked on my wine as she waved them under my nose.

"These aren't yours, are they, so they must be his, right? Or are there any other lovers you're hiding from me?"

"Dan isn't my lover, and you know that full well." I tried to keep my tone light despite the familiar lump building in my throat. I set my glass on the coffee table and folded my arms in front of my chest. Trust Rachel to spoil our cozy Sunday night in with her merciless probing into matters that didn't concern her.

"For a married woman, you still have a surprisingly devious mind."

Rachel pretended to be hurt. "I don't! I'm just saying it as it is. He still loves you, you know."

"If you must know," I enunciated carefully, determined to ignore her blatant announcement and the shiver of confusion it sent through me, "Dan was visiting a few days ago. He was probably playing with Josh and—"

"…and he took his socks off, as one does. I get it." Rachel had that teasing look in her eyes.

"Rachel, stop. Stop it right there." My voice emerged in a tremulous quiver. Tears brimmed at the back of my eyes and I blinked rapidly.

"Dan wouldn't…he couldn't…he knows I can't…"

Rachel pushed herself into a sitting position, grunting slightly as she shifted her weight. Slowly and carefully, she rose and waddled across the room to join me on my sofa. She put her arm around me and squeezed gently.

"Sophie, my love. You're still young. We're only in our thirties! You have to live again. You have to open your eyes and see—"

"I can't!"

There, she had done it. The tears spilled down my face and I swiped at them angrily. "I can't, Rachel, I *can't*. I still miss Steve. I miss him so! He's gone, I know, and I can't have him back but I *want* him back. It hurts, it really hurts, I miss him every day and I want him back, I want him back."

I let the tears run freely now. It would have been futile to halt the emotion; I had to go through this and come out the other side, again.

"Shh," Rachel soothed. "Shh, it's all right, it's okay. I'm sorry."

"It's not all right," I exploded at her. "It's totally not all right. You don't understand, you haven't got a clue what it's like to lose your husband." My voice rose with every word and I ended up shouting.

Rachel yelled right back at me. "I *do* understand. I understand you perfectly. It's you who won't let anyone into your world, won't let anyone near you. And I'm *sick* of seeing you consumed by this endless grief. It's been nearly three years. *Three* years, Sophie, you have to move on!"

We looked at each other in shock, stunned by our sudden outburst. The house was deadly silent and we hardly dared breathe while we waited to hear if we had woken the little occupants. But no, all remained quiet.

"Less than two-and-a-half," I corrected softly. "Two years, three months and twenty-one days, to be precise."

Rachel took a deep breath before she spoke again. "Sweetie, Sophie. That's exactly what I mean. You're still counting the days. You have to stop. You have to move on. Steve wouldn't want this."

I shrugged. She didn't understand, no matter what she said. Nobody understood. How could they, anyway? I had given up trying to explain how bereft and lonely I felt, there was no point.

"I know, I know," I said, as if relenting. "I'll try."

Rachel narrowed her eyes and searched my face. "You promise?"

3

"I promise. Now how's about some kind of snack?" I jumped to my feet and clapped my hands energetically. Comfort food was my emergency Band-Aid and I always had a freezer full of suitably unhealthy meals. "Pizza?"

Rachel snorted with laughter. "Not for me, thanks. I'm already the size of a house. But...*oooh*!"

There was a weird popping sound, barely audible but I caught it anyway. Rachel looked aghast as water ran down her legs, a trickle at first but increasing to a bit of a gush before suddenly petering out. Nonetheless, her trousers were saturated and she lumbered to her feet.

"I think I wet myself," she muttered. "I should have done more pelvic exercises."

I suppressed a giggle and took her hand.

"You didn't wet yourself, lovey. Your waters broke!"

Chapter Two

"My waters broke?"

Rachel sounded mildly hysterical, and I couldn't blame her. After all, the baby would be two weeks early and Rachel's husband was in Dubai right at this very moment with his job. That was why she was staying with me in the first place. So she wouldn't be alone in case… Well, in case. And 'in case' had just happened.

"Your waters broke," I repeated. "But don't panic, it might be hours before you start contracting. We'd better ring Alex, though." I was scrabbling for my phone when Rachel doubled over in agony, panting heavily. She held out a hand to me and I rushed to her side.

"*Ooomph,*" she wailed after a few seconds. "That wasn't Braxton Hicks!" She straightened up and rubbed her back.

"I suppose not," I concurred. "We'd probably best get sorted."

"My baby is coming," Rachel announced, fear and joy dancing in her eyes in equal measure.

"It certainly is," I squealed, infected by her excitement, and we had a quick little hug.

"What should I do now?"

I shrugged. "Get some clean trousers on, first of all. And then... do whatever feels natural. Walk around, sit down...whatever. Leave the organizing to me."

While Rachel went to get changed, I set about the task of tracking down her elusive husband. He was an international security consultant and his work took him all over the world. He hadn't wanted to go on this assignment to the Middle East, but it was supposed to be his last foreign trip before fatherhood, and he was due back in a few days. Only, it appeared, his baby wasn't inclined to wait for him.

Owing to the time difference, I couldn't get hold of Alex so I left a ton of messages with various secretaries and two on his mobile phone. Meanwhile, Rachel had come back into the lounge, dressed in maternity jogging bottoms and a loose shirt. She grabbed the phone off me to try reaching her husband herself, and I scuttled upstairs to gather together a few essentials for her. Thank goodness I had been secretly stocking up for a surprise layette. I also assembled her overnight bag and had a quick look at my peacefully slumbering offspring before venturing back downstairs to see how labor was progressing.

Rapidly, was the answer to that. I had never seen anything like it, and my own two sets of labor had been protracted and painful. Rachel, it seemed, was going for the birthing speed record.

"Are you sure you haven't done this before?" I tried to joke while I rubbed her back through another contraction, but she merely grunted in return. My watch told me that she was contracting every six minutes. It wouldn't be long before we needed to go to the hospital.

"I haven't," she finally spoke. "And I can already tell you, I ain't doing it again."

I smiled but swallowed my response. Instead, I suggested that I should ring the hospital to give them warning of her impending arrival.

Suddenly frightened, Rachel clutched my arm. "How am I going to get there? How am I going to cope? Oh Soph, don't leave me alone!"

I hugged her tightly — well, as tightly as I could, under the circumstances. "I'm going to take you there, and I'm going to stay with you, don't worry."

"Really?"

"Why, of course!"

"But...the kids? You can't just leave the kids!" Rachel's mind latched onto all sorts of little obstacles.

"I'm going to get a babysitter, just hang on a sec." I disengaged from our emotional embrace and picked up the phone yet again. Dan answered on the fourth ring. I could hear guitars and drums and loud voices at the other end; it sounded like Dan was in the studio, but I didn't give him time to speak.

"Hey, listen, I know this is probably *really* inconvenient, but I need you to come and sit with Josh and Emily, like, right now. Rachel is having her baby and Alex is away." My plea emerged rushed and without pause, communicating the urgency of my request.

Having long since become used to the unpredictable demands of parenting-by-proxy, Dan stepped up to the challenge without missing a beat. "I'll be there in twenty," he promised.

Twenty minutes. An eternity for me, Rach, and the baby, but it couldn't be helped. In fact, we would all be lucky if he did make it that quickly, unless he was in one of the recording studios this side of the river.

But luck was with us, and Dan walked in exactly eighteen minutes after he had hung up the telephone. He looked exhausted but radiant and carried a cold take-away pizza.

"Hello, gorgeous," he greeted and gave me a swift hug and a kiss on the cheek. "It's all happening, huh?" He grinned his trademark Dan smile.

"It certainly is," I grinned back. "Thank you so much for dropping everything and getting here so fast. I'm sorry if I pulled you out of the studio."

"It's absolutely fine." Dan was unperturbed. "We had a good session, and we were winding up anyway. Now I get to put my feet up and finally eat my pizza, once it's hot again." He walked through to the kitchen and switched on the oven, rooting in one of my drawers for the greaseproof paper to line the baking tray. A couple of years of coming to my house at any hour of the day or night in response to all manner of emergency requests had given him near-proprietorial familiarity with my home and belongings.

My tummy rumbled impressively and I remembered that neither Rachel nor I had ever had our unhealthy snack in all the excitement. In fact, Rachel probably ought to be eating something to get herself through the next few hours.

As though reading my mind, Dan walked to the lounge door and had a peek. "How's mum-to-be?" he whispered.

"I heard that," Rachel called to him. "Come on in and give a laboring woman a hug."

Dan obligingly strolled through and enveloped Rachel in a tender embrace. "You're doing just fine," he assured her.

"As if you'd know," Rachel grunted back.

"He does, actually," I offered gently. "He's seen me through labor, remember?"

Dan and I exchanged a wistful look. Emily had been born a little over two years after her older brother Josh, but just four weeks after I lost Steve. I was at the height of grief then; I was angry and lonely and very confused. Dan helped me through her birth and didn't once bat an eyelid when I cursed him for not being Steve. He was the first person to hold Emily, and the bond of love between them had been instant.

I forced myself to abandon that train of thought and focus on the present.

"Do you want something to eat before it's time to go to the hospital?" I asked quietly. Rachel pursed her mouth and mimed being sick. "I couldn't possibly."

"You should keep your strength up," I persisted.

"I got pizza," Dan offered helpfully.

"I don't...want...to eat.... *Owww!*" Rachel barely managed to register her protest before the next contraction swept her up. I consulted my watch.

"That's every five minutes," I announced. "Time to go."

Rachel looked at me with wide, scared eyes and sank onto the sofa. "I'm scared. I want to stay here."

"Time to go," I reiterated. "Come on, Dan, help me get her up and into the car."

Dan obligingly held out his arm and carefully pulled Rachel to her feet while I gathered up her things and led the way to my little Golf, parked — for once — conveniently right outside the house. I opened the passenger door and Rachel let herself be settled in the seat. I closed her door and allowed myself a brief moment of catching my breath while I leaned against the car. In truth, I dreaded the trip to the hospital with all the memories it would bring, but I didn't have a choice.

Seeing me hovering, Dan frowned and made shooing hand gestures. "What are you still doing here? Get going, there's a baby waiting to be born."

"I—"

"I know," Dan interrupted me and took my hands in his. "I'll go check on Josh and Emily in a minute. If you're not back by morning, Josh..." he petered out. "Actually, I can't remember what Josh needs to do, or Emily, but I know you've got their schedules stuck to the fridge and we'll all be absolutely fine."

I surrendered and let the moment go, not knowing what I had intended to say in the first place.

"Are you sure this is all okay?" I asked instead. "Only it's too late to call an agency sitter and the kids will be much better..."

"...with their godfather. Yes, it's absolutely okay," Dan assured me. "Now go and take care of Rachel before she sprogs in your car."

Chapter Three

Dan was asleep on the sofa when I arrived back home at six-thirty, bone weary, but somehow exuberant. I crept into the kitchen to brew a pot of strong coffee. There was hardly any point in going to bed as the kids would be up shortly, and besides, I was too wired. I had finished setting out the cereal and fruit on the table when I heard the soft pitter patter of bare feet coming down the stairs. Josh was an early riser and, having found my bed empty, would be searching excitedly for me, thinking I had staged an unexpected game of hide-and-seek. Gleeful shouts of "Dan, Dan" indicated that he had ventured into the lounge first. The tableau that greeted me in the living room was as familiar as it was bittersweet. Josh was astride Dan's tummy, playing jelly-on-a-plate, while Dan flopped about like a stranded jellyfish.

The squeals of laughter from both boys had woken Emily, who started shouting for Dan before she had even made it down the stairs. Dan's face lit up like a Christmas tree when his favorite goddaughter hurled herself at him, covering his face in smoochy kisses. Why this man, who so clearly adored children, had never managed to create a family of his own was a mystery.

Finally Dan noticed me standing in the doorway and flashed me one of his happiest smiles. "Good morning, lovely," he managed between gulps of laughter. "How's Rachel? Is it a girl or a boy?"

"It's a boy." I smiled. "Born at four a.m., healthy and happy. Henry, she's called him. Alex didn't make it, obviously, but he's on his way."

"That's wonderful." Dan huffed and puffed and gently disentangled himself from my children. He sat up, rubbing his face, and tried to smooth his unruly hair. "Shall we have some breakfast?"

"Oh, yes pease," Emily chanted. "Dan stay for brekkie, Dan stay for brekkie."

I filled Dan in on developments in the hospital in between feeding Emily her cereal and buttering toast for Josh. Dan made bacon and eggs for us, and I ate greedily. The kids paid no attention whatsoever to me, focusing entirely on the only man in their lives. Dan basked in their adoration, and he lapped up the unconditional love bestowed on him by my brood. But he had also learned to be a practical godfather, and at eight o'clock, he whisked Josh and Emily upstairs to get dressed and washed while I tidied up the kitchen.

"Why don't I take Josh to playschool and Emily to her playgroup while you catch up on some sleep?" Dan suggested once the three of them were back downstairs, brushed, dressed, and ready for action.

I suppressed a mighty yawn and put up some token resistance. "Are you sure? Shouldn't you be somewhere else, back in the studio, say?"

A belly laugh greeted this inane question. "Sophie, I very much doubt that any other members of Tuscq will surface before midday. I'm due back in the studio at two this afternoon, so I can easily spend some time with my loan family this morning."

I hugged him tight, leaning against his broad shoulder for a second. "Why you guys don't get up early and work normal hours like normal people is beyond me," I mumbled. "If you got in there before nine, you could easily put in a twelve-hour day *and* get some sleep."

"True," Dan concurred. "But we're not normal people, and we like working through the night." He squeezed me gently before letting me go. "Off to bed with you. I'll bring the kids back at twelve."

The front door slammed behind the three of them before I could raise any further objection, and the house turned eerily quiet. It wasn't often that I had three hours to myself, and I was tempted to get dusting and cleaning, or dig out a good book from somewhere. But I was absolutely dead on my feet, so I had a quick bath instead and snuggled gratefully under my duvet.

When Dan returned with the kids at lunchtime, he looked distinctly worse for wear. His very short night was beginning to take its toll, and I suggested it was his turn to have a nap before going back to the studio.

"You are a rock," he told me gratefully and gave me a hug that lifted me clean off my feet.

"How was playgroup?" I asked by way of response to his affection. "Did Ella's mum make moon eyes at you again?"

Most of my mum-friends had taken it in stride when Dan had started helping out in my life nearly three years ago, putting in appearances at play groups and acting as devoted babysitter. Many of them knew vaguely of our history, and it was no secret in Barnes that Dan used to hang out with the Jones family when we were still complete. Yet the occasional acquaintance here or there couldn't quite reconcile the image of Dan-the-rock-star with Dan-the-almost-family-man.

"She did," Dan chuckled. "It was quite entertaining. I made meaningful eyes back at her over the teapot song." He cleared his throat and erupted into song. "I'm a little teapot, short and stout…"

I burst out laughing. "You never. Poor Ella's mum." Ella's mum was a little on the short and stout side herself. "She'll be upset."

"I don't think she got it," Dan mumbled and yawned. "I think I'll repair to your guest room for forty winks, if the offer still stands."

"'Course it does," I declared, "and thank you for giving me a morning off."

While Dan took himself upstairs, I had lunch with the children. Afterwards, I took them to the hospital to meet Rachel and her new baby.

My best friend was still in the first twenty-four hours of full-on hormonal glow and overdrive. Baby Henry was installed in a crib by her bed, looking very tiny and very peaceful, until my own kids blundered in, full of excitement at seeing this brand new life. I shushed them, but Rachel was serene and forgiving.

"Come here, my little darlings," she cooed, and invited Emily and Josh for a big hug each. My children mollified, she carefully lifted a now screaming Henry out of his crib and settled him on her lap for my children to admire.

"He's quite red and ugly," Josh observed with the deadpan nonchalance of his four years.

"Why baby sad?" Emily wanted to know.

"Because you startled him awake," I explained. I looked at Henry's beetroot face, screwed up in indignation and bordering on incandescence. So tiny, and yet so powerful.

Rachel's cheerful serenity crumbled as she failed to calm her unsettled infant, and I deftly took Henry off her, settling him on my shoulder and patting his bottom. He snuffled and continued protesting, but as I had comforted both my kids through endless colicky nights, a tiny newborn wail was water off a duck's back for me.

"He doesn't need feeding," Rachel supplied before I could ask. "And he's had a new nappy. I don't know what else to do." Tears shimmered in her eyes, and I remembered the bewilderment and uncertainty that came with being a first-time mum.

"He's fine," I soothed. "Only a bit disgruntled. He'll settle in a minute." Right on cue, Henry gave a contented snuffle and drifted off to sleep. "There, there," I muttered and transferred him carefully onto Rachel's shoulder. Henry snuffled again and snuggled down for the duration. Rachel smiled at me and breathed deeply.

"Thank you," she mouthed and I blew her a silent kiss in return.

Caught up in the moment of pure mummy-bliss, I noticed with only seconds to spare that my own offspring, by now thoroughly bored, had set up camp under the hospital bed and were working up to an enormous fight over Rachel's fluffy slippers. I performed a swift toddler-extraction maneuver, grabbing a child with each hand and sliding them out from under the bed, before saying a quiet farewell to Rachel and Henry.

"That was fun," Emily announced when we were back in the car. "I like baby. I want baby."

I threw her a look in the rearview mirror. She had plugged her thumb in and was sucking ferociously. She would probably be asleep within minutes.

"Where was our daddy when we were born?" Josh piped up from the backseat. "And will he come back from the airport soon, too?"

"Want Dada, want Dada," Emily chimed in obligingly. As was normal on these occasions, I felt like someone had punched me in the stomach. I tried to concentrate on the road while summoning up a coherent response. And here I was thinking they had accepted Dan as the substitute father figure in their little lives. Ignoring the real question, I offered an explanation I had given many times before.

"Daddy was there when you were born, Josh," I said calmly. "He was very proud. And Dan..." I paused. Not for the first time, I questioned whether it was appropriate to bring Dan into the conversation in the same breath as Steve. Yet he connected our past with our present, and that felt right. "Dan was outside the room. He was the first one to hold you after Daddy and me." I checked his reaction in the mirror. Thumb in, eyes wide open, he was listening.

Taking my grief into the customary stranglehold, I addressed Emily. "Daddy couldn't be there when you were born." I swallowed hard and continued with my rehearsed answer. "He sent you a big kiss, and he loves you very, very much."

"Dan," Emily uttered around her thumb.

"Yes, sweetie, Dan was there with me when you were born. He was the first person to hold you, even before me. He loves you very much, too."

"He's our godfather," Josh supplied eagerly.

I exhaled. "He *is* your godfather," I confirmed. "Both of yours. And look—" I launched into a diversionary tactic as I was reeling with pain and reluctant to go any further with this talk. "There's our favorite pizza place, and it's open *and* it's got a parking space right out front. Shall we go there for lunch?" Not waiting for an answer, I had already pulled in and parked.

"But mummy, we've *had* lunch," Josh offered.

Oh yes. So we had.

"Never mind, let's have *two* lunches today. What do you say?" I turned around to face the kids, and their faces lit up.

Josh initiated negotiations straightaway. "Can I have ice cream for pudding?"

"Cake, me want cake," Emily piped up predictably.

"Yes," I laughed, "yes, you can have ice cream, and cake. Let's go."

Chapter Four

The rest of the week passed in a blur. Rachel was allowed home on the very day Henry was born, and from that moment on, I was on emergency standby for all the little disasters that befall brand new parents. Alex was back from Dubai, of course, but he was just as bewildered as Rachel. Rach, in turn, developed a bout of baby blues, and by Thursday morning, she was a tearful wreck.

"What is it with these damned nappies?" she demanded as she held a sodden Henry up to me when Emily and I walked through the door, forgetting that a pair of little ears would later seize on the swearword.

"What's wrong with the nappies?" I took Henry off her and began undressing him while I waited for a clarification.

"They don't work. The pee seems to run out over the top."

I suppressed a giggle. Her assessment was spot on, and a quick examination of Henry's nappy confirmed my suspicion.

"Rach," I said gently. "You have to tuck his little willy right down, otherwise he *will* pee right over the top."

Rachel stared at me, aghast. Her bottom lip wobbled and tears seemed imminent, but she snapped out of it and burst out laughing instead. "That's so *obvious*, now that you've told me. Why didn't anyone tell me before?"

I finished equipping Henry with a fresh nappy and baby suit and joined Rachel on the sofa.

"Rite of passage, I suppose," I mused. "Nobody told me, either. And you forget about it really quickly. So you leave your best friend out to dry when it's her turn."

"Or to get wet, as the case may be," Rachel offered, a hint of mischief gleaming in her eyes.

"Or to get wet," I laughed. "Indeed."

In this way, the week went by, and by Saturday, I woke up feeling utterly exhausted and wishing desperately for someone to step in and help *me* out for a while.

My wish was granted when Dan turned up, unannounced as was his wont, to see if the Jones family would like to join him for an early dinner at our favorite restaurant. His suggestion was greeted with much enthusiasm by my kids, who preferred pizza 'out' a second time that week to the infinitely more healthy and less appealing meal I had threatened to prepare. We piled into Dan's car and were soon ensconced at our favorite table in the far back corner, where we could see but not be seen. The kids fell gleefully on their dough balls while Dan and I shared a prawn starter and cheesy garlic bread.

"So," Dan began, fiddling with his glass of wine, "how's the week been? You look done in."

"Thank you kindly," I teased him back. "It's been manic. How about you?"

Dan needed no further prompt. As always when asked about his work, his face became animated, and he seemed to grow taller, larger, more exultant. The band had been in the studio for only a few weeks, but the album was coming along great. His excitement was infectious, but our pizzas arrived and cut his update short. For a few minutes, we were both occupied slicing and cutting the kids' food into the right size—my little gourmets required their pizza served *just so*—and suddenly, Josh took over the role of chief entertainer.

"Mummy," he started, "I learned something today."

"Did you," I responded on autopilot, shooting Dan a meaningful look. As he knew only too well, this kind of announcement was often the opening gambit in a roundabout negotiation for a new toy. Not so today, however.

"You know snails?"

Did I ever? I suppressed a snort as I recalled my erstwhile fiancé, Tim, exterminating slugs on a rainy summer's night by the light of a miner's lamp. The neighbors had called out the police, and recounting the interlude to Rachel had cemented her intense dislike for my then boyfriend. Evidently, I had shared the story with Dan, too, because he muttered "exterminator" under his breath. I kicked his shin under the table.

"Yes, Josh, I know snails." I encouraged my son to continue.

"Well, Mummy, did you know their eyes aren't in their heads like yours and mine?"

I had never given this much thought before, but I nodded my agreement.

"How did you find that out?" Dan was genuinely interested.

"On the telly," Josh explained, keen to get back to the key piece of information he was itching to impart. "But do you know where they *keep* their eyes?"

"Where do they keep their eyes?" Dan and I asked as one.

"Snails," Josh started, jiggling excitedly on his seat. "Snails keep their eyes at the end of their testicles."

Dan spat his mouthful of wine across the table, but hastily disguised his amusement in a severe coughing fit. I could feel my mouth twitch with urgent laughter, but I couldn't allow myself to explode. Josh would be crushed. Slapping Dan's back to maintain the coughing charade, I addressed my adorable offspring.

"Do they really keep their eyes at the end of their *tentacles*?" I voiced.

"Yes, mummy, they do, they keep them at the end of their—"

"*Tentacles,*" I prompted, and "tentacles" Josh repeated carefully.

"Ten-ta-cles" Emily chimed in, never keen to be left out, and Dan stroked her hair.

"That's right, my sweet," he praised her. He raised his glass to me. "To your very excellent parenting," he proposed, and I giggled.

Sadly, the mood was broken and our evening cut short when Dan's mobile rang with an urgent summons to return to the studio. Dan dropped us back home and rushed off.

"Sorry about this," he offered before he drove off. I could see genuine regret on his face, but there was also impatient anxiety. He was keen and raring to attend to his emergency.

"It's fine," I assured him. "A rock star's gotta do what a rock star's gotta do."

Later that night, I was in the middle of a strange dream involving Dan, the kids, and a gigantic, multi-tentacled snail when I was woken up by the sound of glass shattering. The scary snail had been going berserk in Dan's garden, lashing out with its tentacles every which way, and for a moment I couldn't determine whether the breaking glass had, perhaps, been part of my dream. I held my breath and strained to hear, but there was silence. Counting to ten and waiting for my heart to slow, I debated whether to investigate. I was always nervous about the downstairs windows which were all too vulnerable, especially in our secluded garden.

With a big sigh, I opted for the responsible action and dragged myself out of bed. As quietly as possible, I ventured downstairs, carefully peeking into each room and breathing a sigh of relief when all windows were intact. However, when I padded back upstairs, I heard it again, very distinctly. Glass breaking, and the grating noise of shards being removed from a window frame. I fled upstairs, checked on the kids, and hid in my bedroom.

Not for the first time in my life, I found myself dialing 999. Whispering furtively, I explained about the breaking glass and being alone in the house with two kids. The lady at the other end reassured me that a patrol would be with me in a few minutes, and I suddenly realized that I ought to get dressed. With trembling fingers, I pulled on jeans and a jumper before venturing back downstairs, holding the phone like a talisman for protection. Within a few minutes, there was a gentle knock on the door. A burly, cheerful-looking and quite young police officer greeted me warmly. Behind him, parked in the street, I saw not a patrol car, but an incident van from which no less than seven other police officers emerged. I swallowed hard. What if I *had* dreamed all of the breakage after all?

Two of the policemen asked if they could come inside to take a look and ensure I hadn't been burgled. The others fanned out along the street, and two disappeared into my garden. Three minutes later, my house had been given the all clear. Miraculously, the kids hadn't even woken up. I felt like an idiot and was about to make my apologies when the burly policeman's walkie talkie crackled.

"Ah, you see? You weren't dreaming," he informed me. "We found the break-in. We must go. Bye for now." He turned and hurried down the road, and I noticed that the police van had already disappeared, presumably going around the corner to the actual scene of the crime.

I crept up the stairs and stood by my bedroom window overlooking the garden. Sure enough, there was action in the building backing onto my property. Cloaked in darkness when I had first woken up, now all the windows were ablaze with lights, and I could see policemen going up and down the stairs. At least I hadn't inconvenienced the law for no reason. Suddenly, I felt shaky. I had always assumed our neighborhood was reasonably safe by London standards, but now I seemed exposed and vulnerable. And lonely. In the throes of the aftershock, I fired off a text to Dan, knowing that he might not receive it until the morning or whenever studio time had finished.

Twenty minutes later, there was another knock on the door. Hoping it might be Dan, I zoomed downstairs, back in my nightie, of course, and flung the front door open.

"Hold it, hold it, young lady," the police officer chided me in an amused kind of voice. "You don't wanna be going 'round opening your door like that in the middle of the night. I could have been anybody."

I bit back a response but wrapped my arms around myself protectively. He cleared his throat.

"Well, right, so, um, I just wanted to tell you that you did right. You should always call us when you're frightened, especially a young mum with two kids alone in her house." He took his hat off and scratched his head.

"Right, so you did hear glass breaking. I thought you might like to know. You didn't dream it. It was a break-in. Only it wasn't a break-in, as such. It was someone who'd locked himself out and tried to get back in."

Ah. I got that stupid feeling again. My neighbor would be very thankful indeed that I had set the police on him. *Not!*

"However," the policeman continued with a wide grin. "However, not to worry you unduly or anything. This is quite unusual around here, but there it is." He cleared his throat before delivering the punch line. "He was dealin' drugs so we nicked him anyway."

Gangbuster Sophie! Oh. My. God. Instant visions of retaliative break-ins, letter bombs, bin fires, and worse crowded my mind.

"You didn't tell him it was me who rang this in, did you?" I burst out, thinking of the kids and my safety before anything else.

"Of course not. Besides, he's gone for a while, so I really wouldn't worry. You have yourself a good night now." He doffed his cap and loped off.

Chapter Five

Too restless to sleep, I sat on my sofa in the dark lounge and pondered. Loneliness and despair swept over me in a big wave. I hated being alone. I hated having to make big decisions for the kids and myself on my own. I hated having to be the responsible adult at all times, with nobody there to soothe my fears in the middle of the night. Thankfully, I was roused from my ruminations when my mobile phone rang. I jumped for it; it was Dan.

"Hey, I'm right outside," he whispered, as though he might wake the kids if he spoke any louder. "Rock star to the rescue. Shall I let myself in or will you open up for me?"

I rushed to open the front door and launched myself into his arms before he could finish his sentence or put his keys in the lock. He stepped inside and locked the door, holding me in his strong arms and stroking my hair. Slowly, he propelled me back into the lounge where he sat on the sofa and pulled me on his lap. Anxious to share the burden of worry, I related the events of the evening. Dan was full of empathy, but, yet again, his pragmatic outlook on life prevailed.

"Sweetie," he began, "there are drug dealers all over the place. There's probably one living next door to me. You can't fret about this. It's just life."

I couldn't quite follow his logic. "But what if he knows it was *me*?"

"How would he?" Dan replied calmly. "How would he know?"

"I don't know," I admitted, taking a shuddering breath. Maybe Dan was right.

"How about a glass of wine?" Dan suggested out of the blue.

"What, now?" I threw a glance at the display of the DVD player under the telly. "It's two in the morning!"

"I know. So what? You're not sleepy. I'm not sleepy. Let's have a little glass of wine and relax."

"Nah," I declined. "Let's not have a glass of wine. Can we simply… sit here for a little while?"

"Okay." Dan reclined on the sofa, stretching out his legs and pulling me down beside him. "There's something else on your mind, isn't there?"

I couldn't see his face in the darkness, but I responded anyway, speaking as if to myself. "I'm so bloody lonely. I always have to figure everything out by myself. It's so hard." I didn't like the whine of self-pity in my voice, but I couldn't help it.

"What do you have to figure out, honey?"

"Josh," I burst out, surprising myself and unleashing a torrent of suppressed worry. "He starts school next month. What will it be like? You know, first day and all that. Will there be lots of happy couples, lots of mums and dads together, and poor old Josh has only me?"

Dan stroked my face; he knew what was coming.

"I miss him so," I snuffled into his shirtsleeve, not for the first time in the past couple of years. "I miss him. I want him back!"

Dan rubbed my shoulder. "I know, my love, I know," he whispered, also not for the first time. "I wish I could bring him back for you."

"Why did he have to go? Why did he have to take the call?" The familiar wave of grief engulfed me all over again. "Why did it have to be Steve? Why couldn't anyone else have gone? He was supposed to be at work as normal. He was supposed to come home to us that night, as always!"

"Shh," Dan soothed, knowing it was futile, knowing we would both have to go through this now, but still trying to stem the flood of pain. "It was his job. He was saving lives. You loved him for it." Dan's voice was oddly strangled, but I was too distraught to ponder the implications.

"He was a *nurse*. He worked in the operating theater. He wasn't even a paramedic. He needn't have gone out. He needn't have died in that blast. He—" The cycle of grief was still intact, and I moved from despair to all-out rage.

"I am so bloody angry with him. I hate him. I hate him for putting others before us, before himself. It was all so bloody unnecessary." I punched a cushion, narrowly missing Dan's body.

Occasionally, I still felt every bit as hurt and lost as the very first minute after I had been told that Steve had been killed. *I'm very sorry to have to tell you…*

The memory rose like an inevitable tide, engulfing me once again in its cold, heartbreaking maelstrom. I felt Dan's arm around my shoulder and I heard his voice as though it came through a long, long tunnel, but he couldn't stop the vision, couldn't save me from sliding back once again to that moment.

The doorbell rang and I grumbled. Josh was asleep upstairs and I needed him to keep to his nap time. I was exhausted. Being eight months pregnant with a rumbustious toddler in the house was no laughing matter, and I had only just put my feet up and flicked the telly on for a bit of relaxing daytime entertainment.

Reluctantly, I heaved my body off the sofa — I was quite sure I hadn't been this big with Josh! — and padded to the front door. As I was leaving the room, I caught the tail end of a news announcement. Some bomb or other had gone off in London and I had goosebumps of terror all over. At times it was scary, living in the Capital.

The doorbell sliced through my thoughts again and I cursed under my breath. Who was so blooming impatient?

I turned the key in the lock, suddenly all fingers and thumbs, and swung the door open cautiously. A policewoman stood on my doorstep and another waited a few paces behind. Both looked pale and stricken, and the policewoman right in front of me held her cap in her hands, turning it over and over and over.

A lump rose in my throat and I had a terrible premonition. Something bad had happened. Something really bad had happened. Mum? Dad? Had they been in an accident?

My knees crumpled and I swayed slightly.

"Mrs. Jones?"

I gulped in some air and nodded.

"Mrs. Steve Jones?

I nodded again and tried to swallow my rising panic. What had happened? What had happened? My mouth opened to ask the question, but my throat had dried up and no words came out.

The policewoman took my hand and met my gaze. Her voice shook ever so slightly.

"Mrs. Jones, I'm police constable Murphy, and my colleague is WPC Parker. I'm afraid we have some bad news for you. Please…may we come in? It…it would be easier to talk inside."

My world disintegrated. Someone had died. Someone I loved had died, and I was about to find out who it was. My heart beat in my mouth and my head swam. Irrationally, unfairly, I found myself praying, please don't let it be Steve. Please don't let it be Steve! Then I realized, with a guilty jolt, that news of Mum or Dad's death would be just as devastating. I didn't want to lose anyone.

Already, tears were pouring down my cheeks and I felt faint. I noticed the two policewomen exchanging a look, pointing their eyes at my bump and then at each other, and very gently, WPC Murphy took charge. She touched me on the arm and turned me around so that I could lead the way into the house. On autopilot, I showed the police officers into the lounge and sat down heavily on the sofa. WPC Murphy immediately sat down beside me, close, but not too close, and took my hand.

WPC Parker came into the room a few seconds later, took in the scene and the blaring telly which, I noticed absent-mindedly, was showing images of ambulances and a blown up building, and she abruptly turned it off.

"Mrs. Jones, I'm very sorry to have to tell you that your husband was killed in a terrorist bomb attack in central London this morning."

I looked at her blankly. Her words entered my brain and skittered around for a little while before they settled into place and made some kind of sense. Involuntarily, I let out a small gasp of relief.

"There must be a mistake. You must have the wrong ID, or something. Steve couldn't have been killed. He was nowhere near the city center this morning, he works in a hospital in Tooting." My words tumbled out fast, and I was dizzy with cautious joy. Obviously it was terrible that someone had died — lots of people, probably — but at least it couldn't have been Steve.

WPC Murphy and WPC Parker traded looks once more. This time, it was WPC Parker who spoke.

"Mrs. Jones, there has been no mistake. Your husband — "

"But there must be! Steve went to work this morning, I know he did, he texted me when he got there!"

WPC Parker swallowed hard. "You're right. He did go to work this morning. A bomb went off in central London just before ten a.m. and there were dozens of casualties. The emergency services were on site within minutes but there weren't enough ambulances and…"

"No, no, no," I wailed. "You got the wrong man. Steve isn't a paramedic, he wouldn't have been there, he doesn't do ambulance shifts, he works as a nurse in the operating theater. Look, I'll call him now and…"

WPC Murphy took over again. "Mrs. Jones, your husband responded to the call alongside three other paramedics — "

"But he wasn't a paramedic!"

Didn't the woman understand that this detail mattered? Steve couldn't have been there. It wasn't his job. Therefore he couldn't have been killed. If I could only get her to understand…

WPC Murphy kept talking regardless of my objection. "As I was saying Mr. Jones responded to the call alongside three other paramedics. The crew was short-staffed. A fourth paramedic was needed. Your husband had the right training. He volunteered and took the call."

"Noooooooooo!" A long, shrill howl of despair filled the room, and it took me a moment to work out that it was mine. My vision blurred and my throat closed up. I struggled to breathe and found myself slumping against the policewoman. Perhaps if I just closed my eyes, this would all go away…

"Parker, call 999. Tell them we have a highly pregnant lady in distress here, do it, now!" WPC Murphy's voice lifted me out of the blackness and I wondered idly who they were talking about.

"Steve," I mumbled. "I want Steve!"

Chapter Six

WPC Murphy made as though to put her arm around me but stopped the movement before she made contact. She cleared her throat instead. For a moment, she hesitated but then spoke again.

"Mrs. Jones, I am really sorry but I think it's best that I tell you what happened, okay?" Her voice was softer now, and the tremor was more distinct. She's finding this really difficult, a detached part of my brain observed.

"Mr. Jones would have arrived at the scene at about twenty minutes past ten. He was assessing a young child with a head wound when another bomb went off..."

"How do you know all this?" I interrupted. "I mean, if he's really dead, then how do you know when he got there and what he was doing?"

WPC Murphy recoiled at my outburst, but only for a split second. "I know this," she supplied gently, "because one of the other crew members told us."

"You mean... you mean Steve died and the others survived?"

In my great terror, I didn't even notice, then, that I had uttered those words for the first time. Steve died. *I was too focused on the notion that someone else should have been there and survived.* Not fair, *my brain screamed.* Not fair, not fair, not fair!

"One of the crew members survived. The other three, including your husband, perished alongside another crew. A second bomb went off while they were attending to those injured by the first bomb, and many of the paramedics and victims on scene were killed by falling masonry and debris. We don't know how many have died, yet, but it's a terrible, terrible tragedy."

A terrible, terrible tragedy. *What a terribly inadequate way to sum it up. I lifted my feet onto the sofa and curled up into a small ball. The baby was kicking wildly in my tummy, probably unsettled by the masses of adrenaline sloshing through my body, and bile sat acidly in my throat. The room swam in and out of focus and I only had one thought. If Steve was dead, I wanted to die, too.*

"Mrs. Jones? Are you with us?"

WPC Parker knelt in front of me, her face at eye level with mine. Without warning, the bile in my throat demanded out and I threw up, explosively, all over the sofa and the carpet. The heaving wouldn't stop and the baby kept kicking and kicking. I moaned in terror and pain, my face wet from tears that I hadn't noticed were still falling, and I wanted Steve.

From a long, long way away I heard the two policewomen talking but I couldn't make out what they were saying. Suddenly more people filled the room, people in familiar green suits, and they were fussing over me, trying to make me better. Surely one of them had to be Steve, if he was on paramedic duty today?

I scrutinized each face hopefully, calling for my husband, but each face turned out to be unfamiliar once it came into focus, and I was alone, alone.

Alone, apart from the baby kicking in my tummy, of course. And Josh, who was still asleep upstairs.

The paramedics fitted me with all sorts of gear, a heart rate monitor for me and one for the baby, an oxygen mask, and they seemed to be getting ready to load me onto a stretcher. Why they wanted to save me if I was just as well ready to die, I couldn't figure out, but quite abruptly, from out of nowhere, a thought pierced my consciousness.

"You can't take me away," I whispered. "Josh is sleeping upstairs. I can't leave him, he's only two..."

And then I blanked out.

The paramedics took me to the hospital for a checkup because the baby was showing signs of distress. Josh and I and the bump ended up in St. George's, the hospital where Steve had worked, and the staff were all in shock. They grieved alongside me and looked after us as if we were family. Within hours, Mum and Dad arrived. Rachel came, too, and she alerted Dan. Everybody was there for me, but still I felt alone.

I stayed in hospital for a few days until it was certain that the baby was all right, and then I was allowed home again until the birth. Mum and Dad looked after Josh in the meantime. They didn't tell him that his father had died. That was my job, in a quiet moment on the first day I returned home, and it was probably the hardest conversation I ever had in my life. Angels and heaven featured prominently, but I cannot recall exactly what I said.

At my ferocious insistence, Mum and Dad left after a week, right after Steve's funeral which they had arranged together with Dan. I couldn't recall anything about the farewell service or the days leading up to it. My memories of that dreadful time resumed with any kind of clarity only at the point when Josh and I had to begin fending for ourselves in the short weeks before Emily's birth.

Rachel was there for me through it all, of course. And Dan. Dan proved to be a real rock. He just quietly turned up and did stuff, like playing with Josh and making sure Emily's nursery was ready. He never said much, and he never stayed long, but he was always somehow there. After my due date had come and gone, he more or less moved in, *without comment and without asking. He entertained Josh and got the house organized and cooked meals. When my labor started, he rang Rachel and my parents to let them know the baby was coming. When labor had progressed far enough, he took me to the hospital. I didn't know what he told the nurses but he stayed with me the entire time. Yup, blood, sweat, tears, gore, swearing and all. He was there, holding my hand and holding Emily right after her birth when I was too distraught to even look at her.*

After the first few weeks of Emily's life, when us three Joneses were eventually home alone together…well, as they say, life goes on. I changed nappies and fed my baby and played with my toddler. I grieved, and I went through denial, and despair, and anger. I recalled blank days and black days that somehow merged into weeks and then months. Denial abated. Despair came and went. But anger was a pretty constant companion.

"I hate him," I muttered weakly. "I'm so cross with him, still."

"You don't hate him," Dan corrected, and I gave a start. How long had I been lost in thoughts?

"You don't hate him," Dan repeated and gave me a little nudge. "You know you don't." He rocked and soothed me as he had done so many times before. Somewhere deep down, I felt bad for him, too. He was an innocent prisoner of this drama, played out all too frequently. I had weeks, months of being happy, almost forgetful, but sometimes little things would send me over the edge all over again. Neither of us had any answers to my questions, never had, and never would; and I knew I had to stop putting us both through this time and again. Somehow, Dan had become my rock, my constant, the link between a glorious past and this unhappy present.

Dan. What was it that Rach had said a few weeks ago? *Rock star extraordinaire, lead singer of mega rock band Tuscq, erstwhile boyfriend and now godfather to my children.* That about summed it up.

I had known Dan practically all my adult life. We had been engaged once, for about thirty-six hours. He helped me through some minor disasters and was my mate-of-honor at my wedding to Steve. When Steve had asked him in private, and without consulting me, whether Dan would like to be godfather to Josh, Dan had been touched and overjoyed, and accepted readily. He became part of the Jones family, and the following two years were the happiest, most perfect period of my life. We had even crept into Dan's music, somehow. Dan wrote a very emotional ballad about the miracle of new life that shot to number one all over Europe and in the States, and stayed there for weeks. I had quite a collection of personalized songs, even if most people were unaware of it.

Dan was always there for me. Of course, he still had his other women, his dalliances, although his highly publicized affairs seemed to have petered out of late. He was absent at times, like when he was touring or recording. And naturally, he tried to keep our friendship out of the papers as much as possible. Initially, when he stepped in after Steve's death and Emily's birth, when he took Josh to playschool every day for weeks and went shopping for nappies, the press had been all over us. But Dan and his agent had released a statement and refused to answer any further questions, and eventually, the interest in his family-by-proxy let up. Periodically, somebody would snap him in the supermarket with a basket full of groceries or in the park with me and the kids, but by and large, it had become possible for him to do normal things with us without too much disturbance. Frankly, I wasn't sure how I would have coped without him.

I nodded off in Dan's arms and was woken by the insistent buzzing of his mobile phone.

"Sorry," he said softly, "I didn't mean to wake you." He struggled to retrieve the phone from his back pocket and held it up to see who had called. The display read, *Jack*. The band manager.

"Shit." Dan muttered under his breath and listened to his voicemail. I could hear Jack's agitated voice, although I wasn't able to make out what he said. Dan sat up and pulled me with him. "Time for bed, methinks. Come on, I'll tuck you in."

I let myself be led upstairs like a small child. In my bedroom, Dan plumped the pillows and threw back the duvet. "In you hop, young lady," he teased, patting the mattress. Instead of obliging, I launched myself into his arms again.

"What would I do without you?" I sniffled into his shoulder.

"You would be fine," Dan assured me, a little gruffly. "Come on, in you hop."

"Do you want to stay?" I suggested in a small voice, thinking only of sleep.

Dan's face crumpled. "I can't stay, sweetheart."

I opened my mouth to object, to plead, to explain that I didn't want to be left alone again. I simply couldn't face it. I was tired of being alone. I wanted company. I needed a friend. I wanted to be held and comforted.

Dan read the emotion on my face and touched two fingers to my lips before I could speak. "I've got to go, Sophie."

Swatting away his fingers, I felt a surge of anger and hot despair.

"Yeah, I bet you've got a hot date," I retorted, even though I knew perfectly well that he didn't. "You'd better hurry."

The light seemed to extinguish in Dan's eyes. He squared his shoulders and rolled his head. "I'd better go," he concurred. "I'll let myself out."

He was gone before I could respond, and I heard the front door click shut. *Damn.*

I wanted to run after him, but I was too proud, too confused, and too angry with myself. The memory of the look in his eyes was killing me. I couldn't work out what it meant. I thought I knew my rock star, but there was a shadow of sadness there that I couldn't explain.

Crawling under the duvet at last and pulling it high over my head, reeling with emotions for people living and dead, I fell into an uneasy sleep before I could reflect any further.

Chapter Seven

Damn and double damn. I groaned as I saw the time on my alarm clock. Only five a.m. My head was sore and throbbing, and I had a big lump of sadness in my tummy. Today, of all days, I had to wake up feeling like a limp dishcloth. It was Josh's first day at school. I wanted to enjoy it, and, most importantly, I wanted *him* to enjoy it. He had been counting down the days, and he didn't need his mummy's emotional turmoil clouding the day.

I rolled on my side and pulled the duvet over me again. It was too early to get up, although I doubted I would go back to sleep. Summoning every happy thought, every cheerful memory I could muster, I spent the next hour reprogramming myself until I was ready to face the day. I rose at six, got dressed, and had a sweet cup of tea with two painkillers.

By the time Josh bounded down the stairs fully dressed in his brand new school uniform, I felt almost human. My breath caught in my throat as I watched my four-year-old buzzing about the kitchen in his gray trousers and red jumper with the white collar of his polo shirt poking out untidily. Points for trying, though!

I straightened the collar and ran my fingers through his short hair in lieu of retrieving the hated hair brush from upstairs. He looked adorable, vaguely rakish, and very cute. How had this day arrived so quickly?

The doorbell interrupted my nostalgic mummy moment, and Josh nearly exploded with anticipation. "I bet it's Dan, I bet it's Dan," he hollered and bounced to the front door like a ping pong ball. Of course it was Dan; it would have been impossible for him to forget the big day after Josh had reminded him every day of the past three weeks: *Remember, remember, the fifth of September*…

Dan bore two wrapped presents and a big, brown paper bag from the local bakery. He flashed me a quick smile and mouthed, "Are you okay?"

"I'm fine," I replied as cheerfully as I could. And I felt fine. Weird, disorientated, but fine. "Thank you for coming."

Dan inclined his head as though to say, *no problem*, and focused his attention on Josh. "Hey, little big man. What's that you're wearing? You look like you're going off to a new job somewhere."

"No, silly," Josh gushed. "It's my school uniform. I'm going to school today!"

"Is that the honest truth?" Dan pretended to be overwhelmed.

"It is," Josh reiterated. "This is my uniform."

"It's very smart."

Dan ruffled Josh's hair and wandered off into the kitchen to arrange croissants and brioche onto plates. Josh hovered in the background, having spied the presents but being too polite to ask. I left the two of them to it and went to help Emily wake up and get dressed. No more leisurely mornings for us; from now on, we couldn't afford to be late.

When I brought a slightly sleepy but obediently dressed Emily into the kitchen, Josh had opened his present, and Dan was reading it to him patiently. It was a book about dinosaurs, and it evidently had gone straight to the top of my little man's chart. Emily hurled herself at Dan and spied the remaining present on the table.

"For me, for me!" she demanded, not yet capable of the restraint that her brother had so unexpectedly displayed earlier. Dan handed her the pink parcel with a big smile. "For my little angel," he announced, and Emily gave him a thank-you kiss before she had even opened it.

"Like it," she promised, and sang to herself while she tore at the paper. "Like it, like it, like it." Predictably, Dan scored another hit with the butterfly coloring book and glittery crayons. My spirits lifted. Maybe with Dan here, this day would be fine.

They sank again, however, as soon as we set off on our first walk to school together, me, Josh and Emily, and Dan. Much as I hated myself for it, much as I realized how ungrateful I was being, I wished Steve was there instead of Dan. He and I had imagined this day together from the day Josh was born; we had played endless scenarios in our heads about the weather and our moods and what we would say and do and feel. It wasn't fair that he hadn't been able to hold up his side of the bargain.

I hung back and observed Josh skipping along, holding Dan's hand and chattering away nineteen to the dozen. They could have been father and son. They didn't exactly look alike, but they didn't look unalike either. I tried to superimpose Steve's image over Dan, tried to pretend, just for a moment, that all was as it should be, and a big lump rose in my throat. *Stop it, Sophie. Now.*

Unwilling to be left so far behind Dan and Josh, Emily jiggled her legs impatiently in her pushchair, signaling that mummy should get a move on. I made myself laugh to reassure her and quash my gloomy thoughts, and we raced after the boys.

At the playground, Josh let go of Dan's hand and joined his friends from playschool, leaving Dan looking slightly forlorn. I stood next to him and nudged him with my shoulder.

"Don't look so glum, you. It's much better this way."

"I know," Dan mumbled. "But it was nice to be needed."

I shot him an amused look. He had never before acknowledged how intense a bond he felt with my children.

Before I could give voice to this thought, an insistent shrilling signaled the start of the school day. Damn, how had that happened? How had I become so distracted when my focus should have been on Josh? And there he was, shooting over like a rocket to give me a hug, then clinging to me, overcome by sudden shyness.

His teacher lined her new charges up to enter Reception, and when the bravest children had disappeared inside under the guidance of the teaching assistant, Mrs. Dean came over to collect the stragglers one by one.

"Hello, Josh." She crouched down in front of him and gave him a friendly smile. "Time to go in now."

"How do you know my name?" my son marveled.

Mrs. Dean winked at him. "I have special teacher powers, *and* I've seen your photograph. Will you come with me now? Say goodbye to your Mummy."

"And Dan," Josh supplied eagerly, giving me and Dan a short hug. Mrs. Dean gave Dan only the briefest of looks while her attention remained fully on Josh. She smiled and coaxed him away.

"That went well," Dan observed. "A bit of an anti-climax, right? What happens next?"

"I don't know," I muttered. Suddenly, I was at a loose end with no idea what would happen next, and I didn't know whether to laugh or cry. "They grow up so fast."

"Time passes too quickly," Dan mused. "Not always a bad thing, but it can take you by surprise."

"You're going all lyrical on me." I grinned. "I bet you're writing a song in your head. I know that look."

"I am, actually," Dan confessed. "Occupational hazard. Sorry."

"Park," Emily demanded when Dan and I continued to stand around. "Emily go to park."

"Okay, sweetie, I'll take you to the park," I agreed, glad of something to do.

Dan sighed. "I'll have to pass. We have a band meeting with the record label this morning. I'd better be going."

Emily erupted in disconsolate crying. "Dan come, Dan come."

Dan smiled at my daughter. "Baby girl," he spoke, squatting to bring his face on a level with hers. "Dan has to go to work now. But I'll come back later and maybe we'll go for a meal. Will you look after your mummy for me this morning?"

He had struck the perfect note, and Emily was putty in his hands. "Of course," she pronounced slowly, copying the exact tone of voice I usually deployed for the phrase.

"That's grand," Dan assured her and offered her a high-five. I laughed as he straightened up.

"Charming the next generation already, I see," I teased. "You do have a way with the girls."

"Also an occupational hazard," Dan retorted easily before turning serious. "I really must be off. Will you be all right?"

"Of course," I replied, exactly as my daughter had, and the irony wasn't lost on either of the adults.

Dan grinned and high-fived me. "See you later."

Chapter Eight

The morning proved to be exceptionally difficult. Initially, Emily reveled in having me all to herself. Even though this wasn't uncommon, Josh having attended playschool most mornings anyway, for some reason, this morning was different.

After she had been on all of the swings, down the slide several dozen times, on the see-saw and the rocking horse, consumed an ice cream and an orange juice, all in the record time of forty-five minutes, Emily became restless and grumpy. The park was boring, she wanted her brother, she wanted to go to school like her brother. She went into full-scale meltdown when I pointed the stroller in the direction of our customary Monday morning Mummy-and-Toddler group, so I took her home instead. Feeling like an awful failure and a terrible parent, I installed her in front of Cbeebies and made myself a cup of tea in the kitchen.

When we picked up an exuberant Josh from school, bursting with excitement at all the fun, new things he had tried out that morning, Emily's mood turned from disgruntled to stormy.

"I want school, I want school," was all she cried during the afternoon, and by four o'clock, I was ready to shoot myself. Figuratively speaking, of course.

Dan came by at five, as promised, to help us celebrate over dinner. He suggested pizza, but, unexpectedly, the kids protested. My little connoisseurs demanded Chinese instead. Dan was only too happy to oblige and took us into Chinatown, to one of his favorite eateries tucked away behind Leicester Square.

I was a little anxious at how the kids would fare in the unfamiliar environment, but, given prawn crackers, prawn toast, egg-fried rice and noodles, they munched peacefully and left us adults to enjoy our own meals.

"You look as though you needed a treat tonight," Dan murmured to me between courses.

"Oh God, yeah. Emily was driving me crazy," I confessed. "Suddenly, I'm no longer enough. She wants what Josh wants. You should have heard her. It was like water torture: drip, drip, drip."

Looking angelic and not at all like the little demon I had described, Emily nudged Dan and offered him some of her noodles. Dan obediently opened his mouth and let himself be fed, rolling his eyes and rubbing his stomach.

"Emily, my pet, how come your dinner is always so much yummier than mine?" he complained, and Emily giggled without responding.

Dan turned back to me. "Why don't you send her to playschool?"

To him, this was the obvious solution, and it had crossed my mind at least a hundred times today. But she was still so young, just barely over two years old.

"You're too hard on yourself," Dan chided. "I know you're proud to be a stay-at-home mum, but maybe Emily has different needs from Josh. She's seeing him having so much fun, so it's only natural she wants to do the same. A few mornings wouldn't hurt, would they?"

"When did you become the expert on childcare?" I snapped, exasperated and bemused at his sudden insight in parent-and-child psychology.

Dan raised his hand in a placating gesture. "I'm not the expert. I just hate to see you so torn. And I think you're too hard on yourself. It's not like you've had an easy ride these past few years. Perhaps you need a break. Perhaps you need a new beginning as well, some time to do something for you."

My turn to throw my hands in the air in a mock-horrified gesture. "How indulgent. How decadent. How selfish!" I intoned.

Dan grinned. "What was that your midwife said when you brought Emily home?" He cleared his throat and spoke in a cheerful falsetto. "Remember, happy mummy makes happy baby."

I burst out laughing. "You have the memory of an elephant."

My hilarity caught the children's attention, and they wanted to be let in on the joke. Grateful for the diversion, I summoned up a quick anecdote. Out of the corner of my eye, I noticed Dan shaking his head. Something about my attitude was making him unhappy, but I was the parent, and I made the decisions, conveniently forgetting that I had bemoaned the burden of lone decision-making on Dan's very shoulder not so long ago.

None of the Jones family were surprised when Dan's mobile phone rang before pudding arrived. "It must be an ee-mergen-see again," Josh pronounced carefully, proud to have recalled such a big word.

Dan shrugged apologetically. "It is, actually," he grumbled when he had finished talking on the phone. "Well, not really. Not a massive one, at any rate, but I'd better go back to the studio when we're done here. How's about..." He furrowed his brow. "How's about you come with me and I give you the quick tour, and after that, a limo can take you home?"

He looked at me across the table, seeking my agreement with his eyes over the overjoyed squeals emanating from the kids. I smiled broadly and nodded. *Yes, that would be a lovely ending to Josh's big day.*

Even though I had derided Dan's idea of putting Emily into playschool, his gentle and serious voice kept playing in my head all night as I lay tossing and turning, unable to sleep. Evidently, Josh's starting school was unsettling the family in more than one way. *A new beginning*, Dan had said. What had he meant by that?

I hadn't considered myself as needy of a fresh start, but now that he had planted the idea in my head, it had taken root and was growing fast. I supposed Emily *was* ready for playschool, even if this hadn't featured in my grand plan. Maybe I had been sticking my head in the sand a little bit, because, after all, what would *I* do when she was away in the mornings?

Evidently, there was a job to go back to. Rick, my former boss, was still willing to have me back at *Read London*, full-time, part-time or freelance, and every so often he would ring and try to nudge me in the right direction. While I could do with the money, I wasn't sure whether I was ready for that level of professional commitment. So what *would* I do?

No easy answer presented itself, and the prospect of having time to read books and watch daytime telly was no longer so appealing now that it could be within reach. I resolved to keep Emily at home for the time being.

Chapter Nine

My resolve lasted until precisely Thursday morning. After three additional mornings of continual whining and the never-ending tantrums ensuing from incurable toddler boredom, I caved in. On Friday, I dropped Emily off for a trial session in the playschool nursery and she shooed me out the door before I even had time to introduce her to the staff.

When I picked her up at noon, she was radiant, tired, and content for the first time that week. Her chatter on the way home revealed that she had done 'dawing', painting, played with play dough and Lego, and also reorganized the role play area. How could I compete with so much stimulation?

I rang the playschool before we had to pick up Josh from school and booked Emily in for morning sessions starting the following Monday. There, I had done it. I was a bad mummy, sending my children out of the house so that I could sit 'round like a lady of leisure.

"You're not a bad mummy," Rachel comforted me over nappy changing and formula making at her house that weekend. "You're simply giving your child what she needs."

"You're not a bad mummy," my Mum advised when we spoke by phone on Sunday morning. "Are you saying *I* was a bad mummy, sending you to nursery from age two?"

"You're not a bad mummy," Dan echoed everyone's thoughts on Sunday night after the kids had gone to bed. We were watching a film and chatting over a glass of wine. "I think you made a brilliant decision, and look how excited Emily is about going tomorrow. She's hardly feeling pushed away, is she?"

No, *that*, she wasn't. All afternoon, she had picked out outfits to wear to her official playschool debut the following morning. Chattering away to the best of her not-quite-three-year-old ability, she had selected and dismissed clothes like a mini-me getting ready for a night out. Dan kept a straight face throughout her entire discourse while I quietly choked into my hanky. Emily was feeling a lot of things, but maternal displacement wasn't one of them.

"Now, you, young lady," Dan broke into my thoughts. "I don't want you moping around your house tomorrow or, God forbid, spend your hard-earned three hours of freedom cleaning."

"I won't," I promised, although I had mentally made a list of all the jobs that needed to be done.

Dan regarded me critically. "I know you. You are planning to wash the curtains and sofa covers, and hoover under all the beds. No way, my friend. You're coming to my house instead."

"I am?" I echoed, surprised.

I hadn't been to Dan's house alone in five years. I had visited, of course, but always together with Steve or at least the kids. We hadn't had any un-chaperoned time together since before I got married. I frowned uncertainly and Dan erupted into one of his famous belly laughs.

"I promise I won't ravish you the minute you walk in the door," he teased. "I only want you out of this house. I'll make some tea and we can have some cake and you can tell me what you think about the new album. How's that?"

That sounded delightful. It sounded like something that the old Sophie would have jumped at, and I was taken aback to feel a finger of excitement deep down in my belly. It would be fun to do something out of the ordinary. It would be fun to be privileged enough to listen to Dan's work once again before the rest of the world got the chance. After almost five years of being a mum and more than two years of being a widow, I was surprised to find little shreds of *me* rising to the surface.

Dan watched my face eagerly, no doubt scrutinizing the display of changing emotion, and he breathed a sigh of relief when anticipation finally emerged.

"Yes," he shouted and punched the air. "I believe there is an excited girl in there somewhere. It'll be like the old days!"

"Ah, but I thought I was due for a new beginning," I teased, reminding him of his wise words in the restaurant.

"New beginning, a re-discovery of self, it's all much of a muchness as long as..." He didn't finish his sentence.

"As long as *what*?" I prompted.

"As long as... As long as that sadness leaves your eyes," Dan whispered, suddenly serious and tender. "It's been breaking my heart seeing you so unhappy. I know, I know." He held up his hands before I could speak. "I know what you've been going through, and you've done it brilliantly. You're an awesome mum and a fabulous friend. You've laughed with your children and turned them into happy little beings. But still, the whole time, you've been sad. And it's killing me."

The great lump in my throat threatened to dissolve into tears, and I swallowed hard. Enough tears, enough crying.

"I don't want to be sad, but it feels wrong to be anything but." I finally confessed the thought that had been haunting me for weeks. "I want to move on, but it's not even been three years, and…"

As I was in confessional mode, I carried on. "Sometimes I can't quite remember what Steve looked like. And I can't recall the sound of his voice. And I feel so guilty." I wrapped my arms around my chest to hold myself together.

"Don't feel guilty. You've got to let go. At some point, you've got to let go. Steve wouldn't want you to be sad—"

I stifled a howl, but Dan continued. "No, he wouldn't want you to be sad and lonely. Gosh, even by traditional standards, not that I believe in them, but even by the most reactionary standards of mourning etiquette, you've done your time. You are *allowed* to move on." He held my eyes, daring me to challenge his words.

"How do you know so much about mourning?"

Dan had the grace to look discomfited. "I did a lot of reading up on it lately. I was getting worried, and I wanted to understand better what you were experiencing and… well, how long you should be putting yourself through this. At what point it's appropriate for a friend to try and extract you from your self-inflicted exile."

"And?"

"Two years." Dan paused. "Actually, one year. One year of heavy mourning, and within the next year, a widow graduates to light mourning, being free to live her life and *court*." He smiled at the old-fashioned word. "So there. No one will fault you or judge you in any way if you come out and have a little fun again. Not with *me*," he added hastily. "That's not what I'm saying at all." He scratched his head. "In fact, I'm not really talking about dating, just, you know, doing things for you. Fun things, things that challenge you, or entertain you, or stretch you a bit."

I took his arm, trying to halt the flood of words. "It's okay. You can stop digging now. I think that hole is deep enough." I giggled. "I know what you mean."

And I did. I couldn't quite fathom *why* his little speech had made a difference, but it had. A small weight had been lifted. A door opened, if only a crack, and there was a sliver of light. Perhaps I *could* permit myself to lighten up and look after myself a little bit every day.

"All right." I returned to our original conversation. "All right. I'll come to your place after I drop Emily off tomorrow. For tea and cake, and to listen to your new music."

"Tea and cake and music," Dan repeated. "Deal."

PART TWO:
FALLING

Chapter Ten

Ten thousand déjà-vu's and a million conflicting emotions crashed in on me as I rang Dan's doorbell the next morning. Standing on his doorstep brought back too many memories. I stamped on them and pressed the bell again. At last the door was flung open and a smiling Dan greeted me. "You came!"

"Of course I came. You made me promise. Now can I come in?"

Dan stood back and held the door wide.

"Work first, or tea and cake first?" he demanded as I stepped into his hallway.

"Work? What work?" No work had been mentioned yesterday.

"Oh, I need your advice on something. You know, the songs. I want to play you my new songs."

Ah, now *that* I did remember. A brief silence settled between us while I pondered options. Technically, I had only just had breakfast and it was too early for cake. On the other hand, it was *never* too early for cake, but it was *distinctly* too early to venture downstairs into Dan's sanctum, his recording studio. I suddenly felt awkward at the prospect of finding myself alone with Dan in that secluded space.

"Cake and tea would be lovely," I finally resolved, and Dan ushered me into his lounge. My eyes were immediately drawn to a lovely cake stand adorned with dozens of little fondant fancies in shades of white, pink, and light blue. The ensemble looked pretty and delectable. I faced Dan with astonishment, but he simply laughed.

"Nothing to do with me. I told the housekeeper you would be coming and she got terribly carried away. I think she likes you. From, you know, way back when."

"But—" I struggled with the logistics. "It's only half past nine. When did she make all of these?"

"Um." Dan blushed. "I texted her last night and she came in at seven. She's off now for the rest of the day, but we can always go for lunch if we get hungry."

"I'll need to collect Emily at noon." I rained on his rather too enthusiastic parade.

"Of course, of course," Dan conceded. "I was just saying. Anyway…" He gestured toward the tower of cakes. "Shall we?"

We sat down on a sofa each, facing each other, and Dan poured tea from a dainty teapot. I lifted one of the bone china cups to my lips, but set it down again before I drank. Dan mirrored my actions and looked at me with a puzzled expression.

"What's wrong, Soph?" His voice was laced with genuine concern.

"It's… I don't know. This is so weird. It's not you, really, or me." I tapped a fingernail lightly against my cup, producing a soft ping. "Before…you know, in the old days…we simply used to dump teabags into mugs and pour milk straight from the bottle. I didn't know you'd gone all posh."

Dan rose and collected the tea things onto a tray. "I haven't. Jenny was simply trying to impress you. Let's do it the normal way."

I opened my mouth to protest, now feeling worse than before, but Dan had already disappeared into the kitchen. I heard him fill the kettle with water and flick it on; the banging of various cupboard doors suggested that he was hunting down cups, teabags, and spoons. Within three minutes, he returned to the lounge bearing two steaming mugs and looking much more himself. He walked carefully around the sofa and sat down next to me.

"There. Better?"

I accepted my mug and sat back, relieved. "Yes, much." We sipped contentedly at our tea, and Dan offered up the cakes again. "Go on, they look delicious."

I took one, he took one. We bit, we chewed, we swallowed. They were fabulous.

"Have another?"

We both took one more, a pink one this time. Next we had a blue one each to see if they tasted different. Twenty minutes later, they were all gone, and I lay back on the sofa, feeling full, fat, and a little decadent. Dan reclined the other way, and we let our feet rub together as though we were dry-cycling.

"Phoar," Dan groaned. "There'll be hell to pay when my personal trainer weighs me next."

"You have a personal trainer?" I was dumbstruck. "When did this happen?"

"A few years ago. Remember when I had some issues with my back after a tour and I had to see a physio, and she recommended upping my core strength and exercising to keep supple. Enter the personal trainer."

After this little confession, I couldn't help looking him up and down pointedly. He *did* look very fit. As gorgeous as ever, in fact. It simply had never occurred to me that he would be working at it these days. My interest was piqued.

"You kept that quiet. So what do you do? And how often?" I had visions of heavy-duty gym equipment, bar bells, and all manner of torture devices.

Dan shrugged. "Pilates, mostly. Three times a week. For half an hour. I didn't want to turn into a bodybuilder or anything like that. I simply want to be able to do my shows without doing my back in. And I want to keep touring for a good few years yet." He smiled his irresistible smile.

I nodded. "Looks like you're doing well."

"Why, thank you kindly, young lady," he retorted in a mock brittle voice. I laughed. It felt good to be back here again. It was lovely not to have to rush around and pick up toys and discarded clothes. I could feel myself relaxing by the minute, and I relished the moment of being *me*.

Somewhere in the house, an alarm clock went off. Dan rose, clapping his hands together. "Time for work," he declared, holding out his hands to help me up.

"You set an alarm? To get to work?" This was getting weirder and weirder. What had happened to my friend, who normally didn't rise before midday?

"Well, I knew our time would be limited, and I really do want to show you my songs so…"

I sprang to. "Let's do it."

Half an hour later, I had listened to some of the most amazing raw material I had ever trained my ears onto. While only roughly put together, there was a new edge, a melodious ferocity to the band's latest work that made me tingle all over.

"Where did all this come from?" I burst out before I could stop myself. "It's... I don't know, different. Edgy, but in a different way than the older stuff. I..." Words were failing me and I shrugged helplessly.

Dan looked pleased. "I take it you like the songs?"

"Heck, yes, I do." I rubbed my nose, a nervous habit I picked up since having the children and that came to the fore whenever I wasn't sure how to say something diplomatically.

"But?"

"Is this *finished* material?"

Whoa; that didn't come out as planned. But Dan wasn't offended.

"No, it's not. Some of it isn't even mixed yet, and none of it has been mastered."

"Ah." I tried to look intelligent. Having heard these terms used many times before, I felt I ought to know what they meant. I had a rough idea, of course, but I didn't understand what was *missing* from the recording I just heard.

"Sit down." Dan pulled a second swivel chair into position next to his own in front of the mixing console.

I sat, taking in the buttons and displays. A few years ago, Dan had conned me into recording a song for him in this very studio, and I had watched him mix and master without really understanding what he was doing. He had been so quick, so efficient, that it all gelled together beautifully. If, indeed, gelled was the right word. The song had been mastered properly in a professional studio later, with the band recording instrumentals and vocals in addition to mine. Anyway, I had watched Dan in action at his console at the time, but today, it seemed, I was to receive a full demonstration.

He hit a button and one of the songs started playing. "Describe the sound for me," Dan challenged. I closed my eyes and leaned back.

"Dull," I eventually offered. "It's kind of... if it were a color, it would be gray. It's... I don't know, it's kind of lifeless. It's a great song, of course—"

"Of course," Dan cut in dryly. "That's not up for debate." Cue cheeky grin. "I want you to tell me what it sounds like, and what you think it *should* sound like. You're critiquing the sound, not the song."

Sound, not song. Right.

"I want more... depth," I offered hesitantly. "Something richer. More..." I still struggled to explain.

"This is good," Dan encouraged me. He was taking notes. "Just throw out some adjectives. Whatever comes to mind."

"Okay," I agreed. Adjectives. I could do adjectives. I thought back to other Tuscq albums, trying to think what made them unique and distinctive.

"I want warmth, and depth. Reds and yellows. Heat. Spark. I want this... dullness gone. Vibrant, that's what I want. You have a gorgeous voice, but everything here sounds muffled. The guitars sound like they're somewhere next door, and the drums are too loud, like they're right in front of me. The bass is like a migraine, pounding away without definition." I was on a roll, but caught myself short when I noticed that Dan had gone quiet. I opened my eyes and sat up straight.

Dan regarded me open-mouthed. He had stopped taking notes and stared.

"I'm sorry." I laughed uncertainly. "Did I go too far? I didn't mean to upset you."

"Upset? I'm not upset. This was awesome. You are awesome. I had no idea you had such great ears. I'm totally blown away." Dan shook his head and scribbled a few things down.

"Right, let's get this show on the road, shall we?" Dan replayed the song, but this time, he started adjusting some of the buttons and dials.

"Sound is made of waves, and the waves come in certain frequencies. Making an album sound great is about getting the mix and balance of frequencies right."

I nodded my understanding, and Dan continued. "I think you've picked up on a couple of distinct issues. One is that I haven't mixed the tracks together properly. So — "

"What does that mean?" I interrupted before I got lost. "You haven't mixed the tracks together properly?"

Dan ran a hand over his face and rolled his shoulders while he contemplated a simplified answer for me. "Okay. So this is a 24-track console, meaning I can feed in twenty-four different bits of sound. My vocals make up a group, and the guitars, and the drums and so on. When you said the guitars sounded like they were next door and the drums were too loud, you were commenting on the mixing, or the lack thereof. I haven't yet balanced the different tracks properly so they work together as they should. Here." He pulled a slider and brought it toward him. "This is taking out some of the drums and this…" He pushed another slider up. "This brings the guitar in more strongly. Listen to it now."

He played it back and the song sounded much more like… a song. More balanced, for want of a different word.

"Amazing." I clapped my hands.

"The other thing that you picked up on is that I haven't *mastered* the track yet. Mastering is the fine-tuning of the sound where you really play with and perfect the frequencies. There are all sorts of things you can do here. For example, you said you want more warmth, and there are dozens of ways of achieving that. It'll take some time, but listen…" He turned a dial. "This is the song with a touch of reverb on the lead vocals. And look, I can bring the guitars into the same room as well." He played with another slider and smiled a boyish grin at me. Already, the sound had improved.

"This is only the beginning. There's all sorts of things we can do to this. We can play with the equalizer, and we can compress and add more reverb or delay…"

I held up my hands, feeling completely overwhelmed. "You've lost me now," I admitted.

"No worries. My God, it takes weeks, *years* to take this all on board. But that's beside the point. You can learn all this stuff. You've got great ears — that's the most important thing."

Said ears were glowing with pride, even though I didn't understand exactly what I was doing so well. Dan's eyes were full of admiration, which was both a new and exhilarating experience. It felt good. *I* felt good.

With a jolt, I realized that I hadn't thought about the kids or the housework or Steve for at least an hour. That had to be the first time in four years I had thought about something totally unrelated to my family. Sadly, the realization also brought the recollection that time was passing, and I would have to pick up Emily very shortly.

Dan grabbed my hand and looked at me intensely. "Come back tomorrow," he pleaded. "Let me play you some more songs, and let me teach you some of these mastering tricks. I think you'd enjoy it. I know *I* would!"

Unsure of what I was letting myself in for, but infected by his enthusiasm and excitement, I agreed. "Yes. Yes, I think I will. That would be fun. If you have the time, that is. I don't want to be a burden…"

"Shush," Dan admonished me. "You're not a burden. You're an inspiration. A muse. And a blank canvas. Let me teach you. Let me initiate you in the art of sound recording and you'll have a skill for life. What do you say?"

"Okay," I said. "All right. Yes. Fine. Brilliant." My voice rose on every word as I was swept away by a wave of anticipation. I was hungry for a new project, new learning. Perhaps this was exactly what I needed.

Chapter Eleven

I was humming with excitement when I collected Emily from playschool. I hadn't felt this elated for as long as I could remember, and the emotion was liberating. Some of the other mums threw me curious looks, and I knew there would be talk behind my back. The more malicious motor mouths would be speculating as to whether I had been *getting it* recently and whether there was a new *boyfriend* on the scene. I was certain of it, because I had heard them dissecting other mums. But I didn't care. Let them talk. Let them assume. Give them something to fill their small lives. I was happy, genuinely happy.

Emily raced toward me with her customary vigor, coat and curls flying, and I found myself crouching down, scooping her up in my arms, then swinging her around in true Hollywood style. My baby girl squealed and wrapped her arms around my neck lest I should set her down unexpectedly.

"More, more," she demanded, and I obediently swung her round again.

"Mummy happy," Emily declared matter-of-factly when as we walked home hand-in-hand.

I choked back sudden tears. I had no idea my children were so clued in to my emotions. My resolve strengthened. Dan was right. It was time to leave mourning behind. It was time to start over, and give myself a break. I *had* to allow myself to be happy and to laugh, especially if it made my children happy.

"Yes, Mummy is happy," I confirmed. "Mummy did some fun work with Dan this morning, and it made me really happy."

Emily giggled. "Dan makes you happy." She drew the obvious conclusion.

I took it at face value. "Yes, sweetie, Dan makes me happy," I agreed.

Josh, too, recognized some sort of sea-change in me when we picked him up.

"Did you have a good day at school?" I asked him as usual, expecting the customary grunted response. My four-year-old already exhibited pre-teen communication patterns. But not today. He beamed at me and gave me a hug.

"I had a good day, and did you have a good day?" he asked back. "You look happy."

You could have knocked me over with a feather. Not Josh, too!

I rallied and smiled. "I had a very good day indeed."

"Mummy had fun with Dan," Emily declared quite loudly, and I laughed.

"Yes, I did something fun with Dan," I confirmed and added, for the benefit of surrounding ears, "we worked on some of his music." The minute the words left my mouth, I cringed. I could practically hear one mum nudge the other, mouthing, *is that what you call it these days?*

Thankfully, my friend, Amelia, came to the rescue. She had an almighty crush on Dan, which was duly and patiently tolerated by her loving husband. "You worked with Dan today, you lucky moo?" she exclaimed. "What did you do? Was the whole band there?"

With a bouncing child at each hand and an excited Amelia in front of me, I suddenly felt like I was on a stage, and the playground tilted ever so slightly under my feet. I stood up that little bit straighter and geared up to speak more clearly. *He showed me how his studio works.* The sentence was clearly formed in my head; lips parted and tongue poised, my brain nonetheless supplied a response that would be less susceptible to misinterpretation.

"I'm writing a feature," I blurted out. "The band is working on a new album, and I'm taking a look at the studio work. That's all."

Indeed. Come to think of it, I *could* always write a feature, a one-off, to turn this little white lie into a red-hot truth. Everyone here knew I used to be a journalist, and Rick would certainly run it if I asked him to. This could be my cover story. I couldn't fathom quite *why* a cover would be needed; but school gate gossip could be vicious, and I had learned the hard way that sometimes it was easier to keep things simple.

"How exciting," Amelia concurred. "Are you going back to work?"

I inclined my head thoughtfully. "In a manner of speaking, you could say that. Yes."

"Even better, it'll do you the world of good," my friend encouraged me, and I smiled. It certainly would.

Later that evening, when the kids had gone to bed and the house was quiet, I sat down in front of my computer. I opened up my word processing application and stared at it for a few minutes. It had been months since I had put fingers to keyboard to write rather than shop or email, and the blank screen intimidated me a little.

Behind the scenes with Tuscq, I typed.
A master class in recording a number-one album

The cursor blinked with encouragement. I rubbed my nose and pondered. I jiggled in my chair, pressing my back against the backrest for a little massage. This was no good. Inspiration wasn't flowing. I had too many ideas but I couldn't find my way in.

I saved the document and began tidying my desk. Then I went to the kitchen to pour myself a glass of wine; *in vino veritas,* and all that. Ready, set, go.

When Dan Hunter, lead singer extraordinaire of legendary rock band Tuscq, invited me to take a look at his studio, I could practically see the innuendo written above his head, I started writing. *Yet I couldn't have been more wrong, for Dan had music on his mind. Music, and a master class in recording it the rock star way. He played me the band's new material and…*

The dam broke, and recollection of today's session poured out in a torrent. For a solid hour, I set down every last detail I could remember and realized I would have to take notes in the future, perhaps take a few photos. Even if the feature was never published, it would serve as a diary of an exciting and unusual experience. Maybe I could blog about it, with Dan's permission, of course.

I read through my evening's work again, correcting a few typos here and there, and nodded contentedly. Yes, this would work. I didn't know what would come out of it, and I didn't really care. The simple prospect of a project, *something to do*, filled me with anticipation.

Chapter Twelve

Early Tuesday morning saw me back at Dan's house, armed with a notepad and a camera.

"Good morning, sunshine," he greeted, only slightly wearily. The early hour was clearly not his cup of tea. "What have you brought today?"

I smiled sheepishly. "I thought I might take some notes and some photos, if that's okay with you."

Dan raised his eyebrows. "Why?"

"Well, I started writing down what we did here yesterday, a bit like a diary, and I noticed I had a ton of questions and couldn't remember everything right. So if you want to show me, perhaps I can learn. You know, properly."

Dan laughed. "That would be cool. I'd love to teach you." He eyed me critically. "And you do look like a student. All you need is the—"

"Glasses?" I cut in, whipping my brand new pair of reading glasses out of my handbag and putting them on. I lowered my head so I could ogle him over my half-lenses.

Dan gave a belly laugh. "Now you look like a 1950s secretary," he chuckled. "What I was going to say was you need a pen stuck behind your ear."

He took the biro out of my hand and slid it behind my right ear. "Like so. There, now you totally look the part."

"Oh." I took my glasses off again, embarrassed. The touch of his fingers sent tingles down my arm, and I was startled by my reaction to an innocuous little gesture. Dan was oblivious. He took the glasses from me and put them back on my nose.

"Don't take them off. I like them." He looked at me with interest, as one might examine an exotic beetle. "When did you get these?"

"A couple of months ago, when I kept getting headaches. They're only for close work and I don't need them now." I swept them off my nose and dropped them into their case and back into my handbag before Dan could interfere again.

He chuckled. "I think they're very cute," he reiterated but I didn't take the bait.

"Shall we get on with it?" I suggested a little brusquely instead, snapping Dan out of his silly mood.

"Okay, yes, of course," he agreed and led the way downstairs.

He played me the song we had worked on the previous day, and the difference was astounding. "I took your ideas and our work to the studio yesterday afternoon and had our sound man master it properly. It's not finished," he hastened to add. "It needs more work, but I wanted to show you exactly what mastering accomplishes."

"It's amazing," I agreed, totally intrigued by the change. "So what did you have in mind? What is it we're doing here, and how does it fit in with the overall recording of this new album?"

This thought had been bugging me all night. We were working in Dan's home studio, and I knew the songs would be mixed and mastered in a 'proper' studio for eventual mass production. I had wondered how our morning session would fit in.

Dan stopped the music and sat back in his chair.

"This is a critical part of the process. I always take home a copy of our raw material to play and experiment with, and Darren does the same. Sometimes Mick or Joe might pop in, or we might all work together. We mock something up, like a demo, and then we take it into the professional studio to talk through with our sound man there. He will do the mixing and mastering on his master files and add his own magic touch, too." He grinned at me.

"Every sound engineer has a certain touch. Our man, Richard, has golden ears, and he's worked with us for years, as you know. When all is said and done, and the band and I are at the end of the road with our suggestions and tweaks, Richard will sprinkle stardust all over the album. That's the art of sound engineering. That's the bit you can't teach, and can't learn. You've either got it, or you don't."

He hesitated. "I think you might have it. You blew me away yesterday. And I want to find out how far we can take you. So…" He turned to the mixing console and retrieved a stack of small USB flash drives, fanning them out on the desk in front of us.

"There are all the tracks. Richard has put them onto flash drives, one each, as a project that I can put on my DAW to play with and—"

"Your what?" I interrupted.

"Sorry," Dan said. "Please stop me if I talk jargon. DAW is short for Digital Audio Workstation, which is what we have here. My home studio."

I picked up one of the flash drives, a little black memory stick with a USB port at the end. "This contains a song, yeah?"

"This contains a song," Dan confirmed. "Richard made a copy of the raw material so I can work on it here, and when we're done, we'll put it back on the flash drive and I'll take it into the studio."

I nodded, and Dan continued. "I'd like us… I'd like *you* to work on a song each morning, maybe the same one for a few days, until you've figured out how you like it. Eventually, I'd love for you to come into the proper studio and watch Richard do his thing, but one step at a time. I can teach you the basics here. It's probably best if we start with mixing before I walk you through mastering. We have plenty of raw material to work with." He rubbed his hands, while I felt a little overwhelmed.

"Give it to me in bite-size chunks," I pleaded. "I'm no technophobe, but I feel completely out of my depth here. It's like learning a new language."

"It is," Dan concurred. "Or perhaps like learning a new instrument. And I will try to make it bite-size. Simply ask if it gets too much or if I move too fast."

Thus we set to work. Dan picked one of the songs—project number six, a song called *White Poison*—and had me play association bingo. "What do you expect of a song with this title?" he prompted for my input.

"White poison," I mused. "That sounds like drugs." Dan gave me a thumbs up. "I'm thinking this could be a hard, gritty piece with shrill guitars and a throbbing base, like a hangover headache. Or it could be a sad ballad, a mellow piece with acoustic guitars. Depends on what happens, I guess, and whether someone's died."

Dan grimaced. "You have a lyrical way of putting things, but yes, you're right. D'you know," he cut into his own thoughts, "it's quite interesting to get a female take on this. You have a different way of looking at things. This will be a great experience."

He pressed play, and it turned out my initial instinct had been spot on. It was a fast piece with loud drums, heavy on the cymbals and bass, and a racing guitar line.

"What do you think of the mix?"

I waggled my head. "It's better than yesterday's but..."

"Yes? Go on, speak your mind. Whatever comes into your head. You have to go with your instinct here."

I took the plunge. "I think it's too mushy. If you're singing about drug abuse, I want to hear a thumping heartbeat. I want the adrenaline, but it needs to start clear and become fuzzy later. You know, alter the quality of the sound through the song so that it does become oppressive and hurtful. Actually..." I paused. "Let me listen to the whole thing first to see where you're taking it and *then* let me think some more."

Dan smiled widely. "I love you," he said sincerely. "I love your style and your honesty. This will be a great partnership."

I blushed at the compliment but smiled back. Dan seemed to value my opinion. Never mind that I was a complete rookie. I had always dreamed of making music. But I didn't play an instrument that would be useful in a rock band, and while I had tried singing, my talent wasn't tremendous. Yet if I could make music *great* in this way, that would be a wonderful achievement. I would do skillful, creative work, musical work. I would be part of the action. I would be in the studio with the band...and I was getting way ahead of myself here. I chuckled to myself and concentrated on the task at hand. *Rock on, Sophie, rock on.*

Chapter Thirteen

"Spill. Who's turned your head?" Rachel demanded over coffee two weekends later. The preceding weeks had been manic. Every weekday morning, I went to Dan's house to help mix and master, and every night, I sat at my computer recording the day's events on paper.

I took a photo of his mixing console and labeled all the buttons and dials on it. To begin with, most of them were a mystery to me, but Dan worked his way methodically through the console, teaching and coaching me on each fader, each slider, each button, every display. By now, I knew the level at which a voice should record optimally, and I knew what happened if you went too far on the reverb or delay.

A couple of times, we took a track completely beyond the pale. Dan said the best way of avoiding catastrophic mistakes was to try them out, one by one, in a controlled fashion. So we turned a ballad into an oompah song. Yes, trust me, it is possible!

For two whole weeks, I saw no one apart from the kids and Dan. I didn't have time to catch up with my parents. I didn't manage to speak to the children's teachers, terrible mother that I was. And I didn't once pick up the phone to speak with Rachel. I was stretched to capacity between my recording apprenticeship, motherhood, and housework.

But the previous night, I received a text from Rachel, informing me I *would* meet her for coffee on Saturday morning or our friendship would be terminated. Thus, this morning, I had driven the kids over to her house and dumped them on Alex, who also was left holding the baby. Now Rach and I were once again installed in our erstwhile favorite coffee hole in Tooting. Old habits and memory lane and all that.

"Spill," Rachel insisted when I failed to respond immediately.

"No one has turned my head," I objected. "I've been busy."

"Busy, my ass," Rachel snorted. "You look like the cat who got the cream. Don't get me wrong..." She stirred two sugars in her cappuccino thoughtfully. "...I totally approve. This was way overdue. Only I don't like being left out in the cold."

"I'm not leaving you out in the cold." Indignation and possibly guilt gave my voice a slightly sharper edge than I had intended. I smiled and softened my expression. "I'm really, honestly, not keeping secrets from you. I've been so busy. Dan and I—"

"*Dan*," Rachel pounced immediately, as I knew she would. "Did you say, 'Dan and I'?"

I nodded, feeling sheepish.

"*No way!* Don't tell me you're rekindling that old flame after all this time!"

"I'm not. *We're* not." My voice came out strong and sincere, and Rachel took note.

"You're not," she repeated. "And you sound like you mean it. Steve's memory is still in the way, huh?"

I flinched, and Rachel caught my look of dismay, but ploughed on regardless. "So all right, what is this 'Dan and I' business?"

"He's teaching me to mix music," I burst out, unable to hold my exciting news in. "He's training me to be a sound engineer."

Now, Rachel was my best friend. Had been so since college. We had gone through an awful lot of stuff together, the best, the worst, and everything in between. We sat at each other's hospital beds and danced at each other's weddings. She was there when Dan crash-landed back in my life when I was twenty-eight, and she cheered me all the way along. She understood the attraction and the sex and the glamour. But she had *never* 'got' the music. Not surprisingly, she looked at me blankly.

"A sound engineer."

I pursed my lips into a goofy smile and nodded. "Yes, a sound engineer."

"Like the chap who sits behind that desk with all the buttons and does weird geeky things."

"Exactly like so."

"And that is exciting because...?"

"Oh Rach, how can I make you understand? It's amazing. It's like doing magic. You've got the great musicians there, and their talent is unbelievable. Yet they put their trust, their faith, their music into your hands to make a fantastic performance outstanding, to add the edge, the sparkle, the fizz."

"I *don't* understand," Rachel confessed. "I always thought sound recording was a bit of a fraud, you know. If the musician is so great, why do they need all that engineering malarkey?"

I took a deep breath, summoning my every wit to try to explain what sound engineering was all about. "A live voice, a live instrument, that's a beautiful thing. It's a living thing with three dimensions. When you try to capture it with a microphone and put it onto a record, you mess with the sound waves, you break them up and parcel them up and reassemble them. It doesn't matter how good the band is, something gets lost and distorted in the process. A voice like Dan's, no matter how powerful, can come out dull and hollow, and it doesn't sound at all like him. The sound engineer undoes that. The sound engineer makes it sound like what it really sounds like."

Inelegant as though this explanation was, Rachel seemed to connect with it. "So it's not fixing the tuning or correcting mistakes. It's more making it true to the original."

"It *can* be about fixing the tuning or correcting mistakes. A sound engineer can do that, but a professional musician will always insist on re-recording a flawed section to improve on it, and that gets spliced and crossfaded into the recording…"

Rachel poked me in the side. "Listen to you. You sound like a pro!"

"Hardly." Although I did enjoy the compliment. "Mostly what a sound engineer does is… I don't know, think about it as a picture gone pale in photocopying and the sound engineer puts the color back in."

"Nice analogy," Rachel approved. "Did Dan teach you this?"

"Nuh-uh, I made that up myself." And it was true, I *had* made it up. Somehow I 'saw' music in color; I was forever making the connection, and Dan was endlessly fascinated by it even though I couldn't explain it properly.

"So that *is* pretty exciting," Rachel concurred after a little thought. "Is it difficult?"

"Heck yes, it certainly is," I burst out. "You have to be light-fingered and golden-eared. You can't just twizzle buttons and off you go. First of all, you have to understand what needs fine-tuning and how. Then there's all your tools, your EQ and your reverb and your delay and pitch and…"

"I get it, I get it," Rachel laughed. "It sounds complicated. But I can see that you've totally got the fever."

"I do." There was no denying it. "It gives me such a buzz. You know, I don't really 'do' music, but mastering and mixing, that's totally my niche. Dan says…" I petered out, suddenly fearful of sounding arrogant.

"Dan says?"

I took a deep breath. "Dan says I've got a real talent for it, and he thinks I've really good ears and a light touch." There, I said it.

"That's high praise, from a rock star."

"Indeed."

"So what's it you two are doing every day?"

Rachel was still not entirely satisfied that we were only working together, so I explained our routine and Dan's grand teaching plan. "It's like an apprenticeship, and when he can't take it any further, he'll talk to Richard… you know, Tuscq's sound man, to see if he can take me on."

"How far *do* you want to take this?" Rachel demanded. "What about going back to *Read London*?"

"I don't know." I hesitated. "I… It feels good to do something different. From, you know, before. Rick wants me back, of course. But…if I could earn money a different way…if I could perhaps gain a small income from doing sound engineering in a few months' time…maybe that would be better."

"Better than a deputy editorship or freelance work for a great newspaper?" Rachel wasn't buying it.

"Well. Yes. Maybe. *Not*, if you put it like that, actually. But..."

"But what?"

I sighed. "It's too painful to go back. I can't do it. It brings back too many memories. It was really difficult, working-part time, and I struggled even with Steve there to help. He changed his shifts and he came home every night at witching hour and..." I gulped but tried to go on. "Without Steve..."

I welled up, angry with myself at shedding tears yet again.

"Oh sweetie, I am sorry." Rachel's voice was gentle but carefully devoid of pity. She had dropped the sympathy act a year ago. Unlike Dan, she had decided a long while back that I should stop mourning and that pitying me would only perpetuate my grief. Therefore, she had shelved the whole empathy angle although right at this moment, I swore her voice wobbled.

She spoke again. "I never made that connection. I'm sorry. Perhaps it is good to make a fresh start, try something new." She grinned wickedly. "Especially if it makes you so happy *and* it involves a totally hot rock star who, let's face it, still has the hots for you. After all this time!"

I rolled my eyes. Why did she keep bringing this up? "He does *not*. He totally doesn't. We're only working together."

"Yada, yada, yada." Rachel pretended to be bored. "I think he has the hots for you, and I am *never* wrong."

"I think you're totally post-birth hormonal and you're totally wrong, not to mention out of order," I responded. There was nothing between me and Dan, and I didn't want her putting ideas in my head that would...complicate matters.

"Methinks the lady protests too much," Rachel teased, but in a good-natured way.

"Methinks the new mum needs to mind her own business," I warned, but also in a good-natured way. "I'm not ready to see anyone else, least of all Dan, and I'm not interested."

Rachel grabbed my hand and looked me squarely in the eye. "Oh God, Sophie, I don't give a damn if he's got the hots for you or not, as long as you have that lovely glow in your eyes, a little spark of life, and you can get excited and happy again."

She might as well have poured a bucket of ice-cold water over my head. Her off-hand, light-hearted comment rocked me to the core, but I tried not to let on.

"You sound like the kids," I commented.

Rachel giggled. "There we go," she concluded. "We're all agreed. I drink to Sophie's new venture, and to falling into a whole new career." She clinked her coffee cup to mine. "And in time, who knows, you might just fall for a certain someone."

"You are a notorious matchmaker," I admonished. "Leave this here widow well alone."

"Widow, yes. Dried-up old prune, no. Mark my words, you shall flower again." Rachel grinned wickedly.

"You and your dirty talk, honestly. Methinks you've regressed fifteen years."

"Maybe I have. Maybe *you* should!"

Chapter Fourteen

Discussing my new career ambition with Rachel gave it greater weight and made it seem less flight-of-fancy. On an impulse, I rang Mum and Dad to tell them about it as well.

"Sophie, love," my Mum exclaimed when she heard my voice and immediately launched into detailed news on all the developments down Newquay way. All the while, I jiggled and twiddled the sofa cushions, nearly dropping the phone a few times and wishing I could get a word in edgewise. Eventually, though, even Mum had to stop for a breath, and I blurted out my news, rather abruptly and completely without preamble. "I've got a new job."

The surprised silence at the other end spoke volumes, but Mum rallied quickly.

"Congratulations, sweetie, that's wonderful news." She halted, probably uncertain where to go next. "I...we didn't think you were ready to go back to work? It's none of our business, of course. You know we're behind you every step of the way... It's only...well, now that you've said it... Would you tell me more?"

I blushed with embarrassment. How come I had put my Mum into a position of apologizing for asking perfectly normal questions? Had I really shut my parents so completely out of my life in the aftermath of Steve's death? They had rushed down to see me, as shell-shocked at the atrocity as the rest of the world and devastated on my behalf. They had given every conceivable form of support. Mum had even moved in with me and Josh and newborn Emily for a while, sharing with Dan and Rachel the burden of propping up the grieving widow. And yet, as soon as I could cope, I had sent her away, and it occurred to me now that I had gone out of my way to avoid seeing her or Dad.

Why? I couldn't honestly answer that question. Perhaps it was too painful seeing my Mum and Dad so happily together after decades of marriage, something that I now would never experience. Or perhaps I was trying to prove a point. I had never once considered that I might be hurting my parents.

I tried to mask my sudden emotional turmoil with a cheery laugh. "A *job* is probably an overstatement at this time. I'm working with Dan right now. He's teaching me to be a sound engineer."

"That's such a wonderful project," Mum offered after a moment's consideration. "I don't quite know what it means, but I imagine it's creative and musical, and it gets you out of the house, and perhaps…"

"Perhaps what?" I prompted when she didn't finish her thought. *Please don't go on about how Dan is such a nice man, Mum.*

"Perhaps it'll take you out of yourself a little. I'm sure it'll do you good."

Exhaling softly so she wouldn't hear my relief, I began explaining what I had been doing and what my plans and hopes were going forward. She didn't ask about *Read London*, so I volunteered my reasons for not going back to my old career, and Mum understood.

"It's probably not my place to say this, but I've been thinking for a while that going back to your old job might not be such a great idea." She spoke hesitantly but firmly. "For what it's worth, I think you are doing the right thing, trying something new. And if you can turn it into a paid position some time, ever so much the better. The only thing that worries me is…"

"Go on, Mum, you can say it, whatever it is," I encouraged.

"If you're sure… All right, I'm simply wondering how the job, were there to be one, would fit around the kids. Don't sound engineers work crazy hours?"

They certainly did, and this was a worry that had been playing on my mind. I knew the hours Dan kept, and I knew a sound engineer had to be in the studio with the band at all times, so if that was going to be my chosen career, how would it work with family life? I hadn't discussed this with Dan yet because, at the moment, the sound thing was merely a project, something that we did in the mornings for the fun of it. But if I wanted to take it further, how *would* I make it work?

"They *do* work crazy hours, Mum," I admitted. "And I've no idea how that would work for Josh and Emily, but maybe I'll figure it out. Or maybe I won't, but for now, I'm simply enjoying learning a new trade. Who knows where it'll take me."

Mum broke into my little speech before I had an opportunity to get mired in self-defense. "It doesn't really matter, does it?" she offered. "You don't have to have it all figured out at all times, do you? Just go with the flow for a bit and let life come to you again. The rest will surely work itself out."

Let life come to you again. She certainly had a way with words. Her joy at talking with me frankly about new beginnings was touching, and I wondered how long *she* had been secretly hoping that I would shelve the grieving-widow act. We talked for another hour about the kids and school and all manner of inconsequential little things. I rang off excited, energized, and relieved. I had been so lost lately that it was good to get approval from people who cared about me; it was good to know I hadn't lost my mind, and it was okay to start a new chapter of my life.

Chapter Fifteen

I was a little late getting to Dan's house the following Monday morning. My alarm clock hadn't gone off, probably because I had neglected to set it the night before. Josh had finally woken me up at quarter to eight, fully dressed and demanding his breakfast. The resulting madness had surpassed any previous Monday morning panic, and I felt grumpy and thoroughly discombobulated by the time I dropped Emily at playschool.

For the tiniest flicker of a moment, I considered bailing out of this morning's sound engineering session, but I gave myself a stern 'buck up' talk. Needless to say, I was thoroughly disappointed when, after all that, I found Dan's house empty. Well, empty of Dan, at least.

Jenny, the housekeeper, let me in and laughed good-naturedly at my disgruntled expression. "Steady on, love, Dan ain't here," she informed me.

My heart plummeted. After all this effort and stress, now I was to go home after all? But no.

"He's left you something to do in that studio of his," Jenny told me. She gave an indignant sniff. The studio was the only part of the house she wasn't allowed to clean, and I didn't think she had set foot in it in all the years that she had worked for Dan.

"Oh. Okay, so I'm supposed to go down there, am I?" I gabbled, slightly at a loss. "By myself, like, right now? Is that right?"

"Looks like it, dunnit?" Jenny concurred. "He must really trust you. The likes of me aren't even allowed to open the door!"

I smiled. I didn't think she was really upset. She normally quite enjoyed ribbing Dan about the sanctity of his studio. But she had hit the nail on the head; Dan really trusted me if he wanted me to work in there on my own. I didn't know whether to laugh, cry, or turn tail. In the end, I did neither, but rather made my way downstairs to find out what Dan wanted me to do.

I found a hand-written note taped to the door.

Morning, sweetness, it read.

Sorry I can't be here this week. Jack has booked us into a studio in Seattle, but I'll be back by the weekend. There's some stuff for you to play with ~ show me what you can do! Loveya,
Dan XXX

I tore the note off the door and, with shaking hands, entered Dan's sanctum and sat in his swivel chair to read his missive all over again. As I took in its full meaning, a bewildering range of emotions assaulted me, one after the other.

Disappointment featured high on the list, although I couldn't work out what exactly I was disappointed about. Was it simply that I had been deprived of my routine morning task spent in agreeable company?

At the same time, I was touched. It was nice to be addressed with 'sweetness' and I simply adored the hastily scrawled kisses and the completely innocent, *loveya*. While there was *obviously* no deeper meaning, it was lovely that someone should care about me enough to use a term of endearment.

There was also a bit of anger in the mix. He had to have known about the Seattle trip for a while. In this day and age, you couldn't decide on a Monday morning that it would be *quite* nice to go the States for a few days. You needed to book flights and arrange visas, and if the band were recording, they probably needed work visas, which took weeks, *months* to organize. So why hadn't he told me? We had seen each other almost every day for the past few weeks. How could a *little* detail like a trip to Seattle have slipped his mind? He wasn't a thoughtless person, or a mean one. Since Steve's death, he had always made a point of keeping me informed of his travels lest I feel alone and abandoned, which was how I felt right now. So what had changed?

Had he deliberately set me up? But why? Had he perhaps not wanted to annoy me, or upset me? Well, I was more upset now than I would have been any other way.

I shook my head. It was a mystery, and would remain so until he got back. There really wasn't much point in getting worked up. It was simply one of those Dan things.

Leaning back in the chair, I used the mixing console for a bit of leverage to give myself a good swivel round. Disappointed, touched, angry, alone, sad. And *anxious*. Dan wanted me to work on something. I was to manipulate the buttons and dials, faders and sliders, all by myself.

A flash drive sat on the side of the console. It was labeled, *Sophie's Project*, yet there were no further notes or instructions, not even a song title. Reaching out, I touched the black plastic casing with my index finger.

"I am to do something with you," I addressed it as though it could help me.

Turning the flash drive over and over, I had another swivel in the chair while I waited for my emotions to simmer down and an overriding response to emerge. When it did, it was excitement. I actually relished the thought of cutting my teeth as an independent sound engineer in the safety of Dan's home studio. I was keen to find out what was on the flash drive and eager to do something with it.

Breathing deeply, I considered the best strategy. In past sessions, Dan had had me explore a number of ways 'in' to the song. We had played the song title association game; we had listened to a whole song before talking about it; we had played with a song on first hearing. I didn't know which way I wanted to turn today, although song title association was not an option as Dan hadn't given me one. A clue, perhaps, that he wanted me to listen to the song first? Or go straight into engineering?

I nibbled at my thumb. *Go with your instinct*, I heard Dan's voice say in my head. My instinct was to get the song playing, first of all. Therefore, my task was to get the DAW working and the song transferred and playing.

Very carefully and deliberately, I pressed the 'on' button and waited for the display to light up. Talking myself through the task at hand, I connected the flash drive and waited for the song to load on to the system. Next, I saved it under "Working Title" and made sure I ejected the flash drive so there was no way I could corrupt my source file.

So far, so good. I put the flash drive to one side, feeling shaky and exhilarated all at once. I had actually put the console to work and managed the first vital task of my project. The song was loaded and ready. Now I could begin my job.

I allowed myself a couple of minutes to collect my thoughts. The whole situation reminded me of being alone in a car for the first time after I passed my driving test, suddenly being in charge of a potentially lethal machine all by myself. It had been an awe-inspiring and frightening moment, and this felt similar.

Yet all of a sudden, I knew how I wanted to proceed. I rooted around in a drawer for a notepad and a pen and installed myself to the left of the mixing console so I could write. Pen poised and pad ready, I pressed 'play' and waited for the music to fill the room.

Drums first, a gentle tapping of drum stick on cymbals followed by a couple of beats on the snare. The sound was slightly hollow, as though the drummer had been in a church. I wrote down on my pad, *Drums. Gentle. Hollow.*

Dan started singing, and his voice was loud, too loud for the drums. I wrote down, *vocals too loud; pull back, reverb.*

And so I continued, taking notes of my impressions through the song. I listened to it several times, adding notes to my music map and starting to write out the lyrics as well. Lyrics mattered greatly, to me and to Dan, and they would hold the key to how I would mix and master the song. I chuckled at myself and told myself to tread carefully. The danger, as Dan had warned me many a time, would lie in feeling over-confident, in settling too fast on a strategy or plan without truly listening with my ears *and* my heart.

In the end, I spent the entire morning listening to the song over and over again. It was a classic rock song, hard and fast, but melodious and lyrical. Or it would be, once I was done with it. I jotted down priorities. Mixing and balancing the tracks was first on my agenda. Dan had left me a really raw recording, and I would have to satisfy my inner sense of 'right' for the song before I could start thinking about effects.

Time flew faster still than it did with Dan beside me, and I noted, with only minutes to spare, that I would have to leave quickly to collect Emily on time. I closed down the DAW and switched off the light before racing upstairs and shouting a cheery 'goodbye' to Jenny, who was hoovering the lounge.

"Wait!" she shouted just as I made it to the front door. "Wait, you're forgetting your keys!" She caught up with me and proffered a set of keys.

I looked at her quizzically. "Won't you be here tomorrow?"

"Nah, I've got the rest of the week off, with Mr. Hunter gone and all that. I'll be back on Friday evening to make sure the house is warm and to prepare some food for the weekend. You'll be all right tidying up after yourself when you work here, won't you?"

I nodded, unable to speak for a moment. The keys lay heavy in the palm of my hand. It was the same set that I had been given before, when I had lived with Dan for a few weeks after a fire had ended my thirtieth birthday party and rendered my flat uninhabitable. When I had first set eyes on but not yet met Steve, and when I had been hoping to engineer a meeting as soon as possible. In the days before grief and sorrow.

"You okay?" Jenny cut in. "Don't worry about the alarm. It's still as it always was."

"I'm not worried about the alarm," I responded. "It's just...these keys..."

"They be bringing back memories of the good old days when you and Mr. Hunter still were considering them possibilities," Jenny chuckled.

I blushed. She meant no harm, I was sure of that. She always said things as she saw them, and she had seen plenty in the relationship between me and Dan that wasn't there, only we had never told her.

"The good old days," I concurred with a smile and stuffed the keys into my handbag. "I'm sure I'll work out the alarm system tomorrow. You have a good week off, now, Jenny."

I waved at her before flying down the front path to my car. I was seriously running late, and I didn't want to risk Emily's tears. It was only when I had picked her up exactly on time, had taken her home and fed her, that I realized I still didn't know the title of the song I was working on. The clue would most likely be in the chorus, although Dan had been known to be a creative titler. I ran the song through my mind yet again and suddenly was struck by inspiration.

"Turn Your Corner."

Chapter Sixteen

"Turn Your Corner" consumed my life for the next four days whenever I wasn't wearing my Mummy hat. I worked on it feverishly every morning, and at the end of every session I used my phone for a sneaky sound-capture so I could review the track at home in the evening. I was a woman possessed.

On Tuesday morning, I addressed the mix and balance, taking the first critical step in the process. It took me much longer than I had anticipated, and I shed a few tears of frustration when I couldn't get the song to sound exactly as I wanted. On Wednesday morning, I returned refreshed and with a new plan of attack which had presented itself to me late on Tuesday evening. Instead of more mixing, I turned my attention to some of the fine tuning tools.

To begin with, I worked on the EQ, or equalization. I wanted the song to be warm and edgy, so I experimented with a slight upper bass boost and some of the high frequencies. Some of the things I tried I liked, while others gave me goosebumps of horror.

By Thursday morning, I had the instruments and vocals sounding nearly how I wanted them, so I had another stab at mixing and balancing, and it proved much easier this time. My self-taught lesson 101 was that mixing and mastering could be iterative; that sometimes, it was worthwhile going back and forth between the two stages.

By Friday lunchtime, I was proud of my little project, and I felt elated and deflated at the same time. I had to leave before noon, as always, and I had no way of knowing when Dan would be back to listen to my effort. I fretted about not being there when he did, because I really wanted to get a firsthand reaction. If he thought I had done badly, I wanted to know.

But there was nothing for it, I had to leave. Reluctantly, I gathered together my music map and notes and put them in my bag. I considered leaving them, but I wanted Dan to listen to the song without any clue as to what he could expect.

I loaded my engineered version on a fresh flash drive and balanced it on the console, exactly as I had found the original drive. I didn't write a note to stick on the studio door, although I considered it. However, Dan deserved a moment of uncertainty — had I or had I not come and worked? — and I rued my rash action of Monday morning when I had torn the note off the studio door in the first place. How cool would it have been to have left it in place, greatly enhancing Dan's confusion on his return? *Two can play your game*, I grinned to myself as I locked up Dan's house. *Just please call me the minute you listen to it.*

Obviously, I didn't expect Dan to be back on Friday afternoon, but I still felt on edge all day. The phone remained stubbornly silent until nearly ten p.m. Yet relief and excitement — my moment of truth was upon me! — were replaced with instant disappointment when caller ID announced Rachel.

Not that it wasn't nice to hear from her, but I *had* kind of been waiting for someone else. I summoned a cheery greeting which stuck in my throat as a tearful Rachel launched herself straight into the conversation.

"Henry has been sick," she cried. "It was awful. He had vomit coming out of his nose and his eyes and I'm absolutely terrified."

I made soothing noises and tried to get to the bottom of Henry's sudden illness. "How's he now?"

"He's gone to sleep," Rachel howled, clearly upset by her offspring's ability to cause utter devastation and drift off peacefully the next second.

"How often was he sick?"

"Just the once."

"Has he got a temperature?"

"No."

"Any funny nappies?"

"No."

I stroked the sofa cushion, as though this random action would calm down my distraught friend. My mind was still turning over possibilities for the cause of Henry's misery.

"What happened before he was sick? Did you feed him? Jiggle him? Burp him?"

There was a small silence at the other end that seemed to radiate waves of guilt. "Um…"

"Yes?"

"Well, you know how he is always so hungry, right? So I made him a bigger bottle tonight."

"How much bigger?"

"Um…double. He's always so hungry and I thought…"

I tried hard not to laugh. "Did he take it?"

"In ten minutes flat."

This time I couldn't help a giggle. "Sweetie, he can't take so much milk yet. He was like a primed volcano. But I don't think you have anything to worry about unless he has a temperature or something."

"No temperature," Rachel reiterated. "So I don't need to call the doctor?"

"I don't think so. Look," I offered to put her mind at rest. "Let him sleep, but take his temperature in half an hour, and again before you go to bed. And if you're worried, call me back. Or better still, call the out-of-hours doctors."

"Okay. Thank you," came Rachel's small voice. "Sorry to bother you with this."

"No bother at all. G'night, sweetie." We rang off, and I felt all wistful. *Ah, the joys of infanthood.* Steve and I had had our fair share of late-night upsets like this.

I tested my memories gingerly. On previous occasions, I usually felt unsettled and lonely. Tonight, I felt nostalgic and a little sad, but mostly calm and mellow. That was a good thing, right? A step in the right direction? Wasn't that what everyone was telling me?

A small cough behind me frightened me nearly senseless. I whipped around to find a grinning Dan leaning in my doorway.

Chapter Seventeen

"What the heck are you doing here?" I shouted. "You gave me a big fright."

"And it's very nice to see you, too," Dan offered. "I just got back and wanted to see how you were."

I rose to my feet. "How did you get in?"

Stupid question; Dan had had keys to my house for as long as I could remember. "I meant, how did you get in so quietly?" I corrected myself.

"Ah, I'm a smooth operator if I have to be," Dan chuckled, but swiftly turned serious. "You were so busy chatting with Rachel...well, I assume it was Rachel, anyway...I could have burgled you, and you wouldn't have noticed. Is everything all right? With Rachel?"

"She's fine, although Henry did a terrific vomiting act on her," I responded. I was about to launch into a reminiscence of one of Josh's spectacular explosions when I got distracted by Dan's appearance. He looked terrible. Enormous bags shadowed his eyes with dark purple smudges, and his face looked sallow and pale. He wasn't well, and I wasn't sure whether it was *only* the tiredness from having flown across the entire continental US and the Atlantic, or something more. Mummy-me wanted to reach out and stroke his face, then tuck him up in bed with a hot water bottle and a mug of honeyed warm milk. I offered neither the hug nor the caress, but rather stood and stared and waited for him to speak.

After an almighty yawn, Dan sat himself down on the sofa and stretched out. "Oh God, I'm so tired," he announced. I rushed to his side and knelt on the floor, bringing my face level with his.

"Are you okay?"

Surprise lit up his eyes, and he waited a moment before he replied, scrutinizing my face intently. "I'm fine," he finally reassured me. "If a bit tired. I only got off the plane two hours ago, and I came straight here. Well…" He petered out while he fumbled in his trouser pocket. "…*almost* straight here. I picked up *this* from home first." He waved the flash drive marked "Turn Your Corner" in my face. I blushed.

"Have you listened to it yet?"

"Did you want me to?" Dan's eyes met mine, searching and teasing.

"Um…yes. Well, no. I don't know." I ran my hands through my hair and rubbed my nose. "Why didn't you tell me you were going to Seattle?" I blurted out, changing the subject before I could stop myself. Dan had the grace to look sheepish.

"I don't really know. It was arranged months ago and I forgot all about it. And then I tried to ignore the fact that I would have to be away. And…I don't know." He was lost for words. "It was stupid, really. I'm sorry."

His honesty completely disarmed me. "It doesn't matter," I soothed. "You're not accountable to me or anything. I was surprised, that was all."

"But I am, though. Accountable to you, and the kids. I promised to be there for you, and I don't even tell you when I'm going away. I don't know why that happened, I feel really stupid. That's why I had to come over and see you tonight. I've been feeling bad all week."

"You might have rung me in the week, if you were feeling so bad," I suggested mildly. "A phone call would have been nice. Or an email."

Dan's face fell even further, and my heart swelled up with worry. Something had happened to this man, and I couldn't work out what it was.

"I know," he mumbled, sounding contrite and apologetic. "But I couldn't get myself to do it. I was worried I would make it worse."

I smiled to myself. Men; they were all the same. Totally unable to think through their emotions rationally and make sane decisions. Dan looked at me as though he could read my mind, and he gently ran a finger down the side of my face.

"Something has changed between us," he whispered. "And I don't know what to make of it." His eyes assumed an intense fervor that I hadn't seen since he had proposed to me in Paris over eight years ago. This was dangerous territory.

"I don't think so," I said softly, deliberately misunderstanding him. "We're still friends, right?"

"We are," Dan confirmed, but wouldn't let go of his train of thought. "But I feel different, suddenly. I feel... I feel like the balance has changed. I feel responsible for you. I want to look after you, I—"

"But you *are*," I interrupted, now seriously fearful of where this conversation was going. "You've been looking after me for years. And the kids, too."

"I know," Dan conceded. "But somehow, things are different now. I...I missed you in Seattle." He laughed uncertainly. "That doesn't sound right. I always miss you when I go away, you know, recording or on tour, but I missed you *different* this time. I can't really explain it. It's all so..."

The phone rang and interrupted his ruminations. I jumped up and answered it before the loud trilling woke the kids. It was Rachel again. She wanted to tell me that Henry definitely didn't have a temperature and they were all going to sleep now, and did I think that was okay?

By the time I had reassured her and finished the call, Dan had sunk down lower on my sofa and was fast asleep. The flash drive that had brought him here had slipped from his grasp and lay abandoned on the floor. I picked it up and stuffed it in my handbag in the hallway. If the kids found it lying around in the morning, it would be drawn on, stomped on, and otherwise destroyed.

Back in the lounge, I contemplated my sleeping rock legend for a few moments. He was deeply asleep; so much so that I couldn't rouse him to move him up into the guest bed. The sofa would have to do for tonight. I raided the guest room for duvets and pillows to make Dan more comfortable. As gently as I could, I eased the pillows under his head and the shoes off his feet. Feeling like a regular Florence Nightingale, I spread the duvet over his prone body and tucked the sides in around him so he wouldn't be cold. On an impulse, I planted a light kiss on his forehead and was perturbed to find it cold and clammy. Dan was definitely not well, but at least he was resting. I tiptoed out of the lounge, switching off the lights as I went.

Chapter Eighteen

Needless to say, I didn't have a very good night. Unspoken words and assumptions floated around my head, mingling in my dreams with a sick Henry and a distraught Rachel. A ghostly looking Dan kept coming and going, alternately drinking beer with Steve in the back garden and whisking the kids away to perform with him on tour.

When I got up and dressed at seven, my pale and hollow-eyed appearance matched both the Dan of my restless dreams and the Dan of the night before. The house was perfectly quiet, and nobody else was up. Even my early riser, Josh, had started sleeping later on weekends.

I padded downstairs to check on the rock god ensconced in my lounge. He, too, was sleeping peacefully. He had curled up onto his side and tucked his entwined hands under his face. The smudges under his eyes had improved. He looked relaxed, and there was some color in his cheeks.

How long I had stood there, looking at Dan and thinking about nothing in particular, I couldn't say, but I snapped to when I felt a gentle tugging at my hand. Josh had joined me in the lounge, still in pajamas, of course, and his little face was wreathed in adoration for Dan.

"Why is Dan sleeping on the sofa?" he whispered as softly as he could manage.

"Because he got here very late and was very tired and he simply fell asleep where he sat," I whispered back, giving Josh a conspiratorial smile. "He's still wearing his clothes, look!" I wasn't entirely sure why I was making such a big deal out of this to my four-year old son who wouldn't care either way, but Josh peered under the duvet when I carefully lifted a corner to show Dan's be-trousered legs.

"Awesome," he enthused. "He's like a cowboy, sleeping in his leather trousers."

"Shall we let him sleep a bit longer and make some breakfast?" I suggested, and Josh nodded eagerly.

We raided the fridge and prepared an improvised luxury breakfast of homemade waffles, bacon, and fresh fruit. Emily joined us halfway through and took great pleasure in scooping gloopy waffle mixture onto the waffle maker, closing the lid, and watching it rise gently as the baking waffles expanded in size.

Amazingly, Dan slept right through the increasing noise levels emanating from the kitchen, and he was still slumbering when we were ready to eat. I ventured into the lounge and considered options. He had fallen asleep by eleven p.m., and it was now nine the following morning. Early, by rock star standards, but ten hours qualified as a good night, even in my book.

Josh had crept up on me again. "Why don't we have a breakfast picnic here in the lounge and Dan can have breakfast in bed on the sofa," he suggested, bright-eyed.

I knelt down to speak with him, a let-down formulated on my lips, but I changed my mind. Why not indeed? What could be nicer than to be woken up by a bunch of smiling people, a huge pile of waffles, and fresh coffee?

"Excellent idea, my gorgeous." I high-fived my darling son and we crept out of the lounge again to get organized.

The kids were brilliant, caught up in their little ploy to surprise Dan. Emily carried plates back and forth, one at a time, doing a kind of stealth-tiptoe each way and setting down her cargo very carefully on the coffee table. Josh took care of the cutlery and the fruit bowl, and I brought up the rear with the hot food and drinks. The kids and I sat on cushions on the floor around our laden table, and we looked at each other with big smiles. Mission accomplished!

The quiet bustle of activity in his immediate vicinity had permeated Dan's consciousness, and he opened his eyes with perfect timing, catching sight of the waffles first, then me, then the kids. He grinned widely, stretched his arms, and sat up.

"What's all this?"

"Mummy said you were very tired, and so we thought we'd make you breakfast on the sofa," Josh burst out, unable to contain his energy or joy at the successful surprise.

"Wow, thank you," Dan issued after a big yawn. He rubbed his eyes and tried to smooth his hair. My stomach lurched at the memory of many a breakfast-in-bed shared by the lovely Dan Hunter and me, Sophie Penhalligan, as I had been back then.

Our eyes locked for a second, and a flash of understanding passed between us. The moment was so fleeting I might have imagined it, but I didn't think so. Yet the kids' noisy clambering for food distracted me from that train of thought, and I let it go.

After a hearty breakfast and a long, hot shower, Dan returned downstairs looking like himself. I breathed a secret sigh of relief at his improved appearance. I had probably overreacted last night, and his tiredness had been a result of the long flight and a stressful week.

"What's next?" I inquired cautiously, knowing that the Jones family would be collectively disappointed if Dan had to leave, knowing also that it would be foolish to assume he would stay.

"I guess I ought to go home and get some fresh clothes and catch up with some stuff," Dan ventured. "We are having the weekend off, though, so I could come back later? If you want?"

"That would be nice," I confirmed, feeling unaccountably shy. "The kids haven't seen you properly in ages. It's always only been me." I blushed and felt annoyed with myself, but Dan was either oblivious to my discomfort or tactfully ignored it.

"We could go out to Richmond Park and see the deer, maybe? Or—I know!" His face lit up with delighted anticipation. "We could fly a kite! Have the kids done that before?"

I shook my head, smiling indulgently. "I'm sure they'd love to, only we haven't got a kite and…"

"Don't worry. I'll bring one. It might be guitar shaped, but I'm sure I've still got it."

I burst out laughing. "You've got a guitar-shaped kite? Really?"

Dan nodded emphatically.

"Why? Where from?"

"Um," Dan started. "I was given it. By the band. As a birthday present. When I turned thirty. Because… you know. Three-oh. Three."

I laughed. "Have you ever flown it?"

Dan looked more sheepish still. "Of course. On the Common, and also in Richmond Park. It's brilliant there for kite-flying, and the band and I used to go quite a lot, at one time."

"The band? Why, are there more guitar-shaped kites about?"

Dan's turn to laugh. "No, but Joe has a drum kit and Darren has a pirate ship."

I shook my head. "How come that's never been in the paper? I can see the headlines…" Adopting a news-reader voice, I made sweeping gestures in the air. "Rock star flies kite as high as a kite…"

"Now, now, young lady," Dan admonished. "We have never done that stuff, and you know that full well. But," he grinned boyishly, "The 'rock star flies kite' bit could be a good angle. Maybe we could take some pictures."

"I'll bring the camera," I deadpanned, half-joking, but Dan took me seriously.

"That would be fab. For, you know…" He backpedalled, seeing my thunderous face and knowing how much I hated the kids and I being dragged into publicity stunts. "… just for me. My godchildren and I. And their beautiful mother."

"Aw, you!" I thumped him lightly on the arm. He could still talk me around to almost anything, this famous rock star of mine.

Chapter Nineteen

Dan never got a chance to listen to my mastered song that weekend. I totally forgot I had put the flash drive in my handbag, and when he left late on Saturday, he left empty-handed. It wasn't until the following Wednesday that we got back together again. I had been asked to help out with a school trip on Monday, and it was my turn to be parent helper at Emily's playschool on Tuesday. For three whole days, I had butterflies in my tummy every time I thought about the flash drive in my handbag. When and how would I get to play the song for him? And what would he say when I did?

My hour of reckoning finally arrived on Wednesday morning. I had just inserted the key into Dan's front lock when Jenny pulled the door open to let me in.

"Morning," she whispered. "Mr. Hunter's down in his studio. He's not in a great mood."

I was a little taken aback by her comment. I couldn't remember Dan *ever* being in a foul mood. Therefore it was with some trepidation I descended the stairs to join him at the console.

What could have happened? Was it something *I* had done? Had I broken something in the studio?

When I carefully opened the door, I caught the tiniest glimpse of Dan slouched in his chair, leaning backwards with his eyes closed and rubbing his cheeks with his hands in a gesture highly reminiscent of Munch's famous *The Scream*. At the sound of my voice, he sat up and put a bright smile on his face, and the visual association faded.

"Morning, lovely," he said, his voice cheerful and strong.

"Morning, gorgeous," I answered back and settled myself in his assistant's chair. Whatever it was that had put him in a bad mood, it didn't appear to have been me.

Dan looked at me expectantly. Eventually, he held out his hand in a 'give over' motion, and I dutifully scrambled to retrieve the flash drive from my handbag. My fingers trembled with nerves as I handed it to him, and I jumped when our hands met for a fraction of a second.

Dan chuckled. "You look nervous. I'm sure you did a brilliant job."

"I feel like I'm about to be judged for an exam," I confessed. "I worked so hard, but what if you don't like it?"

"So what if I don't like it? Happens all the time. Richard doesn't always get it how we want it. Sometimes we make him change it. Sometimes we stick with his instincts. That's what it's all about. Let's hear it!"

He smiled his wicked-boy grin as he connected the flash drive to the console, and my heart soared. He seemed quite happy.

"Jenny said you were in a bad mood," I burst out. "But you seem fine to me."

His eyes darkened for the tiniest moment. "I didn't sleep well," he said. "I can be a bit of a morning grump."

His tone of voice invited no funny rejoinder, and I held my tongue. No need seeing ghosts and bad portents in every little exchange; besides, I knew all about being a morning grump, being one myself. Only Dan had never been grumpy in the mornings, not to my knowledge, not when we had spent nights together. Then again, that was a long time ago.

The DAW had meanwhile accepted the flash drive and "Turn Your Corner" was loading. I wriggled in my chair, full of nerves again, and Dan reached out to touch my hand in a reassuring manner.

"It'll be fine." He smiled, good nature restored. "I look forward to it."

He hit play, and the song started with the drums I had so carefully balanced and filtered. The sound was crisp and gritty and instantly captivating.

Dan closed his eyes and listened intently. His foot tapped along, and he air-played the guitar with his right hand. I doubted he was aware he was doing it. He looked transported and entranced.

All too soon, the song finished. Never before had three minutes and thirty-two seconds passed so quickly and so slowly at the same time. Dan's eyes remained closed as a slow, appreciative smile spread across his face. I held my breath.

Quite unexpectedly, Dan jumped off his chair and punched the air. "Awesome," he shouted at full volume. "My God, this is totally awesome!"

He pulled me to my feet and gave me a hug that lifted me clear off the floor. He made as though to swing me around, but abandoned that plan owing to the confined space in the studio. Instead, he set me down again and gave me the biggest smackeroony of a kiss on the cheek.

"You are amazing. Oh. My. God. You are totally unbelievable. This is great! This is fantastic!" he enthused, ruffling his hair in joyful agitation, then ruffling mine. I grinned, lost for words at his reaction.

Dan turned his attention back to the DAW and started the song again, skipping forward to the bits he particularly liked. "That's an amazing effect, it's utterly brilliant. And..." He forwarded to the next bit that had captured his interest. "Wow. Loud and edgy, I like it. You did all this by yourself, with only a little instruction..."

He gave me another hug. "You must be a genius."

I opened my mouth to speak, but he tilted his head to kiss me at the same time. Our lips met and touched lightly. His mouth tasted sweet and warm, as it always had. I had forgotten how well I remembered his kiss, his touch, as if it had been mere hours rather than years. Dan's musky, masculine scent overwhelmed me and I closed my eyes, giving myself up to the feeling, going with the moment. Quite suddenly, Dan's arms encircled me, one hand pushed into the small of my back, the other travelling up, up, until he cupped the back of my head and entwined his fingers in my hair.

A million remembered moments flooded my brain and drowned out rational thought. That night in the Royal, when we had that bath together and then I had fallen asleep before we could compromise ourselves. The morning after, when Dan had explored every inch of my body and we had sex without having sex. My heart rate ramped up several thousand beats and my loin danced at the recollection of his fingers on me, inside me. I swooned ever so slightly. Instinctively, I leaned into Dan and his arms closed more tightly around me, holding me close, so very close, making me feel safe and wanted.

And still his mouth was on mine, seductive, insistent, exploring. His nose touched my cheek, his ragged breath was hot against my face. I noticed and relished the feel of his hardness through his jeans, pressed hard against my abdomen, and the memories kept coming. The first time we made love... *What goes on tour, stays on tour.* The delicious, heady sex we had had back then. The feel of him on top of me, inside me... I grew hot and dizzy, and there was a longing in my tummy that could only be lust.

For the briefest of instants, I responded to Dan's kiss with wanton abandon, lips tasting lips, tongue caressing tongue, our hearts beating as one. It was fantastic. It was more than fantastic. It was meant to be. Wild. Dangerous. Forbidden.

Forbidden. In a lightning flash, the arousing memories of our love-making morphed into memories of other men in my life...of Tim...and of Steve. *Steve.*

My heart caught in my throat, and I could no longer breathe. I choked on my tongue, Dan's tongue, my guilt. I had caught myself in the act of betraying my deceased husband, and it was an awful feeling. It hurt. *I* hurt. I had crossed a line. The shame was like a physical thing, a thick layer of sand on my tongue and grit in my eyes, a clamp around my heart, a red-hot pain. Pulling back abruptly, I broke my connection with Dan and took a shuddering breath. Confusion and guilt wrestled for supremacy, but guilt won.

Apparently oblivious to my conflicting emotions, Dan inclined his head, taking a gentle step backwards with his eyes fixed on mine. He bumped into the console and put out a steadying hand, accidentally pressing buttons as he did so. "Turn Your Corner" started all over again, and the sudden volume startled both of us. For a second we froze, then Dan turned the music off and silence enveloped us once more.

"Totally awesome," Dan repeated, somewhat breathless, but it was unclear whether he meant the song or the kiss he had stolen from me. His eyes danced with desire and something else, something deeper, but I refused to acknowledge it.

"Thank you," I replied instead, trying to hide my turmoil and inadvertently maintaining the ambiguity.

Dan sent me a goofy smile. "Maybe we should have—"

I never found out what the 'should have' entailed as there was a sharp knock on the door, and someone entered without waiting for a response. Dan held out a hand in greeting, whereas I lowered my bottom into my chair, my knees momentarily ceasing to function in the aftermath of the emotion.

The new arrival looked vaguely familiar. Of tall build, with dark hair and dark eyes, he smiled widely as he took in my presence within Dan's sanctum. "Hiya, Sophie," he opened without preamble.

I shot Dan a curious glance.

"Sophie, you remember Richard, our sound man. Right?" Dan flapped his hands about in a no-introduction-needed gesture.

The sound man. That made sense. I knew I had seen this face before, but it had been a long time.

Richard stepped forward and gave me a friendly peck on the cheek. "How'yer doin', Sophie?" he drawled. "I hear you've been doin' great things with them buttons!"

Dan didn't give me an opportunity to respond. "Wow, wait until you hear her latest production," he announced. "It'll knock your socks off. You ready?"

Richard nodded, and without warning or consulting me, Dan played "Turn Your Corner" all over again. It seemed he couldn't get enough of it. Inwardly, I hugged myself with glee, although a thin sliver of uncertainty permeated my heart with icy spicules. *Why was Richard here?*

The sound man listened with his eyes closed, completely intent on the music. Dan flicked his eyes between one of his oldest friends and long-time workmate, and me, back and forth, back and forth. I became so nervous I stared at a spot a little above Dan's head, mesmerized by an ancient little stain on the ceiling. The song ended, and the DAW clicked off. Silence filled the studio until Richard spoke.

"I'll have her," he said.

Chapter Twenty

Dan let go of a long breath of relief. "I am so pleased," he announced. "Congratulations, Sophie. This is high praise from a tough critic."

I wasn't sure whether I was fully in the frame. "Thank you," I mumbled, ever polite. "What do you mean, 'you'll *have* me'?"

Richard perched on the table next to the console. "I mean," he explained slowly, "I'll have yer as my apprentice. I don't apprentice lightly, and it's been a long time since I last took anyone on."

"It's true," Dan explained, unhelpfully. "Last time Richard apprenticed someone, the chap left after three months. Couldn't take the pressure."

Richard smiled wryly. "He couldn't take the criticism, and he simply didn't have the *ear*. But you are in a league of your own, and it'd be my honor to take yer on. If yer like."

Had my eyes actually been on stalks, they would have swiveled like a periscope on a submarine, left, right, left, right. I wasn't quite following.

"Hang on a minute," I begged the men. "I know Dan said something about training me, but I had no idea you guys had cooked up some kind of apprentice-scheme between you. How do you know that's what I want?"

Both men regarded me incredulously.

"You've got the ear," Richard repeated, being the first to recover. "It'd be a crime not to teach yer to make something of it."

"Sophie, I thought that's what you wanted; a new skill, a new project. I'm not a great teacher. I can't take you much further. You need proper training from the ground up," Dan gushed. I hadn't often heard Dan gushing before. It was quite un-Dan-like, but very sweet. He leaned toward me and whispered conspiratorially. "This is a once-in-a-lifetime opportunity, my sweet. Richard swore he would *never* take anyone else on after the last twerp. You've changed his mind. Go with it. You won't regret it."

"But—but—but—" I couldn't get my thoughts organized. I probably looked like a stranded fish with my mouth opening and closing.

"But what?" Dan prompted, sensing *issues*.

"But… sound engineers, they work crazy hours. I can't do crazy hours. I've got the kids to think of."

Richard gave me a reassuring smile. "Dan's told me all about yer nippers," he assured me. "I know you can't do late-night studio session at the moment. Tell me what you *can* do."

I squirmed, feeling put on the spot. "Um, at this point, I can really only do mornings. You know, a couple of hours while Emily is at playschool. Late evenings, maybe I can manage one of those once a week if I find a sitter. Same for weekends, but not on a regular basis."

My head swam as I tried to compute the logistical implications of all of this. Was I really ready to take this on? I had enthused about this new 'career' to Rachel and Mum and Dad, but suddenly I was facing a whole new ball game. I had vaguely considered the possibility of stepping up the training, but this was *serious*.

Dan grabbed my hand to calm me down. "Don't worry," he soothed. "Richard and I've already talked about this. He simply wanted to hear it from you. I think he was probing your commitment." He shot Richard a defy-me-and-I'll-eat-you kind of look.

Richard laughed. "I'm not really an ogre. I only want to know that yer serious. No point starting if yer gonna bail at the first sign of pressure."

"I won't," I objected stubbornly.

"She won't," Dan concurred at the same time, sounding stubborn on my behalf.

"Cool yerselves," Richard appeased. "We'll do a couple of hours every morning. That's plenty to be getting started with. Dan will bring you, and we'll begin with the basics. In a few weeks, you can sit in on actual sessions. The rest, we'll play by ear. No pun intended." He chuckled at his own joke.

"That sounds good, if it's really all right with you," I exclaimed, excitement and joy surging through me in a giant wave. "*Are* you sure?" I added. "I wouldn't want to be a burden."

"Yer not a burden unless you start messin' me about or not takin' instruction properly. But it doesn't look like that'll be a problem." Richard's voice was dry and patient.

"Just do what you've been doing and Richard will simply love you. He'll eat out of your hands," Dan laughed. "I'm sure of it."

I looked from one man to another, stood straight, and stepped toward Richard, extending a hand for a formal shake. "Okay. I'll accept. I'd love to be your apprentice," I enunciated carefully, sensing the gravity of my decision settle onto my shoulders like… like a lightweight, soft, feather boa. This was the right thing to do.

Richard took my hand and shook it. "Great," he confirmed. "Starting tomorrow."

"Starting tomorrow," I repeated, and Dan gave me a thumbs-up.

Chapter Twenty-One

Richard revealed himself to be a tough-love kind of master. My official apprenticeship as a sound engineer began with the proverbial ice-cold shower, and it took several weeks before Richard and I, teacher and learner, master and apprentice, reached an easy, comfortable mode of being that enabled me to relax and see purpose in my torture.

The portents were all there on the first morning when Dan drove me across to the studio in Central London where Richard was based. I was full of beans and excited anticipation until Dan started making ominous noises.

"Um," was his eloquent opening line. "Um. Richard doesn't mince words. I'm fairly sure that your initiation will involve him taking your mix of "Turn Your Corner" apart." He flashed me an apologetic smile.

"What do you mean, take my mix apart?" I had an odd sensation in my tummy, like I had swallowed a lead weight. "He was totally enthusiastic about it, as were you."

Dan slowly nodded his head. "He was. I was. It is a great mix, for a rookie. It shows potential."

"But?" I waited for a response, becoming increasingly agitated when none came. "But what?"

Still no reply. Dan rolled his head from side to side, as though hoping for inspiration on how to best break the news.

"For weeks, you've been telling me how great I've been doing, and now you're telling me that wasn't true? Is that where you're headed?" I tried to anticipate the blow, aware that I sounded petulant.

"No, of course not," Dan protested. "You are doing fantastically well. But you have a lot to learn still. Your mixing shows an instinctive awareness of common rookie mistakes, but that doesn't mean you haven't committed any sound-engineering crimes."

"Crimes?" Sub-surface hysteria made my voice sound shrill and brittle. "What crimes? I thought it sounded cool!"

"It did, for where you are. I'm sure Richard will take it all apart and tell you," Dan mumbled. "He's the genius. I only hear so much. Just… Just listen to what he has to say. And don't cry."

I swallowed hard. That sounded even worse, *Don't cry*.

Twenty minutes later, I was clinging to those words for dear life. My initiation had been brutal. Dan had delivered me and fled. "I'll see you at half past eleven," he shouted before dropping the briefest of good-luck kisses on my head.

Upon my arrival, Richard wasted no time in playing "Turn Your Corner" back to me, quite loudly. It sounded somewhat different in the studio. Alternately boomy and thin, bass-heavy in places, and too loud on the vocals in others. A week's worth of hard work sounded misdirected and wasted in this different space. But not *totally bad*.

No, *total* annihilation came a little later. Richard handed me some printouts of frequencies that I had mixed, and the sheet looked like a child's scribble.

"This is nuts," was the laconic comment. "For this part of the song, it should be a nice, smooth, even distribution of lines across the frequencies, like waves coming on shore. This shows you how bad your mix really was."

Gulp.

Richard was ruthless in destroying any kind of false confidence or self-esteem I might have mistakenly built while working on my mix. With swift manipulation of sliders and faders, he demonstrated how I had ruined the song, and how it needed to be done properly. My cheeks and ears were burning at the dressing-down, but when all was said and done, I had to admit, he was right.

Nonetheless, the inevitable tears were threatening, and my eyes were smarting from the effort of holding them back. I dug my fingernails into my palms and made myself breathe evenly and deeply, all the while forcing a fake smile to disguise my mortification.

"So..." Richard concluded the session, turning the sound off and relaxing into the ensuing silence. "Are you still happy to go ahead?"

I nodded, speaking not an option for the moment. A single tear escaped from my eye, and I swiped at it before it could roll down my cheek. "I-urgh..." I cleared my throat, trying to get words out after all.

"I'm happy to go ahead. I'm simply a little shocked, that's all. I thought..."

"I know what you thought. And you have to understand that you did well with your mix overall. I wouldn't have invited you here if you hadn't. But I needed you to know that there's a lot to learn. There's *everything* to learn, in fact. We need to go right back to the beginning. You need to learn about set-up and equipment and placement before we can even start to talk about mixing. It's a long and tedious road, but you'll get there. *I'll* get you there," he added, not even remotely modest. "As long as you're prepared for steep hills and rocky outcrops."

"Okay," I whispered. "Okay. I can do that. As long as…"

Richard raised an eyebrow. "Not your place to make demands."

"I'm not making demands." I stood up for myself, suddenly finding my voice again. "Well, just the one. I can do all of this and take the criticism and dressing-down as long as you explain to me exactly where and how I went wrong, and show me how to fix it. And as long as you don't mind me asking a million questions and taking notes and shedding the occasional tear. 'Coz that's how I work."

"That's quite a lot of demands rolled into one," Richard observed, but his smile was kind and genuine. "Yet I like your style and your attitude. We'll get along fine."

Chapter Twenty-Two

"You survived," Dan congratulated me when he picked me up. "Baptism by fire. I imagine it wasn't pretty."

"It wasn't," I agreed, and found myself laughing at the experience. "Richard is the master of taking you down."

"You still look in one piece to me," Dan retorted. "Believe me, I've seen many of his new apprentices leaving in floods of tears after day one. And most of those were men!"

"He reminds me of my ballet teacher," I mused, and Dan snorted through his nose with amusement. "Well, you know, all 'take that chewing gum out of your mouth, young lady, and stand up straight.'"

Dan burst out laughing at my Mrs. Burke impression, and I joined him.

"I survived ballet. I'll survive Richard, too," I predicted.

"I'm sure you will. I'll remind you of that in when you want to throw in the towel." Dan grinned.

"Ha," I countered. "I won't do that. I can be one stubborn lady if I want to, and Richard just pressed my stubborn button."

Dan's response was unintelligible, although I could have sworn I heard something along the lines of 'stubborn, don't I know all about that?' But as we were pulling up outside Emily's playschool, I let the mumbled remark pass.

The next few weeks were a blur of engineering exercises and activities. Most mornings, Dan would join Richard and me in the studio to act as guinea pig and chief sound maker. Richard had me physically positioning microphones, repositioning microphones, positioning and repositioning Dan-the-singer, Dan-the-guitar-player, and even Dan-the-pseudo-drummer in the studio, time and again, until he was satisfied I was starting to comprehend the ins-and-outs of a professional set-up.

At last, it was my turn to sit behind the console and observe Richard making adjustments to buttons, sliders, and faders, while Dan undertook the positioning-routine all over again based on my vocal instructions. At every step of the way, Richard played sound-bites back to me, asking for my assessment, and cruelly informing me how wrong I was.

Several times in the first two weeks alone, I came dangerously close to giving up, but I reminded myself of my stubborn promise and refrained from venting to Dan in the evenings. On the other hand, I relished the fact that I could command this rock star to do this, that, and the other—if only based on someone else's instructions—and that he spent so much time with me when he could have been at home resting or writing songs.

We slipped imperceptibly into a routine where Dan would help me collect Emily from playschool, share our lunch, and disappear to work for a couple of hours before returning for a family dinner with Josh at around five-thirty. More often than not, Dan took part in the children's bath and bedtime routines before leaving the house to join the band in the studio, and I wouldn't then see him again until the next morning.

After a while, Dan suggested that Emily and I should have lunch at his house, which would make it easier for him to do a little work before dinner. Very soon, a trail of Emily's clothes and toys made its way to Dan's house and into one of his spare rooms. Before I knew it, we had fallen into the habit of bringing Josh to Dan's house for dinner, and we would rush home only for bedtime.

None of us commented on this state of affairs. Everything seemed natural and normal. We were simply doing what was easiest under the circumstances, and the kids flourished with Dan's presence in their lives. They even took the altered playschool and school runs in their strides. It was only when Jenny asked me for some kind of weekly food plan so she could shop and cook according to our collective needs that I realized the Jones family had, more or less, relocated to the Hunter residence. I elected not to dwell on the larger underlying question and simply wrote out our evening meal requests. And that, as they say, was that. Until Rachel cottoned on to what was going on.

I hadn't seen much of Rachel in the past month or so. What with Josh starting school and my apprenticeship, I had been pretty busy. Rach, in turn, had been rushed off her feet herself with the mad social whirl that was post-natal group, baby massage, sing-and-sign group, coffee mornings, swimming... It was fair to say that she had left the initial baby blues behind and was throwing herself into a mummy's life with gusto. So, between our respective schedules, we hadn't really managed to get together until one Wednesday afternoon I received a text from Rach telling me she was outside my house and where the heck was I?

I picked up my phone to ring her back. "I'm at Dan's," I declared before she could repeat her question. "Emily, too. Why don't you come over?"

There was only the slightest hint of hesitation before Rachel agreed. No more than fifteen minutes later, she rang Dan's doorbell, clutching a screaming Henry, who gave a distinct whiff of a full nappy. I steered her toward the downstairs bathroom while I made a pot of tea and carried the mugs to the lounge, where Emily was already hosting a tea party for her dollies.

"Well, well, well." Rachel half-whistled when she joined us. "What's all this?" She laid a now gurgling Henry on the rug and rummaged in his changing bag for his favorite cuddly.

"Erm," I started. "Well... It's just..." Telling the story slightly backwards, I filled her in on my apprenticeship with Richard and the gradual migration of our daytime lives to Dan's house.

Rachel's eyes sparkled with glee. "I think it's wonderful," she declared with undisguised hilarity. "I always thought you were meant for each other."

"Rach!" I hissed, before Emily, Jenny, or, God forbid, Dan could hear. "It's not like that. We're simply camping out here during the day because it makes things so much easier."

"Of course it does," my best friend concurred. "I can see that. I'm merely agreeing." She flashed me an amused look over the rim of her mug of tea.

"Cake?" a chirpy voice interrupted our near heart-to-heart. "I got muffins or cupcakes, fresh out of the oven."

Emily launched herself at Jenny with a massive howl of approval. "Muffins, muffins," she sang, well familiar by now with Jenny's prowess in the baking department, which was diametrically opposed to mine.

"Thank you, Jenny," I said politely, as I always did, feeling only mildly uncomfortable by her extra work. Jenny, however, beamed a thousand-watt smile.

"No problem," she laughed. "It's lovely baking for the little ones. Mr. Hunter never really appreciates my baking, although, of course, he is *around* a lot more than what he used to be..." She threw me a meaningful look, set down the plate of baked goodies on the table, and withdrew.

Rachel stared open-mouthed. "Is this for real?" she eventually managed.

I shrugged. What could I say?

"My God, girl, you've got it made here. You totally deserve the break, too. I'd simply move in, if I were you," Rach chuckled while she helped herself to a vanilla cupcake with Jenny's trademark pink sparkly icing. "And Dan's *here* a lot more than what he used to, is he?" She mimicked Jenny's approving tone. "I say, I say."

"You say what?" I challenged. "There's nothing to it. Dan's the children's godfather, and he's helping me out with the childcare while I go through some training. That's all."

Rachel lowered her cake. "I'm sorry," she relented. "I didn't mean to tease you. It's nice to see you so relaxed and happy. That's all."

We regarded each other gravely for a few seconds until Emily broke the mood. "Mummy, why are you fighting with Auntie Rachel?"

"We're not fighting," Rach and I assured my youngest in unison. "We're *talking*."

"Oh." Emily absorbed this piece of information. Seconds later, she picked up her favorite doll and spoke to her sternly.

"Amanda, stop fighting with Erin." Amanda-doll received an energetic wriggle. "But we're not fighting, mummy, we're talking," Erin-doll responded, Emily's voice copying mine perfect in pitch and inflection. Rach and I burst out laughing.

"So that's why you're never at home," Rachel then resumed our earlier conversation.

"That's why I'm never at home," I agreed. "Except, of course, in the evenings. But you know you can always find me here, or text me."

"Cool."

And thus the conversation was closed. Except in my head, it wasn't.

Chapter Twenty-Three

Later that night, I replayed my talk with Rachel over and over again, analyzing every last little word. She had it all backwards, I was sure of that. Dan and I were just friends. No strings attached. No funny business. Well, apart from that amazing...I stopped my train of thought and corrected my assessment of 'that kiss' before I could contemplate whether it would have been nice to pursue the attraction I had felt.

Apart from the *little* kiss we had inadvertently, and completely by accident, had in his studio, we were totally comfortable in our platonic, rock-solid friendship. The kiss meant nothing. It couldn't. I wasn't...I wasn't in the right place for it to mean something.

But oh, wouldn't it be nice if you were? a naughty voice piped up in my head, but I shouted it down. *I am not ready.*

*But...*the naughty voice went on. *But what if Rachel is right? What if Dan still wants you? What if you miss your opportunity* again?

"Shut up," I told the voice in my head, speaking out loud. "Shut up, you. Dan and I, we have seen each other through some of the worst moments of our lives—well, mine, for sure—and there are no misunderstandings or innuendoes between us. Do you hear?"

There. That had done it. That was it.

However, I *was* aware the kids were receiving mixed signals. With no father figure in their lives apart from Dan, and the words *Dan* and *Dad* in such perilous phonetic proximity, I had recently overheard Emily referring to Dan as 'Dad' at playschool ("Dad pick me up") and also calling him 'Dad' to his face. Her pronunciation was still fairly indistinct, but I was certain I hadn't misheard. Dan hadn't noticed, or, if he had, he hadn't commented, but her linguistic slip had sent shivers of worry through me.

Was I doing the right thing, indulging my friendship with Dan simply because it suited my needs and my purposes? Was I confusing the children by moving half our belongings into a house that very patently wasn't ours, nor ever would be? Or was I giving them the benefit of a loving, caring male persona to…yes, to fill some of the holes that Steve had left behind? Wasn't it a good thing that their godfather, who, after all, was so because Steve had made that choice…wasn't it a *good* thing that he had become a much more integral part of our lives? Albeit in a distinctly *godfatherly* kind of way?

But what would happen when he had to leave? When he was touring, which would inevitably happen in the coming months? Where would that leave the kids and me? How would they react? How would I cope?

After all, it was *that* side of a relationship with a rock star that had prompted me to turn Dan down after he had proposed to me in Paris. The anticipated loneliness, the stress, the ever-present potential for betrayal... because yes, I knew all about 'what goes on tour, stays on tour,' I was living it at that time. I had firmly turned those prospects down back then, but was I exposing the kids and myself to the very same risk now?

On the other hand, I had spent the last two-and-a-half years of my life holding off on happiness because of 'what if's' and other obstacles. Perhaps life was too short to miss out on good things simply because they might cease or go away for a short time. I had already learned to carry on, of sorts, with the biggest loss of all. Yes, I didn't want the kids to go through an endless cycle of being upset with missing Dan. Yet surely that wasn't a good enough reason to deprive them of the closest thing to a proper family life that they had ever experienced.

I tossed and turned, unable to determine my motives, unable to disentangle selfish from practical reasons, unsure whether I needed to, unwilling to dig too deep and overanalyze.

Consequently, when Dan suggested the following week after a particularly harrowing day for everyone concerned that Emily, Josh, and I "might as well stay over for the night," I simply shrugged and went with the flow.

Dan produced a couple of airbeds and made the kids a lovely indoor camping den in the guestroom they had progressively been taking over. I installed myself in the guest room in which I always stayed. It was odd, being in Dan's house after the kids' bedtime with Dan absent—off to the studio—and nothing much for me to do, but it was good, too. I watched a movie on the telly and curled up in bed with a book afterwards. I fell asleep strangely content with the light still on and didn't wake until I heard Dan returning home at about three a.m.

For a second, I debated getting up to say hello, but instead, I switched off my light and curled up under the duvet, hoping for a swift return to sleep. Yet my ears strained to hear the sounds of Dan coming upstairs, walking down the landing to his bedroom, except none were forthcoming. Surely, *surely*, he had to go to bed *some* time!

Twenty minutes later, I couldn't bear the uncertainty any longer. Fully awake now myself, I grabbed a dressing gown and padded downstairs. Lights were blazing everywhere, and I clicked them off, one by one, once I had ascertained Dan was, in fact, not present in the kitchen, or the dining room, or even the lounge. Leaving the hall light on, I ventured down to the studio, hoping against hope that Dan wouldn't still be working, unsure what I would say or do if he was.

My heart beat in my throat when I saw Dan passed out in his chair. His head was lolling over the backrest and his hands hung loosely on either side of the armrests, with his legs stretched out and spread wide. It looked like he had simply fallen over backwards, unable to stand any longer. My tummy constricted with worry when I noticed once again those dark purple smudges that had disconcerted me so at my own house a few weeks ago.

Unlike then, however, leaving Dan in that chair was not an option. He would wake up with a crick in his neck, full of aches and pains, and I doubted that whatever sleep he was getting would prove restful. Very gently, I bent over my sleeping friend and planted a kiss on his cheek. I wrapped his right arm around my shoulders and, bending awkwardly, managed to duck my head through his armpit so I could try to pull him upright. His body was heavy but limp, and I couldn't move him an inch.

I disengaged myself and took an uncertain step backward. I had to get this man to bed, but how? Eventually, I resorted to pulling at his arms and shaking his shoulders, and after a small eternity, the action yielded a result. Dan's eyes opened and he looked around, bleary and unfocused.

"Whass gonon?"

"It's time for sleep," I announced, pulling at Dan's arms again to get him to stand up. "Come on, buck up, we need to get you into bed." I tugged some more, and he half-rose with the force of the pull.

"Tired," Dan protested. "Lemme siddown." With that, he let himself droop backwards again. Back to square one.

I wavered for a moment while I gathered my wits. The indistinct slur of Dan's speech disturbed me. I had seen Dan drunk many times, even passed out on the odd occasion, but never had he sounded so...drugged. Yet a surreptitious sniff of his breath suggested a complete absence of alcohol. Unbelievably, he was sober even though he looked wasted. I didn't know what to make of that and determined to mull this over some other time. For now, he needed to get to bed.

"You need to go to bed," I reiterated with determination, pulling him forward again and taking another step. Reluctantly, he fell in beside me, and I grabbed hold of his arm around my shoulders. "That's good," I encouraged. "Keep going."

It took me a good few minutes to maneuver Dan up the stairs and into his bedroom. He was dopey and sleepy and not very cooperative at all, but eventually we got there. I flicked on the beside lamp, threw back the duvet and let Dan sit on the side of his bed. While I bent down to take off his shoes, his upper body melted onto the bed, arms curled up under his face. There was no way I would manage to disrobe and get him dressed in more suitable sleepwear. Thus I simply lifted his legs onto the bed and tried to roll him into a comfortable position.

Without really knowing why, I patted his trouser and shirt pockets, finding and retrieving his wallet, mobile phone and keys, all of which I placed on the bedside table. But there was nothing else. I didn't quite know what I expected; pill packets, maybe, or *something* to explain his weird, flaked out state, but there was nothing. I shrugged and covered him with his duvet. Maybe he was just that tired.

For a minute, I allowed myself to watch my sleeping rock star and I smiled to myself. He was as gorgeous as he had ever been. If, that was, one were romantically attracted to him, which, of course, I was not. But still... I couldn't resist a little stroke of his face, now relaxed in deep sleep. He didn't stir and, quite unexpectedly, I found myself kneeling beside the bed and covering his cheeks, his nose, his eyes, his mouth with gentle kisses. Ah, but that felt nice. Without knowing what I was doing or why, I lay down beside him, curling my body around his and cradling him in my arms. *Just for a second,* I told myself. *Just for a second it would be okay to pretend to be a woman in a relationship with this man, instead of being a widow still paralyzed by grief.*

I breathed deeply and savored the moment. *This is probably wrong,* I mused, *but nobody need know about it and...and...well, I suppose it's okay to —*

Dan stirred and interrupted my train of thought. I quickly let go of my hold on him and withdrew a little, allowing him to roll onto his other side. Now we were facing each other and I held my breath as I waited to see if I had inadvertently woken him, whether my undue presence in his bed would be discovered. Dan flung out his arm in sleeping repose, and his hand landed on my shoulder. I lay perfectly still, not knowing what to do next, half-hoping he might pull me into an embrace, but he shifted and his hand slid off me.

As gently as I could, I slid across the bed so I could get out on the other side. I covered Dan once again with his duvet before turning off the bedside lamp. Shutting the door firmly behind me, I stumbled back to my own bedroom. Four a.m. Great. Another broken night to add to my never-ending catalog of sleep deprivation. And a whole host of disturbing, conflicting emotions to file under the category, "For Later Analysis."

My first, entirely predictable, reaction when my alarm clock went off was, *you've got to be joking.* But my mind was fast to recall the events of the night, and I silenced the alarm quickly in hopes to let a sleeping Dan lie, as it were. I got dressed and snuck into the children's room before they had a chance to make an almighty racket.

"Morning, my lovelies," I whispered into the gloom. "Come on, sweeties, time to get up. But you've got to be *really* quiet!"

My darling offspring rose quietly and without protest. I gathered their clothes, and we all tiptoed downstairs and into the kitchen. Shutting the door softly behind me, I sat the kids on top of the work-surface in the middle island to get them dressed.

"Why are we doing this?" a sleepy Josh demanded to know.

"Dan isn't well," I explained. "I think we should let him get some more sleep, so we need to be *very quiet.*"

"Shh," Emily supplied with her index finger over her closed mouth.

"That's right, *shh*," I confirmed. Right on cue, I heard the front door open. Jenny was early today! I rushed out to intercept her before she could wake the dead with her loud and cheery customary greeting, and pulled her into the kitchen to join the rest of us.

"Dad not very well," Emily informed the housekeeper, who threw me a questioning look with raised eyebrows.

Whether she was perturbed at the fatherly reference or the potential illness of her employer, I wasn't sure, but I focused on the latter.

"Dan had a very late night last night, and he didn't look very well," I offered, hoping I sounded sufficiently concerned yet nonchalant. "I thought it would do him good to sleep in."

Jenny nodded. "I'm sure it would. I've never known Mr. Hunter to get up so early as what he's been doing these past few months. He used to sleep until at least midday. I'm thinking the man must be missing out on a lot of sleep."

I swallowed hard. Dan's lack of sleep was probably in large part due to us. He had been working with me in the morning for weeks, ever since Josh started school. Perhaps something needed to change.

The children remained admirably quiet while Jenny and I whipped up a lightning-fast breakfast. We brushed teeth and hair in the downstairs bathroom, and I bundled the kids into my car for the school run. By the time I delivered Emily at playschool, there was no time to nip back to check on Dan. If I was to make my training session with Richard, I had to drive to the studio straightaway. I was only two minutes late by the time I drew up in one of the parking spaces reserved for staff.

Coattails flying, I let myself be buzzed in through reception and raced down the stairs. "Sorry, sorry, sorry," I gabbled before Richard had time to admonish me. "I drove myself this morning and I got a bit lost."

For the briefest moment, Richard's eyes focused on the empty space behind me where normally Dan Hunter would be bustling in. He looked at me quizzically. "No Dan today?"

I shook my head. "He got home so late last night and looked so terrible, I put him to bed and let him sleep this morning."

Richard raised his eyebrows and tilted his head, and I half-expected some kind of question or comment. However, "Slight change of plan," was all he offered by way of response as he searched for something in a drawer. "Okay. Let's talk mixing 101."

I took off my coat and sat down on the assistant's chair next to him. "Mixing 101," I repeated.

"Right," Richard confirmed. "So you know all about set-up. But no matter what you do, there will always be problems with reproducing the sound you captured, especially the bass."

The problem, or so I learned, was that the "room mode" — the way in which sound waves break in the mixing room itself — could give an engineer a totally misleading impression of the quality of the mix.

"It's important to find the sweet spot in the mixing room," Richard went on. "Although that *can* be a challenge. I know of one studio where that position is exactly sixty-seven centimeters diagonally into the mixing room from the right back corner. That's kind of awkward."

"So the sweet spot could be almost *anywhere* in any given room?"

"That's right. And now I'll teach you to find it."

He produced a flash drive. "This is my reference mix."

"A reference mix?"

"A reference mix. It's one I made myself a long time ago. I'll play it to you on the studio speakers that give me the deepest bass response, and you'll walk around until you find this room's sweet spot."

"And when I've found it? What do I do with it?"

"When you've found it, that's the place you will need to be when you assess and mix bass frequencies in this studio."

I rose to my feet. "But, what if, as you say, it's nowhere near the mixing desk? How do we do that?"

Richard pointed a finger at me like an imaginary gun. "That's why we have several people in the mixing room. *Or remote controls.*" He chuckled. It was the first time he had laughed properly during my training, and I took that as a good sign. I had to be making progress. Dan would be so proud!

"All right, take it away," the sound engineer encouraged me and hit play.

It took me only a few minutes to find the mixing room's sweet spot. I had to close my eyes to listen and fumbled my way around awkwardly, but I got there in the end. Miraculously, the spot was right where it needed to be, namely where Richard kept his chair.

"You found it," he praised when I sat down. "And you didn't cheat, either."

"Cheat?" My pride ebbed, and I frowned. "How would I've cheated?"

"X marks the spot," Richard grinned wickedly and pointed to the floor. Sure enough, there was an 'x' marked in duct tape on the floor under his chair. I had noticed it before, of course, but never considered its relevance. Richard punched me lightly on the shoulder.

"Don't worry. Nobody gets it, not even the people who should. I marked the spot as a courtesy to other engineers working here occasionally, but most people don't notice. You did good."

I did good. My ears glowed with pride, and I couldn't wait to tell Dan.

Chapter Twenty-Four

Unbelievably, Dan was still in bed when I arrived at his house with a buoyant Emily for our customary lunch. I was pretty exuberant until I heard from Jenny that Dan had still not shown his face. All that joy was replaced with acute worry when she filled me in on her employer's continued sleepiness.

"Are you absolutely sure he hasn't crept past you and is ensconced in his studio?" I asked, trying to shush Emily so that I could actually hear Jenny's response.

"Quite sure. Since midmorning I've been getting on with me chores. I've put away pots and pans, I've dusted and hoovered the whole house, and I even put on the radio a bit louder than what I'd normally do. I've tried everything but knocking on his door." She blushed. "That's not really my place."

I considered that a debatable position—suppose he had been taken seriously ill and needed help—but I could also see where she was coming from.

"Look here, why don't you fix Emily some lunch and I'll go and check on Dan," I suggested and quickly clapped my hand on my mouth. This was the first time I had ever addressed Jenny as though I had a right to boss her about, and I instantly felt bad. Jenny, however, hadn't noticed. She sat Emily at the table and started chatting to her about what the little lady might like for lunch. I decided to let my momentary lapse pass. With a last backwards glance, I left the kitchen to find Dan.

He was, indeed, still in bed, although there was evidence he had been up during the night. His clothes lay discarded in a heap. The duvet only half-covered a bare chest, and one pajama-clad leg stuck out over the side of the bed. He looked peaceful and much better than he had at four a.m. Once again, the purplish smudges had faded and the deathly pallor of his skin had receded. He looked groggy, but not ill.

I was debating whether to leave him to it or wake him when he opened his eyes and shot me a sleepy smile.

"Well, well, well," he purred. "There's a sight for sore eyes." He scooched his body into the middle of the bed and patted the mattress in front of him. "Care to sit down?"

I blushed, recalling my little transgression while he was asleep, but perched cautiously on the side of the bed. "Good afternoon, you. Are you all right?"

Dan rubbed his eyes and yawned. "Much better than I was last night, I think. Did I dream this or did you bully me up here into bed?"

"You didn't dream it. I couldn't let you sleep on that chair. You would have been shattered," I explained.

Dan smiled. "Thank you," he murmured and grasped my hand. "That was very kind."

"Any time," I murmured back, only slightly coy. I held my breath, waiting to hear if he was aware of how I had held him a little later, but he said nothing more and I resumed brisk business.

"I suppose now that you're awake, it's time to get up. It's nearly one o'clock. And I do want to talk about you about your sleeping patterns. You—"

Dan sat bolt upright. "One o'clock?" he echoed. "In the afternoon?"

"Indeed," I concurred. "You've had at least…oh, nine hours sleep. Not enough to catch up on everything you're missing, but a start."

"It's one o'clock?" Dan was fixated on that point. "What happened to the session with Richard?"

I grinned. "Oh, that happened. He taught me about room mode and standing waves today. It was awesome."

My gorgeous rock star lay back in his bed, totally confused. "You went? By yourself?"

I nodded.

"And you survived?"

I nodded again, suppressing a grin.

"And you *enjoyed* yourself?"

Another nod, accompanied by an inanely proud grin.

"Wow." Dan ran a hand across his forehead. "You *have* arrived. I think Richard has a soft spot for you. And room mode, huh? Serious stuff." He tickled my side. "You'll know more than me soon."

"That's the general idea," I chuckled. "Come on, up you get."

Dan reluctantly hoisted himself out of bed. He stood uncertainly for a moment, swaying ever so slightly, and I rushed to his side to steady him.

"Why, hello there," he murmured suggestively, wrapping an arm around me. "It's nice to have a beautiful lady throw herself at me first thing."

I swatted away his arm with a playful nudge, even though my heart beat furiously and eagerly in my chest.

"Now, now, Mr. Hunter, behave yourself," I admonished but Dan laughed and didn't look in the slightest put out.

"Yes, Ma'am," he mock-saluted before making his way into the bathroom. I left him to it and went back downstairs.

When he finally joined us in the kitchen, all traces of the night before were wiped out. He was bright-eyed and sparkly and joined Emily in her lunch of scrambled egg and bacon on toast as though it was the most normal thing in the world. It probably was, to him. After all, it could have been breakfast.

Even though Dan stayed at home for the rest of the afternoon, I didn't get a chance to talk to him about working and sleeping and looking after himself. He busied himself playing with Emily and offered to collect Josh from school.

"This proxy-parenting malarkey is completely ruining my rock-star lifestyle," he joked, his eyes dancing.

When he and Josh returned from the school run, they brought home all the ingredients for home-made pizza and pudding. Dan made the tomato sauce and had the kids spread the pizza dough into one enormous party-pizza. The kids garnished their sections to their own taste, while Dan looked after his and mine. Needless to say, he didn't consult me on what I wanted. I had been a double-pepperoni-with-pickled-chili girl for as long as he had known me.

Dinner was a carefree, golden family moment with cheerful chatter, candles, and wine for the adults. Never mind it was a school night, the kids stayed up well past their bedtime, and I ended up putting them to bed in Dan's spare room yet again. When the little monsters were fast asleep, I insisted on doing the dishes, even though Dan told me that Jenny would take care of them in the morning.

"I don't feel comfortable leaving all this work to her. It's not right," I explained, and he let me be.

He retreated to the studio while I clattered with pots and pans, but re-emerged when all was quiet on the kitchen front. Without discussing it, we settled on the sofa to watch a movie, and this time, it was Dan who gently prodded me awake halfway through the evening and suggested it might be time for my beddy-byes. He dispatched me upstairs with a little kiss I was too tired to object to. And I wouldn't have wanted to object, anyway.

I was nearly asleep when I heard the front door open and close, then being locked, followed by muffled footsteps down the front path.

Chapter Twenty-Five

"We're like Tom-Tom's family," Josh announced quite out of the blue during a Saturday morning breakfast a few days later.

Dan looked up from his complicated task of spreading strawberry and apricot jam in little neat quarters on Emily's toast. "Who's Tom-Tom?"

"And more to the point, what's Tom-Tom's family like?" I interceded, inwardly rolling my eyes. Trust a man, however smart, to get hung up on the details of lesser importance.

"Tom-Tom is my new best friend," Josh declared and reached for his milk. "His mummy and daddy live in different houses, like we do, but they see each other all the time, and Tom-Tom says his mummy says his daddy says he wants to live in a new house together."

Dan shot me a look across the table. "Does he now," he mused, leaving it unclear whether he was referring to Tom-Tom or his daddy.

"He does," Josh beamed, "and I've been thinking we could, too." He spread his hands out wide in front of him, and I couldn't help wondering where he had seen that gesture. But the punch-line was still to come. "I mean," he continued with the innocence of a four-year-old, "we live here anyway, really, don't we?"

A million and one questions and quagmires opened in my mind.

Dan caught the despair in my eyes and cleared his throat. "Of course you do," he declared. "So that means you have *two* houses to live in. Because sometimes I come and sleep at your house, don't I? So really, that's pretty cool, if you think about it, isn't it?"

Josh gave that some thought while I held my breath. Perhaps, just perhaps, Dan had struck the right note. A reluctant nod followed by a slow smile indicated he had.

"But," Josh persisted, "are we a family?"

Once again, it was Dan who took the bull by the horns. I was unable to speak, my throat having dried up completely. I gulped down some too-hot tea and burned my mouth.

"Of course we are a family. Sophie is your mummy, and I am your godfather."

"But not my real daddy," Emily piped up.

In for a penny, in for a pound. Dan continued without blinking. "No, my sweet, not your real daddy. Your real daddy is in heaven."

"But he did ask Dan to look after us all," Josh supplied, remembering well the discussion we had had in the car.

"He did," I concurred.

"Will you go to heaven soon?" Emily's face puckered with sudden worry.

Dan burst out laughing and pulled her little body onto his lap. "I hope not, my buttercup, not if I have anything to do with it."

Emily's arms flew round his neck in a protective gesture and Dan beamed delightedly.

"How's about we go to the zoo today." I launched into an abrupt diversionary tactic, knowing my offspring could persist on this line of discussion for some time yet, and also knowing they could be easily deflected onto more pleasurable pursuits with three little letters. Emily immediately abandoned Dan's lap and danced round the kitchen. "Yes, pease!"

Josh also started a mad voodoo-style dance before dropping to his knees.

"Look at me, I'm a lion," he roared, then straightened up and flapped his arms. "Can we feed the lorikeets?"

"Of course," I agreed and started stacking dishes.

Dan cleared away bread and jam and whistled a little tune. For the first time ever, I felt a little awkward. With all the secret thoughts I had been having, and after my little stolen moment of one-sided affection the other night which kept playing on my mind… With all that going on in the background, I felt like the wife of a rock star who wasn't really the wife of a rock star and who had to broach the subject of whether her man would spend the weekend with her and the kids, or whether he would be doing rock-starry things. And I didn't quite know how to handle it. But of course, I had no real claim on Dan. And I didn't know, couldn't work out, whether I wanted one. Whether *he* would want me to have one. What would he feel if he could see inside my head? What a quandary.

Dan resolved it for me. "I'm off to the studio later," he informed me casually, as he would have done on any other day. "I can't join you guys at the zoo, but I can be back for dinner. Would that work?" There was genuine concern in his voice that my wishes should be met, that his little almost-family should be happy.

146

I gave him a hug. "That would be lovely. But tell you what, why don't we have dinner back at our...*my* house today?" I lowered my voice. "I think it would do the kids good to be back at home for a change, and you can come and go as you please, and that'll be just...how it is." I tailed off lamely, not sure how to explain my motivation.

"Fabulous. You've got a deal." He returned the hug and topped it with a little kiss.

This turned out to be the beginning of a new routine. If anything, it was probably even more reminiscent of Tom-Tom's family life, but it was clear, unambiguous, and suited everybody, *and* it freed up time for Dan to work and rest. During the week, I let Dan be after our morning recording session. He often came to our house for dinner a few nights during the week if he could manage.

Friday and Saturday nights, however, the kids and I typically stayed at Dan's house. Dan made every effort to spend mornings and evening mealtimes with us. On Friday nights, Dan went out as usual at around eight, but Saturday nights he spent with me, curled up on the sofa or occasionally going to the cinema or theater if Jenny agreed to babysit. Always we slept in separate rooms even though on the odd occasion here or there, I wondered whether maybe... Well, whether *maybe*. I never got any further than that as I kept a tight lid on those thoughts.

I *had* to, otherwise I would have fallen apart. I couldn't admit to myself that Dan put the butterflies back in my tummy. I couldn't acknowledge that perhaps I was experiencing a renascent physical attraction for Dan. If I did, I would be turning my back on my husband and I wasn't ready for that. On the other hand, I was a widow, not a nun. Would it be wrong to want some human affection, some sex? It wouldn't necessarily imply love, or abandoning the memory of my husband, right?

But still, I couldn't go there. I simply didn't know what was right for me, or for my family, at that time. So I let my confusion fester unattended in that locked-away folder in a corner of my brain, and allowed myself—and the kids—to simply go with the flow for a while.

And as such, everything was perfect.

It was quite blissful.

It lasted for a month.

Chapter Twenty-Six

I got the first inkling something was wrong when Dan caught a cold that simply wouldn't shift. It started shortly after Josh went back to school after his first half-term. He came back with a dreadful cough and sneeze during the first week, and the entire family succumbed within days; Dan included, of course. Except where the three Joneses shook their viruses off in a matter of days with the help of copious amounts of hot water with lemon and honey, Dan's cold clung on. The timing was dreadful as the band was still recording.

Dan went to his doctor to get some medicines that would enable him to keep working, and he was on a hefty regime of decongestants, painkillers, and some sort of throat tablets. He had been told to come back if symptoms persisted after five days. Being a man, he ignored that order and carried on popping the pills while the prescription lasted. No amount of bullying by me made him see the light, and I held my tongue in the end.

Quite soon, Dan looked like the lead actor in a zombie movie. Yet he kept going, and cheerfully at that. I was mystified.

He carried on as normal, working with me and Richard in the mornings, joining me and the kids for dinner, going out recording or partying at night. If he got more than four hours sleep on any given day, it would have been a miracle. And still, the worse he looked, the more hyper he got. He continued to refuse to talk about his health and though I was worried sick— pardon the pun—I didn't know what to do. So I cooked healthy meals, refused to serve any alcohol, insisted on plenty of tea instead, and let him crash-nap on the sofa whenever he fell asleep.

The build-up to a big party at the Hyde Star Inn brought with it a new level of feverish activity. The band was scheduled to perform three of their new songs as a kind of preview gig, and for the week preceding the party, Dan practically disappeared as the band ceased recording and rehearsed instead. For the first time in months, the kids and I barely saw Dan. We returned to our Jones-family-only life at our own house, and although we missed Dan sorely, we were okay.

On the Saturday morning of the big promo party at the Hyde Star Inn, the kids and I were delighted when Dan turned up at our house for breakfast at nine. He simply walked in, sat down and joined us as though he had come down from the bedroom rather than driven partway across London. His eyes were red-rimmed and bloodshot, and he was unshaven, but his demeanor was bright. Over-bright, in fact.

The kids babbled on cheerfully while I focused on feeding and watering my adrenaline-powered rock star. I kept piling bacon and eggs on his plate, and he wolfed them down without really noticing. He already had the biggest mug in the house, and he drained three helpings of sweet tea with lemon, and still he was asking for more. I didn't know whether to be delighted he was refueling, or concerned at the extraordinary quantities consumed.

"When did you last eat?" I asked while I brewed another pot of tea.

"Hm?" Dan wasn't really listening.

"When's the last time you had a proper meal?"

"Oh." Dan shrugged. "I don't really know. Yesterday lunchtime, I suppose."

I suppressed an expression of horror and played it positively instead. "That's good. And...good rehearsal last night?"

"Hm-hm," Dan responded, temporarily unable to speak through a mouthful of food. "We finished rehearsing at about ten and went to a party."

I breathed deeply to stop myself from making a scornful remark. Instead, I stirred the tea and removed the bags before I made a brew so strong it would send us both through the roof. When I rejoined Dan at the table, the kids having long since left to go play upstairs, I surreptitiously examined his appearance all over again. Listening to him chatter away, I could be forgiven for thinking he was simply a little overexcited about the upcoming gig. A pre-launch was a big deal, after all. But looking at him, I felt duty-bound to put him on immediate bed-rest. I didn't say any of that, of course.

What I said was, "That sounds like fun."

Dan regarded me with confused eyes. Evidently, too much time had elapsed between his last statement and my response for him to make the connection. "The party," I reminded him. "That sounds like fun."

"It was all right," Dan mumbled. "A bit late, but you know how these things go."

I did indeed. *Well actually,* I corrected myself, *I didn't.* I had never seen Dan like this, not even when we went on tour together. I had never known him to stay up all night and give up on sleep altogether. He had always been too aware of his health and the physical demands of touring or promoting, and he had always taken care of himself. *Always.*

Then again, he hadn't had a proxy-family to look after in days of old, and he would have slept in the mornings. Dan had been burning the candle at both ends for weeks on top of this dreadful cold, and he looked as though he was about to drop. I felt bad. I felt awful. *This had to stop.*

We had to talk about this. I had to get him to see reason and to look after himself. Us Joneses, we could look after ourselves while he was busy, like we had done before. He didn't need to run himself ragged over us, and I would order him to stop. Now, however, was not the time. *Let him get through the day and talk tomorrow,* I decided. *At least he's had lots of food and plenty of fluids.*

"What's the plan for the rest of the day?" I chatted, taking great care to leave my voice light and unconcerned. "More rehearsals? Sound check? Interviews?"

Dan sat back in his chair and patted his belly.

"We're resting until the party," he announced. "We prepped the stage yesterday at rehearsal and we'll have another quick sound check before we go on, but the whole thing isn't until late so I don't have to be anywhere until about nine."

My heart soared. Finally, someone had seen sense.

"Resting. Good idea," I gushed, but pulled back immediately. *Don't overdo it.* "Would you like to…" I didn't finish my sentence. I really wanted to offer him a bed here, where I could keep an eye on him and make sure he actually did rest. But would that be too forward?

"What are your plans?" Dan cut into my thoughts.

Think, Sophie, think. "Um... We don't really have any plans," I bumbled. *Nicely done.* "I was thinking of taking the kids to the park and...uh..." I flailed, unsure how to proceed. Was Dan more likely to stick around if I said we were out? Or would he simply take himself off if we weren't in? Or the other way round?

Dan looked at me, his tired eyes dancing with unnaturally intense merriment. It was like I was witnessing a supernova right there in my kitchen, but the implications were disturbing. What would happen when he burned out?

"Cinema," I suddenly burst out. "Perhaps we'll go to the cinema. Would you like to come?" *Genius plan. If I get VIP seats for all of us at the back, he can kip without losing face and I'll know he's safe.*

Dan gave an almighty yawn. "Cinema sounds great, and I'd love to, but..." He had to stop talking while he waited out another monster yawn. "D'you know, I would love to grab some sleep. I—" Yet another yawn incapacitated him, but inwardly I was dancing. *Sense at last.*

"Upstairs?" I suggested, sensing impending collapse.

"Upstairs would be lovely," Dan agreed, swaying with exhaustion. "Only I haven't got my stuff for tonight..." His eyes were half-closed already. As I had done at his house, I wiggled my head under his armpit, draping his arm across my shoulder, and helped him stand up.

"I'll get your stuff from your house," I offered. "I'll get a selection of things. I've seen you launch often enough. I'll find something. Trust me."

"With my life," Dan muttered, very nearly asleep. How could anyone go from manically hyper to crippling fatigue within seconds? It was like a switch had been thrown and the electricity had been shut off. Alarm bells were ringing somewhere deep in my brain, and I resolved to look into this kind of erratic behavior, even if I just Googled it. Tomorrow. I would look into it tomorrow, when I had the time, when this day was done with, but before I would broach the subject of sleep, work and play with him.

"Come on," I cajoled. "Up we go."

Chapter Twenty-Seven

I spent the afternoon in a blur of worry, despite all the entertainment I laid on for the kids. The local cinema was running a series of special screenings of Disney films, and today's offering was *Finding Nemo*. The kids were mesmerized, clutching my hands excitedly while I let my mind wander. Afterwards, we swung by Dan's house to collect a variety of outfits for his big night. I picked his favorite leathers, trademark silky blue shirt, and cowboy boots. To be on the safe side, I also added a couple pairs of jeans, four alternative shirts, and two extra pairs of boots. Dan rarely wore jewelry, but I took a few rock star accoutrements anyway, just in case. Having deposited my loot in a handy hold-all, we piled back in the car and drove home to see how our Rock God was faring, the kids singing "Beyond the Sea" the entire way.

Our Rock God was faring well, or so it appeared. The sounds of singing and splashing water greeted us when we entered the house. Dan was evidently up and in the shower, and in high spirits at that. I delivered his clothes to the spare bedroom and loitered outside the bathroom. Should I go in and tell him we were back? Or should I wait until he came out?

This situation hadn't presented itself before. In the dim and distant past, when mutual bathroom episodes featured in our lives, it had always been only us. In the more recent past, Dan had always been discreet about showering, and he had never hogged the family bathroom before. But I couldn't simply barge in. For one, the kids would probably follow right on my heels, which might prove a tad overwhelming. And for another…I just wasn't sure whether I could trust myself.

So I loitered and bit my nails and eventually settled on knocking on the door and announcing our presence. The singing stopped, as did the splashing. "We're back," I repeated, lest he hadn't heard the first time.

"Brilliant," he shouted back. "I'll be out in a few minutes." His voice was steady and strong, and he sounded cheerful. I prayed he had slept and rested and had turned some kind of corner.

He came downstairs a few minutes later, wrapped in my dressing gown—which was, of course, a little on the short side, quite apart from being pink—with wet hair and sparkly eyes.

"I feel good," he remarked, sounding quite surprised. "That was just what was needed."

"Sleep always helps," I retorted. "You should try it more often."

The barb passed Dan by as he settled on the sofa to watch telly with the kids, struggling to safeguard his modesty in my too-short dressing gown. I threw him a blanket and he accepted, spreading it across his legs and snuggling down. My fingers were itching for the camera to document this extraordinary scene. Nobody, but nobody, would have recognized Dan Hunter in this display of familial coziness. I didn't, of course. I fixed dinner instead.

Dan got dressed before dinner, selecting a pair of jeans and a dark shirt from amongst the clothes I had brought.

"Thank you," he said, putting his arms around my waist and planting the briefest of kisses on my cheeks. "You are a star."

I smiled, and the kids giggled at our half-serious display of affection. The oven timer broke the mood, announcing dinner was ready. Dan let me go and made a show of sniffing the air. "What's that gorgeous smell?"

"Chili," I announced proudly. I adored making chili con carne with my secret recipe. In deference to the kids' taste buds, it wasn't terribly hot, but it was tasty and juicy, especially if served with lashings of melted cheese. "Would you like to join us?"

Assume nothing, hope for the best. I kept my tone light and my face neutral, suddenly aware that I was treating Dan like a gazelle who was liable to shy away and take off at the slightest scare.

"I'd love to," he agreed.

Dinner passed quickly, time running through my fingers like sand, and all too soon, Dan announced he would have to get ready to leave. He went upstairs, singing one of his new songs, and returned a half hour later in his leathers and the silky blue shirt, top buttons undone, as always.

My heart jumped into my throat as I took in his appearance. Oh my, he was a gorgeous man. Always had been, always would be. My nose caught a waft of his aftershave, and I held onto the kitchen counter to stay upright while my legs threatened to buckle in a momentary swoon. I could feel a slow blush start on my cheeks and work its way down my neck. What on earth was going on? I was behaving like the star-struck teenager I had once been. Why was it, after all this time, after everything that had happened between us, everything we had been through together, my wedding, Steve's death—how come after all this time, I suddenly got a dizzy spell again just because Dan put on the full rock-star act?

The kids were in awe. They had never seen Dan in his full glory, not face-to-face, and they danced around him as though he was a god descended from heaven.

"You look like someone on telly," Josh announced. "You look like a rock star."

Dan shot me an amused glance as he bent down to speak to Josh. "That's because I am a rock star," he said and burst out laughing. "D'you know," he addressed me as he straightened up, "I don't think I've *ever* said that to anyone like this before. 'That's because I am a rock star,'" he mimicked himself, laughing again.

I stepped across and ruffled Josh's hair. "Sweetie, you know what Dan does. You've seen the albums and the photos, you've heard the music?" It was a question more than a statement.

"I know," Josh explained himself, jiggling up and down impatiently. "I know all that. But this is really real!" He raced off around the room like an airplane. "I can't wait to tell everyone at school that a real rock star has been to my house!" And he flew upstairs, Emily in his wake.

Dan perched himself on the side of the sofa. "What was that all about?" he reflected, somewhat dumbstruck.

"I don't really know," I confessed. "But kids are like that. Your albums and your photos, that's all a bit abstract for them, I suppose. But seeing you like someone they might recognize on the telly, that makes it real. As absurd as that actually is."

Dan shook his head. "Well, at least I can still wow the next generation," he chuckled.

"You certainly can," I agreed. "And the current one, too."

Dan looked up. "Is that so?" he teased, his voice gentle and low. His blue eyes, no longer bloodshot or red-rimmed, brimmed with mischievous excitement.

"Is that so," he murmured again, leaning in to nibble at my ear. His breath was warm against my neck, and for one short second, I nearly forgot once again who I was or where I was.

Only nearly, though, for the heavy clatter of feet on the stairs announced that airplane Josh and entourage Emily were on the return journey, and Dan and I shrank apart hastily. The smile remained in Dan's eyes and he poked my side playfully.

"We're gonna talk about this later, young lady," he threatened.

"Maybe." I fiddled with the sleeve of my jumper and tried my best to backpedal from the moment.

Dan arched his eyebrows, but said nothing more. He wouldn't have been able to anyway as the kids now buzzed around us with noisy laughter. Josh had retrieved his kiddy camera and was asking to take pictures, and Dan preened obligingly. Emily looked on adoringly. Dan really was wowing the next generation.

He left at eight-thirty after helping put the children to bed. There was a hint of reluctance in his eyes as he shrugged on his leather jacket. "Wish you could come," he said.

"Me, too," I confessed, but made light of my inexplicable disappointment. "Maybe next time, right?"

"Definitely," Dan said. He leaned in and kissed me on the mouth, surprising us both. For a moment, I savored the feel of his lips on mine. The heady scent of his aftershave mixed with that of his masculinity filled my universe and dulled any rational response. My body responded to his affection with a hot flush starting on my cheeks and racing down to my toes. My heart beat wildly and I enjoyed the adrenaline rush. Pressing myself against Dan eagerly, I raked my hands through his hair.

What are you doing, Sophie? a small part of my brain wondered somewhat belatedly, but I ignored it and kissed on. Dan wrapped his arms around me, and the very heat radiating from his body made my knees weaken. This man was hot with desire.

We remained locked in this embrace until we needed to come up for air. Confused despite my arousal, I took a step backwards and broke free of Dan's arms. He was panting heavily, taking ragged, shuddering breaths. His face was flushed, and his eyes had a feverish glitter to them.

My God, maybe Rachel is right, I suddenly thought. *Maybe he does still want me. I certainly seem to be having an effect on him!* I smiled softly to myself.

"You are quite something," I whispered. "But I think it's time you went." With the intention of planting a chaste farewell kiss on his brow, I cupped his face in my hands tenderly. Yet feeling the dry, intense heat in his cheeks projected me abruptly into concerned mummy-mode. I touched his forehead, and the back of his neck. Hot, too hot.

"I think you have a fever," I declared. "Let me get a thermometer. Maybe…maybe you shouldn't go tonight?"

Dan shook off my worry with levity. "If I have a fever, it's because you're burning me up inside," he joked, half-quoting a line from one of his songs. "But seriously, I'm fine. And I really ought to go." His face flickered with regret and anticipation. "It's weird, being with you," he suddenly remarked. "It's changing everything."

Before I could begin to compute the implications of what he had just said, he roused himself and rushed to the door. "I'll be off, or I'll never make it," he threw over his shoulders.

"Have a great time," I shouted after him, but I didn't think he heard me.

Chapter Twenty-Eight

It wasn't until the door had shut behind him that I realized I didn't even know whether he would be coming back to my house, going home, or staying at the hotel. I poured myself a glass of wine as I settled in front of the telly and surmised that, based on previous experience, he was most likely to stay at the hotel. He had always done so in the past, even when he was going out only miles from his very own bed.

I giggled and blushed as I recalled a night we had spent together at the Royal Hotel over a decade ago, getting very nearly, but not quite, up-close-and-personal. Yup, on balance, he would probably stay in a suite at the Hyde Star Inn.

I went to bed at eleven with only the slightest sense of unease, having spent all evening convincing myself that Dan would be okay, would probably have finished the gig already and be happily partying. Stretched out under my snuggly duvet, I fell asleep instantly and dreamed vivid dreams involving the kids and Dan playing a noisy game of hide-and-seek.

The house was dark and the alarm clock read three a.m. when a particularly loud bang woke me up. I lay in the darkness and steadied my breathing, suppressing recollections from my inadvertent drug bust and resulting fears of retribution. *There is nobody in the house apart from you and the kids*, I told myself calmly. However, the distinct and unmistakable sound of heavy footfalls coming up the stairs told me otherwise, and I stuffed a hand in my mouth to keep from screaming. For the fraction of a second, I considered that it might be Dan, but I dismissed the thought. He would be staying in the hotel. And anyway, the irregular, heavy thumps didn't sound like him at all.

The footsteps reached the top landing and silence ensued. My mind was racing, and I was paralyzed with frustration at not being able to recall where I had left my mobile phone. The landline handset by the bed would beep when I lifted it off the cradle, and I really didn't want that to happen. My bedroom door was only ajar, as always, and the man was sure to hear any noise I made. Hell and damnation, but did I never learn?

The silence was oppressive and I was shaking with fear. Seconds seemed to stretch into minutes before there was a massive thud, followed by a groan, followed by more silence.

The groan, however, was familiar, and I leapt out of bed. Nearly tripping over my own feet in my tired haste, I pulled open my bedroom door but ground to a halt at the threshold. Dan was sprawled across the floor at the top of the stairs. He had barely made it all the way up before collapsing. My first reaction was anger. How dare he to get so blindingly drunk and come back to my place, frightening me and quite possibly the kids, too?

Thoughts of waking the kids galvanized me into action, and I tiptoed across the landing to close their bedroom door. But when I returned to Dan, I had to shelve my anger. This man wasn't drunk. Something else was wrong.

Even by the scant illumination from the nightlight on the landing, I could tell that Dan was white as a sheet, as ghostly pale as I had ever seen anyone, but with a bright heat burning red in his cheeks. I sank to the floor beside him, using the sleeve of my pajamas to wipe his brow. He looked at me and mumbled something incoherent. His eyes were feverish and unfocused with enormous dilated pupils. He was drenched in sweat and shaking violently, his breathing shallow in between bouts of hoarse coughing.

"Dan," I whispered. "Dan, it's Sophie. Can you hear me?"

No response.

My heart jumped into my mouth and a thousand thoughts chased each other around my head. What was I to do?

I stroked his forehead and tried to make eye contact, which was difficult as Dan's gaze skittered all over the place. Primal fear took hold of me, and I rose to my feet abruptly.

"I'm calling an ambulance," I declared and turned to go into my bedroom for the phone. A desperate, violent gurgling sound stopped me in my tracks.

"No. Please, no." Dan's words were barely audible between his ragged breaths and I paid no heed.

"Dan, you need medical attention," I reiterated and took another step away from him. Unexpectedly, Dan's hand shot out and clamped around my ankle with surprising strength. I nearly fell over with the motion.

"No," Dan rasped again and tried to speak on, but his words drowned in another coughing fit. He held onto my ankle for dear life while his lungs heaved, and I slowly sat down again. The act of restraining me and the effort of coughing had worn my rock star out completely. His hair was matted with perspiration and the brightness in his cheeks shone even stronger than before. Dan desperately needed a doctor. Evidently, he didn't want one. What was going on?

"Dan, let me get you to bed at least." I grasped at the next reasonable course of action. He had to get off the landing for his own sake, as well as mine and my family's. If the kids woke and saw him like this….

Dan tried to speak again, but this time his tongue merely lolled in his mouth and no further words came out. I swallowed hard, trying to control my panic. I stroked his face some more, but his eyes were closed and his eyelids barely fluttered in response to my caress.

"Dan," I said again, speaking a little more loudly. "I need to get you into bed, okay?"

Dan rolled his head from side to side before pulling his legs up into a fetal position as his body was consumed by a violent attack of the shivers. I held his face in both my hands, simultaneously trying to stem his quaking and make him look at me.

"Dan!" This time, my voice was nearly a shout. "Dan, look at me!"

No response again. His eyes remained closed and his mouth worked furiously as if he were chewing. Next thing I knew, he tried to bring a fist up to his mouth. He was uncoordinated and clumsy, and he never made it, but the act caught my attention.

"What have you got in there?" I demanded. "Let's see."

Dan made an incoherent sound. There was a sinking feeling of foreboding in my tummy, and I was watching the two of us as though I was detached from the scene. I saw myself take Dan's hand, shaking and clammy, and pry away his fingers, one by one, until I revealed a small, orange-tinted but transparent plastic bottle half full with small pills. I took in a sharp breath as I turned the bottle over and over in my hands. There was no label on it, which I took to be a bad sign. Something was very seriously wrong here. And I needed help with this; I needed help helping Dan.

Dan was becoming more agitated by the second. With apparent effort, he opened his eyes again and looked around wildly until he finally saw the bottle in my hand. Weak and disorientated though he was, he nonetheless tried to grab the pills back out of my hands. Anger rose in my throat alongside bile, and I whipped the offending pharmaceuticals out of his reach. "Oh no you don't," I hissed. "You've done far too much damage already, you stupid man."

I stuffed the bottle into the breast pocket of my pajamas and did the third weightlifter heaving-rock-star-into bed impression of my life. Momentarily too furious to be compassionate, I yanked at Dan's arms and upper body until I had him almost upright. When he stumbled and refused to cooperate, I slapped his face to get him to focus.

"Get up and walk, dammit," I hissed. "If the kids see you like this, I'll kill you." I didn't mean that bit, of course, but it got a reaction. Dan made a grand effort, and together, we stumbled the few steps into my bedroom, where Dan collapsed yet again and passed out like a dead weight. I closed the door and switched on my bedside light. For a minute, I sat on the floor and wept.

I pulled the vial of pills out of my pocket and looked at it again. My hands now shaking almost as much as Dan's had, I fumbled with the cap until I had the bottle open and shook some pills into the palm of my hand. They were white and looked fairly innocuous, almost like sweets, but they weren't stamped with any pharmaceutical company's logo or make number, and that in itself was the worst piece of news. Humble painkillers, they were not.

"What am I to do?" I wailed, purely for my own benefit as Dan's eyes were closed and he was very much passed out. He was breathing but he was shaking all over, and I knew I had to do something. Well, not something. Dan needed an ambulance, he did, he really did. But he had begged me not to make that call.

Was I to listen to my friend, or to my gut instinct? How much time did I have to make that decision? Could I risk losing another of the men in my life?

I grabbed Dan's wrist and tried to take his pulse. It took me ages to find it, and when I did, it was thready and fast, but it was there. I gave myself permission to make one more call before summoning the medical services. One more minute. Just to be sure I was doing the right thing for him.

Rachel answered after the second ring.

"Sophie?"

"Rach," I whispered as loudly as I could. "You have to help me. I'm sorry to wake you."

"I wasn't sleeping," she soothed me. "Henry is teething, and you know what that's like. What's up?"

"It's Dan," I sniffled but forced myself to get a grip. I related events as coherently as I could, ending on the hateful orange bottle of little white pills.

"I don't understand," I muttered. "What's going on?"

Rachel responded with a volley of quick-fire questions. Had Dan been working hard? Had he seemed strange? Up and down, perhaps? Hyper, at times?

I answered each question with a simple 'yes,' desperate to cut to the chase now. "What's going on? I have to call that ambulance, right?"

Rachel spoke quickly, urgency in her every word. "Dan's been taking something. He needs a doctor fast."

"I know! But Rach, he begged me not to call an ambulance—"

"Call 999, now. He's done drugs, and you need to help him."

"I—"

"Sophie, he may be dying! Hang up, ring that ambulance, and I'll be round as soon as I can. Do it. NOW."

The line clicked dead as my friend hung up and the shock propelled me into action. Feeling stupid now for indulging Dan's request, I dialed 999 with clumsy fingers. *He may be dying. He may be dying.* Rachel's words ran round and round my head and I barely managed to stop myself from howling in despair.

Chapter Twenty-Nine

While I waited to be connected, I retrieved a thermometer from my bedside drawer were it lived in continual readiness for child-related crises, and I took his temperature. He was running a fever of forty degrees centigrade, the equivalent of one hundred and four, and I panicked even more. *Hurry up, operator, I have a sick man here!*

Although it seemed an eternity, in reality, I spoke with an emergency operator in mere seconds. The dispatcher was great. She asked me short, relevant questions, reassured me, gave me advice, and told me an ambulance would be there within minutes. Meanwhile, I was to make sure that Dan didn't choke in the event of vomiting and stay with him in case he woke up or had a seizure.

"I'll be staying on the line with you until the ambulance arrives, Ma'am, I'll be right here, okay?" the operator assured me after finishing her instructions. "Okay?"

"Okay," I breathed, "thank you." It was a relief having her there, like a lifeline. Although it was a little awkward struggling into my clothes while holding the phone. Then again, if I were to go to the hospital with Dan, I didn't want to do it in pajamas. I put the phone on the bedside table, face up so I wouldn't inadvertently hang up, and got myself organized.

Quite suddenly, Dan shifted in my bed and rolled on to his side. He started coughing and retching. His breath rattled ominously and it sounded as though he was choking on something. Without warning, he spat out a few globs of foul-smelling, rusty-colored phlegm. The sputum soiled his shirt and the sheets, and more kept coming, but Dan choked on it and swallowed some down. Then he started vomiting. He coughed and spluttered and heaved, and the bilious brown vomit kept on coming, wave after wave it.

"Ma'am? Ma'am, what's going on?" The headset on my bedside table emitted the operator's voice, and I gave a little start. In the shock of the moment, I had forgotten that the line was still open.

"He's coughed something up and then he was sick." I snatched up the phone and spoke quickly. "He's stopped now but there's sick everywhere."

"Are his airwaves clear? Is he breathing okay?"

I nodded in response but remembered that the operator couldn't see me. "Yes, he's breathing freely. Well, it's ragged and raspy as before, but he's breathing."

"Good. Keep him on his side, okay?"

"Okay," I agreed, glad of someone to tell me what to do. I put the phone onto speaker and put it on my bedside table. Then I sat by Dan's head and stroked his hair, his face, holding him steady on his side as he heaved again, making sure all the come-back was clear of his airwaves and mouth and talking to him all the while.

"Good, you're doing great," the operator praised me. "It won't be long now until the crew get to you."

After a couple of minutes, Dan was finally spent and the vomiting stopped. He was awake, but barely conscious, and he didn't seem to recognize me. I nipped out to the bathroom to retrieve a washcloth and wiped down his face, noting again how hot he was to the touch. *Hurry, ambulance, hurry!*

My mobile phoned beeped. It turned out that it was under the bed and I seized it swiftly. Rachel had texted to say that she was outside my house.

"Rachel is here," I explained to Dan and added for the benefit of the operator, "A friend's here. She...she'll be sitting with the children if...if..." I couldn't finish the sentence. "I'm just going to let her in."

"You do that, Ma'am," the operator acknowledged my statement.

Downstairs, Rachel gave me an enormous hug. "You okay? You look beat."

"He's been sick. Like, everywhere. And he's running a fever, a really high one. I'm so worried."

"Did you call the ambulance?"

I nodded. "They should be here any minute. And the operator is still on the line, too."

"Good. All will be well. You're doing all you can. Where's your bucket and mop?"

Rachel was pragmatic as always. I let her get on with collecting some cleaning stuff while I hurried back to Dan's bedside. I had barely been gone two minutes, but he had been sick again. Because I hadn't been there, he had simply spat where he lay and he was covered. The phone was talking incessantly.

"Ma'am? Ma'am, are you there?"

I spoke for the benefit of the operator as well as my own, explaining what I was doing while I stepped over the puddle, pulled Dan away from the vomit and checked hastily but carefully that he was breathing. The operator acknowledged my every action with a calm, "Good." Only when Dan was back safely on his side and away from the pool of sick did I pick up the phone, disengaging the speaker phone as I did so.

"I'm frightened, really frightened." I nearly cried.

"Keep calm," the operator advised. "You're doing great."

"I…I need to make sure he stays on his side. I need to hold him steady. Will you stay on the line?"

"Yes, Ma'am."

"Okay. But…I…I just need to put you down a minute, okay?"

The operator was unflappable. "You do that, I'll be right here for you."

I put the phone back down again and kept a hold of Dan. Rachel entered the room and grimaced but said nothing. She didn't need to. Her entire body told me that this wasn't looking good. Still, she set to work, scooping big gloops of vomit into a plastic bag with my dustpan, sponging the floor and sprinkling liberal amounts of bicarb of soda over the affected area.

"I'll have another go when you're gone, but you might want to get this professionally cleaned," she ventured. It seemed callous and cruel to talk carpet logistics, but we were both holding on to practical things while we were waiting for the medics. Yet there was something on my mind, something that I needed to talk about before the ambulance arrived. I reached across and pressed the mute button on the phone so the operator wouldn't be able to listen in for a moment.

"Dan doesn't do drugs," I told Rach, simply because I needed to get that fact straight.

And it was true, Dan had never done drugs before, ever. Never, ever, ever. I was one hundred percent certain of that. The band had always been fantastically proud of their clean lives.

Rachel looked up from her scrubbing. Her eyes flicked to the phone and her face said, *are you crazy?* I shrugged and mimicked holding the phone while placing a finger to my lips. Rachel widened her eyes in response and nodded.

"Well, he has now." Her voice was low and gentle, as if untrusting of my phone's mute function. "It adds up. His tiredness, his hyper activity, the sudden crashing, the extreme cheerful moods..." She let that hang for a moment before continuing. "I would guess that he's been taking boosters."

"Boosters," I echoed numbly. "Boosters don't sound too bad, right?"

Rachel was blunt in correcting me, but there was no judgment in her voice. "He's been taking Ritalin, or E."

"Ritalin? E?" I stroked Dan's hair in agitation while I digested this piece of information.

"*E*, as in Ecstasy? It can kill people! Why would he do that?"

Rachel sighed. "They're stimulants. They keep you going and going until your body pulls the plug and you drop. Looks like Dan's dropped."

I swallowed hard, recalling the metaphor of the supernova that I applied earlier that day. I had worried about when he would burn out. I had had no idea how close I had been to the mark. If only I had *thought* properly. If only I had spoken with Rach before. If only...

I didn't get a chance to voice my thoughts because the ambulance arrived at that moment. Rachel ran downstairs to let them in while I stayed glued to Dan's side.

Within seconds, my peaceful little bedroom was full of people. There were three ambulance crew members and they got to work immediately. Two of them looked after Dan while the third one quickly closed the call with the operator before addressing me with a sequence of questions that I answered as best I could. No, I wasn't his wife. No, I wasn't next of kin. Yes, I was a good friend. Yes, he had come to the house under his own steam. No, I hadn't been with him during the evening. All the while, I watched in dismay as they inserted an IV into Dan's hand, attached a saline drip, fitted an oxygen mask.

The paramedics began assessing his condition. "How long has he had this high temperature?"

"I don't quite know. He felt feverish when he left earlier this evening, but I didn't take his temperature. He seemed all right. I think he knew he was hot, he—" I bit my lip.

"He what?" prompted the medic.

"He made a joke about it. He said…he said I was burning him up inside." The medic looked at me blankly. "It's a line from one of his songs," I supplied.

"Oh, right. Well, from the state of him, I would assume his temperature has been too high for quite some time. Is he taking any medication?"

I stared at the wall, avoiding Rachel's gaze. "He…he's had a prescription for some things from his GP, but I don't know exactly what for. He's had this really bad cold, and he needed to keep recording so…"

The medic gave me a searching look. "Anything else? Alcohol? Drugs?"

"I don't know," I tried to evade. "He was at a party tonight. When I first found him, I assumed he was drunk. I'm sure he drank." It would have been foolish to deny that Dan was full of booze.

"Drugs?" the other medic persisted.

I shrugged. "I've never known Dan do drugs, and I've known him a long time. This isn't like him." I connected two truthful statements that didn't really answer the question.

Dan was unconscious through all of this, although he was agitated and occasionally mumbled incomprehensibly. Rachel grabbed my hand and squeezed it.

The second paramedic, the one who had insisted on the drug question, looked up at us.

"He's exhibiting all the signs of having taken something," he stated matter of fact. "It would help if you could tell us. We can treat him faster."

Rachel and I finally exchanged that tell-tale desperate glance.

"We're not the police. We only want to help him," the first medic chipped in. Rachel cleared her throat as though to speak, but I got there first.

"He had this in his hand." I proffered one of Dan's pills. "He wanted to take it, but I didn't let him."

The first medic took the pill from my outstretched hand, peering at it closely before putting it into a plastic bag without comment.

"Thank you," the other medic said. "You might have just saved his life. We're ready to go."

They lifted Dan onto a stretcher and covered him with a blanket.

"May I... Please, can I come with him?" My voice wobbled at the prospect of being turned down.

"Of course. Please do." Medic One smiled encouragingly. "Give us a minute to get him into the ambulance." The two medics stretchered Dan out of the bedroom and down the stairs.

Miraculously, the kids were still asleep. In the tiny moment of being alone with Rachel, I gave her a big hug.

"Thank you," I whispered. "I had to tell. I'm sorry. I couldn't not."

"You did the right thing," Rachel said. I smiled, briefly, and hugged her before I went down to join Dan in the ambulance.

Chapter Thirty

"Your friend has a severe case of pneumonia." The doctor's face was calm and exuded confidence as she smiled and extended her hand to greet me. "It looks bacterial, but we'll have to wait for the test results to be sure. Meanwhile, we're giving him antibiotics. He's also on a drip, and he's still receiving extra oxygen. He'll need to be in hospital for a few days."

She paused and cleared her throat. "He has a lot of alcohol in his system, and we're also testing for other drugs. He's not in a great condition, and, to be honest with you, it's a little touch and go at the moment. He should pull through, but I can't say for certain until I know what he's taken, and how bad the pneumonia is."

I could feel tears pricking the back of my eyes. "When will you know?"

The doctor gave me a sympathetic look. "Well, his temperature is coming down with the medicine we're giving, so that's good. His heart rate is steady, and his breathing has eased with the oxygen. Those are all good signs. I would say the next twelve hours will tell us more. We're doing everything we can."

"Do people really die from pneumonia, in this day and age?" I simply couldn't contain my panic.

The doctor looked me plainly in the eyes. "A very small number of people do die from pneumonia, even in this day and age. Sometimes, we can't save them." She paused and rubbed her eyes. After a little sigh, she resumed speaking.

"I don't think your friend will die. But I can't tell you that he will pull through for sure until the drug screen is back and I have an idea what other damage might be harming his system. I need to know that the medicines are working before I can reassure you one hundred percent. I wish I could give you better news, but we will simply have to wait. He is young, though, and you say he doesn't smoke. He looks to be fit and healthy otherwise. This will all work in his favor." She tilted her head. "Why don't you go and see him for a moment?"

"Is he awake?" Sudden hope blazed in my soul, only to be dashed instantly.

"No. But it will still do him good to hear your voice." She handed me a mask. "You'd better wear this, in case he's contagious."

Deflated, worried sick and sporting the proffered mask over my mouth and nose, I trudged after the doctor as she led me to Dan's room. I had been waiting for this moment for three hours, and I was woozy with exhaustion.

Dan looked pale and fragile against the white sheets. Tubes snaked into his veins and nose, and the telltale purple smudges were lodged under his eyes again. Every now and then, his eyelids fluttered as though he was waking up, but he was probably dreaming. The doctor pulled up a chair for me and encouraged me to sit.

"Take your time," she advised. "Talk to him. He will hear you. It will help." And with that, she left.

At first, I didn't know what to say. I simply looked and prayed and let a million thoughts run free in my head. At length, the tears came, one or two at first, followed by a veritable torrent. I was terrified at the loss of my friend, my rock, my rock star. Grasping his hand in both of mine, I stroked his palm, his fingers, his wrists. His skin was warm, yet clammy, but at least he had stopped shivering. His hand lay limp and unresponsive in mine, even though I had irrationally hoped he might squeeze back. My vision blurred as yet more tears came, and I wanted to lie down beside Dan and howl.

Of course, I did no such thing. I simply sat and cried until there were no more tears left. In my mind, I was speaking, I was ranting. *Please don't leave me. Don't leave me. I can't bear to lose you. I can't bear to lose another man I love. Don't do this to me. I'm sorry, Steve. I'm so sorry, but I need this man, now. Don't leave me, Dan. You promised to look after me. And the kids. Don't go. Don't go.*

The urgency and despair in my head surprised me. Yes, I had been shocked, terrified even, when I had found Dan collapsed on my landing, but I had been too busy trying to deal with the situation to figure out how deeply my feelings ran. Yes, I had once again been harboring a secret fantasy, a physical attraction for this man for some time now, even though I had been in conscious denial about it. Yes, I had arguably been cavalier about my own feelings, and his. But I simply hadn't understood what was going on. I hadn't comprehended what had happened to me, slowly, gradually, imperceptibly.

I was in love with Dan all over again.

The realization hit me with full force. I had fallen in love all over again, even if it had taken a trip to death's door for me to see the truth, plain as daylight. How could I have been so blind?

Worse, I knew he loved me, too. I knew he had always loved me, had never stopped. I had known all along. I had known from the songs he wrote and from the way he had always been there, other women or not. I had known from the way he looked at me, even on my wedding day. I had known from the way his heart had broken for me when Steve died, and from the way it mended when he held Emily in his arms. I had known it when Rachel told me, I just hadn't been able to acknowledge it.

Two people—two stupid people—in love with each other, unable to see, to say, to do something about it. Would we have figured it out, would *I*, had it not been for this dreadful interlude?

I sat back in my chair and laughed. I laughed and laughed and laughed, loud, clear peals of merriment. I was in love. *We* were in love.

I had no idea what to do with this feeling. I had no clue where we would go from here. Would we ever be lovers? Or would we invent a new art form of unhappiness, the mutually unfulfilled love? If and when he woke up, could I tell him? *Should* I tell him?

I gripped his hand again. "Do you know what you've done?" I whispered. "Do you know what you're feeling? Do you have a plan?"

Of course, I didn't get an answer. I didn't expect one. Pushing back my chair, I got up and took a few steps along the bed. I bent down and put my mouth by Dan's ear, stroking his face with my hand as I spoke words only for him.

"I don't know if I'll ever tell you this face-to-face when you're awake, you great big fool of a man. But I love you. I love you."

Chapter Thirty-One

"How is he?"

A pale and tired-looking Rachel greeted me when I returned home shortly after six a.m. She wrapped her arms around me and led me to the sofa. "Here, sit down. I'll make you a cuppa. You look as though you could do with one."

"That would be lovely, thanks." I smiled, feeling every bit as wan and tired as my best friend looked. It hadn't been a restful night for either of us, although, mercifully, the kids still appeared to be asleep.

"He's got pneumonia, they say," I informed Rachel when she pressed a steaming mug of tea into my hand. "They were still running tests and drug screens and all that when I left. They know he'd drunk a lot, but..." I fizzled out.

"Pneumonia?" Rachel reiterated. "How'd he come by that?"

"I don't know yet. I didn't know people still got pneumonia, really. And..." Tears pushed inside my eyes as I recalled the conversation with the doctor. Rachel took my hand and rubbed it gently.

"And what? What is it?" Her voice was full of concern.

"He might die." There, I said it. It sounded as bad spoken aloud as it did running endlessly around in my head.

"He might die? Of pneumonia?" Rachel's face showed her shock and surprise. "Surely not. I mean, come on, this is the twenty-first century."

"I know, that's what *I* said, but the doctor said that until she's certain that the medication works and until she knows exactly how bad it is, she can't say for certain that he'll pull through."

"Oh, Soph." Rachel squeezed my hand a little harder, but said nothing more. There was nothing much *to* say. We sat in silence for a few minutes, and, distracted though I was, I registered the sound of the boiler springing into action in the kitchen. Six-thirty. We were on borrowed time. The kids were bound to be up any minute. I needed to get a grip.

I squared my shoulders and sat up straight. Rachel mirrored my stance, and we looked at each other somberly. The concern and confusion in her eyes pushed me over the edge.

"I love him." The words slipped out before I could stop them. "I love him, and I can't bear the thought of losing him. I can't lose him. I can't." My resolve to buck up ran from my body alongside the tears that coursed down my cheeks, and I sagged against Rach. She put her arms around me again and stroked my hair, making indistinct soothing noises.

"He mustn't die," I sobbed, all restraint gone. "He mustn't. Why does every man I love die on me? He can't die. I don't want to lose him."

"I know, darling, I know," Rachel whispered. "I know you love him. You won't lose him. I promise. He'll pull through. He'll be all right."

I sat back and met her gaze again, hope fighting against pessimism in my chest. "But will he? What if—"

"Shh," Rachel soothed again. "Shh. He'll be all right."

I let myself be comforted by my best friend, accepting her calm reassurance at face value. There was nothing else I could do right at that moment, and it felt good to be held. I vaguely wondered at her quiet acceptance of my love declaration for Dan. *I know*, she had simply said.

How had she known, when I had only just realized? Was that where she had been guiding me lately, trying to push me in the right direction? Had I been too absorbed in my grief and my obstinate refusal to take charge of my life to notice what was right in front of me? Had I missed my opportunity? What if he did die? What then? I shuddered and found fresh tears to shed. Rachel produced a tissue and wiped at my face.

"Shh," she made again, putting a finger to my lips, trying to stem my sobbing. She listened attentively. There was a thump upstairs, followed by a series of lighter mini-thumps.

"Somebody's up," Rachel stated.

"Oh God," I groaned. "Look at me. I'll frighten them to death." I grabbed the tissue off Rachel and ran it over my face, mopping up the floods. No doubt my eyes would be red and my skin blotchy, but that couldn't be helped now. I took a few deep breaths and sat up straighter, fixing a watery smile onto my face. And sure enough, Josh appeared in the doorway, looking sweet, sleepy, and innocent. His face lit up at seeing me awake, and he ran across the lounge with his arms wide open, skidding to a halt in front of me when he noticed my rumpled appearance.

"Why are you crying?" he asked before throwing himself on my lap and putting his little arms around my neck. Oh, the unconditional love of a child!

I gave a muffled half-sob, half-laugh and opted for the truth. Well, a child-appropriate, edited version of the truth. "I'm crying because Dan is very poorly, and he's been taken to hospital."

Josh sat bolt upright. His face crumpled and his bottom lip wobbled. "Will he die, like daddy?"

Cursing my insensitivity, I ruffled his hair.

"No, he won't," Rachel jumped in, her voice light and cheerful. "He's poorly, but it's only a bit of a bad cold, really, and he'll be fine. They're giving him lots of medicine."

I shot her a feeble smile, glad she was there to face the crisis with me. Josh, however, was not reassured. He fiddled with my hair while he pondered the situation, and I knew something was coming.

"But if it's only a bit of a bad cold," he slowly and carefully repeated Rachel's words, then delivered the killer conclusion. "If it's only a cold, why is Mummy crying? And why is he in the hospital?"

Where had the innocence of childhood gone? No longer would a simple explanation suffice. My inquisitive son didn't miss a trick and wasn't fobbed off easily. I pulled him round so I could look at him.

"You know how Dan has had this cold for, like, weeks? We all had it, didn't we?" Josh nodded. "Well, Dan's not had a chance to get rid of it, like we have. He's been working really hard, and he's not looked after himself properly."

"You mean, he hasn't been eating bananas for breakfast and apples for lunch, and broccoli with his dinner?" my son inquired.

Despite the sadness of the situation, I caught Rachel suppressing a soft giggle. I inclined my head, pondering my response.

"Well," I said, "I think Dan's been eating some fruit and veg, because, you know, that's really important, and he knows that too."

"But he didn't eat enough?"

"No, he probably didn't eat enough. But he also did a lot of singing and a lot of working too hard. And sometimes, when that happens, a cold can get really bad, and you need to go to the hospital so the doctors can give you super-strong medicine to make you better."

Josh looked terrified. "Will I go to hospital next time I've a cold?"

"Of course not." I sighed, unsure how far to go, how to pitch my explanation. Recalling my own parents' approach of forthright factualness, I took the plunge. "What's happened to Dan is that his cold infected his lungs. And now he can't breathe properly. That's called pneumonia, and that's why he's in hospital. But it doesn't happen to everyone. In fact, it's quite rare, and I'll be here to make sure that your colds don't turn into pneumonia, so don't worry."

Relief momentarily lightened Josh's face, and I hugged him hard. But we weren't done.

"And Dan?" he persisted. "Will he be all right?"

"He'll be absolutely fine," I said vehemently.

"He really will," Rachel offered, too.

"But why are you crying?"

"I'm not crying anymore." I tried to divert his line of questioning, and it was true. Somehow, facing my child and talking it through had calmed me down. Simplifying the situation had restored my own hope and belief that everything would, in fact, be well, and I felt a lot calmer.

"But you *were*. I can see it." Josh wouldn't be satisfied until he understood what had upset his mummy.

"I *was* crying," I conceded. "I took Dan to the hospital and it upset me to see him so poorly, and I got a bit worried, but that's all. I promise."

"Ah." Finally appeased, Josh gave me another hug and snuggled down on my lap. I smiled at Rachel over his little head. My best friend smiled back, then erupted into a giant yawn.

"Sorry," she apologized when she got over it. "I think I might go home now, if that's okay."

"Of course!" I gently sat Josh on the sofa so I could get up. "Thank you so much for coming and everything...for listening, and all that."

She punched me lightly on the shoulder. "That's what friends are for, you old sop. Don't go funny on me now! I'd love to stay, but I suppose I'd better see how Alex and Henry have been getting on."

We hugged. "Get some sleep," I advised her. "I'll phone you later with news, if I have any."

"You should get some sleep, too," Rachel mused. "How will you manage?"

I shrugged. "I had... oooh... four hours before Dan came home so... I've gotten through days on less. I'll be fine." Catching sight of Josh, still in his pajamas and looking quite tired, too, I had an idea. "We might have an outrageously decadent telly morning at this house, watch a film or two and relax. I'll be fine by lunchtime. Although..."

Another thought wormed its way through my addled brain. "I want to go back to the hospital sometime this afternoon, and I don't think I can take the kids. Would—"

"We'll be home," Rachel interrupted without hesitation. "Drop them off whenever you need to."

"Cool, a play at Rachel's house," Josh enthused. "Can I take Woodie?"

"Of course," Rachel and I replied together.

"Thank you again, and already," I whispered. "You are the best." My sentimental voice earned me another good-natured punch on the arm, and Rachel left.

Chapter Thirty-Two

Later that afternoon, a nurse intercepted me before I could enter Dan's room. He had been placed in a private room, although I didn't know whether that was because he was potentially infectious or because he had private health insurance.

"Are you Mr. Hunter's friend, the one that called the ambulance this morning?" she asked just as I placed my hand on the door handle.

I hesitated and let go. "Yes, I am. My name is Sophie."

She scribbled a little note on her pad before offering me a quick smile. "Mr. Hunter's doctor would like a word, if you don't mind. If you take a seat," she indicated a waiting area opposite the nurse's station, "I'll page him for you."

"Oh, okay," I consented hesitantly. "Is everything all right?"

"Mr. Hunter is resting comfortably," the nurse said. "The doctor will tell you more. Wait a moment, please, and take a seat."

My heart thumped loudly in my chest, and I staggered to the seating area on wobbly legs. What had Dan done? What had they found in his blood? What was I to say? Or was there something even more sinister waiting for me? Had his condition deteriorated? Had he maybe slipped into a coma? Anxiety nibbled at my very soul with sharp, angry bites, and I swallowed hard to suppress looming tears. Darn, but it was difficult to be calm and rational when you had had no sleep, and you were on the brink of losing a loved one.

"Mrs. Jones?" A man in a white coat with the obligatory stethoscope hanging round his neck broke into my thoughts. I gave a start and rose.

"That's me." I met his eyes, a clear blue surrounded by crinkly laugh lines, and I immediately felt better. They were open and friendly.

The doctor held out his hand. "I'm Dr. Smith. Won't you come with me for a moment where we can talk in private?"

There, the worry bites were back again. Why did we need to talk in private? What was going on?

The doctor picked up on my concern immediately. "Please, don't worry. I'll explain. Mr. Hunter is doing well, but I have a few questions I'd rather not discuss right here. If that's all right."

His professional frankness was disarming, and I followed him obediently. He took me to a small family room a couple corridors away from Dan's ward, and offered me some tea.

"Tea would be good, thanks," I consented, realizing that I was likely to keel over any minute without sugary fortification.

"How did you know my name?" I blurted out once we were seated on either side of the coffee table.

Dr. Smith smiled. "You gave your name as next of kin when Mr. Hunter was brought in."

I did? Oh God, I must have been really out of it. I cleared my throat.

"I… I wasn't paying attention. I'm not actually next of kin. I'm just a really good friend."

Dr. Smith took this information in his stride. "That doesn't matter either way. He collapsed at your house, and you brought him in. Isn't that right?"

Collapsed. I used that very same word in my mind when I saw Dan on my landing, but it sounded more serious when it was said by a medical professional. I gulped.

"That's right. Won't you tell me what the problem is? Has his pneumonia gotten worse? Why can't I see him?" The questions tumbled out higgledy-piggledy, and Dr. Smith offered a reassuring pat on my arm.

"You may see him, of course you may. I only wanted to clear up a few details. But first things first." He consulted a chart. "As you know, we ran several tests on Mr. Hunter this morning when he arrived. We also did a chest x-ray and more blood tests. Mr. Hunter has very high levels of white blood cells, pointing to an infection." He paused and stuck an x-ray on the light box on the wall. He used his pen to point out a white blob. "See this?"

I nodded. "That wedge is bacterial pneumonia in Mr. Hunter's right lung. The sputum test confirms that this is caused by pneumococcus."

I nodded again as though this meant something. It didn't, really, but between them, the children had caught enough 'coccuses' for me to understand that this was some sort of evil bacteria. Dr. Smith continued.

"Mr. Hunter's condition has stabilized. He's responding well to the antibiotics, and his fever has come down. However." He paused for a second.

"The infection is quite severe and we have now placed Mr. Hunter on a ventilator to help him breathe and raise the oxygen levels in his blood, so it may be a little unsettling when you first see him. We're hoping he can come off the ventilator later today, but we'll have to see. He's still receiving fluids through an intravenous drip."

I clenched and unclenched my fists, trying to get a grip on the situation. It didn't sound good. My mind fastened on to the least important detail and I blurted out a question.

"Dan's a singer. This ventilation…will it harm his voice?" Dr. Smith raised his eyebrows, and I gabbled on. "You have to understand, music is his life, and if he can't sing…"

"A ventilator can cause hoarseness in patients, but this usually subsides within a matter of days. Prolonged intubation may cause swelling and edema of the vocal cords, or granuloma, which is a kind of ulcer in the vocal folds. But this is unlikely to happen, and it's a little early to worry about it." He paused briefly while I digested this information.

"In either case, Mr. Hunter will need to rest extensively before he can resume his career. Let me ask you about the drugs, though." Dr. Smith moved on to his bombshell question, and I reeled from the impact.

"Drugs," I repeated flatly.

"You gave the paramedics a pill Mr. Hunter attempted to take." The doctor regarded me seriously, and I tried hard to sit still and look calm. I said nothing.

"It was MDMA. Ecstasy. Were you aware that Mr. Hunter has a drug problem?"

"He doesn't!" I objected. "I'm sure of it. Look, I'm not in denial here, and I know he walked into my house last night with that pill, but I've known him for years, and I know, I am certain, that he's not a user."

Mr. Smith nodded. "Our tests bear that out. His liver does not show the damage associated with habitual drug abuse. Nonetheless, he took amphetamines last night. The evidence is irrefutable. We also found evidence he took some sort of caffeine booster pills and paracetamol, and there was plenty of alcohol in his blood, too. A pretty dangerous combination."

He looked at me again, as if waiting for some kind of response. When none came, he prompted me. "Is there anything you can tell me about his physical condition over the past few weeks?"

I took a deep breath and explained about the cold and the doctor's prescription and Dan's crazy schedule and heavy workload. Dr. Smith listened carefully and took notes.

"It adds up," he concluded. "He ignored his symptoms, used painkillers and energy boosters to keep going, and essentially ran himself into the ground. It's no surprise the pneumococcus took hold. Still, I daresay he didn't know what he was doing to his body."

I latched onto another detail irrelevant to Dan's immediate health, but potentially explosive for his career. I cleared my throat, but I knew I would go mad if I didn't get an answer to this question. "Will you...do you have to report this?"

Dr. Smith held my gaze for a few seconds, and his silence prompted me to speak on. "I...I don't mean to sound callous or anything. I'm desperately worried for Dan, but...I need to know. Will this go to the police?"

The doctor's silence continued for a little while. "I can't condone drug abuse," he eventually spoke. "However, I am not obliged to report it. In Mr. Hunter's case, there is no indication that he is a regular user. Moreover, we don't even know yet if he took the drug knowingly, or if it was something that was simply given to him without explanation. That's a conversation you will have to have with him, and I shall trust you to initiate appropriate action if necessary."

I let out a sigh of relief. "Of course. Thank you."

"Thank you for your time and candor." Dr. Smith rose. "I see you understand why it was necessary to have this conversation. Now let's focus on making Mr. Hunter better."

"May I go see him now?" Urgency and fear made my voice raspy, and Dr. Smith patted my arm again.

"Of course. But remember, he is on a ventilator. If he's awake, he won't be able to speak, and you'll have to do the talking for him. Be cheerful and positive, and tell him everything that's happening in the world. If he gets tired, let him rest."

"What happens next?" I was eager to hear that everything would be better soon.

"We'll have to see. The next twelve to twenty-four hours are crucial. I can tell you more then."

Chapter Thirty-Three

Dan was asleep when I entered his room, donning the obligatory mask. The rhythmic swooshing of the ventilator and beeping of his heart monitor were the only sounds that greeted me. I stood by the door for a minute to gather my composure before taking a seat at Dan's bedside.

He looked very pale, and the purple smudges under his eyes had not eased. His hair was matted against his forehead, soaked from the fever ravaging his body. He still had an IV drip attached to his right hand, and there was also a sturdy white plastic clip attached to his ring finger. I had seen those on medical dramas on TV and assumed the device was measuring his oxygen levels. It was a little scary, but it was the sight of the ventilator that shocked me most, even though I had been warned about it. Dan looked fragile and vulnerable. And very, very ill.

I took his free hand and stroked it. It was warm to the touch, but he didn't respond to my caress. Not even the tiniest hint of a squeeze. I reminded myself that the kids didn't squeeze my hand either when I kissed them in the middle of the night, simply because they were so deeply asleep. I hoped that Dan, too, was simply deeply asleep.

"Hey, you," I started after a moment. "Afternoon! Well, it is afternoon although you probably don't know that. You gave me quite a fright, you know."

I paused. The ventilator continued swooshing and the heart monitor beeped.

"You've got pneumonia, the doctor says. That's why you've been feeling so poorly and why you had that fever. I hope you got through the gig at that party all right, somehow."

My God, the pre-launch party — I had no idea how that had gone. I hadn't been on the Internet or listened to the news. I hadn't even seen the papers. I had no idea what had happened. A finger of dread lodged in my tummy. Was his poor state all over the news? Would there be a massive media circus about this? And Jack — did he even know? So many questions... There was only one way to find out.

I rose to my feet and walked over to the window, keeping up my chatter with Dan while I fumbled for my mobile phone in my handbag. I knew I was probably not supposed to use it in here, but that hadn't stopped me in the past, and the doctors seemed to be carrying mobiles, too. If I put some distance between me and Dan's monitors and did the quickest of Internet searches...

My fingers flew over the buttons while I prattled on. "So, that party...was it good? You never told me. Ah, here, look, I found something on the Internet about it."

Trusty Google, shortcut to all desired information. I scanned the search results.

"It was a success, it seems. You all got rave reviews. Look, there's a photo of Tuscq performing. Don't you look dashing..."

I petered out as my heart caught in my throat. From the looks of it, no one could ever have known how poorly the front man and lead singer of Tuscq had been that night.

"Oh, there's a YouTube video here, too." I carried on my one-sided conversation. "Shall we have a teensy look? And I'll switch the phone off before I get into trouble. Yeah?"

There was no response, of course, but I clicked play anyway. On the tiny screen, Dan sprang into song. He was excellent, his voice as strong and powerful as ever. The beads of sweat on his forehead could easily have been due to the exertion of performing, although I suspected otherwise. But there was no indication for the world to see that Dan Hunter had been on the brink of collapse. Or, indeed, that Dan had taken drugs. Small mercies, right?

I interrupted the clip and switched off my phone. It had only been the quickest of searches, but bad news and gossip traveled faster and more extensively than positive publicity, so I was fairly certain Dan was in the clear. Pulling the chair closer to his bed, I sat down again.

"That was awesome. I wish I could have been there. I love the new songs." Of course, I had been mixing quite a few of them, so I was intimately familiar with every key change, every riff, every drum roll.

And on I prattled. "Do you know, I wonder how different it is to mix sound for a live concert. I mean, I know the effort that went into making the songs sound as they do in the studio... How does Richard replicate that on stage? How does he figure out room modes in such a big venue with such poor sound conductivity? The sound must be bouncing and breaking every which way from the ceilings and the windows and the tables... I really must ask Richard about that some time."

There was a twitch in Dan's fingers. It was a tiny movement. It could have been a reflex, and I very nearly missed it, but nonetheless, there was a twitch. I held his hand tighter still and kept talking.

"Oh ho, I felt that, my friend. Are you trying to tell me something? It was nice — "

My words dried up when I saw Dan's eyes flutter open. Thank goodness, he was conscious. I rose and bent over him slightly so my face would be in his field of vision, pulling down the mask to reveal my face properly, never mind the risk.

"Hi," I whispered.

Dan's eyes roamed and tried to focus on me. I wasn't sure he could see clearly, so I gave him a little reminder.

"It's me, Sophie." That got another twitchy reaction from his hand, and my heart soared. I was confident he was responding to my voice.

His eyes rolled some more, and he was having trouble focusing. Was I supposed to do anything here? Raise his head up, perhaps, or call a nurse? But oh — there, Dan held my eyes with his. I smiled.

"Hi, you," I said again. "Fancy meeting you here."

Dan rolled his head from side to side, and his right hand came up to his face. He feebly clawed at the tube in his mouth with a look of panic in his eyes, the blood-oxygen clip-thing clunking hard against the tube and frightening him further. I grabbed hold of his hand, drip, clip, and all, and stroked it gently.

"Shh," I soothed. "It's all right. That's a tube in your mouth. It's a ventilator to help you breathe."

Dan shook his head to the extent he could. It looked as though he was trying to evade an angry insect. Confusion and fear were written all over his face.

"You're in hospital," I explained, in case the past twelve hours were a black hole in his memory. "You have pneumonia, but you'll be fine, just fine."

Damn that bloody tube. I knew it served a purpose, but right now, it was making Dan extremely anxious. The beep rate of the heart monitor was speeding up steadily, indicating Dan's stress. "Do you know, I think I'll call for a nurse. Maybe she can tell us if we can get rid of this thing now. What do you think?"

Amazingly, Dan's grip on my hand tightened, and his eyes opened wide with concern. I understood his meaning, or at least, I thought I understood his meaning.

"Don't worry. I'm not going," I reassured him, and his face relaxed immediately. "I need to press that red button there. Hold on a sec."

I let go of his hand and reached for the call button. Immediately, a bell went off outside Dan's room, and I could see a red light flashing above the door. I hoped I had done the right thing.

"I bet there'll be a nurse here any second now," I issued as though we were sharing a secret. On impulse, I smoothed the matted hair away from his forehead and stroked his face. He tried to grunt, and it sounded painful.

"Don't speak," I interrupted. "You can't speak around this thing. Let's see if they think they can take it out now. Hold on, and be brave." I spoke as I would to my children, but it worked. He relaxed and stopped trying to speak.

Brisk footsteps announced somebody was coming, and within a few seconds, Dr. Smith himself appeared in the doorway. He took in the scene quickly.

"Mr. Hunter," he greeted Dan. "Good to see you're awake. I'm Dr. Smith, your doctor."

Dan made a weird sound again, and Dr. Smith cut him off. "No, don't try to speak. Let me see if we can take you off this ventilator now."

He walked across to the bank of monitors at the head of Dan's bed and tapped a few buttons. "Well, your blood oxygen levels are up," he informed Dan. "I'm willing to have the tube taken out. I'm going to ask one of the PACU nurses to do that for you now."

Dan opened his eyes wide to indicate his agreement. My heart bled for him. This had to be torture for someone who relied on his voice for a living. He waved his free hand about until he caught hold of mine, and he held on tight. Dr. Smith saw the gesture and smiled.

"It's a little unusual, but Mrs. Jones may stay if it puts you at ease. If she wants to, that is. It may be a little disconcerting to watch," he addressed me.

"Of course I'll stay," I informed both men, and Dan squeezed my hand again.

"Okay. The nurse will be with you shortly, and I'll check on you again later." He left, and a few minutes later, a cheerful nurse entered the room.

"Good afternoon, Mr. Hunter," she greeted Dan. "I'm Nurse Margaret. I'm a PACU nurse. That means I work in the post anesthesia care unit. I'm here to extubate you and make sure you're okay without your ventilator." She paused for a moment to allow Dan and me to absorb this information before she continued with her friendly chatter.

"Isn't it nice to see you awake. But let me get you off this thing, first of all." She indicated for me to take a seat on the other side of Dan's bed, and I moved the chair there and sat down. Even though it wasn't me who was affected, my heart was hammering hard in my chest, and I could only imagine how Dan would be feeling.

The nurse busied herself with the tube in Dan's mouth. "I'm suctioning the tube before I remove the tape holding it," she explained, following through swiftly. Dan squirmed uncomfortably and looked at me with frightened eyes.

"Right, there we are," the nurse continued. "I'm going to disconnect you from the machine, then give you a few big breaths, okay?" She worked as she spoke, and once the tube was no longer connected to the ventilator, she attached what looked like a bellows to it. "Here we go...and one...and two... Good." She squeezed on every count, supporting Dan's his first few breaths. "Here, let's deflate the cuff...and..."

She stood behind Dan's head, looking at his face while she addressed him. "I need you to breathe out as hard as you can, all right? Ready...go." Dan's chest rose and fell as he exhaled, and the tube slid out in one fluid motion. I breathed out, too. I hadn't been aware I was even holding my breath.

Dan gurgled and rasped, and the nurse stroked his forehead soothingly. "Concentrate on breathing for now. You can speak in a moment. Let me listen to your lungs a minute." She placed a stethoscope on Dan's chest, first the left side, then the right. Next, she listened to his throat and checked the blood oxygen readings on the monitor. "You're doing really well." She smiled.

Dan breathed and swallowed and prepared to speak.

"Sophie," he eventually rasped. He sounded hoarse and in pain.

"Hi," I said for the third time in half an hour. "It's nice to hear your voice."

The nurse checked various monitors and turned to speak to Dan. "I agree, it's lovely to hear your voice and it's good to see you awake and breathing unaided."

Dan gave a wan smile. He still looked every bit as pale and poorly, but without the tube in his mouth, he looked more like himself. The nurse filled him in on his condition, explaining his course of treatment, outlining that he would likely need to stay in hospital for another few days, and reassuring him that his voice would be perfectly fine in a couple of days.

"But take it easy on the talking for now, and definitely no singing," she joked. "I know all about you!"

Dan smiled again. "I'll be good," he croaked. "May I have a drink?"

"Of course," the nurse agreed. "I'll get you some water." She bustled out.

Dan turned to me. "Sophie," he grated once more, and we both gave a little laugh at the sound of his scratchy voice.

"Don't talk," I admonished him. "You heard the nurse. I'm so glad to see you awake. I was terribly frightened."

"What happened?" Dan issued. "How did I get here?"

"I'll tell you," I offered, "but you mustn't speak. Nod or shake your head, okay?"

Nurse Margaret returned with water, and Dan took a few eager sips.

"I'll leave the water here, but go easy," she advised. Addressing me, she continued. "Ten minutes, and then Mr. Hunter needs to rest, yes?"

I nodded.

Once alone, I gave Dan an edited version of events. I left out the drugs. I figured we could address those some other time. Also I wanted to see if he brought them up on his own, and now was not the time to go there. Dan held my hand as we spoke, and his eyes were full of emotion. He was still very hot to the touch, and even in the ten short minutes that we 'talked'—or rather, that I talked at him—I could see his face drooping with exhaustion. I wrapped up my tale and gave him a kiss on the cheek.

"You'll be better soon. You'll see. I've got to go now, but I'll be back soon. I promise."

"Today?" The single word cost him a lot of effort.

"If I may. I'll check with the nurse. Else I'll see you first thing tomorrow. I promise. Cross my heart and all that..." I smiled my biggest smile, hoping to reassure him.

He smiled back, barely managing to lift the corners of his mouth. He was one exhausted patient.

Thus, it was with mixed emotions that I made my way to Rachel's house to collect the kids. I was massively relieved to see Dan awake and talking, sort of. Yet I was deeply disturbed to see him so weak, so worn out after barely half an hour of being awake. He would recover. I felt sure of that, but it would take a long time.

Chapter Thirty-Four

Rachel, Alex, and my kids were all greatly relieved to hear of the small improvement in Dan's condition. I put a more cheery spin on the situation for the kids than was perhaps warranted, but even in the more truthful update for Rach, I couldn't deny I felt cautiously optimistic. Being the star friend that she was, Rachel hadn't only entertained my brood while I visited Dan, she had also knocked together a quick dinner for all of us, and so it was bedtime by the time the kids and I returned home.

Amid much protest, I put the children to bed as swiftly as I could and rang the hospital to check up on Dan's status—stable, and improving slowly—before crawling under the covers myself. Breathing in the scent of fresh laundry, I blessed Rachel from the bottom of my heart. Apart from the faintest whiff of wet carpet, there was no trace of the violent sickness that had taken place in my bedroom a mere eighteen hours earlier. She had washed and dried the bedding and remade the bed, and she had sponged and disinfected the carpet and tidied up all the debris. A friend, indeed.

I was drifting off to sleep when a phone rang. It was neither the soft, ululating trill of my landline, nor the piercing three-tone shrill that heralded a call on my mobile. Disorientated, I switched on my bedside light and surveyed the bedroom. There, a strange mobile lay on the far bedside table, ringing incessantly. I scooched across the bed to make a dive for it. Caller display read, *Jack*. It had to be Dan's. Presumably, it had fallen out of his pocket somewhere in the house, and Rachel had put it in a safe place.

I answered it without a second thought. "Hey, Jack."

There was a surprised silence, which I felt obliged to fill. "It's Sophie here."

"Sophie," Jack repeated. "Hey. What's up? Can I speak with Dan? I've been ringing him for hours."

For somebody who couldn't know about Dan's illness, Jack sounded terribly agitated, and I got that heavy sense of foreboding in my tummy. "Dan is—" I began, but Jack talked right over me.

"What was he thinking?" he bellowed. "It's all over the bloody Internet. Facebook, Twitter, everywhere."

My tired brain struggled to follow what he was saying. "What is all over the Internet?"

Last I checked, it had been all good news. What had I missed?

"'Rock star collapses with drug overdose after party at Hyde Star Inn'," Jack intoned. "That's one of the headlines. 'What happened to the squeaky clean Dan Hunter?' is another. Where on earth is he?"

The bottom fell out of my world, but only temporarily. My mind raced. There had been no press at the hospital. Nobody knew what had happened to Dan apart from me, Rachel, and the staff. Had there been a leak at the hospital, there would have been reporters outside when I got there this afternoon. God, how I hated the press sometimes. Right at that moment, I was embarrassed to have been a member of that profession. I cleared my throat.

"Dan's in St. George's. He—"

"What?" Jack exploded. "Don't tell me this is true!"

"It's not true," I shot back. "Will you let me explain? He has pneumonia. He came to my house last night and collapsed. I had him admitted to hospital because I was so scared for him, but *nobody* there has even told the press he's there, or why. I swear. I was there this afternoon again, and the place was calm."

I could hear Jack taking deep breaths at the other end. "You'd better start at the beginning," he invited, sounding calmer and more reasonable.

So I explained, starting with the cold Dan caught a few weeks ago and leaving nothing out, not even the E's. Jack listened in silence and remained quiet for a few moments after I finished.

"This is a disaster," he mumbled. "How could he have been so stupid?"

"It's hardly a disaster," I disagreed, and a thought popped into my head. "It's a setup, that's what this is. Somebody gave Dan those drugs, hoping he'd do something stupid, like taking them for everyone to see, or passing them on, or collapsing at the party. And when he didn't, they fed the story to the press and the social media anyway. There is no earthly way anyone could have substantiated the story because there's nothing much *to* substantiate. It's all a lot of hot air. He didn't even take a lot, certainly not enough to collapse. And!" I pounced onto this last detail with gusto, recalling something Dr. Smith had said and holding onto it for dear life. "We don't even know if he knew what the pills were. We haven't had a chance to ask him yet."

"Oh, he knew," Jack said darkly. "Regardless of what you say about him being ill, he would have known. He's not dumb. The band gets offered stuff all the time. They don't take it. They know I'd eat them alive."

The sentence hung between us for a second before I jumped to Dan's defense again. "Be that as it may, he was in very bad shape when he came out for the concert that night. I shouldn't have let him go. I feel bad about it. Can you honestly say whether he was in his right mind afterwards? With a raging fever and a painful set of lungs, do you think he was capable of rational thought? And whatever happened, this drug story is a setup. It *has* to be. Dan didn't take an overdose. He collapsed with a fever and because he was desperately ill."

"Hm," Jack replied. "You must be right. It doesn't make sense. So many years in the business, so many temptations...I was shocked and horrified to think Dan would have gone off the deep end last night. And disappointed."

"Well, shelve those emotions. We've got to do something about this setup, and fast." *But what?* I was running through options in my head. *Think, Sophie, think.*

"I'll write a refutation," I suddenly burst out. "I'll set the record straight. I'll get the doctor to release a statement and..." Stroke of genius! Never mind I wasn't working with *Read London* anymore, Rick would run it, I was sure. He had always run my articles.

"You can't," Jack cut into my thoughts. "It wouldn't work. For one, you'd be considered a biased source. And for another, you'd drop Dan right in it. The hospital would be swamped within minutes."

I didn't even pause for breath. "True on both counts," I conceded. "But something along those lines has to be done, and fast." I sat up straight in my bed, trying to clear my head. The solution was within grasp, if I could only...

"I know. *I'll* write the piece, but I'll get Rick to publish it under his own byline. That gets me out of the picture. And as for the hospital...let me ring them and talk to Dr. Smith, if he's still around. There must be procedures for this kind of thing. Or maybe he has another idea. Anyway, let me get onto it. I'll call you back." I hung up and got busy.

Tackling the most urgent job first, I rang the hospital. Miracle of miracles, Dr. Smith was still on duty and came on the line instantly. I filled him in, but he had already heard the news.

"I was going to get in touch with you tomorrow," he explained. "There have been phone calls, and a few reporters have been snooping around. Security has sent them packing, and we have made no statement. Yet."

There was my opening. "Do you think you should? Would? Could?"

"It's highly irregular. It breaches doctor-patient confidentiality, unless, of course, that is waived. Mr. Hunter isn't really in a good enough condition to talk about this kind of stuff right now." While willing to be helpful, Dr. Smith sounded doubtful.

"What if his manager gave you the all clear to make a statement?"

"Uh-huh, not good enough."

I changed tack. "Look, let's have a think about what you might say, first of all. Evidently, the truth would be best. How about something like this..." I paused for a second, marking the beginning of my proposed statement for Dr. Smith with a small clearing of my throat. "'I can confirm that Mr. Hunter was admitted to this hospital in the early hours of Sunday morning. Mr. Hunter suffers from severe pneumonia and is currently undergoing treatment, to which he is responding well.'" I petered out. "Let's not even mention the drugs. This is simply a factual statement. I'm sure Dan will be fine with that."

Dr. Smith coughed uncertainly at the other end of the line. "I'd love to help. But I'm not authorized to make this kind of statement."

I suppressed a groan. "Who *is* authorized to make that kind of statement? It would be best coming from you, as his doctor, really. It's the only way to put an end to the nasty rumors before they spread out of control." There was no reaction from the doctor, and I tore at my hair. "Look, why don't you ask him. He's been in the business for years. He'll know word will get out about something or other. He'll want to set the record straight. Trust me."

Dr. Smith wavered. I could feel his resolve crumble through the telephone line. Alas!

"It's rather late." He put up another obstacle. "He might be asleep. Patient care has to come first. I can't wake him."

"Then don't," I was quick to retort. "But he might be awake. Why don't you go see? Please?"

A big sigh signaled the collapse of Dr. Smith's resistance. "Okay. I'll check on him now. If I deem him strong enough, I will ask him, as you suggest. If not, you'll have to come up with something else. I'll ring you back. Give me your number."

I rattled off my home number and thanked him profusely. I knew he was going above and beyond the call of duty, but he was clearly willing to interpret patient care in the widest possible sense here.

While I was waiting to hear back from the doctor, I rang Rick on my mobile. He didn't sound the least bit surprised to hear from me. In fact, his opening line was, "I'll run it. When can you get it to me?" I could have kissed him, and I was grateful my old editor had enough faith in my rock star to know the vicious rumors were all bogus.

Repeating Jack's words about how I would be considered biased, I gently asked whether Rick could run my article as his own. If Rick was astounded by my request, he didn't let on.

"I'd have to speak to Jack, at least, to verify the story," he mused. "Or to the hospital. It would be unethical to publish a piece that I hadn't a hand in at all."

"By all means," I agreed. "Substantiate away. Meanwhile, I'll knock together my copy and email you. Oh, hold on a sec." My landline was ringing. God, what a crazy night.

Dr. Smith was back on the other line. He had talked to Dan briefly, and Dan had unreservedly agreed that the doctor could make whatever statement was necessary. He had even signed a piece of paper to that effect. Apparently, Dr. Smith had woken the legal department to get this all squared off. "I'm ready," he said. "And so is the staff. I've issued instructions to repeat this statement verbatim, and nothing else. No press will be allowed in the hospital. Anyone trespassing will be escorted off the premises by security."

"Thank you," I offered before asking on impulse, "why are you doing this?"

"Let's just say I may have been to the odd Tuscq gig or ten," Dr. Smith whispered. I nodded even though he couldn't see me.

"Right, right." I nodded some more, while considering the two phones I held in my hand, connected to two men who currently held Dan's fate in *their* respective hands. Perhaps...if I could press the right buttons... I spoke before I had the idea clearly formulated. "Okay. Dr. Smith, I have the editor of *Read*

London on the other line. He will be printing your statement. Would you mind if I patched him into our call?"

"That was quick work," Dr. Smith responded. "But yes. Might as well."

I spoke briefly to Rick and pressed the conferencing button on my landline. *Please work, please work.* It was an age since I had last made that happen, but there…yes. Rick was coming in on my landline, too. I was a genius.

Afterwards, things happened very quickly. Dr. Smith made the statement exactly as we had discussed, saying neither more, nor less. Rick took note and ended his call. I thanked the doctor again and rang off, switching my laptop on at the same time and tapping away at the keyboard. Jack rang a few moments later to confirm he had spoken with Rick. All systems were go pending my copy. And so I typed. Short, sweet, and to the point.

Dan Hunter Collapses with Pneumonia

Don't believe everything you read on the Internet. While it is true that lead singer of legendary rock band Tuscq, Dan Hunter, collapsed after an album pre-launch party at the Hyde Star Inn in London on Saturday night, drugs had nothing to do with it. Sources confirm that Mr. Hunter had been unwell for weeks and finally yielded to his illness in the early hours of Sunday morning. Mr. Hunter's physician, Dr. Smith of St. George's Hospital, offers the following statement…

I closed the article with a quick, vague summary of Dan's prognosis, and that was it. *Go viral,* I prayed when I submitted my copy to Rick, *and work your antidote.*

By midnight, the small piece was already live on the *Read London* website and blog, adorned with a powerful image of Dan singing his heart out on stage. Rick had added a short and very clever comment from Jack, thanking Tuscq's fans for their messages of support for their ailing rock star. Of course, there had been no such messages yet but...I chuckled despite the gravity of the situation. Jack really was the master of public relations. If this didn't get the fans on our side, I didn't know what would.

Rick plastered the article all over Facebook and Twitter, too. The next day's edition would lead with this news item blown up on the front page, and some of the other dailies would hopefully pick it up, too. The media would be awash with news of Dan's illness.

A swarm of reporters descended on the hospital within thirty minutes of news of Dan's pneumonia hitting the social media, but was kept at bay by security. Jack instructed a private firm that very night to support the hospital's cadre of security staff and contain the circus. As my refutation piece went viral, get-well messages from fans all over the world started pouring in, obliterating the smeary drug allegations. With a bit of luck, the crisis was averted. Now I only needed Dan to get better.

Chapter Thirty-Five

Needless to say, I was absolutely knackered from my second broken night in a row. I had stayed up until four a.m., monitoring developments on the Internet, and I slept right through my alarm on Monday morning. If it hadn't been for Josh bouncing into my bedroom bright and early, I probably wouldn't have woken until midday.

Bleary-eyed and jelly-boned, I somehow managed to get the children fed and dressed and delivered to their respective educational establishments. After I waved Emily goodbye, I stood on the pavement uncertainly, competing priorities fighting for dominance with my conscience.

I needed sleep. I was supposed to work with Richard in the studio. I had promised to go and see Dan first thing. I ought to somehow contact Dan's sister, Jodie. She was bound to have seen the news by now. Ditto for Jenny; while she was 'only' the housekeeper, she was the pinnacle of Dan's domestic existence, and she would worry and fret. I had to get some food shopping done, not to mention tidying the house. I *really* needed some sleep. I desperately wanted to see Dan.

Feeling thoroughly overwhelmed and incapable of coping, I sat on the nearest bench and wept. People traipsed by and I could tell by the way their footsteps accelerated when they came past me that they were disconcerted by the sobbing creature on the bench. I probably looked like a loony, but I really didn't care. Worry, exhaustion, and self-pity needed out, and out they poured in torrents.

Eventually I sniffed. I had to get a grip. Some of the tension had drained from my body alongside the torrents I had shed, and I felt lighter, somehow. I only needed to blow my nose and dry my eyes and —

"Are you all right?"

The voice was full of concern, and vaguely familiar. A trace of a Northants accent with a hint of a transatlantic twang acquired in years of living in LA. Could it really be?

I straightened up and raised my eyes just as Jodie sat down beside me.

"You all right?" she repeated, smiling uncertainly.

"Jodie," I snuffled, perplexed. "I was thinking of you a minute ago. Do you know about Dan? What are you doing here?"

She exhaled slowly and answered my questions in turn. "Yes, I read about Dan on Facebook. About the drugs, first of all, and next a brilliant piece from *Read London* which had your handiwork written all over it, even though it's not your byline. Pneumonia, huh? How did he come by that?"

"I'll tell you in a moment. But...how come you're here? I was worried I'd have to summon you all the way from LA."

Jodie was a fashion designer and spent most of her time jet-setting around the globe, dividing her not-traveling time between London and LA. Although mostly she lived in LA because the weather was so much better.

Jodie smiled. "I've been in London these past few weeks, preparing a show."

"Oh God, you must think me awfully rude. Everything happened so fast. I was going to get in touch. I promise. I simply haven't had a chance. How did you find me *here*, on this very bench?" My mind was all over the place.

"I wasn't quite sure what to make of all the weird news. I went to the hospital earlier, but it's madness there, and I couldn't face the photographers before I even knew what was going on. Isn't that sick? Can't visit your own brother in the hospital. Bloody fame. *Bloody press*." She said that last utterance with considerable venom, then gave a start and grabbed my hand. "Sorry! Present company excepted, of course."

I squeezed her hand back and begged her to go on.

"Anyway, I dropped by Dan's house, after I'd *not* been to the hospital, to see if I could find out what was *really* going on. He wasn't there, obviously. Jenny is most a-tizz. She said *you* would probably know for sure, you two having become...*quite* close again of late." Jodie gave me a meaningful look, but pressed on with her thought. "Jenny pointed out the schedule that you'd stuck on the fridge about the kids' school times and stuff. So when I couldn't find you at home, I figured you'd probably be on your way back from dropping Emily off." She waved her smartphone at me. "Google maps is a wonderful app. You can find anything, anywhere."

We chortled, despite the situation.

"You look done in," Jodie finally observed. "Why don't I take you home, and you can fill me in and grab some rest? And I can go and brave the press at the hospital and see how Dan is."

I sighed. "I want to go see Dan, too. I promised I'd be back first thing in the morning."

Jodie observed me critically. "You'll frighten him to death if you go looking like this." She pondered for a moment before rising and pulling me up with her. "Come on. I'll drive you home and initiate you in the Jodie Chase fifteen-minute-power-nap routine. When you've rested up, we'll both go to the hospital together."

"I...I...well, I'm supposed to be working this morning, and I need to buy some food, and..." Confronted with a decision, my brain churned out all the other to-do's on my mammoth list. Jodie was not perturbed.

"Forget work, you have a crisis. Ring in and explain. Make me a shopping list, and I'll get your food while you nap. No problem, come on."

She tugged at my hand, and I let myself be led to her car. I had barely fastened my seatbelt when Jodie drove off, nearly, but not quite, burning rubber in her great haste. She handed me her smartphone while she drove. "Shopping list. Dictate it. Go on."

I looked at her phone in confusion. I was a little behind the times, and my own gadget wasn't nearly as fancy. "What do I do?"

"Just talk," Jodie instructed. So I talked to the phone, listing milk, bread, honey, Weetabix, and other critical foodstuffs I needed to restock, watching in stunned amazement as the items turned up on the phone's screen, one by one. I knew phones were smart, but I hadn't known they had become *that* smart.

Jodie pulled up in front of my house, jumped out of the car, and solicitously opened my door. "Come on, come on," she urged again. Together, we ran up the garden path, and Jodie clicked her tongue impatiently while I stabbed my keys at the front door lock. We were barely inside when Jodie took my handbag and coat, dumping both on the floor by the front door.

"Jodie's Power Nap," she began. "One, thou shalt go and take a very hot, three-minute shower. Three minutes, no more, and as hot as you can bear. Two, thou shalt wrap yourself in a towel and climb into bed, wet as you are. Three, set your alarm clock for fifteen minutes hence. Four, pull the duvet up as high as you can. Lie on your back, hands beside your body, palms up. Close your eyes and breathe. Think about nothing. Five, rise refreshed. And we shall go to the hospital. Meanwhile, I'll go shopping, as promised."

I didn't know whether to laugh or cry. "A three-minute hot shower and a fifteen-minute nap in a wet bed? You're kidding."

"I kid not. Trust me, it works. Now, off you go." She made shooing hand gestures, but I remained rooted to the spot.

"I must at least ring Richard. He'll be wondering what's going on."

That had Jodie's attention. "Who's Richard?" she asked, eyes wide.

"He's the sound engineer. I've been training to become one, and I'm due in the studio this morning."

For the smallest moment, my news left Jodie speechless. She rallied quickly. "Well, well, well." She grinned. "What a brilliant idea. Stroke of genius. You become a sound engineer and you and Dan can..." She didn't complete the sentence.

"Dan and I can—what?" I prompted, reacting to the glint of intrigue in her eyes. What had Dan been telling her about me?

"Work together," Jodie muttered. "Just work together. That's all. And that's all there is, right?" she teased, and I blushed.

"Go on, ring your Richard man, and then have your power nap. I'm off shopping."

Jodie was like a whirlwind of activity, and I wasn't sure whether she was simply driven by anxiety and eager to go and see her brother, or whether she was genuinely that hyper. Either way, she compelled me into action, and I did as I was told.

Richard had seen the news, of course. He was incredulous at the drugs allegations and devastated to hear about the pneumonia. We agreed I would take a week or two off, and I promised to keep him in the loop on Dan's progress.

Still doubtful of the promised effects of Jodie's power nap, I nonetheless trudged upstairs and stood under a hot shower for three minutes. Obediently, I went to bed barely towel-dry, lay back, and breathed deeply.

Chapter Thirty-Six

"Oh. My. God."

Jodie and I were both shocked at the sight that greeted us when we approached St. George's Hospital. The place was positively under siege by reporters, photographers, and a couple of film crews. However, the hospital security staff and the firm that Jack had hired were doing a stellar job of keeping the media contained behind barricades, and it looked as though they had the situation under control.

We hung back out of sight while we had a little conflab about how to get in.

"This is ridiculous," Jodie seethed. "He's my brother. I simply want to go see him without the world looking on."

I said nothing for a moment but observed the situation. "Look," I pointed out. "There are people going in and out without bother. They must be relatives visiting other patients. Come to think of it..." I grinned, and Jodie regarded me with bemusement.

"Come to think of it, I'm not exactly sure what the press is waiting for. They don't know you're his sister. They may or may not remember me. Dan has no wife or anyone who's been in the spotlight who's likely to turn up here. The other band members won't go anywhere near the hospital right now. So I'm not sure what exactly they're expecting. A miraculous appearance by the Rock God himself? Surely not."

Jodie elbowed me. "You're the expert. What would bring you here?"

I shook my head. "I wouldn't be here. There's nothing to gain. If you're worth your salt, you'll get your story firsthand somehow. You don't have to rely on hanging about in doorways and all that. I bet my bottom dollar there's no reporter from *Read London* here. Anyway…" I pulled the hood of my coat up and wound my scarf around my neck, half obscuring my face. "As it is the middle of November and very nearly freezing, I suggest we wrap up and walk in."

Dan's sister bellowed with laughter. "You've certainly acquired a certain nous since you've been hanging out with my brother," she giggled. "I like your style. Let's do it."

Chatting amiably, heads high and blatantly disregarding the press, we sauntered toward the hospital entrance as though we didn't have a care in the world. We didn't make eye contact with anyone and sailed through, no questions asked.

"That was easy," Jodie exclaimed once we were safely inside. "Now to the ward."

"I think *that* bit will be harder," I muttered back. "At least, I hope it will. If they let just anyone up to Dan's room, there'll be trouble sooner or later."

We wandered up to the bank of elevators. Unless Dan had been moved, he would still be in the main complex, and we had to get up to the second floor. When I pressed the call button, a be-suited man stepped forward to address us. He had been so discrete at loitering, he had completely escaped my notice.

"I'm awfully sorry to bother you, but may I ask who you're looking to visit here today?" His voice was deep and firm and invited an answer.

"I'm Sophie Jones," I introduced myself. "I'm here to see Dan Hunter. This is Jodie Chase. She's his sister."

At the mention of Dan's name, the man produced a clipboard and scanned down a list of names. He looked up and smiled. "Thank you, ladies. Up you go. Have a good day."

"Nicely done," Jodie complimented him and smiled back. The man merely inclined his head and melted into the background, ready to address the next visitor.

"Well, he's *not* hospital staff, that's for sure," I remarked as we traveled up. "Jack chose well."

"He did. He would. Dan's his meal ticket."

"Whoa, that's a cynical way of looking at things. I always thought of them more as friends," I teased.

"They are friends. But business is business, and at the end of the day, Jack gets paid to look after the band's affairs. That includes crises such as this one. I'm thankful that Jack is such a fabulous person. Not every band manager has been known to respond to…issues as successfully, promptly, or discretely. But look, here we are."

The elevator doors opened and we stepped out. I led the way toward Dan's room, retracing my steps of the previous day, and we fell silent as our footfalls echoed on the polished floors. Jodie briefly took my hand and squeezed it hard. How I hoped Dan would be better.

Dan's room was unmistakably marked by another security officer stationed in front of it. Like the one in the lobby, he looked professional and friendly. He examined us and checked our names against another list before inviting us to go in.

"You go first," Jodie suggested. "I'll be right behind you."

"I...you're his sister. You should go in first," I objected. "You haven't even seen him yet."

"He won't care about me half as much as he'll care about seeing you," Jodie retorted. I wondered at her meaning, but it wasn't the right place or time to probe. "Go on," she continued. "Make his day." She opened the door and gave me a gentle shove.

Dan was awake.

His face was pale, but not as pale as it had been, and he looked less feverish. He was breathing unaided, although he was still attached to a drip. His eyes were trained on the door, and he saw me immediately. There was no delay, no confusion, no lack of focus in his reaction. A smile spread over his face, and he raised a hand, reaching out for me.

For a moment, I forgot all about Jodie right behind me, or the security man, or the hospital room. My knees went weak, and my heart was in my mouth while I took the four steps into the room and straight to Dan's bedside. I took his hand and held it tight, never looking away from Dan's eyes for even a single moment. He was better. He would pull through. I didn't need a doctor to tell me that. I could see the improvement. No doubt. He wasn't out of the woods, but he would make it.

Dan still smiled.

"Soph," he said, and his voice sounded better, too. Still a bit raspy, but more Dan-like.

"Dan," I replied softly. "Hey."

We held each other with our eyes for a few moments while I struggled to find words that would adequately convey my feelings.

"How are you feeling?" I ventured eventually. *Epic fail!* What about, "I love you," or at least, "I'm so glad you're better?" Anything to let him know I cared for him more deeply than he understood? *Quick, Sophie, say something else.*

"I—"

"I'm feeling much better," Dan offered before I could make any dramatic declaration. Then he caught sight of Jodie hovering in the doorway. He laughed quietly, but the sound quickly turned into a coughing fit.

"Jodie!" he exclaimed when he had recovered. "Cor, now I really know I've been poorly. Come in, come in, let me see you, sis."

Jodie stepped forward. She looked shaken and worried and gave a watery smile.

"You big oaf! How on earth did you get pneumonia?" she admonished, her voice gentle and light-hearted and entirely belying the fear on her face.

Dan shrugged and puckered his mouth. "Don't I get a kiss? I haven't seen you in months."

Jodie pecked him swiftly on the cheek before sitting down on his visitor's chair. All of a sudden, I felt surplus to requirements. This was family. They hadn't seen each other for a long time, and they had just had a big scare. I had no place there. Feeling self-conscious and a little uneasy, I squirmed on my feet, fumbling for something to say.

"Um."

Brother and sister were still looking at each other, and my resolve strengthened. I had to leave them alone.

"Um. I…well…um." I fiddled with my hair. "I think I must be going now. I…um."

Dan and Jodie regarded me with wide eyes, and the family resemblance was striking.

"Things to do," I blurted and made to turn.

"Sophie." Despite the residual rasp, Dan's voice was sweet as honey. "Don't be silly. Sit down. Please don't go."

"Don't go," Jodie echoed, sounding sincere. "Come on, we've got so much to talk about! This useless lump here isn't up to much, so I'm relying on you to tell the story."

I wavered. I didn't really want to go, of course. At the same time, I didn't want to make a nuisance of myself and intrude on family time.

Dan coughed and reached for the glass of water on his bedside table.

"Eight years," he grunted. "Eight years we've known each other. Seventeen, if you go back all the way to Edinburgh. And you're *still* worried about making a nuisance of yourself?"

How did he know?

Jodie backed him up. "It's written all over your face. Come on, don't be daft. Sit down. You're practically part of the family anyway. If it hadn't been for you…"

She didn't finish the sentence, and it occurred to me that she seemed to know more than she let on. Anyway, the desire to stay won over my social politeness, and I grabbed a chair and sat down. Dan smiled.

"There's no need to look so smug," I teased him, but very gently. "I was worried sick. And I have a bone to pick with you, Dan Hunter. Next time I tell you to go back to the doctor's, you'll jolly well not ignore me, do you hear?"

Dan pretended to be crestfallen. He dropped his eyes and furrowed his brow. "Sorry," he mumbled. "I was really stupid."

Stupid, indeed, but *not just* for not going back to the doctor's. I suppressed the question I was yearning to ask and turned to Jodie instead.

"Has he always been this stubborn?"

She giggled. "He used to drive Mum nuts. One time, he went outside to play in the snow in his pajamas, without shoes, I might add, because he'd gotten bored of lying in bed with a fever."

"Now, now," Dan admonished. "If you're gonna dish the dirt on me, sis, I'm going to have to ask you to leave."

And thus we chatted easily, the three of us, for a short half hour before Dan practically fell asleep in mid-sentence. A nurse had checked in on him twice while we were there, and when she saw his eyelids drooping on her third visit, she unceremoniously threw Jodie and me out.

"Come back this evening," she advised. "You may visit the patient between six and eight."

Chapter Thirty-Seven

It was another four days before I next found myself alone with Dan during visiting time. To begin with, Jodie was camped out in the hospital. While the two siblings rarely saw each other, they always stuck together in times of crisis, and she wanted to be absolutely certain that Dan would pull through without further complications before she relinquished her space at his side. Seeing the affection between brother and sister was touching. It reminded me woefully of what I had missed out on as an only child, and made me doubly glad that I had two kids of my own. Whatever happened, they would have each other.

Of course, I didn't really mind Jodie's presence at the hospital. How could I? She never once made me feel superfluous or unwanted, and in a weird way, it was as though this occasion made me become absorbed into Dan's family. But it was tough, never having a moment alone with Dan.

If Jodie happened to be absent for a while, a nurse or a doctor would bustle in. Jack visited, of course, as did sound man, Richard, and even Rick, my old boss. And when the media frenzy was diverted toward a footballer who had been tweeting with his girlfriend while his wife was giving birth to their first child, the rest of Tuscq quickly ventured into the hospital to visit their poorly front man. On the one occasion where absolutely nobody else was with Dan, I had brought the kids who were clamoring to be convinced that Dan would get better.

In this manner, I had had no opportunity to talk with Dan privately. Four days wasn't a terribly long time in the grand scheme of things, but they had been so fraught; so busy with dividing my time between the hospital and the kids, so up-and-down with Dan's fever rising and falling, but generally refusing to yield completely to the medication, that my re-discovered love for Dan had taken a back seat. Where I had longed to burst out with the realization on first seeing him again, that moment had passed, and I didn't know how to broach the subject. *Whether* to broach the subject.

So I was unsurprisingly a little tongue-tied when, on the morning of the Friday after Dan had first been admitted with pneumonia, I suddenly found myself alone with my rock star.

"Morning," he greeted me with a strong and almost cheerful voice. His bed was raised, and he was sitting up, reclining regally against a pile of cushions and finishing up his breakfast. For the first time, there was a little color in his cheeks, and it wasn't the unnatural glow of a high fever. His eyes were sparkling, and his hair was freshly washed. The improvement was so marked and so sudden that it was a lot to take in.

"Morning," I mumbled back, retrieving the visitor's chair and sitting down. "You look so much better." Suddenly, I noticed the biggest tell of all. "Your drip's gone!"

Dan grinned and wriggled his unencumbered right hand. "It certainly is. My, what a relief. Fancy a hug?"

He held out both arms and I rose to let myself be enveloped in a clumsy hug. It felt good. Without noticing, I closed my eyes and breathed in deeply. *Hmmm.* How I had missed him.

Dan let me go and held me at arm's length. "Are you all right? You look like you've seen a ghost."

"I'm fine," I responded automatically. "Fine. I'm just so happy that you're on the mend. You gave me such a fright." I made to sit back on the designated chair, but Dan patted his bedside.

"Please, sit here. I can't bear you being so far away. Plus," he flashed a cheeky grin. "I'm supposed to rest my voice so I mustn't talk loudly. Much easier, therefore, if you sit here. *Close.*"

By golly, he was recovering fast. I nudged him gently on the shoulder, but obligingly sat on the bed. Dan took my hand.

"I'm sorry I gave you such a fright," he said. "I didn't mean to."

"What happened?" The long overdue question came out before I could hold it back again. "What happened at that party that night?"

Dan's face fell. "I...I don't really remember. I wasn't feeling too good and..." He paused, gathering his thoughts.

"I know you weren't feeling good. You looked as though you had a fever when you left my house. I should never have let you go," I mused. "I feel bad."

"Please don't," Dan objected. "It's not your fault. I would have gone even if you'd begged me not to. It was a big deal. I couldn't just bail. You know I've done whole concerts with ear infections and some such. Doing a few songs with a small fever didn't seem unreasonable."

"And yet...you ended up collapsing on my landing," I pointed out. "There was more going on than a small fever."

"But I didn't know that when I left, did I?"

"So what happened?" I prompted again. I was like a dog with a bone. I *had* to know. This was the right time. "You did the show and...?"

Dan let go of my hands. He was becoming agitated and laced his fingers together, clenching them into a tight heap of digits. The gesture almost resembled a prayer.

"I did the show and things looked up for a while. The songs went down well, and I came off on a real high. Jack introduced us all to the audience, as if they didn't know us, and we had to mingle. I had a beer. You know how I like beer."

I grinned. I didn't want to, but I did. "I know how you like beer," I concurred. "But there was more, right?"

Dan shot me a rueful look. "You're like the Spanish Inquisition this morning."

"You turned up in my house with a bottle of E's. Of course I'm like the Spanish Inquisition." *Oops.*

My accusation came out sounding harsh and bitter, surprising me as much as Dan. He looked as if I had hit him. He said nothing for a moment, and I held my breath. I hadn't meant to confront him this way. I had hoped he would tell me on his own, but I had jumped the gun, and now the statement was out there, hanging between us like an ice-cold dagger.

"Oh God, I'm so sorry," Dan finally uttered. "I was...I wasn't with it anymore. I knew I was in deep shit, and I needed help, and you were the only place I could turn to."

I took his hand. Rage and fury notwithstanding, it hurt to see him so torn up. "And you *should* have come to my house. I am so grateful that you did. If you'd gone to your house, on your own..."

That desperate scenario had played in my head a thousand times, and I couldn't bear to think about it. It hadn't happened, thankfully. I snapped to.

"I'm angry because you took drugs," I clarified. "I'm pissed off that you brought them to my house, into the very place where two young children were sleeping, innocently and peacefully. If *they'd* found you before I did…If they'd got hold of the stuff…"

I swallowed hard. *That* scenario had also played in my mind a thousand times. I picked at a corner of Dan's duvet, unable, for the moment, to meet his eye.

"I am so, so sorry," Dan repeated. The choke in his voice made me look up at last, and Dan was crying. "I…there is nothing I can say to make this better. Other than, I had no place else to go, and I knew you would make it all right."

The emotion in his words touched me deeply. He had been a desperate, sick man, and he had turned to me. He had needed me. And now he was coming clean.

"I… After I had had a few beers, I was feeling rough. I was so tired. I sat down on a sofa somewhere, and I believe I dozed off. Jack found me and told me to buck up. I guess he thought I'd just drunk too much." Dan smiled ruefully. "As if. Anyway, I went to the loo to take some painkillers and some other stuff that I'd gotten from the pharmacist to keep me awake."

Caffeine boosters, Dr. Smith had said. I didn't say anything, but I nodded.

"That worked for a while, but I drank more, and I had another dip. I went back to the loo and this chap followed me. He…"

Dan paused and took a sip of water. "He offered me stuff. Amphetamines. *E*. I'd had one, once or twice before. I know, I know, we've always sworn we don't do drugs, and we don't, really."

I felt like my world was about to disintegrate, but then I told myself off. *He's a rock star*, I reminded myself. *What do you expect? Lots of ordinary people do drugs on the weekend. I bet Rachel does. And anyway, where is the line? I drink alcohol. I take painkillers. Those are drugs, too.*

A black hole of thoughts and convictions threatened to swallow me, and Dan must have seen the confusion on my face.

"Oh God, Soph, I feel like you've discovered my clay feet after all this time. Listen to me." His voice was urgent, and he touched my face to make me look at him.

"I don't *do* drugs. *The band* doesn't do drugs. But that doesn't mean that, very occasionally, we don't…um…well, take something. Something…err…recreational. It's impossible not to, sometimes. *Everybody* does it."

"Not me," I objected in a small voice. "Never."

"I know," Dan wailed. "You're…you're like an oasis of goodness. Do you have any idea how precious that is? How amazing you are?"

I swallowed hard. I had been naïve, really. I *was* naïve. Always had been. Presumably always would be. I was foolish to expect everybody in my life to abide by my standards. Perhaps I was foolish to close my eyes to the realities of life *out there*. What would I do when the kids came home one day, spliffed and high and *on* something? Never having experienced that myself, how would I react? How would I know the right way to handle that situation? What was the right way to handle the present Dan situation?

Wringing my hands in despair, I looked Dan squarely in the eye. "I'm just a bit…shocked, I suppose. I'm sorry. I'm not your judge or jury. I'm just me, and of course you can do exactly as you please..."

"Sophie, don't do this. I'm still the same old me, the same Dan who lo—" He bit his lip abruptly. "I'm still the same Dan who's been your friend all these years. I would never do anything to jeopardize our friendship, or you, or the children. Saturday night..."

"Sunday morning," I interjected, grasping at the detail as though it mattered.

"*Saturday night*," he corrected gently, "I was in the shit. I needed help. That chap in the loo, he offered those pills, and I knew what they were, of course I knew what they were, and the night was so young, and I still had so many people to talk to, the pills seemed like a lifeline." He spoke increasingly fast, rushed, as though he needed to get his confession over and done with as quickly as possible.

"I took one. Then I took another. That's all. I took two. They hit me...my God, they hit me like a speeding train. I was alive. I was wired. The world was soft and cheerful and colorful. There was laughter everywhere. I could move again. All the pain in my chest was gone. I was light as a feather, and I could talk and laugh and schmooze all those people."

He took a breath. "I drank more, I think. Somebody gave me a cocktail, and it was so pretty, and it didn't really taste of anything, so I had it and then I had another. Things got a bit blurry after that."

I listened, dumbstruck. How could this have happened? He had to have been completely off his trolley. How hadn't anyone noticed? How come *this* wasn't in the papers? How could Jack not have known? He had sounded all innocent and worried when I had spoken with him on Sunday night. He had never mentioned anything about Dan being high as a kite and seeing the world in cheerful colors.

"Blurry, huh?" I pondered. "How come you got away with it? How didn't anyone notice?"

"I don't know," Dan admitted. "Maybe I was still functioning on some level until the very end. Anyway, yes, blurry. I knew I'd had it then. I'd never been that wasted before, ever. I *swear*, you have to believe me."

And somehow, I did.

"So how did you get to my house?"

"I needed to get out of there, fast. It was late. Jack had disappeared. The room seemed to be spinning, so I legged it. I went outside and jumped into a cab. I threw a few notes at the driver and gave him your address. We got to your house and I fell out of the taxi. I practically crawled up your garden path." He grimaced at the recollection.

"You had a whole bottle of pills in your hand when I found you. What were you going to do with that?"

Dan raised his eyebrows. "Truthfully?"

"Truthfully."

"I was going to show you. I was frightened. I knew I'd gone too far. I kinda hoped you'd do the right thing."

"And yet when I said I was going to ring for an ambulance, you begged me not to."

Dan shrugged. "I don't remember that at all. I must have been way out of it."

"That's one way of putting it." I chewed my thumb. "You frightened me to death. Do you remember anything that happened after you fell on my landing?"

Dan shook his head. "Nope, that's it. Until I came around in this room some time. With you there, talking to me. My God, you are amazing, Sophie.

Surprisingly, I wanted to hit him. Yes, I was relieved at hearing the story. Yes, I was relieved that he was getting better. But I was also angry, confused, disappointed, and furious. And I felt very stupid.

"Do you know, I swore blind to your doctor that you *never* took drugs? That this was a disastrous aberration? You could have killed yourself."

Dan hung his head but said nothing.

"I...I have to go and think about this," I mumbled. "I can't get this straight in my head." Rising abruptly, I grabbed my handbag and coat and headed for the door. Tears welled in my eyes, and I couldn't be in Dan's presence for one second longer until I had figured out my emotions. Deep down, I knew he was telling me the truth. Deep down, I knew I was getting hung up over the wrong thing. He hadn't been admitted to hospital with an overdose, as I myself had pointed out to millions of people. He was in here because of pneumonia. Yet his casual confession at 'recreational' drug use had rocked my world. Naïve though I was to the signs of drug abuse, I knew what E's could do, even just one, and until I could get a handle on Dan's more cavalier attitude to this, I couldn't look him in the eye.

As the door clanged shut behind me, I heard Dan calling out to me.

"Sophie, don't go. I—"

Chapter Thirty-Eight

I spent the rest of the day being the worst mummy in the world. I was so absorbed in the thoughts chasing round my head that I nearly forgot to collect Emily from playschool, and I was grumpy with her when I did. Unable to engage with my darling daughter, I made her a quick lunch and settled her in front of the telly. A desperate measure, and the guilt nagged at me even while I tuned into Cbeebies, but I really couldn't help myself.

Things didn't improve after we collected Josh from school. The only difference was my two kids entertained each other, having quickly come to the conclusion that their mummy was a lost cause. I defrosted some Bolognese and served it with overcooked spaghetti. If the kids objected to the mushy texture, they never let on.

After dinner, Josh, with the wisdom of his approaching five years—his birthday would be in January—decided to take care of mummy. While I was tidying the kitchen, he ran a bath and managed to get both himself and Emily into the water, and splashing with plenty of soap by the time I came upstairs.

Having checked the temperature and ensured that the water wasn't too high, I let them get on with the fun while I sat on my bed and brooded some more. Within a few minutes, the kids turned up, wearing pajamas and sporting dripping hair, with a book each and ready for a bedtime story. Their eager faces and concerned eyes finally jolted me out of my gloomy apathy, and I rallied.

"Aren't you the two most wonderful children in the world," I praised them, hugging them tightly. "Let's get your hair dry and then cuddle up for the stories."

Probably to compensate for my extremely negligent parenting during the afternoon, I read them not two, not four, but six stories. We were all snuggled up in my bed under the big duvet, pretending to be sloths that never got up. It was a magical, peaceful interlude and it helped restore my inner balance and perspective. I gave the kids big kisses each when I tucked them into their beds, glad yet again to have their powerful presence in my life and marveling at the personalities that were emerging.

After all was quiet upstairs, I sat down with a small glass of wine and toasted Steve's photo on the mantelpiece. "Who'd have thought our kids would come to the rescue like this. You would be so proud of them. I just hope I'm doing a good enough job."

I stared at Steve's picture for a while, wondering what he would make of my situation. There was a twang of nostalgia, but the pain of missing him had receded, and I felt oddly detached. Suddenly, I was able to think of him like a much beloved, close, but sadly absent friend, rather than a deceased husband, and it was a good feeling. I carried on my conversation.

"I can't get my head around this Dan thing. I mean the drugs. Is it a big deal? Am I making a mountain out of a molehill?"

I paused and let myself think quietly for a while. I was listening for Steve's voice in my head, wondering if some forgotten nugget of conversation would pop up and remind me of what he would say. It didn't.

Sighing, I sipped at my wine and sat back, allowing my thoughts to freewheel. I was quickly coming to the conclusion that I wasn't going to find a satisfactory answer. I wouldn't be able to reconcile drug abuse with my own opinion, my *fear*, on this matter. Yet who was I to judge anyone?

Round and round I went, until all the questioning became background noise and eventually paled and faded in the presence of one emerging certainty. I needed Dan. I loved him. I didn't want to lose him again.

"Forget about today," I advised myself aloud. "Think back to all the time you've known this man. Has he *ever* given you cause for concern or doubt? Has he ever behaved weird or irresponsibly?" I paused dramatically before giving myself the answer. "*No.*"

That was what it boiled down to. The answer to all those questions was *no*. The Dan I knew was honest, kind, responsible, and caring. He had never let me down, on the contrary. If, amongst all of that, there had been E here or there, he hadn't been near me and he hadn't brought it home. Wasn't that what mattered most? How he behaved around me and the children?

"Sophie, you're being an idiot." I looked at Steve's photo again while I spoke, daring him to contradict me. Of course, he didn't.

"You've already told Dan you're neither his judge nor jury. So get on with it. Go see him."

Oh God, I had to see him. Right there and then. The need was overwhelming, the urgency constricting my throat. I had left him this morning without a backwards look, without another word. I couldn't leave it like that. What if something happened in the night and I never got a chance to see him again? I, of all people, knew that life could quite literally be too short, could change in a heartbeat, and missed opportunities would become lost opportunities.

I started trembling all over with anxiety and urgency. My hands shook so badly I had trouble dialing Rachel's number, but I managed on the third attempt. It was only half past eight. With a bit of luck, I could be with Dan within the hour and back within two.

Predictably, Rachel assumed the worst when I asked her to come and sit with the kids. "What's happened? Has Dan taken a turn for the worse?"

"No, nothing like that," I assured her. "I... I was being stupid earlier, and we had a bit of a disagreement. And I simply have to go see him. I *have* to."

Rachel digested this in silence. I could practically hear the little cogs turning in her mind, but she asked nothing. "You owe me big time, my friend, but it's your lucky day. Alex is here to look after Henry and I'll be with you in twenty minutes," she said.

"I won't be long, I promise. Thank you, thank you, thank you."

Rachel laughed. "Enough already. One day, you'll actually make yourself happy and that'll be the day it's all worth it. Anyway, let me hang up so I can get out to see you."

I flinched. *One day, I'll actually make myself happy?* Rachel seemed to think I was going wrong somewhere, but what was I to do? Throw myself at the man, after all this time?

"No, silly, tell him how you feel," Rachel enlightened me when she turned up, a coat hastily thrown over the pajamas she was already wearing. "Watching the two of you pussyfoot around each other over the past few months has been doing my head in."

"Wha?" The utterance half stuck in my throat with shock. Rachel laughed and shoved me toward my front door. "If you can't see for yourself the moon eyes Dan's been making then you'll just have to wait. Now, off you go." She put my coat over my shoulders and opened the front door.

"Oh God, I've had a glass of wine. I probably shouldn't drive," I suddenly wailed.

"How much wine?" Rachel inquired calmly. "Your usual thimble's worth?"

"Well, yeah. I didn't even finish it."

"You're fine. Go!" Rachel pushed me out of the house and shut the door behind me.

Chapter Thirty-Nine

I strode into the hospital as if I belonged. That was one of the first lessons I had learned while hanging out with Dan and Tuscq. Act as if you belong, and you don't get challenged. It worked every time without fail, and it worked that night even though it was nearly nine p.m. and well past visiting hours. The receptionist didn't give me a single glance when I flew past her, and the security body stationed at the elevator banks remembered me from my previous visits.

The corridors on Dan's ward were deserted, but the lights were still on. It wasn't *quite* bedtime yet for the patients. I slowed my step, suddenly unsure whether I was doing the right thing. Dan might be sleeping, for starters. My exuberance faded and was replaced with a dull dread. I didn't want to turn back now that I was so close.

While I was loitering, a door opened and a man stepped out. He turned and came my way, and I recognized Dr. Smith.

"Mrs. Jones," he greeted me amiably.

"Dr. Smith," I responded. "I...I know it's late, but I was hoping to see Dan. If that's okay. Only..." I shrugged and fiddled with my hair. "I left a bit suddenly earlier and...well...I wanted to apologize for something."

Dr. Smith smiled kindly. "I should think Mr. Hunter will be very glad to see you. He's been a little agitated all afternoon. By the way..." He hesitated for a moment before imparting a critical piece of information. "I might as well tell you, Mr. Hunter will be discharged tomorrow."

I opened my mouth to express my joy, but was cut short by Dr. Smith raising his hand.

"Don't get too excited. He's not recovered, not even nearly. His manager has arranged for a private cottage in Devon with a live-in respiratory nurse to look after Mr. Hunter while he convalesces."

My face must have been a question mark because Dr. Smith elaborated. "The cottage is within half an hour's drive of a private hospital, I recommended it myself." He gave me another look and hesitated for a second before volunteering yet more information. "I recommended the respiratory nurse, too. Peter is highly qualified and very experienced." Dr. Smith placed particular emphasis on the caregiver's name, then shifted on his feet as if he was worried about overstepping a boundary. "Just in case you were wondering."

"Ah. Right. Good," I muttered, trying to wrap my head around all this information. "I'm just surprised at the speed of events, that's all." Truth be told, I felt completely out of the loop, but yet again Dr. Smith stepped in to reassure me.

"This was all arranged quite quickly this afternoon after I agreed that Mr. Hunter would be well enough to leave the hospital providing he had sufficient care *and* he would rest for at least four weeks."

"Right, right." Nodding maniacally, I plastered a smile on my face. "That sounds…good. If he's well enough to leave, that's good. Right?"

Dr. Smith took my hand. "It is good. And he will be well looked after. He'll be allowed visitors, of course. Just no work. And certainly no singing."

"Thank you for everything." I pumped the doctor's hand up and down. "I guess I probably won't see you again."

"Not unless you come in with pneumonia yourself sometime, which I rather you didn't," he joked and let go of my hand.

"I won't," I promised and realized I actually liked this forthright doctor. "Bye."

"Goodbye," Dr. Smith echoed. "And off you go to see him. Just don't stay too long, okay?" With that, he resumed his walk down the corridor, off to the next patient or quite possibly home.

Squaring my shoulders and fixing the smile more firmly onto my face, I approached Dan's room and knocked gently on the door. Too gently, probably, for there was no response. Very carefully, I depressed the handle and crept into the room, which was dark. My heart sank.

"Sophie?" Dan's voice came out of the gloom, and with a sudden click, the bedside lamp came on.

I closed the door behind me and smiled even wider. "Dan." This time it only took me three steps to get to his bed, and he pulled me straight into his arms. Down, down he pulled me until my elbows rested on either side of his head and my upper body half lay on his torso while I balanced on one leg, with the other raised awkwardly in the air.

"I'm so glad you came back," he mumbled into my hair.

"Me, too," I mumbled back, fighting the urge to giggle at my rather bizarre contortion. I breathed in a few times then straightened up before I succumbed to a cramp.

"I'm sorry I walked out on you earlier." My eyes sought Dan's and bored into them so that he would understand what I was saying, and more. "I wasn't thinking straight and...well, I shouldn't have walked out. That was really rude of me."

"Don't worry," Dan reassured me. "I probably deserved it. No, scratch the 'probably.' I..." He lowered his eyes for a moment then looked at me again. "Do you want to talk about it? The...stuff?" He couldn't quite get himself to say the words again.

"I don't actually, if that's okay. At least not right now. Maybe some other time. Maybe...maybe I'll need your help if the kids ever get in trouble." My words tumbled out hard and fast, and Dan took my hand as though to stem the flood. His eyes softened and his mouth curved into a smile.

"Of course that's okay. But I just want you to know that I won't...go there again, ever. And if you want to talk about...what I said earlier, or if you have any questions or if you're worried, you can ask any time. *Any* time. Do you hear? Anytime."

"Okay. Thanks. I will." I returned his smile. There was an awkward silence while we both wore goofy grins on our faces.

Then Dan chuckled. "If you could see your face..."

"If you could see yours!" I retorted with a snort.

"You look like a star-struck teenager all over again," Dan elaborated.

"You look like a smitten sugar daddy," I shot back.

"I'm only ten years older than you," Dan defended himself. "That's never mattered to you before."

His last statement was more of a question, and I longed to pour out the answer, but somehow, I couldn't. I plumped for a weak put-down instead.

"Says who?"

"Says...well, I suppose I could be wrong." Dan was momentarily perturbed, but rallied quickly. "Nah. You're pulling my leg. It's never mattered in the past, and it doesn't matter now. This is smoke and mirrors. There's something you're not telling."

He was fishing. My God, he was fishing. He knew, and he knew that I knew he knew, and he wanted me to come out and say it. The mind boggled.

I looked around the small hospital room. I took in the emergency life support equipment still stationed by Dan's bedside, and the faded curtains. My eyes wandered along the slightly battered walls, painted a shade of pale blue, and rested briefly on the door to the bathroom.

Here? Now? Expectation hung in the air between us, palpable like a living thing, and I broke out in a sweat.

"Possibly." I evaded an outright answer eventually. "And I'm only saying maybe. But if there is, you're not well enough to hear it."

Dan arched his eyebrows. "Come again?"

I touched my finger lightly to his nose. "You're weak and dependent and you're not yourself and—"

"Gee, thanks. I'm not on my deathbed yet," Dan objected.

"I'd rephrase that to 'you're not on your deathbed *anymore*'." I amended his meaning pointedly. "And I don't think you quite know what you're saying at the moment and therefore..." I raised my hand to silence him before he could interrupt again. "Therefore I declare you unfit for rational emotional conversation." *Take that.*

Stunned, Dan burst out laughing. "'Rational emotional' is an oxymoron, my sweet, and you know it."

My turn to suck in a breath. "Don't you smart-aleck me, Mr. Hunter," I said in a mock-offended voice, and somehow, the awkward moment passed.

"I wouldn't dream of it, my darling," Dan joked back and yawned. He clapped his hand to his mouth. "So sorry."

"It's fine," I reassured him. "You are, after all, still recovering. Talking of, what's this fancy cottage I hear about?"

"Ah. That. Well…Jack thinks I ought to get out of here and go somewhere more pleasant and private. He's found some posh cottage down Devon way and arranged for some kind of person to come and look after me while I…convalesce." He placed an odd emphasis on this last word, as if he couldn't quite get his head round the notion that he would need more time to recuperate.

"Well, I think that's a splendid idea," I issued. "I'm quite envious, actually. I'd quite fancy a month in a little cottage by the sea myself."

"I'm not quite sure it'll be as nice as your little runaway jaunt to Langeoog that time," Dan observed. "I can see you getting all dreamy. But you're welcome to visit, of course. I'd…I'd like that."

"I'll see what I can do. I've got the kids and everything… a lot will depend on where this place is and where we could stay."

Dan nodded, but looked crestfallen all the same.

"I'm not fobbing you off," I reassured him. "God, to think of not seeing you for four weeks…" I shuddered, and Dan grinned. "But shall we get you down there first of all and see what it's like before we make any grand plans? Who knows what your caregiver has in store for you. You might be knackered and in bed every night at eight!"

"God, I hope not. I thought the whole idea was to rest!" Dan looked dismayed at the prospect of physical therapy.

"I'm sure it is. Chin up, you do what the doctors say and you'll be good as new before you know it." I half-clambered on the bed again to give him another hug and he pulled me close.

"Come on up and lie down," he cajoled in a soft, gentle voice, wiggling his body to one side of the narrow bed to make some space for me. I giggled like a teenager.

"If you insist! But on your head be it if you get in trouble with the nurses." I wiggled my feet to kick off my shoes and carefully lay down beside Dan, snuggling into his arms. He raised his duvet to pull me under, but I drew the line there.

"Don't do that. It'll look *really* dodgy if someone walks in. Let me just lie here, in your arms. That's good."

We lay there for a good hour, holding tight and just breathing. Every now and then, a rattly breath from Dan's chest would speak of the lingering illness which, while better, was not vanquished. Yet overall, the mood was peaceful and relaxed, a tonic for my bruised and battered soul. I stored every moment, every sensation in my memory to stock up reserves for Dan's impending absence.

Eventually, Dan's breathing became slower and deeper, and I knew he was asleep. Very gently, I clambered off the bed and put my shoes and coat back on. I switched off the bedside lamp and waited for my eyes to adjust. When I was certain my bustling about hadn't woken Dan, I pulled the duvet up to his chin and tucked him in, good and proper. I laid a kiss on his forehead and whispered a farewell before I left.

"Take care, my love."

Chapter Forty

"Are we nearly there yet?" Emily's voice piped up from the backseat, sounding bored and slightly petulant. The initial excitement at going off to Devon to see Dan in his little house by the sea had worn off a mere hour into the journey, and she was getting increasingly restless and fraught.

"Not long now, my sweet," I assured her for the twenty-seventh time since we left the motorway behind in Exeter. "Remember? I said it would be about an hour after we left the blue road" — the blue road being the motorway — "and I'm just about to turn off the green road unto the yellow road and then it's just a few more turns."

Josh held up the giant mapbook I had given him and traced his finger along the route marked in red pen so that Emily could see where we were. It didn't mean much to either of them, but it had kept Josh entertained. Alas, if only it *were* as easy as turning off the green road unto the yellow road. Very shortly, I would have to abandon the comfort of named and numbered roads and brave the little white roads.

Dan's hired cottage was on the Devon coast just before Plymouth and the Tamar estuary. His instructions sounded easy, but with two fractious children in the back, calm navigation was beyond me.

"Help Mummy out." I tried to involve my son in the driving effort. "We're looking for signs for the Cliff Road."

"Cliff Road," Josh repeated. "With a curly 'c' or a kicking 'k'?"

"Curly 'c'" I clarified.

So absorbed was I in sounding the word out for him that I nearly missed the turnoff. "Ooh, look, there it is," I exclaimed just as Josh burst out, "I see it, Mummy, there, there, turn, quick."

Emily began bouncing up and down in her car seat. "Nearly there, nearly there," she shouted.

I followed the road around, slowing down so we could take in the stunning sea view that had opened in front of us. And okay, it was late November and bitterly cold, but the sun was shining and the sea was as blue as ever.

"Can we go to the beach, Mummy, please?" Josh latched onto this notion, remembering summer holidays in Cornwall at my parents' house.

"We can go to the beach if Dan is well enough, but we won't be bathing, and we might not be able to build any sandcastles." Best to down-manage his expectations before he could throw a tantrum. "And here we are."

I pulled up in front of a cottage called Cliff Heights and stopped the engine. Silence enveloped us for a moment, and I breathed a sigh of relief. I had made it.

It was two weeks since I had last seen Dan in the hospital. He had called and texted every day, filling me in on the draconian rest and exercise regime his caregiver was putting him through and begging me to come see him. "There are plenty of bedrooms here. There is enough space. It really won't be a problem," he kept reiterating until I finally caved.

"Let's go in, let's go in." Emily and Josh were clamoring to be released from their car seats.

Our arrival hadn't gone unnoticed, and Dan was opening the front door to the cottage just as I released the children from the car. Emily spotted him first and fairly flew into his arms.

"Dad, Dad," she yelled, and a lump caught in my throat. Whether she continued to confuse the sounds or whether she actually considered Dan her dad, I couldn't know, and it didn't matter. Even if she had shouted *Dan*, the emotion in her voice spoke volumes.

"Emily, sweetheart, it's so lovely to see you!" Dan's voice emerged loud and clear, and he swept Emily up in a hug.

"And Josh, too!" Dan pretended to be surprised. "My, haven't you grown in the last few weeks. You'll be taller than me soon." He grinned, and Josh homed in for a cuddle of his own.

"Me go inside?" Emily was impatient to explore, and Dan let both kids go. "Of course, go and have a look."

He straightened up and held his arms out to me. "You made it."

"We did." I stepped into his embrace and basked in the light shining in his eyes. Dan wrapped his arms around me, and we stood for what seemed an eternity. Eventually, he started shivering, and I disengaged myself from his hold.

"You're cold. Come on, inside with you. I'll just get our bags from the car."

"Let me help," Dan offered, his teeth chattering.

"I'll manage," I admonished him. "Get warm, or I'll get in trouble with the nurse."

Dan grinned. "You will, too. All right, if you're sure you can manage…" He retreated into the cottage while I retrieved our bags.

'Cottage' was a bit of an understatement, as I discovered when I trudged through to the bedroom allocated to me. For starters, the building was a bungalow, albeit with a steep cottagey roof. Having crossed an open-plan lounge-diner-kitchen with a massive fireplace and phenomenal views across the bay, I discovered a sumptuous, tastefully decorated bedroom with ensuite for my use and a smaller bedroom with two single beds for the children right across the corridor. One bed sported a Fireman Sam duvet, and the other Hello Kitty.

"Do you think they'll like them?"

Dan's voice made me jump. I turned to face him.

"I'm sure they'll love them. How fortuitous that…" I petered out when I saw the beaming smile on his face.

"*You* got them for us?"

Dan shrugged. "Well, technically Peter did, but I had the idea."

"You…" I couldn't put my feelings into words and took another tack. "They'll never want to leave, you know."

"Good," Dan observed. "I don't want you all to leave."

I punched him lightly on the shoulder. "We've only just arrived. Shall we have some — "

"*Mummy!*" Emily's shrill shriek interrupted me, and goosebumps trickled down my spine.

"Emily! Where are you? What's happened?"

"*Mummy-y-y!*" My daughter's voice went up a pitch and near hysteria threatened to engulf me.

"Where is she?" I demanded of Dan, but right at that moment, Emily came flying down the corridor.

"*Mummy-y-y-y!*" She screeched to a halt in front of me, looking undamaged, but overexcited.

"What is it, sweetheart?" My voice wobbled slightly, still fearful to make a dreadful discovery of hurt or broken limbs…if not on Emily's part, then Josh's.

"Swimming pool, Mummy. Look, look!" Emily took my hand and pulled me impatiently in the direction from which she had just emerged.

I threw Dan a look. "A swimming pool?"

He shrugged. "I didn't hire this place. But before you ask, there's a sauna, too."

"A sauna?" I knew I was sounding slightly unhinged, but this was somewhat unexpected. *A cottage*, I had been told. Not a one-person luxury spa resort.

"A sauna. We could try it together later?" There was a glint of mischief in his eye before he amended his statement. "Peter makes me go in there for ten minutes after my afternoon swim. It's medicinal, you see. Steam is good for the lungs, or something."

"Come *on*, Mummy." Emily was oblivious to the sparks flying between the adults, and I laughingly yielded to her call to be shown around the rest of the cottage. We found the swimming pool, where I also met Peter, who was in earnest conversation with my four-year-old. Dan stepped to my side.

"Peter, this is Sophie. Sophie, this is Peter," he introduced us with the customary back-and-forth hand-waving.

Peter smiled and held out his hand. He looked to be in his late thirties, probably slightly older than me but just a little younger than Dan, with a shock of blonde hair and piercing blue eyes.

"Nice to meet you," he drawled in a deep West Country twang, and I shook his hand.

"And you, too. That's quite some set up you all have here."

Peter grinned. "I know. I couldn't believe my eyes when I arrived. And I really couldn't believe it when my patient arrived." He laughed. "This is quite the plum job. Apart from keeping Dan from singing, of course, and from making him do his exercises."

"Are you being a difficult patient?" I teased Dan.

He had the grace to look embarrassed. "Only occasionally. I do most things Peter asks me to do."

"You look so much better," I burst out. "Worlds apart from the hospital. You're up and dressed for starters." I reached out a hand and stroked his woolly jumper. "This get-up suits you. You never wear clothes like this in London."

"It's not as cold as this in London. Just wait until we go outside later. There's a wind blowing in off the sea that'll chill you to the bone."

The children had been half listening to our conversation while they took it in turns to walk around the pool.

"Outside, outside," Josh suddenly piped up.

"Swimming, swimming," Emily objected.

I grimaced, sensing impending disagreement and resulting tantrums but I was rescued from an unexpected side.

"Lunch," Peter declared firmly. "It's lunch time and we'll have lunch." His voice invited absolutely no argument, and, confronted with so much natural authority, my children gave in immediately.

"Lunch," their voices echoed eagerly. And, "What is for lunch?"

Chapter Forty-One

Lunch was a simple but wholesome meal of soup and sandwiches. The kids tucked in hungrily, displaying impeccable manners for once and doing me insanely proud. Dan presided over the table, and the joy at seeing us there radiated from every pore. I was doubly glad that we made the journey.

After lunch, Peter ordered Dan to go for his hour's bed rest.

"Food, and rest, and exercise, and rest, and more food, and more rest," Dan commented. "That's what he makes me do, every day, according to a strict schedule, and he never lets off."

"It seems to be working miracles," I observed, winking at Peter. "I quite fancy that kind of holiday myself."

Dan loitered at the table like a truculent teenager. "Can't we make an exception, just today? I haven't seen Sophie and the kids properly in such a long time…"

Peter merely raised his eyebrows, and I stifled a giggle. The man was adorable. He was just like a matron out of a carry-on film, and I had no doubt that he was excellent at his job.

"Tell you what," I offered to diffuse the situation. "I'm done in. I could do with a rest myself. Why don't we *all* have a little lunchtime nap?"

The kids made to protest, but I spoke over their little voices. "*After* we've had a nap, we'll do whatever Dan needs to do next... walking, swimming, whatever. And *if* you both have a nap, you can stay up later after dinner."

The caregiver helped out again. "After midday rest, it's a walk to the beach, and then a quick swim in the pool. And I know some fun games to play in the pool." He made a meaningful face at my kids, who were putty in his hands.

"Okay," Josh agreed. "But where do we sleep?"

Needless to say, the squeals of joy at their own little bedroom were every bit as loud and exuberant as I had expected, and I doubted much 'resting' would be done by my children. Nonetheless, I closed their door and ensconced myself in my own bedroom. Snuggled under the duvet, it didn't take me half a moment before I fell asleep.

When I woke an hour later, I discovered that the kids, too, had succumbed to sleep after all. It was thus a rested and sparkly eyed bunch of people that made their way to the beach, wearing hats, gloves and scarves, and wellies. Out the back door we went, through the garden, and onto a sandy path up the dunes, then straight down to the beach. Before long, the kids ran ahead, splashing their be-wellied feet in the surf and giving great whoops of joy. Peter, Dan, and I walked at a more sedate pace.

Peter took us the length of the beach below the cliff road until we could see no more houses. The wind was blowing in strongly from the sea, and Dan pulled his scarf up high to cover his mouth and nose. "The air tickles me," he explained in a muffled voice. "I hate coughing. But Peter assures me the salty air heals my lungs."

Peter said nothing, but kept walking. I had the feeling that Dan hadn't proved to be the most accepting of patients.

After another half hour, just when the kids started showing signs of fatigue, Peter headed up a narrow path into the dunes. "This way takes us back through the village and to the house," he explained for my benefit. "It's much shorter this way, and we'll be home in fifteen minutes or so."

Sure enough, before long, the cottage loomed in front of us.

"What's next?" I asked Dan and Peter, but the kids got in there first.

"Swimming, you promised swimming," they chanted, and both Dan and Peter grinned.

Within half an hour, the kids and I were splashing in the shallow end of the pool while Dan completed his mandatory lengths. Peter produced balls and floats and lilos and showed the kids how to paddle. He had a floating football goal, and the kids and I amused ourselves by trying to score against Peter. Dan joined in as soon as he was done with his exercises, and the little indoor swimming hall filled with shrieks of laughter as dusk fell outside the enormous plate glass windows.

"Enough, enough, enough," Dan finally begged, half laughing and half coughing. "I surrender." He exchanged a look with Peter, who inclined his head ever so slightly toward a door marked 'sauna.'

"I must go and sweat for my sins now," Dan explained when he caught me staring. "Do you want to come?"

I found myself blushing and picked self-consciously at the strap of my swimsuit.

"You can leave that on," Dan elaborated hastily. "And the kids can come, too."

No sooner said than done. Within seconds, the Jones family, Dan, and Peter all sat or lay on the wooden benches in the little sauna room, where Josh took great delight in adding cold water to the hot coals in the grate to make more and more steam. Peter set a maximum temperature and a timer, and slowly we all grew quiet as the heat worked its magic.

After a long windswept walk, energetic water play, and the unfamiliar heat therapy of a sauna room, my offspring drooped and lolloped about languidly when called to the dinner table. Dan had organized pizzas for all of us, although the amount on offer seemed a little on the stingy side.

"Is this enough?" I mused, ever in housewife mode, as I helped dish up.

Dan threw me a conspiratorial look. "Shh," he whispered. "Just pick lightly. We'll eat something…"

He stepped away as though retrieving the cheese when Peter came within earshot, and he finished his sentence on an unexpectedly loud and somewhat incongruous, "healthy." We'll eat something healthy, too. Like… salad?" He turned to Peter. "We got salad, right?"

Peter looked from Dan to me and back again. I tried to keep a straight face, and Peter simply shrugged. "Of course we got salad. Here, let me help."

For the second time that day, we sat around the large dinner table in the open-plan lounge. Peter had lit a fire in the enormous fireplace, and the warm glow of logs, the discreet lighting, and many candles contrasted wildly with the black darkness outside. The weather had turned, and rain lashed against the window in intermittent gusts. I felt a sudden longing to curl up with Dan in front of the fire…alone.

Dinner passed quickly, and the kids had a second wind when Dan produced a bag of marshmallows and a stack of roasting tongs. He speared marshmallows for all of us and showed the kids how to hold theirs to the fire so the sweet would melt, but not burn.

We sat back and let them get on with it for a moment, and Dan smiled at me wistfully. "Remember Greetje's cottage?" he whispered.

I nodded. How could I forget one of the most memorable nights of my life? Newly engaged to my beloved Steve, on a gorgeous, if remote island in the German North Sea, freshly united with my three best friends, and in delicious anticipation of a terrible storm. We played games and drank wine and toasted marshmallows all through the afternoon, Dan, Rachel, Steve, and I.

"That was a great night," I whispered back. I probed my heart for emotions. Would the memory of that innocent time bring back the grief and anger at having lost Steve? Waggling my head from side to side as if weighing options, I discovered sadness and regret. A vague longing. But most of all, there was fondness and nostalgia and remembered happiness. I was learning to remember Steve without shedding tears and descending into gloom. I was able to talk about good times without feeling bitter.

"It was a great night," I repeated.

Dan took my hand. "You okay? I didn't mean to bring up sad things," he mumbled. "I just...it just came to mind."

"I'm fine," I assured him. "It came to my mind, too, and do you know? I...I don't mind. I can do this now."

Dan raised his eyebrows, but said nothing more, just squeezed my hand a little harder.

Meanwhile, the kids had finished the marshmallows and were looking distinctly worse for wear. The clock on the mantelpiece read nine p.m., and it was definitely time for bed. For the kids at least.

But—"Time for bed," Peter announced, startling me. He had been so immersed in a book, tucked away on a sofa in the corner, I had totally forgotten he was there.

Dan opened his eyes wide at me as if to impart some secret meaning that I completely failed to grasp. In a moment, the gesture was gone and he rose, stretching his arms high above his head.

"Time for bed, indeed," he yawned. "That was a wonderful day. Thank you all for coming."

The kids rushed to him for big hugs, as was their custom at bedtime. "Night, Dan," Josh muttered sleepily. I chuckled to myself. I had expected a riot, but the kids were absolutely exhausted and quite willing to go off to sleep.

"Night, Dad," Emily echoed her brother, then came to snuggle with me.

Me, I was confused. Dan, to bed, willingly, at nine p.m.?

But there was nothing for it, so I took the children to my bathroom and supervised brushing of teeth before tucking them into their beds. By half past nine, the cottage was in complete silence.

At ten p.m., I opened my bedroom door a fraction to gauge if there were any nocturnal goings-on, but I was met with nothing but a dark, empty corridor. Resigned, I retreated to bed and crawled under the duvet. I *was* quite tired.

"This is so totally weird," I chuckled to myself. If word got out that Dan Hunter was living the healthy low-life... Still, he evidently needed it. I switched off my bedside light and turned to face the window. I was just feeling myself drift off when a whisper from outside my door roused me all over again.

"Sophie? Are you hungry? Come and eat!"

Chapter Forty-Two

My bedroom door opened slowly and Dan crept in. All thought of sleep forgotten, I flicked the light back on and was met by an astonishing sight. There was Dan, the rock star, legend for his antics on and off stage, clad in a demure pair of checked pajamas with a button-up top and a mismatched, stripy dressing gown. His feet were stuffed into fluffy slippers, and he clutched a bottle and two glasses in his hands.

"Come on," he whispered. "Dinner is served."

I giggled and left my bed, grabbing my own stripy dressing gown and a pair of thick socks.

"What are you doing?" I breathed into his ear, but he simply took my hand and pulled me down the dark corridor toward the open-plan lounge.

"Have a seat," he invited me and gestured at the dining table, which was once again laid, although only for two, complete with candles and napkins.

He set down the bottle and glasses and scurried off to shut the lounge door so we wouldn't alert the kids or Peter.

While he busied himself in the kitchen, I basked in the heat from the fire, which Dan had re-stoked, and observed my rock star with some degree of amusement.

Within a few minutes, he brought a dish of smoked salmon bites to the table, followed by crusty bread, a cheese board, various cold meats, olives, pickled anchovies, and prawns with some sort of aioli dip. He popped the cork on the bottle of champagne, poured two glasses, and sat down, satisfied at last.

"*Now* we can eat," he announced. "Tapas. What do you think?"

I raised my glass. "Cheers," I giggled. "So that's what you meant earlier. I think it's amazing. It's like a midnight feast. I'm just waiting for matron to discover us and give us detention. Why all the secrecy?"

Dan speared a prawn and pointed it at me. "Well, for one, as you say, matron will certainly come and give us detention. Peter is very strict on my sleep regimen, you see." He dipped the prawn into the aioli before popping it into his mouth. The beatific look on his face and his scrunched up eyes suggested he was enjoying this humble treat far more than was warranted.

He swallowed and cleared his throat. "And for another, I'm on a strict diet. Every last bit of cheese gets weighed, the carbohydrates counted, the sugar added up. It's really tedious." He grimaced.

I helped myself to some bread and salmon. "Tedious indeed, I can see that. But *why*? I thought you were supposed to eat lots and get better." I chewed greedily, my tummy having given an impressive rumble.

Dan speared another prawn and added a mountain of cheese and bread to his plate. "Bliss," he murmured before explaining further. "I'm supposed to eat *healthy*, not lots. So Peter has taken it upon himself to reform the bad eating habits of a lifetime. Bless him, it's what he's paid to do. I've been going along with it, and I have to admit, I'm feeling pretty good. But…"

He grinned his school-boy grin, took a big mouthful of food, washed it down with a large gulp of champagne, and finished his thought. "Well, it gets boring. And I wanted to do something special with you. On my own."

I burst out laughing, but quieted down when I saw the alarm on Dan's face.

"Sorry," I whispered.

"Peter's bedroom is right next door there," Dan whispered back. "And he's a light sleeper." He pointed his finger, and we sat in silence for a minute, straining to hear.

"I think we're okay," Dan finally concluded and resumed eating.

"God, this is worse than trying to entertain with just the kids in the house," I giggled softly. "Naughty, naughty us."

"Ha, we're not naughty yet," Dan shot back, speaking softly, as well. "I was working up to that part."

He winked, and my heart skipped and jumped. He didn't mean—he couldn't mean what I thought he meant?

"What do you mean?" I bumbled, hoping for clarification, but Dan was enjoying himself.

"All in good time," he teased. "Let's finish our meal first."

So we tucked in and chatted away. Our low voices, the roaring fire, and the champagne glasses glinting in the candlelight produced a date-like atmosphere, and my spine tingled in delicious, lusty anticipation. Would he? Would *I*? Was he ready? Was *I*?

Finally, I sat back, defeated by the food. "That was delicious."

"Uh-huh," Dan groaned back. "God, I needed that." He reclined in his chair for a moment. Suddenly, he jumped up and grinned at me yet again.

"Now for the naughty part... No, stay there!" he instructed as I half-rose to get up, assuming that...well, that my bodily presence would be required. He did an exaggerated tip-toe stage-walk back toward the kitchen and disappeared from sight behind the counter. From the noises he made, I assumed he was looking for something in the freezer. Sure enough, there he was, straightening up and carrying something. I clamped my hand over my mouth when I saw what it was.

"*This* is really naughty." He hiccupped with suppressed laughter when he set down the most enormous ice cream bombe on the table between us. He handed me a spoon. "Dig in."

"What, like this? Just so? Really?" I indicated my spoon and the heap of ice cream in the dish.

"Yup, just like this. Really. Otherwise it wouldn't be naughty." He demonstrated what he had in mind by dipping his spoon in deep to extract a huge helping of double-chocolate ice cream striated with luxury vanilla. "Hmmm yum!" he moaned and had another mouthful.

I readied my spoon and followed suit. "Where did you get all this?" I inquired through a mouthful of melted bliss. "And how did you hide it from Peter?"

"Aha!" Dan laughed. "I have a smartphone. I have Internet access. I got a food delivery when Peter was out getting something in Plymouth."

"Back up, back up, your phone is still at my house. I never thought to give it back." I remembered that Dan's phone was still parked on my bedside table this very moment, having long since run out of juice and never having been recharged. "I'm sorry."

"It's fine. Jack insisted I had to have a new one anyway." Dan brushed my concerns away with airy insouciance. "So anyway, I got a food delivery, and I stashed it all before Peter came back."

"But...how come he didn't see it all in the fridge?"

"I did the old window-refrigeration trick," Dan explained with evident glee. "You know, like when you were a student? I had it all in a plastic box below my window sill. It's been cold enough and Peter never thought to check. And as for the ice cream... well, Peter doesn't believe in frozen food so he never uses the freezer."

I shook my head. "Unbelievable, the lengths you go to."

"All for you, my love, all for you." He spoke lightly and toasted me as he said the words, but there it was again, that undercurrent of emotion. I broke out in goosebumps all over.

A thumping noise from the next room shattered the mood. Dan and I looked at each other with frightened eyes.

"We'd better tidy up," I whispered. "Quick!"

We rose and hurriedly cleared the table, putting the sparse evidence of our crime into a black refuse bag and stuffing it deep into the kitchen bin. I loaded the dishwasher while Dan ran back and forth with dishes and cutlery. He blew out the candles and poked the logs in the fireplace apart so that the fire dispersed. There was another bang from next door, followed by the distinctive sound of a door being opened. Dan dove toward the bank of light switches in the kitchen and plunged the large room into darkness. He pulled me down into a crouch behind the center island and put a finger to my lips.

I had barely gotten my breathing under control when the lounge door opened.

"Anyone here?" Peter's voice carried through the dark room. Then the lights came on. I flinched and screwed my eyes shut, as if that would make me invisible. I hoped he wouldn't see us in our impromptu hiding place because our position was…incriminating to say the least. Dan had wrapped his body around me, and I half-sat on his lap. Depending on the angle of sight, our stance might easily be misinterpreted.

Peter's footsteps crossed the lounge and a grating, crackling kind of sound suggested he was busy at the fireplace.

"Must have been a log falling," he muttered to himself. "I thought we put the fire out properly."

He paced the room some more, and I broke out into a sweat of hysteria. I had to open my mouth to breathe because my nose had blocked up and was making snorty noises. Digging my fingernails into my palms to keep myself quiet brought tears into my eyes, and Dan touched them lightly with the tip of his nose. Once more, I envisaged how very much we would look 'caught in the act' if Peter stumbled upon us, and I started to shake with silent giggles. I could feel Dan's hand moving infinitesimally against my back, trying to calm me down, and I buried my face in his shoulder.

Round and round Peter went, straightening chairs and plumping cushions, from the sound of it. Several interminable minutes later, he finally concluded his examination of the lounge. He switched the lights off before closing the door behind him, and I exhaled sharply.

"Wait," Dan breathed into my ear, barely audible despite his immediate proximity.

"Let him go back to bed first."

We held on to each other in our cramped and awkward position for another few minutes. With the fire extinguished, the room grew cold, and I started to shiver. Dan responded by pulling me closer against him still, and the shift in our center of gravity finally caused us to topple over. Dan extended an arm backwards to break our fall so Peter wouldn't hear the thud of our entwined bodies crashing onto the floor, and we slowly lay down in a tangled mess of limbs, me on top of Dan.

Very gently, he pulled my face down until our lips met. Softly at first, and increasingly greedy, we kissed. His mouth was warm against mine and his ice cream sweet breath took mine away. His tongue flicked out to trace the shape of my mouth, lick my lips, probe my own tongue, teasing. Where I had been shivering with cold a moment before, I was now trembling with desire, and I gave a low moan. Suddenly, Dan's hands were in my hair and he yanked me down so I was flat on him, against him, feeling his ribs move, rise and fall with every healthy breath. I let my weight melt my body against Dan's, mouth connecting against mouth more ferociously than ever before, his hardness hot and strong even through our double layers of clothing. My loin was fizzing with heat, and my ladyship quivered with a long forgotten, long neglected need. Forget the kitchen floor, the cold, and the caregiver next door. I needed this man. I *wanted*. I was hot. We were both desperate to connect.

Our breathing came in hard bursts, completely synched. I could feel Dan's pulse in his lips, beating as one with mine. I was dizzy with desire and rubbed myself against Dan greedily. Dan pulled open the front of my dressing gown, then tugged at my pajama buttons.

"Take it off, take it off," he whispered urgently, and I raised my upper body so he could liberate me from the offending garment.

"Mummy?"

Emily's tearful voice rang out tremulously, and I froze.

"Mummy, are you there?"

I swallowed hard, trying to get a grip on reality.

"Yes, sweetheart, I'm here." My voice came breathy and raspy. I spoke while I rolled off Dan, refastening my dressing gown and thanking my lucky stars that Dan hadn't gotten anywhere with the buttons.

"*Mummy?*" The fear in my daughter's voice caught in my throat, and I pushed myself off the floor.

"I'm right here, darling," I spoke in a soothing voice that sounded more like Mummy and less like wanton-abandon-sex-goddess. "What's the matter?" I crossed the kitchen and found Emily at the lounge door, shaking with cold and fright. I scooped her into my arms and sat down with her on the nearest sofa.

"I scared. I had bad dream." Tears spilled down my daughter's cheeks, and the last remains of lust in my loins evaporated, to be replaced with guilt and shame. How very stupid of me, of us, to get carried away *here*, in an unfamiliar house with the kids only a few doors away.

"I'm sorry, sweetheart. I was thirsty and wanted a drink of water. That's why I wasn't in my bed." More guilt! How easily the white lie tripped off my tongue. But I couldn't really admit to my midnight assignation with 'Dad', could I?

"Why's Dad here?" Emily asked through her tears, momentarily distracted from her fear. I followed her gaze, and, despite the darkness, could make out Dan standing in the kitchen, looking reasonably composed. He loped across the room to join us on the sofa and wrapped us both into a hug.

"I fancied a drink, too," he whispered. "Your Mummy and I, we've been very naughty."

I inhaled sharply and tried to dig him in the ribs but failed, Emily's little body being in the way. Dan shot me a look and grinned.

"You see, we've been having a secret midnight feast, and Peter wouldn't be very happy if he knew about it."

Relief washed over me in a great wave. I hadn't really thought Dan would give my daughter the down-and-dirty, but with Dan, you never did know.

"Midnight feast?" Emily's eyes grew wide with excitement. "I want, too!"

Dan laughed. "Shall we see what we can find?"

"Yes, pease!" Emily was all agog, but still remembered her older brother. "I get Josh?"

Dan looked at me, and I shrugged. We were committed now. "Why don't you do that," I whispered. "But don't wake Peter!"

Emily traipsed back to her bedroom, her little feet making nary a sound.

"You gave me the fright of a lifetime," I confessed to Dan. "I thought you were going all honest and liberal on Emily."

Dan didn't respond to my remark, but simply took me in his arms. He stroked my hair and planted a quick kiss on my lips. Already, we could hear the excited whisper of two children approaching down the corridor.

"There's no way Peter is going to sleep through this," I warned, but Dan still didn't react. Just before the kids arrived in the room, he let go of me.

"You got me falling," he said in a low, seductive voice. "I just hope you'll catch me."

"I—"

I didn't get a chance to offer my reply as the children bounded in. "Midnight feast, midnight feast," they chanted as quietly as they could.

"Right, let's see what we've got," Dan announced and rubbed his hands together. "I think we can find some chocolate here somewhere."

I watched as he charmed my children yet again with his easy-going, cheerful, confident demeanor. It really was no miracle that Emily had given up calling him 'Dan' altogether. Josh, too, was attached to the only man in his life. And Dan? Well, one thing was for certain. He was learning to take unexpected interruptions to his amorous intentions in his stride. We were like a family, even if we weren't a family.

Chapter Forty-Three

We stayed with Dan almost all of Sunday. Peter let Dan off the hook for the day, resulting in an unexpected lie-in, and we didn't have breakfast until ten a.m. It was sleeting and thoroughly uninviting outside, so we extended our morning repast until lunch, let the children play, and generally lounged around like in days of old.

When the kids got too restless, we had another splash in the pool and Dan hooked up the Wii thoughtfully supplied by the cottage owner, letting the children mess about with games and balance boards while we looked on indulgently. Emily tired of the technology first and demanded to play dress-up. Josh immediately jumped on the bandwagon and suggested they could practice his play.

"What play?" Dan queried, amused. "Are you in the school play?"

Josh grinned. "I'm the innkeeper."

"The innkeeper?" Dan was lost.

"In the nativity."

Dan opened his eyes wide and clapped his hands. "The *nativity*. Of course. Is it really that time of year already?"

"It is," I confirmed. "Two weeks to go. Emily is an angel in hers, aren't you, sweetheart?"

Emily nodded and swept around the room in her rendition of an angel-ballerina dance.

"So...can we practice?" Josh was eager to show off his inn-keeping prowess.

"Sure," Dan agreed. "What shall we do?"

Thus, under Josh's keen direction, Dan and I took turns at being Mary and Joseph, party guests and kings. Emily brightened proceedings with a spirited chant of "fear not, fear not", flapping her arms like wings and dancing around us like an excited butterfly. The afternoon flew past, and before we knew it, I had to bundle the children into the car amid many protests and emotional tears, and we were on our way back to London. I felt thoroughly discombobulated and out of sorts myself, desperate for a moment alone to ponder the sexy near-miss of the previous night.

Two weeks and thirteen phone calls with Dan later, I was even more confused. My initial certainty that we would *probably* have made love right there on the kitchen floor had been replaced by doubt when there was no hint of innuendo—subtle, crass, or otherwise—during our long-distance chats. I longed to confide in Rachel, but something kept me from doing so. I wanted to keep the moment precious, even if—*especially* if—it was never to be repeated. So I stewed and wondered and kept getting on with my daily life. And there was plenty to be getting on with.

For starters, I resumed my training with Richard, and I was astounded to discover how much I had missed this professional purpose in my life during the weeks gone by. With

Dan out of the picture, Richard was working with another band, and I got to cut my teeth on a different, much more grungy kind of sound. I didn't particularly rate the music, but I enjoyed playing with it and mixing it to Richard's specification.

Then there were the nativities. I made costumes and practiced lines with the kids, learning songs and movements and even stage directions, wondering all the while at the logistics of it all and how I would pull it off. Because, naturally, Josh's and Emily's nativities were scheduled for the same day, if not exactly for the same time.

"*Obviously* they're going to be on the same day," I ranted at my mum when I found out. "Why on earth would a school and a playschool coordinate their dates so that fraught single mummies can see their children in their respective nativities?"

"Calm down, calm down," Mum soothed. "What's the big deal? You go to one first, and then the other."

Grrr. Why did Mum have to be so reasonable about this? "I don't want to be rushing around like a headless chicken. I wanted to…you know, *enjoy* their performance. I'd kind of hoped that one would be on one day and one on the other, and I could make a big fuss of each of them in turn."

Saying it out loud, my reasoning sounded lame even to me. Mum simply laughed. "Thirty-six and still discovering that the world doesn't always turn your way. Sweetheart, get over yourself and get on with it."

"Yah, well, thanks Mum," I sulked, then laughed. "You're right. It's just that I'm exhausted, and all this running around for them on my own…"

"It's tough, I know," Mum conceded. "But you'll do it. I know you will. And anyway, isn't Dan…?"

She didn't finish her question, unsure, as always, whether she had already said too much.

"I don't know." I sighed. "He hasn't said when he'll be back, even though we've spoken every day. He sounds much better…"

"But he knows about the nativities, right?"

"He does. I'm fairly sure we mentioned the date." *At least seven hundred times.* I was working hard at not getting upset on the children's behalf that Dan would miss these performances. There was *no* reason he should be there, no obligation, no expectation. The kids had asked a couple of times but took my evasive answer in their strides. After all, they knew Dan was away at the moment. So it was only me who felt rankled, but I didn't want Mum to know that.

"Sophie, these things have a habit of working themselves out. Don't fret," Mum advised before she rang off.

"Don't fret," I repeated to myself and pulled a face. Easier said than done.

With two days to go, "Don't Fret" became my mantra, and I even passed it on to the children.

"Don't fret, angel cakes, you'll remember your lines," I reassured Josh when he was in tears the night before the nativity.

"Don't fret, sweetheart, of course you'll remember to walk slowly and regally," I soothed Emily, who was also going to pieces.

"Don't fret, Sophie, you'll get through the day," I instructed myself at bedtime, feeling restless and agitated.

Finally, the big day arrived. I rose early and got my two stars ready, dropping Josh off first, then Emily, and returning home for an hour before rushing back to playschool to claim my front row seat. I had just made myself a cup of tea and switched on early morning television, having taken a day off my sound apprenticeship yet again, when I heard the front door being unlocked and shut. I didn't have time to contemplate what was going on, and at a deep level I knew who had arrived even before his voice rang out, firm and strong.

"Hello? Anyone here?"

I set my cup down on the coffee table and flew into Dan's arms. He held me tight, stroking my hair with one hand and securing my body against his with the other. We said nothing at all, just hung on to each other like two drowning people.

We started to sway, and Dan let me go. His eyes shone, and his face was one big smile.

"You made it," I stated. I tried for a casual tone but failed miserably. The high squeal in my voice told Dan exactly how excited I was to see him.

"I made it," Dan reiterated. "I wouldn't have missed the plays for the world, and besides, my Devon exile is finished. I am officially a healed man."

"That's wonderful!" I jumped up and down like one of my children.

Dan burst out laughing. "It's wonderful to have someone so happy to see me."

We hugged again, simply because we could.

"Have we got enough time for—" Dan began, a certain glint in his eye, but I didn't let him continue.

"—a cup of tea? Yeah, we have about half an hour. I just made myself one. Would you like one?"

Dan belly laughed. A loud, long, proper laugh, free of crackles, coughs, or convulsions. His skin glowed with a healthy color in his cheeks, and he had put on just a little weight. It suited him better than the hollowed-out look he had sported before.

"You have a very low opinion of me, Sophie Jones," he teased. "A cup of tea was all I was after."

"Of course. Right." I felt flustered and caught off guard. I *hadn't* imagined that look in his eye. I knew I hadn't. I knew this man.

He's flirting with me.

The realization hit me with a bang, and I sloshed boiling water all over the counter rather than into Dan's mug because I giggled so much. Dan was flirting with me, innuendo, tease, and wide-eyed denial. It was as if he was turning the clock back eight years and starting all over again. The butterflies in my tummy told me I liked that idea. Very much. I was ready. But they also told me I was wildly out of practice and had no idea how to play the game anymore, so I opted for blithe ignorance.

"Here's your cup of tea," I announced brightly but calmly, cheeks flaming but hands only shaking mildly.

Dan gave me a curious look when he accept the mug. "Everything all right? Are you feeling okay?"

"Fine," I squeaked. "Just fine. Anyway, drink up, we need to go soon."

My rock star raised an eyebrow at me, but gulped down his scalding hot cup of tea. I busied myself in the kitchen, feeling awkward all of a sudden. There was simply no time to get all flirty and coy. The last thing I wanted was to be blushing and bumbling in front of the other parents at Emily's playschool, let alone my daughter. *Cool* and *composed* had to be my watch-words for the day.

"And not just for today, either," I muttered to myself while I put our cups in the dishwasher.

"What *are* you whittering on about?" Dan appeared perturbed by my distance so I flashed him a bright smile that literally sent him reeling across the room. Talk about mixed messages!

"Nothing," I sang. "Come on, let's go."

My heart flipped happily in my chest while I sat next to Dan at Emily's play, having claimed two front row seats. The overriding emotion was relief. Relief, at having Dan healthy and smiling at my side, and relief at sharing this special occasion with someone who meant so much to me and to the kids.

The children acted and sang beautifully, if just a little out of tune, and Dan smiled the entire time. I noticed his eyes scanning the group time and again, examining each and every angel closely, finally moving on to Mary and even the shepherds.

"Where is Emily?" he grumbled. "Has she been taken ill or something?"

I shot him a confused look, forgetting for a moment that he hadn't witnessed the drama of the past two weeks when Emily had experienced a diva-style traumatic change of heart regarding her allotted part.

"What do you mean?" I hissed back. "Why would she be ill?"

"Wasn't she meant to be an angel?"

"Shh," an angry voice interrupted from behind us. Dan and I turned as one, doing a superb double act of indignant parenthood. The dad whose stern admonishment had silenced us so abruptly gestured toward the state-of-the-art video camera he was pointing at the stage and then placed a finger on his lips again. I suppressed a giggle and turned to face the front. Dan nudged me, also looking forward with a stony face indicating an imminent explosion of laughter. I could feel his shoulders shaking.

Just then, Emily finally made her grand entrance alongside the other two kings. Her blue eyes sparkled brightly in her blackened face, and her crown wobbled as she took the regal steps she had practiced at home. Dan stared a question at me but said nothing.

"I bring thee Frank and sense," Emily enunciated as clearly as she could, handing Mary a cone made out of gold foil with a small man drawn on the side. The children's solemn dedication to their cause was touching. I felt tears brimming in my eyes, and they weren't just from withheld laughter at Emily's unexpected reinterpretation of Casper's gift for the baby Jesus. I didn't dare look at Dan for fear of losing my composure completely, which would have been wholly inappropriate. Digging my nails into my palms, I breathed deeply and tried to commit the occasion to memory.

"Frank and sense?" Dan queried sotto voce when the play concluded, the applause faded, and the parents started mingling, waiting for their de-costumed offspring to appear for home-time.

"It's a big word," I defended my daughter.

"It sure is," Dan agreed. "I thought she was going to be an angel?"

"She decided last week she didn't want to be an 'airy-fairy angel,' she wanted to be someone high and mighty and with some power. And anyway," I continued my imitation of Emily's belligerent revolt, "'being a girl sucks'—no idea where she got *that* from—and so she swapped roles with one of the kings."

Finally, Dan let go of the laughter that had been building between us for the past twenty minutes. He barked and hollered and was wiping tears of mirth from his eyes when Emily emerged, jubilant, and threw herself straight onto his lap. No thought spared for Mummy. My daughter was an opportunist and knew which side her bread was buttered.

"Dad!" Her little voice carried loudly through the room and several heads turned. "Dad back!" She cuddled him, and I smiled. Dan had certainly made both Jones ladies' day.

275

"Sweetheart, you were a lovely king," Dan complimented her.

She took a proud bow. "Kings rock," she declared. "Girls suck."

Dan ruffled her hair. "Do they now? Well, then you won't be wanting the Barbie ballerina I brought for my angel..." He petered out, putting on a distressed face.

Emily scrutinized his frown lines and downturned mouth with all the intensity of a two-year-old. "Barbie ball-ina?" she squealed after a moment's thought. "Me like Barbie ball-ina. Pease?"

"Okay," Dan laughed. "It's waiting for you in the car. Shall we go?"

And just like that, he had my daughter eating out of his palm all over again. They held hands as we left the hall, and I caught a few more curious glances. The mother of one of Emily's playmates touched me lightly on the arm.

"Dad?" she asked curiously. "Since when?" She knew about Dan, of course, as did almost everyone there.

I shook my head and giggled to defuse the moment. "For some reason, Emily gets very confused with pronouncing 'Dad' and 'Dan'," I explained. "It's been going on for a while, but he's not her dad."

"Ah." A shadow of embarrassment passed over the woman's face. "I'm sorry, I didn't mean to pry."

"You're not prying. I bet all of the mums will be wondering after Emily's rather...noisy love declaration. But it's just what it is. Anyway," I stole a glance at my watch, "I must dash. We got to get some lunch, and then it's Josh's play straight after. See you 'round!" And I hurried off before anyone else could intercept me.

An hour later, Dan, Emily, and I rushed into the hall at Josh's primary school, securing seats in the second row. Dan kept Emily on his lap, partly because I had only two tickets and partly because Emily wouldn't let go of him. We had had a hurried lunch in a coffee shop, and the excitement of the morning, combined with a pleasantly filled tummy, overwhelmed Emily before Josh's play even began. Within a few minutes of sitting down, her head dropped onto Dan's shoulder, her thumb went in, and her eyes closed. One sleeping king.

Dan shifted in his seat, shuffling his bottom and stretching his legs until he was in a comfortable position, then regarded me with an amused smile on his face.

"I thought she was looking forward to the show?"

"She was," I confirmed. "But it was probably all a bit much. We'll give her twenty minutes and see if she won't wake up."

Dan nodded, and, seeming quite unaware that he was doing so, stroked Emily's back. He looked quite the dad, and I wondered how many more tongues we would set wagging this afternoon. *Hey ho, that's nobody's business*, I thought, and concentrated on the play.

Josh was magnificent. Even though I had taken him through his lines time and again, I hadn't fully comprehended the scale of his part. He was quite the star, introducing the play and returning as quasi-narrator every so often when another batch of party guests arrived at the overcrowded inn. I had had no idea that my son was such a convincing comedian. He carried off the funny-grumpy innkeeper beautifully and got a round of standing applause at the end. Emily, who woke up halfway through the play, was beside herself with glee and joy, and she clapped as loudly as she could for her big brother. Dan high-fived Josh exuberantly and Josh, like Emily, threw his arms around Dan's neck as if he hadn't seen him for years.

"We're all together again," he exclaimed. "That's so lovely. Can we go for dinner somewhere to celebrate?"

I exchanged looks with Dan and he inclined his head, *yes*.

"Why not," I conceded, not wanting to give into my children's demands quite so easily. "That would be nice."

"Pizza!" my children exclaimed as one, and Dan agreed on my behalf.

"All right, all right." I tugged at Josh's costume. "It's a bit early though, and you'd better get changed."

"It's never too early for pizza," my son contradicted me, sounding quite in-role still, before scampering off to change. I shook my head.

"They're growing up so quickly," Dan observed. "It's unreal. It seems like only yesterday they were babes in arms…"

"…and now they're feminists and budding comedians with wise-crack repartee," I concurred. "And it's only going to get worse."

"Wha's a femist?" Emily chimed up, and Dan ruffled her hair yet again.

"A feminist," he repeated the word slowly for her benefit, "is a little girl who thinks it's better to be the king than an angel."

Emily regarded him with big eyes, and I simply knew she was storing this nugget of information for future reference, but she said nothing.

"Can we go now?" Josh burst into our little scene, fully, if haphazardly, dressed, and Dan grabbed his hand.

"Let's go," he declared, leading the way with a child at each hand.

Chapter Forty-Four

We got three more days with Dan before he disappeared again, having been summoned to the studio to start making up for lost time. I warned him to take it easy, but he brushed my concerns away, making promise after promise not to burn the midnight oil like he had before. Consequently, we didn't see him much at all, not even on the weekend. I received texts and took telephone calls, and I spoke with Jack several times, beseeching him to send Dan to bed at a reasonable hour, but I had no insight into whether my rock star was being sensible. The only aspect of his life I could control was whether or not he ran himself ragged trying to fit the Jones family into his schedule, and I blocked that avenue one hundred percent, much as it pained me.

In actual fact, with Christmas being so close, days flew by without me having time to draw breath. School and playschool broke up for the holidays, and I kept us busy with making Christmas decorations, baking cookies, going to carol concerts, and even braving a panto, Peter Pan. I cried real tears at the very bad and very saucy jokes, while the children were beside themselves with glee at the funny acting and outrageous capers.

When the cast erupted into a spirited rendition of 'Gangnam Style', Josh stood on his seat and danced, and, amid many giggles, I had to persuade him to come down and dance with both feet on the floor. It was a resounding success, and we were all worn out with laughter and shouting by the time we arrived home. I put my overexcited kids to bed at nine, promising them a trip to the Christmas market the following day, Christmas Eve.

"So much excitement and busy-ness in the time that's meant to be the quiet coming of Christ," I mused to myself, not for the first time, as I settled in front of the telly with a glass of mulled wine. Since Steve's death, Christmas had been one of the most difficult times for me. The first year, my parents had tactfully invited us to spend the holidays with them, away from our familiar surroundings, memories, and the inevitably empty space by the tree. Steve's parents had made a similar offer, and so we had oscillated between the two well-meaning sets of grandparents, the kids duly distracted, me barely coping with the loss.

It had gotten easier, of course, and the previous year, we had even been quite jolly. But this year, my parents had booked a cruise in the Caribbean, completely taking me by surprise when they had asked my permission *in March* to be absent for this year's Christmas so they could fulfill one of their lifelong dreams. *Of course* I had sent them booking the cruise of a lifetime and hadn't given the twenty-fifth of December another thought. Gradually, I had become used to the idea of spending Christmas in London and had gracefully but firmly declined Steve's parents' invitation.

Lately, I had secretly wondered...nay, hoped, that perhaps we might see Dan over Christmas. After all, he kept calling us his loan family and we had all become so close over the past six months, even though we hadn't necessarily seen him very much recently... But still, I had hoped. *I should've simply asked him*, I surmised. It was entirely possible that Dan was hoping for the same, but didn't want to intrude. It was, in fact, quite likely that the both of us were simply being too polite or too confused to make that call. One way or another, I hadn't asked, and he hadn't said anything. I was trying very hard — if unsuccessfully — not to feel hurt about this, reminding myself that we had no real claim on him.

So now, on the eve of Christmas Eve, I was questioning my judgment of facing the festivities alone with the kids. In a house that was dark and quiet, with a gaudily bedecked Christmas tree sparkling silently in a corner of the lounge, I couldn't help wondering whether I was doing the right thing. How would we get through the next two days? Would it even occur to the kids to wonder where their father was? Would *they* still feel the pain? Would I be *enough* for them?

The phone rang at this very opportune moment and I pounced on it gratefully without even looking at it. If it was Steve's mum again repeating her offer of Christmas asylum, I might just accept.

"So...tomorrow," Dan's voice emerged from the handset somewhat unexpectedly and without greeting or preamble. "When are you all coming?"

My mulled-wine brain struggled to catch this curve ball. "Tomorrow? Coming where?" I repeated, befuddled.

Dan laughed. "Sweetheart, I got the tree waiting to be decorated by the two young Joneses, a deli feast waiting to be consumed in the evening, and a turkey prepped and ready to be cooked on Christmas Day. I can't do this on my own. I thought you were all helping me?"

My spirits soared. Christmas with Dan, after all?

"That would be awesome," I gushed while a tiny voice at the back of my head muttered, *it would be awesome, but what message will the kids take away from this?*

Dan picked up on my infinitesimal hesitation. "What's the matter?"

"Nothing, nothing!" I tried to reassure him as much as myself. "We'd love to come. How…What did you have in mind?"

"Surprise! Get here when you can and leave the rest to me." There was a definite smile in his voice, and I found myself smiling also, even though we couldn't see each other.

"I kind of promised the kids to take them to the Christmas market on the South Bank tomorrow. Shall we get to you when we've done that? Or before? Or…" I petered out, getting the distinct feeling that there was a hurt vibe coming down the line. "Why don't you come with us? The kids would love that. I'm not thinking straight. I'm saying everything back to front here. So sorry, I…I was having a funny moment, and when you rang, I didn't quite get my head 'round it all and…" Verbal diarrhea carried me through the awkward moment.

Finally, Dan laughed. "I was beginning to think you didn't love me anymore," he teased, and the 'L' word carried clear with his strong timbre. A trickle of goosebumps ran down my back, but I didn't get time to enjoy them.

"Tell you what, get here when the kids are up, and then we'll see what we fancy doing. They shall have their Christmas market, don't worry. We'll play it by ear. What do you say? It *is* Christmas Eve, after all, time for taking it easy and making merry," he coaxed.

It was my turn to laugh. "Okay, we'll come over for breakfast," I agreed.

"Don't forget your PJ's," Dan instructed, a distinct hint of mischief in his voice.

"Pajamas?"

"Well, unless you plan to head off tomorrow night and then be back with *sleeping* kids first thing on Christmas morning?"

"Oh. Right. Of course." I wasn't doing well at playing this gracefully, but Dan forgave me.

The kids had a little lie-in the following morning, so I hastily loaded the car with their presents, then threw blankets and bags with clothes over the top. By the time my offspring rose, the car looked as though we were departing for a two-week holiday. I told the children we were headed for Dan's, and they got dressed quicker than ever before, all thoughts of Christmas under our own, lovingly decorated tree completely forgotten.

The smell of freshly perked coffee and croissants baking in the oven greeted us when we arrived at Dan's house, and Christmas rock songs were playing on the iPod in the kitchen. Dan wore a reindeer apron and a set of antlers on his head and quickly outfitted us with similar accessories. Needless to say, the kids were ecstatic, more so when, after breakfast, Dan let them loose on the enormous, but bare, Norwegian spruce that graced his lounge. There were boxes and boxes of ornaments scattered about the sofas: baubles, tinsel, angels, stars, pine cones with silver snow, handmade fabric bows, lacquered apples...a riot of styles and themes, but my children fell on the lot and got decorating with gusto.

Dan pulled me down on the sofa to watch, his eyes full of vicarious excitement. "This is grand," he whispered, sounding a little choked. "I've always wanted to do this."

"It'll be gaudy and lopsided," I warned him.

"I don't give a monkey's what it looks like. Look at their faces!" Dan was still rapt.

I took in the scene through his eyes and I had to agree, it was picture book perfect. "Thank you," I said softly. "This means a lot."

Dan put an arm around my shoulder and gently pulled me into him. "Thank *you*," he retorted. "It means the world to me."

It took Josh and Emily the best part of an hour to trim the tree. Then Dan heightened the magic further.

"Perfect," he announced when Josh declared the job done. "Now for the candles. But that's a job for your mummy and me." He produced another box from under a sofa, this one filled with silver clip-on candle holders. "The candles are over there," he pointed, and I spotted a box of tiny white candles on the sideboard. It was our turn to adorn the tree while the children watched us from the sofa, and we performed our task with such ease it felt as though we had done it many times before.

"Real candles," Josh enthused when we were nearly done. "We've never had real candles before. Can we light them?"

"No, let's wait until tomorrow." Practical me immediately tried to manage the situation, thinking of wax and drips and messy floors, not forgetting the risk of fire from burned-down candles and the ensuing need to replace them from ditto. But Dan had other ideas.

"Of course," he agreed. "Wouldn't be much fun otherwise."

He handed Josh and Emily a long safety-taper each and let them light the candles that they could reach, not flinching even once when wax dripped onto his wooden floors. He swiftly finished the job off with the higher candles and turned the electric lights off. The tree looked spectacular, if predictably lopsided.

"It'll be even better when it gets dark," Dan promised the children, then launched into the next phase of his plan. "Now then. I think your mummy deserves some pamper time. I hear you wanted to go the Christmas market. What do you say, I take you, and we leave Mummy to relax for an hour or two?"

Huge screams of joy indicated the kids were more than happy with this plan, and Dan shot me a meaningful look. "Are you okay with that? I...there's something I need to get and I don't want you to see. I've fixed the guest room properly for you. It's all yours. I even got your favorite bubble bath. You don't need to do anything, no cooking or anything, it's all taken care of. Just relax. My first present to you — what do you say?"

Needless to say, I said 'yes', although it felt slightly odd being left behind in Dan's house while Dan and the kids went off on a secret mission together. I had no idea what he had planned but actually, I was excited by the prospect of not being in charge. Singing Wizzard's classic Christmas song at the top of my voice, I unloaded the car and hauled the presents and clothes upstairs.

On account of having my hands full, I had to push the door to my customary guest room open with my bottom, and I nearly dropped my cargo in shock when I stepped in. 'Fixed the guest room properly for you' was the understatement of the century. 'Created your own personal haven' would have been more accurate. Gone were the pine bed and big wardrobe. In their place, a white four-poster bed waited for me, with gauzy curtains and a colorful quilted cover. It looked at once elegant, dreamy, and decadent.

The far wall was hidden behind a row of mirrored wardrobe doors, and there was a brand new white carpet with red and blue rugs scattered around tastefully. Last, but not least, there was a dinky antique dressing table and a big, squashy armchair by the newly opened and restored little fireplace. This was my dream bedroom, had I but enough money to furnish my own sleeping quarters in this manner.

I set my bag down and ventured into the other guest room, which also had had a makeover. Dan had installed a massive bunk bed of sorts, but the bottom bunk was at a forty-five degree angle to the top bunk and stripy canopies turned both beds into secret hideaways. There was a big children's wardrobe, a brand new dark blue carpet—sensible choice—and a big storage unit with cheerful plastic boxes for storing toys and bric-a-brac. The kids would be over the moon. They would never want to go home!

Completely overwhelmed, I sat down on the bottom bed and fingered the pink bedding absent-mindedly. What did this mean? Granted, at one point the Jones family had spent a lot of time in this house, but I had put a stop to that since Dan was back, to keep him from burning out all over again. What was he proposing?

Proposing...proposing...posing... The word echoed around my mind, bouncing off the walls and fading slowly. I was feeling dizzy, but I pulled myself up short. Dan had always been a face value kind of man. It was obvious, and had been for some time, that he thought of the children and I as his kind of family-by-proxy, and I presumed he was simply indulging this idea. Whether there was a hidden agenda, a deeper meaning to his action...

"Probably not," I ruminated, rising to my feet and padding back to my own room. "He's probably just wanting us to be comfortable when we do stay. And anyway..." I kicked off my shoes and succumbed to exhilarated joy. "Who cares? This is fab!"

I did a good movie-heroine impression of launching myself onto the four-poster with a squeal and bouncing up and down. My next stop was the ensuite bathroom, which had also had a bit of a makeover, and I found my favorite bubble bath waiting for me as promised. I turned the taps and squirted a liberal amount of shiny, pearlescent bath essence into the water before discarding my clothes and diving in.

Chapter Forty-Five

I was still in the bath when the doorbell rang. Feeling lazy and rather enjoying my bubbles, I elected to ignore it, but the ringing wouldn't cease. If anything, it got more persistent until I finally relented. I wrapped myself into a fluffy bathrobe and padded downstairs, leaving little wet footprints along the way. Being ever cautious, I attempted to look through the spyhole first, but the view was obscured by something large and white. I was debating whether to zip round to the kitchen to take a peek out the window when the buzzer went again, and I swung the door open in the sheer desire for the noise to stop.

"*Finally,*" a muffled and highly impatient voice greeted me from behind a large cardboard box. "I thought there were nobody here."

The cardboard box began to move forward and I stepped back before I got squashed.

"Where you be wanting this then, love?" the voice continued. "In the kitchen?"

"Um…what is it?"

The cardboard box stopped moving and turned a fraction, then tilted sideways as the owner of the voice tried to look at me. He wore a chef's hat.

"What *is* it? Are you joking?"

I tied the cord of my dressing gown more firmly around my waist, as if the gesture of propriety would help, and shook my head.

"This is your Christmas dinner," the man informed me. "Where do you want it?"

"In the kitchen, I suppose," I ordered, pointing toward the door to the left. I was still computing the implications of the unexpected arrival of food when another cardboard box walked in, followed by another, and another. A veritable army of home delivery chefs was invading Dan's house, and I had no idea whether they were in the right place. After the last chap had shuffled past me, I closed the door and followed them into the kitchen, where I was met by a hive of activity. Tray after little tray of food was being unpacked from the cardboard boxes, some placed on the side and others stacked in the fridge.

"This is your turkey," the original voice suddenly informed me, and I turned to inspect the bird. "It won't fit in your fridge. Do you have anywhere else…?"

Thankfully, the front door opened before I had to come up with an answer, and Dan and the kids bounded in.

"Ah, the food's here," Dan enthused, and immediately took charge of placing the turkey into storage. The kids rushed at me, sporting tinselly bopper-headbands and chocolate-covered mouths, and told me all about the fabulous time they had had at the Christmas market.

"Dan says we're going to have a big party tonight," Josh gushed, and Emily nodded, her shiny boppers accentuating her every move.

"Are we now?" I asked. "I was beginning to get that impression."

Dan flashed me a look across the kitchen. "Only a *little* party," he corrected. "Only with the band.

"Ah. Only the band," I repeated.

"Well, and their families. They're due to arrive any minute—"

He never got time to utter the "now" as the doorbell rang again. Dan laughed. "That'll be them. You might want to…" He gestured loosely at my dressing gown attire. I let out a gasp and scurried up the stairs as quickly as my feet would carry me.

"Party…party…he never mentioned a party, what am I supposed to wear? I didn't bring any clothes for a party," I muttered under my breath as I sorted through the small amount of clothes I had brought. "Jeans and a top will have to do." Holding up my current favorite black top shot through with golden thread, I shrugged and got on with getting dressed and made-up.

When I got back downstairs, the caterers had left, the band and their families had arrived, and Dan was busy administering a game of charades in the lounge. Darren, Joe, and Mick sat on one side while their wives or partners sat on the other. We were obviously playing in teams. The kids—mine and Joe's and Mick's—were playing with a train set that had materialized under the Christmas tree, and with the fire going and Christmas music playing, it looked like the perfect seasonal soiree.

The afternoon passed in a riot of laughter, food, and music. I couldn't remember the last time I had felt so at ease on this day. Perhaps it was because the universe of comparison was so far removed from anything Steve and I might have done. Perhaps it was because this group of people was linked to a time in my life before Steve. Or perhaps it was simply because everybody was having a genuinely fabulous time. When the kids began to get restless, Dan and Mick started carrying in platters of food, and there was everything imaginable to please little and grown-up gourmets.

Joe opened a couple bottles of bubbly, and everyone sang "We Wish You A Merry Christmas." The kids clamored for a taste of the 'fizzy drinks' and, taking my lead from the other parents, I let Josh and Emily have the tiniest of sips each. Josh pretended to like it. Emily scrunched up her nose and sneezed, the bubbles having caught right at the back of her mouth. Everybody laughed with her, and she gave a little ballerina twirl. Two-and-a-half years old, and already an accomplished entertainer.

It seemed natural, somehow, to be at Dan's side, and there seemed nothing wrong with the fact that his arm would wrap around my waist occasionally, that he should pull me into him with a laugh when we all toasted a Happy Christmas and sang another carol. Nobody commented, nobody even seemed to notice, and I filed the sudden feeling of 'couple-ness' for later analysis, alongside all the other bits of emotion already germinating at the back of my mind.

By nine-thirty, all the kids were drooping, and, one by one, the band members and their families called it a night, leaving among many hugs and kisses and best wishes for the festive season. Dan carried a drowsy Josh upstairs while I took care of Emily. The two of them were so exhausted, they barely noticed the new bedroom that Dan had prepared for them and simply curled up under the duvets with sleepy goodnight kisses for us. I shut the door gently behind me and followed Dan back downstairs, where he had already begun to tidy up the debris of the party.

"Hello, gorgeous." Dan stopped what he was doing and smiled at me. "You look wonderful tonight. Did you have a nice evening?"

I crossed the room to give him a hug. "I had a fabulous evening. The best. Thank you!"

Dan returned the hug and we held on to each other for a fraction of a second too long. I cleared my throat and pulled away before I found myself incapable of letting go altogether.

"Now then...where shall we start?"

Dan rallied, too. "Let's collect up all the rubbish, first, and then carry the dishes into the kitchen. It'll only take a few minutes, you'll see."

We worked in companionable silence, the music turned low and a glass of wine on the go each.

"I love the bedrooms, by the way," I suddenly burst out, remembering that I hadn't thanked him for the generous makeover. "You didn't have to do that."

Dan set down his rubbish bag. "I know that," he admonished. "But I wanted to. Nobody ever stays here anymore apart from you." He scratched his head and smiled, then sat down on the sofa and pulled me down next to him.

"It's not like in the old days before, you know, everyone had families. When the band would camp out here for days on end, and we'd have wild, raucous parties. That doesn't happen anymore. Not very often, at least." He grinned to soften the inadvertent melancholy in his comment. "I guess we've all moved on. And the only people that stay here regularly are you guys, the Jones family, my...my borrowed family. I wanted you to have a little bit of a home here so that when you *do* stay, it's...well, it's nice for you. Especially for the kids. I mean, blow-up beds are great, but..."

He faltered and ran a hand through his hair. "I'm not...I'm not suggesting anything. I just...simply...well, I could make the rooms more beautiful for you, so I thought, why not?"

"They are beautiful," I assured him. "I love them. Just you wait until the kids wake up in the morning and take in the change properly. They'll be so excited, they'll never want to go home."

I felt a bit woozy and let my body sag against Dan's for a moment. Dan put his arm around my shoulder, and I relaxed into him even more. It seemed the...natural thing to do.

"We'll cross that bridge when we come to it," my rock star suggested and hugged me closer. I closed my eyes for a moment, enjoying the sensation. The fire was still crackling gently in the grate and there was a distinct hint of Christmas magic in the air. Never mind the bin bags lined up in a neat row by the door, and the piles of plates stacked on the coffee table waiting to be taken through to the kitchen.

Dan caressed my face with the ball of his thumb, tracing my cheek, my eyebrows, lightly touching my nose.

"Mmmh mmmh." I made soft noises of enjoyment, and Dan turned me around so I half lay on him. "Mmmmh mmmmh mmmhhh," I responded and Dan kissed me.

His hands were all over my body, on my back, in my hair, under my top, on my breasts. It was amazing how swiftly his hands could move, and every stroke, every touch sent a delicious tingle through me. In turn, I covered his face in kisses and ran my hands up his chest, alighting on his nipples, still hidden under his shirt, and tweaking them teasingly. Dan went wild and bucked beneath me, grinding his hardness into my loins.

"It...is...a...good...thing that...we...are...still...dressed," he panted between heavy breaths. "Otherwise I...wouldn't be...accountable...for... my actions."

"Is that so?" I teased, and removed my top with one swift moment. Dan groaned and pulled me down onto him, licking my nipples then sucking them until I practically melted with desire. I was hot and cold all over and could feel my ladyship dancing through my jeans. We writhed and turned and fell off the sofa, landing on the floor with a loud crash and sending a pile of plates flying. Nothing could have killed the sexual moment between us faster than the resulting explosion of noise, and we sat side by side as if frozen, waiting to hear if we had woken the kids.

Gradually, my breathing slowed and eventually I dared to look Dan in the eye.

"Sorry about the plates," I muttered.

"No need to apologize," Dan retorted. "Goodness knows where we would have taken each other if we hadn't fallen off the sofa."

"On the sofa, presumably," I deadpanned, but was met with a blank stare.

"We would have taken each other on the sofa," I elaborated.

Dan raised an eyebrow. "Would we now?" he mused. "And would that have been a good idea?"

"It would have been naughty," I surmised.

"*Very* naughty," Dan agreed, the lightness in his voice belying the meaning of the words. Suddenly he turned serious. "And are we quite ready for *very naughty* yet?"

I picked at the hem of my black top, which I had swiftly pulled back over my head when we unleashed the wave of noise into the house.

"I don't know," I replied at length. "Are we?"

Dan didn't respond at first. He scrunched up his forehead and rubbed his hand across it. "Do you know, this reminds me of something…" He shot me a grin. "Do you remember that time on the coach? That was *just* as awkward."

I giggled. "It certainly was."

"At least you can't fob me off with that virgin excuse again." Once again, Dan spoke lightly, but there was a probing undertone.

"Um…no." Taking a deep breath, I took the plunge. I didn't exactly know I would do so, but the words came out before I could stop them. "And I don't know how long the widow excuse will stand up, now."

There. I had said it. Not one but two raised eyebrows met this comment, and the look on Dan's face was priceless. After a small eternity, he cleared his voice. "Well…uh. *Hrgg.* Maybe…maybe we've…uh…pushed the limits far enough tonight, don't you think?"

He rose abruptly and busied himself with collecting plates. "I'll just take those through to the kitchen, and we should probably take care of the breakage, too."

I fell to my knees, starting to pick up broken bits of plate.

"Don't!" Dan's voice made me jump. "That's not what I meant. I don't want you…er…inflicting injury on yourself. I'm going to get the dustpan and brush and…"

"Well, now *that* reminds me of something else as well," I chortled, and the awkward atmosphere finally passed.

"Oh, yes. The champagne glasses at that wedding." Dan laughed, too. "Well, then you'll remember I'm good with a dustpan and brush. You carry those other plates into the kitchen, and I'll be right back."

"Yes, sir." I gave a mock salute and clicked my heels together, earning myself a leftover piece of quiche flung accurately at my face.

"You deserved that," Dan justified, fleeing into the kitchen before I could take aim with a soggy napkin.

Chapter Forty-Six

"*Mummy!* Mummy-mummy-mummy!" Both my children's voices penetrated my consciousness, and I stole a quick glance at the alarm clock at my brand new princess bedside table. Six thirty a.m. Not bad for Christmas morning.

"*Dan!*" My offspring were demanding the attention of the other adult in the house, too. "Dan, Dan-Dan-Dan! Mummy, Dan, look what happened!"

There was a faint voice of hysteria in the kids' voices, and I suddenly realized that they weren't even coming from downstairs, which is where I thought they would be. I jumped out of bed, clutching my sore head to steady my vision, grabbed my dressing gown, and raced the few steps down the hallway to the children's bedroom, nearly colliding with Dan who looked to be in the same state.

After we had finished tidying up the previous night, Dan had opened another bottle and we joyfully arranged the children's presents under the Christmas tree, some from me, but some also, I had been touched to note, from Dan. In fact, his presents seemed larger than mine! Mission accomplished, we had snuggled up on the sofa and watched a Christmas movie together, and it was quite late by the time we finally went up to our respective beds.

We exchanged a glance and Dan pushed open the door. Josh and Emily were bouncing on their beds, clutching a stocking each, and wearing the biggest smiles imaginable.

"Santa bringed stockings…" Emily waved a rather large and bulky-looking stocking about. She could barely lift it in her little hands.

Dan nudged me in the side to stop me from saying something stupid.

"That was awfully good of Santa," he said for my benefit, and I wanted to hug him. Fancy him remembering what the kids' negligent mother had forgotten!

"And Santa brought us a whole new bedroom," Josh enthused. "Look, new beds and everything. Isn't it cool? Can we just live here now?"

Dan sat down on Emily's bed and pulled the children onto his lap. "Actually," he said, "you might not have noticed it last night, but it wasn't Santa who brought your new bedroom. That's a little out of his remit."

"His what?" Josh was quick to pounce on the unfamiliar word.

I leaned against the doorjamb and folded my arms across my chest, curious to see how Dan would handle the situation.

"His…er… responsibilities. It's not exactly what Santa does, but he did bring the stockings. Look."

"Who did the room?" Josh persisted.

Dan shifted uncomfortably. "I did. Well, I had it done, for you, because I wanted you to have a nice bedroom here."

"It's nice, much better than our room at home," Josh supplied, keen to please Dan and utterly unaware about the dagger he was driving through my heart. I cringed.

"Now, I think you have a fabulous bedroom at home, and this is just your away bedroom for…when you stay here. Which isn't all the time, 'cause your home is…at home." He threw me an apologetic glance for the lame finish, then resorted to diversionary tactics. He had learned from the best—me!

"Don't you want to have a look in your stockings? And… do you reckon perhaps Father Christmas might have left something downstairs?"

Well done, that man. With great whoops of joy, the kids swooped downstairs, clutching their unopened stockings, to see whether Santa had visited. And of course, he had.

"How'd you manage to light the candles before we got down here?" I whispered to Dan while the kids enthused about the pretty tree with the stack of presents underneath.

"I set my alarm for six," Dan whispered back. "You said they'd be up!"

I grinned. "Thank you. This is magical!"

"You're quite welcome." He smiled back, his eyes dancing. "Merry Christmas."

"And Merry Christmas to you, too," I added.

We let the children unwrap their presents before breakfast. There really was no stopping them, but we made them take their time and look at one present in turn. I had knitted Dan a long stripy scarf, and Dan surprised me by giving me a lovely scarf-hat-and-gloves combo from my favorite shop.

"Great minds," he chortled as he wrapped his scarf around his neck, and I giggled, too. I was relieved that Dan's gift was a small and innocent one. I had been worried that he might do his usual over-the-top all-out treat-Sophie routine, and I would have felt uncomfortable with that, especially given all he had already done for us. But he had read my mind and kept it simple. For that reason alone, I felt a little tearful and desperately in need of a hug, but I put on my hat and scarf instead and gave a little bow.

"Now all we need is some snow to try out our new winter attire and it'll be perfect," I joked.

Dan jumped up with alacrity. "We haven't even pulled the curtains yet," he exclaimed and rectified the matter as he spoke. I sucked in my breath, feeling my heart soar. Before he could even tell me, I knew from the bright quality of the light that spilled into the room that it had, in fact, snowed overnight.

"Oh my God!" I squealed and joined him at the window.

It hadn't just snowed the normal light London dusting of tiny flakes. It had snowed good and proper, and everything was white. In fact, more of the heavenly stuff was still falling, and it was quite magical. Alerted by my apparent joy, the kids joined us at the window, and, for a moment, all four of us contemplated the winter wonderland outside Dan's window.

"This is, like, the best Christmas *ever*," Josh declared.

"Snow, snow, snow," Emily sang, taking quite after her mother in her love for the elusive white stuff.

"Can we go sledging?" Josh begged, tugging at Dan's pajama sleeve.

"Of course, little man," Dan agreed. "But how's about some breakfast first? And I suppose we better get dressed, too. It looks quite cold out there!"

And so it was, after a scrumptious and quite leisurely breakfast, we togged up, all four of us — Dan and I sporting our respective Christmas gifts — and went out in the snow. By some small miracle, Dan discovered an ancient wooden sledge in his attic, and we took turns pulling the children on the snowy pavement on our way to Clapham Common in search of the tiniest remnant of a hill or a slope that might be suitable for sledging. After an hour's energetic sledging, we returned to Dan's house and built a snowman in the garden. Quite suddenly, Dan remembered that he had forgotten to put the turkey in the oven and dashed inside frantically. I gave the kids firm instructions to play nicely and followed him inside.

In the kitchen, Dan was wrestling the turkey into the oven. "Fit, damn it, or I will make you," he admonished the obstinate bird.

I giggled. "It'll never cook," I offered, somewhat unhelpfully, but Dan wasn't perturbed.

"It doesn't have to cook," he replied. "It's already cooked. It just needs to heat through again."

I cast a look at the kitchen clock. "It's nearly midday. When will we be able to eat?"

"Oh, about two o'clock, I should think," Dan declared. "Enough time to warm up, play a few games, and have some mulled wine."

"What about the veg? You know, potatoes, sprouts, that kind of thing? Do you need me to get peeling?"

"It's all taken care of," Dan reiterated. "All the trimmings will go in the other oven about half an hour before we eat. Easy." He wiped his hands at his apron and gave the oven door an energetic shove. "There. Done."

And so it was. A catered and already-prepared Christmas dinner was a real revelation. I marveled when Dan opened trays of sprouts with pancetta, crispy-looking roast potatoes cooked in goose fat, little cocktail sausages, baby carrots and peas smothered in garlic oil, Yorkshire puddings, and, of course, gravy and cranberry sauce. The bird, when it came out of the oven, looked and smelled fantastic, and the children um'd and ah'd. Miraculously, they ate too, tucking into a little bit of everything except for sprouts.

Dan observed our mini gourmets with wry amusement. "They're doing well," he whispered sotto voce, lest he break the spell.

"I think it must be all that cold, fresh air and vigorous exercise," I replied, equally softly. "Note to self—wear little monsters out before feeding them big feast!"

After lunch, Josh and Emily went back outside for half an hour to add to their family of snowmen, then came inside to watch "The Snowman" on the telly.

"I haven't watched this in *years*," Dan enthused. "I'd forgotten all about it, in fact."

"Ah, well, Christmas with kids, it brings back all those memories. I give you ten minutes before you're on the floor with Josh building his Lego police station."

"What a brilliant idea!" Dan dropped to the floor and tickled Josh. "Hey, young man, shall we take a look at that Lego of yours?"

So the boys did boy things and us girls played with Emily's new dolls and doll house, and the afternoon passed in a contented, warm haze. I was glad we were there, with Dan, the children's godfather. We hadn't had a Christmas like this before, ever. It was as close to perfect as I could imagine it being, all things considered.

Chapter Forty-Seven

"Merry Christmas," Dan toasted once again after we had put the children to bed and re-lit the fire in the lounge. "Thank you for a wonderful day."

"And thank you, too," I responded, hearing the emotion in my own voice. "It was fabulous. We had such a great time. It was...perfect." I swallowed the 'nearly' before it could come out.

"You look radiant," my rock star commented. "I haven't seen you looking like this for a long time."

Trying to hide my embarrassment at this unexpected compliment, I took a large sip of wine to buy myself some time.

"Thank you," I eventually offered. "I *feel* good. It was almost magical, you know, with the snow and the candles and the kids so happy."

"Only almost?" Dan teased.

"Well...uh...it sounds so weird saying something was magical. Soppy, you know." I tried and failed to explain my feelings.

"Soppy?" Dan smiled widely. "This is getting better and better. Why soppy?"

"Not soppy," I corrected. "Because, you know, I stayed rational. Adult."

Dan waggled his head from side to side. "Yeah. Indeed. You've still got those feelings of yours in a stranglehold."

I set my glass down on the coffee table with more care than was warranted and turned to face him. "And what's that supposed to mean?"

Instead of a response, Dan, too, placed his wine glass on the table, then lunged and tickled me. "I watched you, Sophie Jones. You very nearly let yourself have a perfect day today. I wish you'd just let go!"

He caught the soft spot on the right side of my back, and I giggled helplessly as he dug his index finger in deeper.

"That's better," he commented, mercilessly persisting with his tickling.

I was flailing wildly, and my hand caught hold of a sofa cushion. I grabbed it eagerly and used it to bash Dan on the head.

"Oi! Wench! Right, you want a fight..." Dan snorted with laughter as he, too, got hold of the nearest cushion and started hitting back. We got to our feet and circled the coffee table, feigning here and there like sword fighters. Suddenly, Dan took a flying leap and hop-stepped over the table, tackling me to the floor and pinning my hands above my head in one swift motion.

"Do you surrender?"

"Never surrender, *never* give up," I panted, straining to breathe as Dan lay atop me. He mock-roared.

"Actually, that wasn't right, I meant to say — "

I never got an opportunity to correct myself as Dan pressed his lips onto mine. Skin connected with skin, warmth flooding warmth, and his tongue caressed my mouth until I yielded and let our tongues dance together. A corner of my mind rapidly went over the spatial arrangements in the house. The kids were in their room upstairs, passed out with exhaustion from the day, and their door firmly closed for once. The lounge door was closed, too. We were on the rug in front of the fireplace—handy how *that* had happened—and the sofas probably shielded us from immediate view, in case anyone *should* enter the lounge. Short of locking ourselves in, we were as safe as we could be in a house with two young children. Finally, I gave myself up, in every sense of the word.

Dan ran his hands through my hair and down the side of my face, raising himself onto his elbows and planting light kisses all over my cheeks. His eyes were wide and mellow, and they shone with that very special light that I had seen only a few times before, a long time ago. Without speaking, he tugged at my jumper and pushed it up to reveal a dainty, lacy bra. He raised his eyebrows in appreciation.

"Beautiful though it is, it shall have to come off," he murmured. He slid his hand under my back to undo the clasp and tugged at the straps until he exposed my breasts. *There.* Lust was written all over his face, but he paused and examined me silently for a minute. I could feel a vein pulsing impatiently under the delicate skin of my suprasternal notch but I lay completely still, almost submissive. Abruptly, Dan discarded the redundant garment with a flourish so that it landed elegantly onto the sofa. Then he looked at me some more, drinking me in with his eyes.

My breathing grew ragged and shallow. The burst of air on my skin made my nipples harden and pucker, and they stood out proud and pink like little rose buds. Slowly and teasingly, Dan bent forward until his mouth hovered above my breasts. His eyes held mine all the while. I swallowed hard and licked my lips.

Dan moaned and licked his own lips. Then he inclined his head so his mouth could reach my nipples and his tousled hair fell on my face. I closed my eyes.

Lazily at first, Dan flicked his tongue over one, then the other nipple, alternating between the two until I pulled his head down and held him in place so he could have a good taste of one at a time. *More. I wanted more.*

I shifted beneath him and raised my hips to meet with his loin. There it was, his delicious hardness pressed against me again but protected, as before, by two layers of jeans. I ground against it impatiently.

Dan got my meaning and ceased his nipple titillation. He sat back on his haunches. With a gentle, determined experience, he unbuttoned my jeans and pulled them down over my hips. His eyes searched mine; *is this okay?* I nodded, and the trousers came away completely.

"Yours, too," I whispered, my voice surprisingly hoarse, and Dan obediently, if all too slowly, removed his own. His thick hardness sprang forth, hot and defined against the pale skin of his belly. I gasped and giggled.

"You went commando? On the coldest day of the year?"

Dan lowered himself down onto me, and his rock hard erection pressed against my naked abdomen. The shockwaves spread from the point of impact until it felt like I had red-hot lava coursing my veins. I grew dizzy with desire, my heart pounding fast and my breath echoing in my ears.

"Of course I didn't go commando on the coldest day of the year," my rock star breathed into my ear. "I...just felt a bit...needy earlier and..."

He didn't finish his confession, but thrust himself inside me, almost brutally, then withdrew slowly, slowly, until I could feel my own moistness letting him go. I moaned in protest.

"Shh," Dan soothed, then once more grasped one of my nipples between his teeth. He bit down just enough to hold it and tugged, tugged until I couldn't take any more.

"Do it," I begged. "Just do it. Do it now."

In response, Dan placed his hand over my mouth to stifle my cries and finally entered me all over again, slower this time, with controlled determination, until I bucked and rose to meet him. We joined completely and lay down together, his manly weight overwhelming me, his hips grinding strong and powerful against mine. Stars exploded behind my closed eyelids and all awareness of my surroundings, of my past, my future, my present, faded into nothingness as wave after wave of pleasure rolled over me.

Chapter Forty-Eight

"Are you okay? You look…different. Like the cat who had the cream." Rachel held me at arm's length and observed me critically. "You're positively radiant. There's a certain glow to you. I *know* that glow. Have you —"

Her eyes widened and she drew in a breath, swiveling her gaze from me to Dan and back again. Dan, I noted, looked studiously casual. *Bad tell.*

"How's about you let us in," I suggested as it was still snowing and freezing cold. "Happy Boxing Day!" I gave her a quick peck on the cheek and pushed past her to get into the warmth.

"I'll speak to you later," she threatened, then stood back to let Dan and the kids in.

Rachel's house was a funfair of bright Christmas decorations hung in unusual places. I bumped my head on several ornaments as I was walking through the hallway, and Alex smiled apologetically.

"They're hung low so Henry can see them," he greeted me, hugging me and planting a mulled-wine scented kiss on my cheek.

"Oh...right." I resisted the urge to smack myself on the forehead and reminded myself that I, too, had once been a new parent trying to pander to my infant's every cognitive need. "Good idea." I smiled and sidestepped another low-hanging seasonal implement on my way to the kitchen.

Alex poured me a mug of mulled wine, and Dan and Rachel joined us. There was a short awkward silence as we four adults stood around contemplating each other, but then the oven timer went off and Rachel sprang into action.

"I made a gammon joint," she explained. "Everyone loves ham, right?" We nodded our assent and she continued assembling the meal.

"It's been such a long time since we've seen you properly. So glad you could make it." She stopped in her food preparation and raised her mug. "Happy Christmas."

"Happy Christmas," the rest of us chorused, and I offered to help with the food while the men laid the table.

All through the afternoon, I caught Rachel looking at me when she thought I wouldn't notice, and she would smile indulgently, like a mother hen who is watching her chick take off for the first time. Once or twice, she went on a fishing expedition, but I didn't take the bait, and Dan deflected her not-so-subtle questions like a Teflon shield.

"I think Sophie quite enjoyed sleeping in her new guest bed," he answered deadpan when Rachel asked if we had spent a *nice night* together. What he didn't add was that he had enjoyed it, too. And when Rachel went all out, declaring that there was a definite aura of *lurve* around us, Dan toasted her back. "There certainly is, my sweet. To *lurve* and the magic of Christmas." He winked at me over his glass, but this little clue Rachel failed to notice.

At the end of the day, Dan took us back to his house as though it was the most normal thing in the world. I hadn't planned on a stay this long, and we were all running low on clothes, so Dan offered to stuff everything in the washer and have it dry by the morning. "I suppose I could drive you to your house," he said, "but truth be told, I really don't want to. It's too cozy in here, and I'm too lazy."

Needless to say, the kids loved going back to Dan's house and all their new toys, and for the next few days, we once again led a quasi-family existence. Dan and I were physically addicted to each other as if making up for lost time, which, in a way, we were. Nothing was said, nothing was discussed, the 'L' word wasn't mentioned by either of us, but it was present at all times, and we both knew it. It was as if, by mutual unspoken agreement, neither of us wanted to break the spell we had magically found ourselves under again.

By New Year's Eve, Dan and I couldn't even be bothered to keep up a separate bedroom charade for the kids. They saw us hug and kiss—gently, on the lips only—and they responded well to this new level of connection between me, their mummy, and Dan, their...godfather. In fact, 'responded well' didn't quite capture it. They were positively blossoming with the attention lavished upon them by Dan.

I couldn't quite put my finger on it, but they seemed calmer, somehow, less clingy, less in need of constant reassurance. Or perhaps that was an illusion created by the simple fact that there was somebody other than me they could lean on, and therefore, they didn't rely on me quite so much.

Having learned the hard way to take life as it came, I refused to overanalyze these developments or fret about the consequences when Dan would disappear on tour in January. We hadn't discussed this subject in great length yet, but we didn't need to. It was clearly marked on the Tuscq-themed calendar for the coming year that had appeared in the kitchen during our Christmas stay. *U.S. Tour* started on January second and ran all the way into April. I knew that because I had checked when Dan wasn't looking. And even then, I had refused to let my heart sink. This was how it was, how it would be, always.

"Isn't it funny how life alters your perception of things?" I challenged myself while I was brushing my teeth the night I found out about the impending tour. "You turned Dan down because of exactly this...and now you're living it anyway." I offered a wry smile to my reflection in the mirror.

How true that was. All those years ago in Paris, after Dan had proposed, I had imagined what our life would be like, and I had concluded that I couldn't cope with all the absences. "Although," I pointed out, stabbing my toothbrush in the air triumphantly, "I always assumed there would be infidelity." Imagined adultery on Dan's part had been the definite deal breaker, back then.

"But there most categorically isn't, now." I whispered this last part, struck by a sudden realization. Yes, Dan had had many other women while I had known him. He *had* been a serial womanizer and had never made a secret of it. Yet, while I had featured in his life, while I had a starring role, there hadn't been a single transgression. Well, all right, there had been *one*, in Paris, after he proposed and before he knew my answer. But he was younger then, and anyway, that was water under the bridge. The point was, since he had looked after the Jones family of three, he had not had a girlfriend. The other women had simply vanished.

How come I hadn't noticed this before? Suddenly, I had to hold onto the sink for support. I could deal with absences. I could deal with tours and recording and performances. I would talk the children through it, make them understand that Dan's spells away from us were only temporary. I had always known I could figure all that out as long as he was *mine*. And it seemed like...he...just *might* be. Maybe. If I didn't mess it up all over again.

My hands shook so badly I couldn't finish brushing my teeth, so I rinsed my mouth out instead. Now that I had the knowledge, what would I do with it?

"You all right?"

Dan's voice startled me. I hadn't heard him come in and I jumped, sloshing water all over me. Dan snuggled into my back, wrapping his hands around my waist, resting his head on my shoulder to peer at me in the mirror. I laughed.

"I'm fine. I was just...I didn't hear you come up the stairs." I broke eye contact and shifted my body. I hadn't quite recovered from my blinding insight yet, and I certainly wasn't ready to share.

He turned me around and enveloped me in his arms again.

"I've had the most magical time." He nuzzled my neck, and I could feel him getting excited.

"Me, too," I agreed. Unspoken words hung between us, and Dan kissed their weight away.

"Tomorrow is New Year's Eve," he whispered in between planting kisses all over my face.

"I know," I giggled.

"Will you come to the show?"

I pulled back, scrutinizing his face. He had mentioned the New Year's Eve show when he first came back from his stay in Devon, and I had duly filed the knowledge for future reference, wondering whether I could, whether I *should* go. Of course I wanted to, *but*. And there were the kids to consider…

Dan mistook my hesitation for concern. "It's only a half-set," he told me once again. "I'm not going to overdo it. It's a short hour, and it's a small venue we've booked for an invitation-only gig in Covent Garden. It's not like a massive arena…"

I placed my finger over his lips. "I know all that," I reassured him. "I just…I'd love to come. I'll see if I can get a sitter."

Dan recoiled in horror, his eyes as wide as saucers. "*No!*"

For the second time in ten minutes, I jumped. Dan was contrite. "Sorry, that came out a bit loud. But no, don't hire a sitter. Bring the kids."

My turn to recoil. "Bring the kids? To a licensed venue? They're only two and four. I'll get done for…something. Plus it'll be too noisy." Emily became very distressed when exposed to loud noise of any kind.

"You can sit in the private family area. And they can wear earplugs or…" He grinned, suddenly. "I know! Joe figured this out years ago for his own children. They can wear those little cute kids' earmuffs and they'll be just fine. They come in pink, blue, or yellow…" He petered out, and I laughed.

"You do know your way 'round a child's mind these days," I commented. "Kids' earmuffs, indeed. They might work, though."

I scratched my head, feeling excitement bubbling inside me. It would be *awesome* to see the show and take the kids along. They had never really seen Dan in action.

"And you're sure that's okay?"

Dan nodded. "No problem. I'm fairly sure Joe and Mick will bring their kids, too, and…" He waved a hand to stave off my obvious comment. "I know they're a little bit older, but it's going to be all right. And if it all goes horribly wrong, I'll have a limo ready to take you home."

Ah. Now there was a thought.

"Speaking of…what happens after the gig? I mean…" I caught myself, twiddling with my hair, uncertain how to proceed. This was the tricky territory I had always been worried about. I didn't want to sound like a whiny wife. But I did want to know whether Dan would be coming home with us, or shortly after us, or whether he would be out partying all night.

Dan planted a kiss on my nose. "Sweetie, you are so cute when you're trying to be cool. In the past, as you well know, we used to do an all-night show with a party lasting into the New Year."

"Uh huh. I know." *That was why I was asking.* I recalled the gig Steve and I had attended together, the one where Dan had conned me onto the stage to sing. That seemed a lifetime ago.

"But things are different this year for obvious reasons. And afterwards, everybody's doing their own thing. I suspect the rest of the band will disappear off home, too. You know, what with the tour and the traveling…" He shook his head, realizing too late we hadn't discussed that yet. "Anyway," he ploughed on swiftly, "I'll come back with you after the show. We'll all come here, you, me, and the kids. He pulled me close and held me tight. "What do you think?"

"I think it sounds fabulous," I finally confessed. "Roll on tomorrow."

Part Three:
Finale

Chapter Forty-Nine

"This next song goes out to Sophie and my lovely godchildren, Emily and Josh."

The crowd roared then hushed as the stage was momentarily clad in darkness. Josh jumped up and down next to me, waving and shouting "Dan, Dan." I had to hold on to Emily's jumper lest she climb over the balcony railing.

We were sitting in a cordoned-off area on the mezzanine with the other band members' partners and their children. My kids were proudly wearing protective earmuffs, Josh's blue and Emily's a predictable pink. They were a loan from Joe, whose children had outgrown the need.

A spotlight picked out Dan, and Josh's cries went up another frenzied pitch, carrying clearly above the muted murmurings of the expectant fans. Dan waved in our direction and blew us a kiss, and the crowd laughed. Dan played to the audience.

"The next generation. Love him to bits," he grinned, lowering his guitar momentarily. "I should point out that he's here with his mummy, and he *will* be going to bed soon."

"*No I won't,*" Josh yelled back, and the audience erupted in laughter again. I could feel my cheeks flaming in the dark, and Joe's wife, Ellen, nudged me affectionately.

"They're lapping it up," she whispered. "It's good for them."

She didn't elaborate whether she meant the fans or the band, and I didn't get a chance to ask as Dan started strumming the guitar. I pulled Emily off the railing and gathered her in my arms. Together, we listened to one of my favorite Tuscq ballads, and for some inexplicable reason, I found myself welling up with tears.

Though I had been skeptical until the last minute, it had been a wonderful idea to bring the children. The presence of the other band members' families had meant we hadn't stuck out like sore thumbs and also reassured me I wasn't a bad mother for taking my children to a rock concert. Josh and Emily had been excited beyond belief and absorbed the atmosphere with wide-eyed enjoyment. They would probably treasure this memory all their lives. To begin with, they had been incredulous that the showman on the stage, singing and rocking and projecting an amazing presence, had been *their* Dan. I reckoned he had moved from hero to God-status in their little eyes, and would remain there forever more.

Emily wrapped her arms around my neck. "Mummy sing this song at home," she informed me and I squeezed her gently.

"I sure do," I confirmed. "It's one of my favorites."

"Me like it, too." My daughter beamed at me, then put her head on my shoulder and plugged in her thumb. Somebody was getting tired. I rocked her in time to the music. The show was nearly over. It was almost ten o'clock, and my baby girl would be in bed within the hour. Very late, but not unreasonable for New Year's Eve.

At ten to ten, the band invited their fans to join in with a rocking rendition of "Auld Lang Syne" and Dan wished everyone all the best for the coming year. "See you on tour, I promise!" he shouted before launching the band into the final song of the night, Tuscq's very first number one.

The crowd went wild and everybody danced and sang along at full volume, even the kids and partners in the family area, including my erstwhile sleepy Emily. The night went out on a bang, and, even though the concert had been short, I experienced that familiar, delicious euphoria of having taken part in something really special.

We retreated to the backstage area and waited for Dan to come find us. We didn't have to wait long, and it made my heart lift with joy to see my rock star back to his usual, glowing, buzzing self. His eyes shone with delight, and every fiber of his being oozed post-show exhilaration, that fantastic, addictive high that made the musicians go back time and time again.

Dan enveloped me in a hug and gave me a smacking kiss on the lips, then scooped the children up, too, and thanked them for coming. Within minutes, he had security whisk us outside and into the waiting limo, and we were home at his house by ten thirty.

Together, we put the children to bed, having had a quick, secret exchange as to whether or not to leave them up until midnight. On balance, they were too far gone to remain upright for another hour and a half, and we decided to end their evening on a high note rather than a tired temper tantrum. Of course, they mounted a protest, but they were rather half-hearted about it and fell asleep while we were still singing their customary bedtime song.

"Imagine that," I whispered as we shut the children's bedroom door. "Having a lullaby sung to you by a world-famous rock star. These kids have no idea how lucky they are."

Dan kissed me on the ear. "It appears their mummy does, though. Know how lucky *they* are, and possibly even how lucky *she* is."

"Am I?"

"Aren't you?" Dan's eyes brimmed with meaning, and I held him tight.

"I guess I must be."

The innuendo was flying thick and fast, and I savored the moment. I loved flirting with this rock star of mine, even though we were arguably well beyond the flirting stage. Again.

"But is it my lucky night?"

"It could be," Dan retorted. "Do you want it to be?"

I feigned nonchalance. "Well, if you're offering…"

He swept me off my feet and carried me to the bedroom, closing the door firmly behind us. There were fireworks for the New Year at Dan's house, in more ways than one. And I rather liked them all.

The mood changed drastically over the next few days. According to the calendar, the band was supposed to have left for the States on January second, but a delay in the visa process meant the travel date was pushed back five days. Jack was furious, and Dan was stressed. While the tour itself wouldn't start until March, the delay impacted recording time that had been booked and also reduced rehearsal time. Dan filled me in on these developments on New Year's Day, and we had a long chat about how long he would be gone, where he would be going, and how he would stay in touch while the band was Stateside.

"I'll miss you," Dan stated over a glass of wine on the evening of New Year's Day. "It'll be so hard. Harder than ever. You have no idea…"

"I'll miss you, too," I confessed, suppressing tears. "And so will the kids. But that's how it is, and…" I shrugged, unable to complete the sentence.

"I know." Dan took my hand. "I know, my love, I know. I remember the talk we had on that plane back from Paris. I've been replaying it in my head over and over again, word for word."

I swallowed. *He remembered?*

Dan touched my chin with his finger so I would look him in the eye. "I need you to understand something, Sophie." His turn to swallow and clear his throat. "Things have changed. I still make music, obviously, but…but you won't…wouldn't be second to the music, the tours, the albums. I don't want to hurt you, or the kids. And there certainly are no other women. I—"

"You recall all that? Every word I said?" I was incredulous.

Dan nodded. "As I said, they've been playing on my mind these past few weeks while I've been getting ready for this tour. I *have* to go, but…I will be in touch as much as I can, I promise. There will be no funny business with anyone and… And you can see me every day. Look."

He pulled a gift-wrapped box out from under the sofa and gave it to me.

"What's this?"

"Open it and see."

I tore at the pretty Christmas wrapping until I got to the box. It was a tablet. I sucked in a breath.

"*Dan!* I thought we weren't doing big presents for Christmas."

He chuckled. "It's not a Christmas present. It's a staying-in-touch present. Look, it's got Skype all ready and set up. You can connect wherever you are, the Internet contract's up and running, and it doesn't matter where you or the kids are. You can always take my call and see me, or the other way 'round. Any time of day or night. Except on stage, of course." He grinned.

"See? I don't want you to feel alone. I *have* to leave, but I'm taking you with me. Sort of." He gave a little start and assumed a faraway look, as though he had an idea, but the moment passed and he carried on talking.

"Please, you have to accept this. It'll be our lifeline and the few months will pass really quickly, and it'll almost be like we're all together. I don't want you to feel like you're second to my career, not for one single minute. Not anymore."

I smiled a tentative smile. His vision sounded so lovely, so brilliant, so easy, and it was tempting. At the end of the day, it wasn't like I had a choice, so I accepted the tablet and we amused ourselves having a play around with it to make sure it worked. And then we played with a few other buttons while we still could.

So instead of getting onto a plane on January second, the band went to ground in a London studio for a two-day marathon work-ahead session, and Dan only came home to grab a few hours' sleep. At least, that was what he told me. I couldn't know for sure because the kids and I had returned to our own home with the start of the new school term.

The upside of all this trauma was that Dan was around for Josh's fifth birthday on January seventh, a Saturday. He actually emerged from the studio for a few hours to be with the birthday boy. Alas, he had given us no warning, so the house was full of children when Dan turned up at our front door, dressed in his customary studio garb of jeans and shirt and carrying two enormous boxes.

Chapter Fifty

"Thank God you were here this afternoon. I couldn't have done this without you." I heaved a sigh of relief as I finished emptying the dishwasher for the second time. Dan, meanwhile, had taken down the decorations and hoovered all of downstairs.

He laughed. "Why didn't you *tell* me? We could have had some professional help."

"I don't *need* professional help to run a children's party, thank you very much. But a second pair of hands came in very handy!"

"I'll say," Dan commented. "Can't remember the last time I played DJ for musical bumps."

"And a fine job you did, too." I closed the cupboard door and threw myself at Dan, catching him slightly off guard. "Thank you."

"You're welcome. It was fun. I think Josh enjoyed it, as well."

"Josh *loved* it. He'll never forget this. You are quite the star."

I was still holding on to Dan, reluctant to let go, aware that I was being clingy.

"Do you think the children understood I'm going to be out of the picture for a while?" Dan mused. "I hope they do."

"They do. They will. As soon as we've had our first Skype call, all will be well. Trust me."

Dan had sat down with Josh and Emily before bedtime and explained about being away for some time. He had shown them the tablet and made the mistake of opening the games folder, after which the kids got so engrossed in Mario's adventures they didn't give Dan's impending departure another thought.

"And you will be all right? Will you cope?" Dan gave me a probing, knowing look.

I smiled my brightest smile. "Of course I will. I'll..." *Dare I say it again?* "I'll really miss you, though."

"Oh sweetheart, I'll miss you, too. You know that."

There wasn't really any good place to go from there, and we regarded each other in uncomfortable silence for a minute.

"God, I hate goodbyes," I finally burst out. "I never know what to say."

"I hate having to leave you right now," Dan confessed. "I wish there was more time but..."

"You have to pack and rest, and your flight is at seven a.m., I know. There's nothing for it."

"I could...I can always catch up on sleep on the plane?" Dan suggested with a glint of mischief in his eyes.

"You could, but you won't. Why start an exhausting trip already exhausted?"

"You sound like my mother." Dan belly laughed.

"I couldn't possibly comment on that, never having met your mother, but I'm sure I sound like *a* mother. It's amazing how kids alter your take on life."

"You're right, you're right," Dan concurred. "It's just that I can't get enough of you."

"And me of you either." We launched ourselves at each other by unspoken consent and clung to each other like there was no tomorrow. I could feel my resolve crumble. His strong arms, the scent of his skin, his breath against my face… Maybe…just perhaps…

"I'd better go then, before I forget myself." Dan's voice was hoarse and low. While his face looked composed, his clenched fists gave away his inner turmoil as he broke off our embrace.

I, too, took a step back, increasing the distance between us. The front of my body, deprived of Dan's heat, felt curiously cold and numb.

"Four months," I mumbled, suddenly overwhelmed by the length of separation.

"Three-and-a-half months only, and they'll go really quickly." Dan tried to put a positive spin on things but failed miserably.

"We'll have the tablet, and Skype," I rallied.

"And Facebook and email and texts and…"

"It'll be like we're not apart at all," we chorused together, but we didn't fool each other.

Dan hugged me again, briefly. "Bye, Sophie love," he murmured into my hair.

"Bye, Dan," I whispered in return, just barely preventing my voice from breaking.

We did a clumsy hip-joined sidestep to the front door and suddenly, I was desperate for him to go. I simply couldn't go on with this goodbye-ing malarkey any longer, or I would break down and cry. I fumbled with the door and opened it abruptly, my eyes brimming. Dan touched his thumb to my cheek and kissed my nose.

"I'll call you tomorrow," he promised. "From the airport. Before we board. Make sure you've got your phone on."

"I will." Somehow, this promise sounded tangible and made the impending four months seem less scary. We would speak tomorrow, after all. I would hear his voice.

Dan turned and walked down my front path, waving ever so often without looking back. It was dark outside, and his silhouette became indistinct in the obscure orange streetlight before he even reached his car. Tears filled my eyes and blurred my vision even more. I snorted, half laughing at myself, and waved after Dan's car until it turned the corner of my street.

January was a miserable month. Dan called as often as he could. He had kept his promise and rang me from the airport on that first day of the band's trip. As promised, we Skyped. We emailed. I followed Tuscq's progress on their Facebook page. The kids received letters and little presents sent via the Internet. Dan was as present as he could be, but he wasn't *there*, and we missed him sorely. If I was sad, the kids were sullen and sulky until I read them the riot act about taking the rough with the smooth, enjoying the good times for the sake of getting through the bad, and being thankful for what they had rather than ruing what they didn't. They looked at me with big, confused eyes and went meekly to play with their toys.

First-rate parenting, I scolded myself while I observed their hunched figures sloping off to the playroom, already regretting my outburst. *They're a little young for this level of philosophical stoicism. And you might as well take your own advice while you're at it.*

And thus I tried. The very next day, I resumed my sound engineering training. Richard left my apprenticeship in the capable hands of a mate who would be holding the fort for him while he went on tour with Tuscq, and Dean worked me extra-hard just to prove his mettle. However, at Richard's insistence, I was now being paid a very small wage, and I was inordinately proud of this achievement, even though the money was peanuts, really.

Thus I went to work, the kids went to school and playschool, we had dinner, we read stories, we waited for Dan's call, we went to bed. That was January.

February got worse. In February, we were ill. Josh brought home a nasty virus from school, and by the time he felt better, Emily had caught it, and, of course, I didn't escape it either. I found myself trying to launder my daughter's duvet and bedding in between bouts of my own sickness, and I felt very sorry for myself indeed. Rachel offered to help, but I told her to stay away. This virus was the last thing she or baby Henry needed.

When the sickness finished, the flu arrived. After only four days of being almost back to normal, Emily came down with a really high fever that wouldn't budge. For two nights, I sat with her, mopping her brow, feeding her medicine, and wishing someone else was there to help out. I caught Emily's flu just before Josh did, and for a couple of days, the three of us curled up in my bed together for want of any easier solution, and we slept and sweated and shivered and coughed in turn. Mum and Dad were back from their cruise and highly concerned about us all, but I refused to let them come.

Dan got incredibly worried with every passing day and eventually summoned his housekeeper Jenny to come to our rescue. One morning, she appeared at our front door with a set of meals for the day, already cooked, which she left in the kitchen with re-heating instructions. I was tremendously grateful for this small mercy. Actually, it was a huge mercy, for I wasn't in any fit state to shop or cook. She came back again the next day, and the day after that she took care of the laundry and cleaned the downstairs.

"You'll catch your death in our house," I warned her, feeling guilty about exposing her to our germs and yet grateful that someone was helping out.

"No, I won't," Jenny contradicted me. "I'm disinfecting everything down here, and I'm not coming upstairs just yet. But you do need someone to take care of you all, and there's nothing much for me to do at Mr. Hunter's house at the moment anyway, so I might as well make myself useful."

I shook and shivered and held on to the banister while I finished my short conversation with this domestic gem. "You've no idea how much I love you right now. You should be available on the Health Service."

Jenny flashed me a grin. "You be going back to bed now, young lady. I'll finish up down here, and I'll be back to see how you are tomorrow."

I went back to bed with the children, and we slept through the rest of the day. Dan Skyped us at seven p.m., and I thanked him profusely for sending us help.

"Sophie, love, this is nothing. Jenny is glad to do it. But I so wish I could take care of you myself. I've been going mental here."

Joe's face appeared behind Dan. "He has, too, and he's been driving us all up the wall," he shouted.

"Hiya, Joe." I waved weakly. The downside of the tablet-Skype-conversation was that Dan was very rarely on his own as he snatched moments at lunchtime or before a show, when the rest of the band was present.

Joe grinned and blew me a kiss. "You'll be better soon, you'll see." He disappeared from view again.

"Sorry about that," Dan mumbled, but I laughed. Well, I tried to, at any rate, as the laughter turned into a massive coughing fit.

"You sound like you've been smoking forty a day," Dan commented. "Don't you think it's time you all saw the doctor?"

"The doctor doesn't want us anywhere *near* the practice," I explained, my frustration clearly audible in my voice. "You know what the Health Service is like with flu. If you're not dying, you stay at home, and don't bother anyone with your germs." I coughed again, and Dan grimaced.

"Anyway, I think we're over the worst. It's just getting back on our feet now." I swiveled the tablet around so that Dan could see a peacefully sleeping Emily and Josh.

Dan grinned. "I know it's grim, but you do look rather cozy back there, all snuggled up together."

"Yeah, well, it was the easiest way."

There was a commotion at the other end, and Dan turned away briefly. "I gotta go," he announced when he faced the camera again. "I'll call you again later."

Possibly as a result of Jenny's good home-cooked food—she had served us chicken soup that day—and the relief of having someone else take charge for a little while, and possibly also as a result of the fevers finally breaking, we had an unbroken night's sleep that night, and things began to improve gradually.

February bled into March. The kids returned to school, and I returned to work. The incessant rain stopped, and there were signs of spring everywhere. Little crocuses and daffodils were pushing up through the soil, and most days, the sun put in a little appearance in the still-cold blue sky. We had weathered the halfway point of Dan's absence.

Over in the States, the band had finished recording. The album was released early in March, and naturally, the Jones family received a signed copy by courier before the album hit the shelves. By the time the tour went underway, we had fallen into a comfortable routine of chatting and catching up, sometimes altogether as a family, and sometimes just the adults. Dan sent us pictures and reviews for every show, and even made the occasional clip for us to watch. Meanwhile, the children were invited to birthday parties, and we made plans to spend Easter down in Newquay with my parents. Days whizzed past, and I gathered hope.

Chapter Fifty-One

"*Please* can I take my Lego police station to Granny and Grandad's house?" Josh begged for the fifteenth time, looking at me with imploring eyes, and I resisted the urge to snap at him — just. Packing the kids into a car for a two-week holiday with my parents in Newquay was already stressful enough without Josh making continuous left-field demands. I suppressed a sigh and crouched down to bring my face on a level with his.

"Sweetheart, there's so much stuff to play with at Granny and Grandad's, I really don't think you need to take your Lego with you. Plus," I seized on an inspiration, "you wouldn't want to lose any pieces, would you? It's already difficult to keep them together here at home."

Josh looked crestfallen and my resolve nearly crumbled. "Why don't you...why don't you go find Scooby. He would be a good thing to take." Apart from his addiction to Lego, Scooby Doo was his new major love, and he had been given a cute cuddly toy he wouldn't be parted from at night.

"Good idea," Josh agreed and raced off to collect his dog.

I straightened up and turned to pick up our bags to put them in the car. I collided head on with an unexpected solid object.

"Oomph." The solid object gave an amused gasp and wrapped me in his arms. Fear, confusion, and joy raced through my mind in quick succession as I computed his presence in my house. How? Why? *What?*

"Dan!" I couldn't keep a high-pitched squeal of excitement from my voice. Dan laughed and scooped me off my feet, swinging me around my small kitchen. I wrapped my arms around his neck and nuzzled in.

"What are you doing here?" I mumbled into his chest, hardly believing he was real. His warmth, his scent, his lovely Dan-ness. *Hmmm-hmmm.*

"I thought the tour was going on for another couple of weeks?"

Dan set me down and regarded me with those big eyes of his.

"Aren't you due in...LA and...New York...and Washington?" I scrabbled to recall the exact schedule, although I had it imprinted on my brain at one point.

"I've just come from Washington," he informed me, "and I'm due in Seattle tomorrow for rehearsal. The next show's on Monday. But I simply had to come see you."

I took a closer look at him, noting that he looked a little tired but healthy, with eyes brimming with excitement and...something else. I also clocked his five o'clock shadow and slightly whiffy appearance. "You're just off the plane?"

Dan nodded.

"Just to see us?"

Dan shook his head. "Not *only* to see you. I've come to collect you. You're coming with me on the rest of the tour."

"*Wha – ?*"

I couldn't finish my question, and no doubt my mouth was hanging open in an unattractive 'O', but the children had heard Dan's voice. Footsteps that sounded like a herd of elephants trampled down the stairs, and within seconds, Emily and Josh were rushing at their godfather, nearly toppling him off his feet. He sat down on the floor and gathered them both in his lap, mischief now dancing in his eyes. He ruffled their hair in response to their many excited exclamations and waited for them to calm down before he launched the killer question.

"How would you two like to come with me and your mummy on an airplane to America and see the rest of my tour?"

"*Yay!*" Josh jumped to his feet and punched the air, superhero style.

"Yes, yes, yes!" Emily remained on Dan's lap, but jiggled up and down gleefully.

Dan laughed and clapped his hands. The noise level was astounding.

Joy rose in my heart and brought a lump to my throat. How exciting, how unspeakably thrilling to go on tour with Tuscq again. Possibilities and thoughts jostled for attention. A second tour. *A second chance?*

I stamped on that notion hard and fast, and my knees grew weak with confused emotions. I sank into a kitchen chair and wrapped my arms around my chest to hold myself together. Dan watched my every move and gave me an encouraging smile when he saw the fruit machine of thoughts come to a standstill on my face.

"What do you think?"

"Er..." I had to clear my throat before I could speak. Where to start? *How* to start? "That would be lovely and very exciting, but do you really think it's possible? I mean, the kids are so young…"

"We want to go!" Josh was quick to put a stop to any of my objections on account of their age.

"Want to go," Emily echoed. Oh heck!

"It's fine," Dan reassured me. "It's absolutely not a problem. Joe and Mick have brought their children on many a tour and—"

"Will Ellen come, with the kids?" I pounced on that idea. I really liked Ellen, and if she was bringing her kids, then that would somehow make it more…okay. My notions of responsible parenting clashed violently with the idea of taking the kids on a rock tour.

Dan shook his head. "They were going to," he explained. "But James has chicken pox and…"

Enough said; I felt oddly deflated.

"What about Mick's family?"

"They've been out already. They came in the February half-term for a couple of weeks."

Ah. Well. My mind seized gratefully on the notion that Mick's kids had gone out to the tour, and that Ellen would have brought hers had it not been for chicken pox. Maybe it was all right. But…

"When? I mean, it's the school holidays and all, but…When did you imagine this to happen?"

I noticed the kids had gone absolutely quiet, watching our exchange like spectators at a tennis match, eagerly awaiting a positive outcome. Dan moved Emily onto his other leg and shifted his body around slightly. No doubt her increasing weight was killing him, but he never said a word.

"Today," he said. "Now."

"*What?*" This time, I got the word out whole, even though Emily and Josh erupted into a quick cheer.

"*Today?*" I repeated incredulously. "But...but..."

Dan grinned at me. "I see you've already packed, as it happens, so why not?"

"We're...we're going to my parents. Oh God, I can't just stand them up. They'll be devastated. They made all these plans..." My heart sank to the boots I wasn't wearing. I could definitely feel it in my big toe, throbbing away.

"Ring them," Dan said with an impassive face. "See what they say."

"But...but..." I sounded like a sick parrot. "Even if they're okay with it, we have no tickets, no visa..."

Dan shifted his weight again so he could raise an arm off the floor. He scrabbled around in the back pocket of his jeans and whipped out a sheaf of papers.

"Et voilà," he pronounced with a flourish. "Tickets..." He fanned out three sets of airline tickets in his hands. "And visa waiver forms." He added three more pieces of paper to the fan.

I must have looked at him completely blankly, because he gave the papers to Josh and said, "Here, bring these to your mummy." Josh took them carefully and transported them the three steps across the room.

"Mummy, please?" he wheedled as a precautionary measure when he handed me the paperwork. "Please say we can go?"

I waggled my head instead of a response and looked at the documents. There were three tickets, economy class, one in each of our names, to leave from Heathrow for SeaTac International airport.

"*Today?*" I whispered. "At three o'clock?"

Dan nodded.

I cast a look at my oven clock. "In...like... *five* hours?"

Dan nodded again.

I examined the other documents. They were printouts of something called ESTA.

"Electronic System for Travel Authorization," Dan offered before I could ask a question. "Remember the old green immigration cards you used to have to fill in on flights to the US?"

My turn to nod. It had been a long time since I had traveled to the States.

"Well, they don't do those anymore. Instead, you have to fill in this stuff online ahead of time, and it's a case of going through immigration at the other end."

I perused the documents more closely. "These have our names and birthdates and passport numbers and everything."

"Sure. It's got to match, you see. It's all done and paid for. We can't do anything more than present you three on the other side."

"But..." I was stuck on that word again. "But how did you know our passport numbers? How did you even know the kids *had* passports?"

It was, in fact, a small miracle that they did have passports. Steve's parents had insisted, when Emily was a year old, that I should have passports made out for both kids, because I could never know when the mood to travel might take me. I had laughed at the time, but now I saw the wisdom of their words. Nonetheless, how did Dan know all of that?

"I had help," he grinned.

Something stirred in my mind. A little thought. A conversation I had had with my Dad not too long ago. Something about banks and life insurance and...

I looked Dan squarely in the eye. His entire face was wreathed in smiles.

"Dad?" I said uncertainly. "Is that why he wanted our passport numbers a few weeks ago?"

Dan nodded, almost gleefully.

"Dad's *in* on this?" I repeated, just to be clear. "You've talked to him about this?" More nods on Dan's part. "He knows about this plan?"

"Why don't you just call your parents?" Dan suggested again.

"You know, I just will," I retorted and went to the lounge to retrieve the phone. Mum picked up on the second ring, almost as if she had been waiting for me to call.

"Sophie love! Is he there yet? I hope you're not being obstinate and coming up with all sorts of reasons *not* to go?" She launched into the conversation without preamble, without even a hello.

I laughed. "You really do know about this?"

Mum made an 'uh-huh' noise of confirmation.

"And you've played along with all these plans for the kids and me to come down for Easter because…?"

"Well, it was just perfect, wasn't it? Aren't you all packed and ready to go on holiday?"

"We are, but—"

"No 'but.' I expect you'll have to go to the airport quite soon." Mum was brisk in her dismissal of any of my unspoken concerns. I could hear a riot of laughter in the kitchen, but I couldn't make out what the source of the hilarity was.

"Mum…do you really think that's a good idea? Going on tour again? Taking the kids and all?"

There was silence at the other end, and I held my breath.

"Sweetheart," Mum eventually spoke. "Only you can answer that question. You have to follow your heart. But I don't see a really good reason *not* to go. I mean, it's like the holiday of a lifetime, isn't it? Think of all those beautiful cities you'll get to see..."

Dan had obviously filled them in with a lot of detail about the tour he wanted the Jones family to join. Mum was going all dreamy and faraway on me.

I tried a different tack.

"Don't you think it's terribly irresponsible, taking the kids into that environment?"

Mum chuckled. "I don't see why. You took them to the New Year's show and they were fine, weren't they?"

"I know, but this is different. It's—"

"Don't be silly. You don't think Dan would let you or the kids come to any harm, do you?"

"Err, no, but—"

"Sophie, if you 'but' me once again, I'll personally come down there and shove you on that plane. Just go!"

Whoa! I recoiled from the handset and looked at it in shock. What had just happened? I hadn't heard my Mum raise her voice to me since I was a teenager. Mum spoke again, more softly.

"Just go. Have fun. Show the kids what sights you can. Make the most of it. You deserve it."

I swallowed hard. "I love you, Mum."

"I love you too, sweetheart."

Another thought occurred to me, although I suppressed the 'but' before Mum could blow a gasket. "What about you and Dad? What are you going to do over Easter?"

Mum laughed. "We've a list of invitations for Easter parties as long as my arm, and we might just have a few days in London or something."

"You didn't plan for us to come at all, did you?"

"Nope," Mum confirmed dryly. "We knew you'd be otherwise engaged."

Suddenly, I couldn't hold the joy in anymore. At the end of the day, this was a dream come true—again. Dan had obviously moved heaven and earth for us to join the band in the States. The tickets were there, the visas were there, the suitcases were packed. All that remained was to retrieve our passports and we could go.

"Mum?"

"Yes, sweetie?"

"I gotta go."

Chapter Fifty-Two

"And did you pack these bags yourself?" The officious check-in agent cast her eyes over our luggage. Mine, and the kids, that was. Dan didn't have any, although that wasn't obvious in the humdrum collection of suitcases and bags.

"I certainly have," I piped up. Josh and Emily stood silently beside me, overwhelmed by the hustle and bustle of the airport and the vastness of the terminal building. Their eyes, however, gleamed with excitement.

"Excuse me, sir, madam?" Another airline official approached us from behind the counter. She spoke very quietly and blushed slightly.

"Are you...aren't you Dan Hunter?"

Dan smiled at her graciously. "I am," he whispered back, mimicking her secretive voice. "It's very nice to meet you, Lilly." He used her name as though he hadn't just read it off her name tag. What a smooth operator. Lilly thought so, too. She nearly giggled and touched her hand self-consciously to her hair.

"Would it be incredibly rude if I asked you for an autograph?"

Behind-the-counter lady shot Lilly an aggrieved look, but according to her name tag, Lilly was the senior check-in manager and evidently outranked the other agent.

"Not at all," Dan obliged. "Have you...?" He motioned for a pen and a piece of paper and wrote Lilly a little message. Lilly blushed and smiled.

"Um...are you all traveling together?" she asked.

"Sure," Dan explained. "This is my friend, Sophie, and these are my godchildren, Emily and Josh."

Lilly's eyes widened. "Godchildren. Wow. I had no idea." Dan smiled, and we all stood there awkwardly for a moment. Then Lilly spoke again.

"If...um, without meaning to be...intrusive or anything, but...um, how come you're traveling economy with us today?"

Dan gave a belly laugh. "Not intrusive at all. I don't often travel economy, do I?"

Lilly had meanwhile gone back behind the desk and was tapping away at the computer terminal. "No, I can see that," she agreed. "You've been doing rather a lot of flying with us these past few weeks. So how come...?"

Dan shrugged. "This was a last minute booking and, well..." He shrugged. "Budgets," he mumbled under his breath, but we all heard him anyway. I felt a little uncomfortable. I hadn't even considered the cost of it all. I shifted from foot to foot and tried to look inconspicuous. Dan picked up on my emotion.

"Ah, there you have it. I knew you'd be embarrassed when you'd think about the tickets," he mumbled. "It's okay, really. I want the kids and you to come, and don't you start talking about paying me back."

Lilly listened to his little speech attentively. I said nothing but simply pulled my shoulders up to my ears in a 'well, I'm here and I'm cool with it' kind of gesture.

"Hrr-humm," Lilly cleared her throat from the other side of the counter. "As it happens, I'd like to offer you all an upgrade anyway," she announced calmly. "You're a valued customer, Mr. Hunter, as well a frequent flyer, and so would you like four seats in First?"

Our first check-in agent looked somewhat scandalized, and I couldn't say I blamed her, but Dan took it in his stride. His voice was honey-sweet, yet sincere, and carried that mesmerizing Dan Hunter timbre. "We would love to accept an upgrade, of course, but I wouldn't like you to think…"

Lilly looked from him to me and the kids and back again. She smiled. I was really getting to love her smile.

"I think I see what's happened here," she said simply. "Let's get that upgrade sorted."

Three hours later, I was blessing Lilly from the bottom of my heart and resolved to send her some kind of thank you token when we got back. The journey was proving long and exhausting with another seven hours to go, but at least we had the comfort of space.

We had stocked up on magazines, sticker books, and travel games before boarding and were working our way steadily through them. Dan sat with Josh and I with Emily, although we had swapped around twice already. The kids were delighted at the cute seats and the in-flight entertainment system, but I was holding off on letting them loose on the video games and television until a little later. The children's whoops of joy at the first snacks had raised a couple of bemused eyebrows from the other first class travelers, but they relaxed slightly when I quieted the kids down immediately.

"Sorry," I mouthed to the man across the aisle. "They'll be fine in a minute or so. We'll try not to bother you." The man gave me a half-hearted smile and plugged his headphones in to watch one of the in-flight movies.

At four hours in, Emily curled up on her seat and fell asleep. I had a look at my watch, which I had already put back by eight hours to reflect Seattle time, and worked out that it was nearly seven p.m. in the UK. A little early for Emily's bedtime, but given the excitement of the day, probably not far off what she would normally do at home. I covered her in a blanket and took a deep breath. One down, one to go.

"Sophie?" Dan's voice emerged in a whisper from the seat behind me. I twisted around then raised myself onto my knees on the seat so I could look over the back at Dan.

"Right here," I whispered back and suppressed a giggle. Josh, too, had fallen asleep in his seat, his legs on Dan's lap and his upper body sprawled against the backrest.

"Aw, bless him. Just lift him across. He won't wake." I smiled at Dan. "Actually, maybe I could move Emily next to him and then you and I can…talk."

Dan grinned. "Good idea but…" He motioned at his lap. I looked a little closer.

"Are you wet?"

My rock star nodded. I looked at Josh and then again at Dan, and clapped my hand on my mouth. "Oh God, I'm so sorry," I mumbled through my fingers. "He probably forgot himself, what with all the excitement and all the juice."

I scrabbled to my feet to assist my stricken men. "Here, I brought some pajamas for the kids anyway, let me go and sort Josh out while you…um…sort yourself out." I fought the urge to giggle at the absurdity of the situation, but Dan did it for me.

"That's a definite first," he chortled. "This could be seriously misinterpreted!"

"I'm glad you see the funny side," I snorted.

Dan shrugged. "What else can I do?"

I lifted a still sleeping Josh and carried him to the bathroom while Dan made his way to the other bathroom, a napkin discreetly placed over the wet patch. Josh barely woke up while I removed his trousers and shirt, washed him down with a soapy washcloth, then changed him into pajamas. I took him back to his seat which a thoughtful flight attendant had meanwhile transformed into a bed. After I snuggled Josh down, she and I had a quick conversation, and she turned the seat next to Josh into a bed, too, while I took a sleeping Emily off to the bathroom to change her into her PJs. By the time I had settled Emily in her bed and returned to my seat, Dan was back—cleaned-up and nearly dry—and dinner was served.

"Welcome to my world, again!" I observed wryly as I sat down next to him. "Thanks for keeping your cool."

"Welcome to *my* world," Dan retorted, raising a glass of bubbly. "Thanks for coming."

I shook my head, still trying to catch up with my reality. "This is…mad. *Good* mad, but mad."

"Hm." Dan was thoughtful. "It brings back memories."

"It certainly does," I chuckled and clinked my glass to his. "Seventeen years it's been since we first met. My God, what a lot has happened."

"It certainly has." Dan was also in a reflective mood. "Some good stuff, and some not so good stuff."

I tried to keep the mood light and grabbed at the first thing that came to mind, inspired by my current beverage. "We've certainly had some entertaining moments. Do you recall that time when you broke all those champagne glasses?"

"'I daresay that's several hundred pounds of damage you've just inflicted, young man','" Dan intoned, mimicking perfectly the voice of a slightly batty old Great Aunt we met at a wedding we both attended a few years previously, before Steve came into my life.

"'I don't know, the help sitting down with the guests','" I continued the joke. "'What *are* we coming to?'"

"I don't rightly know," Dan responded, suddenly serious.

I sipped at my champagne nervously. The parallels of days gone by were so clear, so obvious—never mind the children and everything else that had changed us both—that there was a sense of expectation in the air, and I was certain I wasn't imagining it. Dan took my hands and looked at them thoughtfully. I still wore Steve's wedding band, although I had moved it to my right hand a short while after his death. I had wanted to keep him with me, always, but I had also needed to remind myself that I was no longer a married woman, as such. It had been a really weird moment, but it had felt right, and I hadn't given the ring much thought afterwards, until now.

Dan touched it and turned it gently between his thumb and index finger.

"Rings," he mused after an eternity. "They're quite heavy on symbolism, aren't they?"

I nodded, needing a moment before I could speak. "I…it would feel wrong to take this one off. But it doesn't mean…"

Dan grasped my hands more intensely, but I ran out of courage. "I still have yours," I stated instead, as a diversionary measure. "Well, my half of it, anyway."

"And I still treasure my half." Dan's voice was solemn and slightly hoarse. And that about summed up the complexity of our relationship. We looked at each other for a long while, unsure how to proceed, where to go next. As the seconds stretched by, the poignancy slowly faded, the small opening grew smaller and eventually closed, and the moment slipped away. And yet, something had passed between us, a certainty, an understanding, perhaps, and I felt oddly at ease. Dan let go of my hand, and I flexed my fingers as though waking up from a trance. We smiled.

"So. Tell me about the tour. How's this going to work?" I was first to break the silence, and Dan released a breath I didn't know he had been holding.

"Right. The tour. Well..."

And so he filled me in on the schedule. There were five more shows planned: Seattle, San Francisco, LA, Chicago, and New York. The band would be rehearsing most afternoons, followed by a quick radio or TV appearance in most places, then a sound check prior to dinner at the concert venue before the various shows. Afterwards, there were a variety of events ranging from interviews to after-parties. Non-show days were spent traveling, punctuated by early-morning and lunchtime promotional gigs—more radio and TV appearances, meetings with local record bosses, and other obligations.

There was a two-day gap between the show in LA and the next gig in Chicago, and Jack had booked the band into a studio in LA to lay down demos for new songs with some of the local big names. The schedule was grueling, to say the least, and I was breathless just hearing it.

"But that's us," Dan laughed when he saw my face. "You guys are along for the fun part of the ride. I'd think you get up when you're ready, and then go and do some sightseeing in each of the cities until the early afternoon. If you want to join us for rehearsal or sound check, then please do. I'd definitely like to see you all for dinner, and I'd love for you to be at the shows, kids'n all. We'll work something out. After-parties and all that malarkey…Again, we'll work that out. Depending on where the action is, Joe and Mick sometimes used a hotel babysitter or simply put the kids to sleep in a quiet room at whatever place we would hang out. It's all different and you'll have to learn to trust me and to go with the flow a bit, but it's perfectly okay."

I laughed. "All the stuff I used to worry about, way back when. And it's all going to be okay."

Dan laughed, too. "Absolutely. And I can't tell you how happy I am you guys are here with me."

Chapter Fifty-Three

It was nearly seven p.m. local time by the time we arrived at our hotel in downtown Seattle. Immigration at SeaTac had taken a little while, and the kids had been very cranky, having been woken from their slumber at landing, but there were no mishaps, and we all enjoyed the twenty minute cab ride from the airport to the hotel, taking in the unfamiliar boulevards and relishing the occasional glimpse of open water.

"The hotel is only a few blocks away from the waterfront. If you wanted to do something exciting tomorrow, there are ferries going across the sound. They're mostly commuter ferries, really, but you could always check them out, I know how much you guys like your boat trips," Dan told us, and the kids squealed excitedly.

"Let's do it now, let's do it now," Josh chanted, suddenly wide awake even though it was technically the middle of the night for him.

"We'll do it tomorrow," I replied. "Let's get to the hotel first and settle in and grab something to eat."

Dan had booked a family suite for us with two bedrooms and a little sitting room, as well as the obligatory fabulous bathroom. The kids were beside themselves with glee, and I wasn't far behind. It was a stunning room, bright and airy and very luxurious. Dan joined me at the window and put an arm around my shoulder, pulling me snugly into him.

"It's a bit odd, this, isn't it?" I mused, voicing my thoughts.

"Is it?" Dan threw me a probing look. "Why?"

"Well...no more separate suites, no more connecting doors, no more pretense. We're just...here. Together."

Dan planted a little kiss on my cheek. "Is that a problem?"

"Of course not," I protested. "It's just...after all this time...it's a little weird, that's all."

"I don't think it's weird." Dan's voice was deep and calm. "I think it's long overdue. You are the closest thing I have to a real family. I missed you all. I wanted you here. Right here, not next door. This is what it should be like."

Oh my God. I experienced a weird tingling sensation all over at hearing these words. Yet I was hearing them without really taking them in, because my heart rate picked up so dramatically that the muffled pounding in my ears drowned out all sound and thought. I felt a little dizzy, too. Was he really saying what I thought he was saying?

I disengaged from his arm so I could look at him properly. He was smiling, his eyes full of love, his face content.

"Um..." Faced with a highly poignant moment, I was my usual eloquent self. But Dan rescued me.

"It's ridiculous, really, that it's taken us so long." He grinned and wrapped his arms around me once more. He held me tight, and my face was pressed hard against his lovely chest. Mmmhh-mmmhh.

"Taken us so long to do what?" I mumbled into his shirt.

"This." He let go of me with one arm and made a sweeping gesture. "Being honest with ourselves about staying together. Gosh, if only we'd done this first time 'round..." He didn't finish his sentence, but put his arm back around me instead.

As before, I had this sense of certainty. We were headed some place, and I knew where. The unspoken thing was there between us, growing, stretching, emerging into something beautiful, and we were both watching it develop, waiting to see when it would burst through the surface. But this wasn't the right time, it appeared. For one, we were jetlagged, dirty, and hungry. And for another, there were two kids involved who rarely, if ever, would give two adults more than five minutes' uninterrupted talking time.

"Mummy, mummy, I want to go in the bath, it's got nobbles in, and it sprays, and it makes waves!" Josh bounded up to us and pulled at both our sleeves while we were still mid-embrace.

I looked at Dan, confused, and he laughed.

"That would be the spa tub," he explained. "It's all singing and dancing. It makes bubbles and everything. Or so I'm told. Let's go check it out."

So we ran the children a bath, complete with mad amounts of bubbles, and let them splash to their hearts' content. Meanwhile, Dan and I took turns in the shower to freshen up, too. Once clean and dry, we dressed in our pajamas. Dan ordered a room service dinner—steaks and chips for the adults, and burgers from the special children's menu—and we feasted in front of the telly, feeling weary and exhilarated all at the same time. At nine-thirty, the kids started drooping again, and I put them to bed in their room while Dan made a few rapid calls to Jack and the band to confirm the schedule for the following day.

Afterwards, unreasonably early by local standards perhaps, we crawled into our king-size bed, luxuriating in the fresh sheets and the thoughts of a long night's sleep ahead to stave off the worst effects of jetlag. I nuzzled contentedly into Dan's bare chest and dropped off to sleep before a single naughty thought could cross my mind.

Dan was gone by the time I came around the following morning. There was a note on the pillow signed with fifteen kisses, explaining the band was due at a radio station by seven a.m. He left me his detailed itinerary for the day along with a set of mobile telephone numbers to contact him or Jack, but there was one item he had circled in red: *Final rehearsal, The Arena, 4 p.m.~See you there?*

I smiled to myself. Four o'clock wasn't a long time away, and I was certain the kids and I would find something to do for the few short hours. Once we were dressed and ready to go, of course.

The kids woke up shortly after, looking refreshed and happy and not at all jetlagged — yet. They raced into my bedroom and made to jump into bed to hug me, but got diverted at the last minute.

"Look, look, *look!*" Josh's excited voice emerged from somewhere under the bed. Emily immediately joined him, and they both emerged brandishing a chocolate Easter egg.

"It's an Easter egg," I stated, somewhat superfluously and not a little dumbfounded.

"Let's see if there are any more," Josh suggested to his sister, and they commenced a frantic search of the room.

Meanwhile, my addled brain had latched onto a vital detail. It was Sunday, of course. Easter Sunday! And Dan had obviously come here prepared. I broke out into a giant smile I simply couldn't wipe off my face.

"What's so funny, Mummy?" Josh wanted to know when he noticed my wide grin.

I giggled. "Nothing, sweetheart. I'm just glad the Easter bunny found you here, all the way in the States."

"It's amazing," Josh agreed and resumed his hunt. All in all, there were twenty-four eggs and four chocolate Easter bunnies to be found in the suite, and the kids assembled their loot in one of the hotel's fruit bowls, having unceremoniously moved the fruit onto the coffee table. Easter-bunny Dan had truly outdone himself. I was so stunned, I couldn't even feel guilty about forgetting the whole thing myself, and I allowed each child one chocolate egg before we went down for breakfast.

In actual fact, I was a little nervous about braving the breakfast room on my own with two young children. This was a first for us, but they excelled themselves. They sat nicely and calmly, remembered their please's and thank-you's, and ate like champions. The hotel staff responded in kind to their good manners and treated us like royalty, and I felt inordinately proud.

When we were ready, we went sightseeing. It was an overcast day but at least it wasn't raining, and we made our way to the waterfront, taking in the gentle lapping of the waves against the piers and the dramatic juxtaposition of cityscape with mountain views. Well, *I* did. The kids were more fascinated by unfamiliar cars and all the marine vessels moored by the pier. One of them, Josh deciphered, offered trips around Elliott Bay and, predictably, once the kids had discovered this fact, we had to buy tickets and get on.

An hour later, we returned to shore, excited, cold, and hungry, so we found a little eatery for lunch. During our meal, we debated whether to go the nearby aquarium next or whether to check out the Space Needle. Emily wanted to see the fish, but Josh convinced her that space was much more exciting. On balance, I tended to agree with him, not bothering for the moment to correct his expectation, and we flagged down a cab to have ourselves taken to this amazing monument.

Obviously the kids were overwhelmed with the sight of this spectacular structure, rising high above us into the sky "and with a spaceship at the top," or so Josh said. When I told them we could go up all the way to the observation deck, they could hardly believe it and tugged eagerly at my hands to get inside.

It was a momentous afternoon, and time flew so quickly that I nearly missed our four o'clock appointment at The Arena. I piled the kids into another cab, even though we could probably have walked to the concert venue, and we screeched to a halt in front of the gates at just a few minutes to four.

Taking a deep breath, I smoothed back my hair, took each child by a hand and walked confidently up to the security office. It occurred to me too late that I had nothing to prove I was entitled to go *in*, no pass, no identification, not even Dan's little note. It was just me, a slightly wild-eyed mother, and her two kids.

"Sophie Jones," I announced myself boldly. "With Emily and Josh. The band is expecting us."

I received exactly the kind of skeptical look I had feared, but the chap checked his clipboard anyway. Interminable seconds seemed to pass before he looked up and smiled.

"Of course. Come on through." He pressed a button to release a door lock and we were in.

"This is cool," Josh whispered, evidently becoming more aware of our exalted status that granted us access to places most people could only dream of seeing.

"I know," I whispered back, squeezing his hand excitedly. "I used to do this all the time, but I'm kinda out of practice."

Emily hop-skipped happily next to us while I tried to get my bearings. "If in doubt, follow the music," I lectured my young children, and together, we did just that, until we emerged inside the auditorium to find the stage.

Chapter Fifty-Four

"They're here!" Dan's voice carried through the arena and it sounded as though all of Seattle would hear. Joe gave a drum roll, and Mick and Darren played a dainty riff on their respective strings. I grinned and waved, taking a deep bow. The kids whooped and clapped their hands.

"Sit down, sit down," Dan encouraged us from his vantage point on the stage. "We'd love you to watch this rehearsal. We're going to do a full run-through for you!"

We clapped and cheered and picked some random seats. I wasn't *entirely* sure whether the kids would last for a whole set, but then again, there was plenty of space for them to run around if they got bored. A thoughtful roadie rushed out to meet us and handed me two sets of earmuffs, one pink, one blue, and I held them up high in the air for Joe to see, mouthing, "Thank You." I had no idea whether he saw my words, but he got my meaning anyway and gave another drum roll. The kids put on their earmuffs, and we settled down to take in the show.

Needless to say, it was amazing, and the kids were mesmerized and lasted the entire two hours. Toward the end, I had to cuddle Emily on my lap as the jetlag threatened to engulf her, but she refused to yield and watched every last song, every last moment. I saw the show through the kids' eyes, marveling at the jokes and the stage walks, delighting at the fireworks, shouting for all my worth at the customary sing-along challenge sections. Enormous video screens framed the stage, alternately focusing on the band and showing animated clips of swirling colors, psychedelic night skies, montages of the band's album covers that combined into a funny cartoon, and cheering crowds with a tickertape identifying the venues: Ontario, Nashville, Las Vegas…

The showmanship was breathtaking and once again, I was in awe of 'my' rock star. I hugged my daughter hard, noting with amusement that Dan didn't fail to enchant the next generation, and smiled inwardly. As I had worked out on the plane, it had been seventeen years since my fateful train journey to Edinburgh to visit the band backstage after they had extended a random invitation at a gig a few days previously. For more than twenty years, Tuscq had provided the musical backdrop to my life, seeing me through the highs and the lows, whether they had known it or not. I was thirty-six years old, and yet Dan and his band still made me feel like a teenager.

Rehearsal finished at just after six, and just in time, as well. Emily could barely keep her eyes open, and Josh swayed in his shoes as if drunk. It was time for my darlings to go to bed, and I didn't feel too hot myself. We sat tight until the band came off stage to see us, and I hugged every one of them hard, still feeling irrationally emotional. Dan scooped up Emily and held her close, and she snuggled into his neck and dozed off instantly. The rest of the band was much amused.

"Look at you," Joe chuckled. "That's an unexpected effect you have on this young lady."

Dan rose above the banter and simply smiled, looking as happy as I had ever seen him.

"What's next for you guys?" I inquired cautiously, not wanting to put a dampener on the mood, but also needing to extract myself and the kids quickly.

"Dinner," the band shouted as one, startling Emily out of her slumber. Dan shifted from foot to foot, and I sensed that this wasn't a situation he had anticipated. His face spoke volumes. He hadn't reckoned with the jetlag, and he had assumed we would tag along. He tightened his grip on Emily and stroked her back, clearly telling me he didn't want to let go.

"Where are you going?" I asked, stalling for time. Maybe we could work something out.

"Steak," Mick opined immediately.

"Burgers," Joe bellowed at the same time.

"Beer," Darren chimed in.

I laughed and raised my eyebrows. "Tell you what," I said to Dan, gently taking my sleeping daughter out of his arms. "Why don't you guys go let off some steam over burgers and beer, and I'll see you later?"

Dan looked crestfallen and torn. "Are you sure? I don't want you to feel like you're not welcome!"

The other band members nodded, and I grinned.

"Aw, guys. I know I'm welcome. Heck, I hung around even *before* I knew I was welcome," I joked, and of course the band erupted in protest. I blew Dan a kiss.

"Look, any other night, I'd say, yeah, let's do this. But tonight..." I gestured at the kids and pulled an apologetic face.

"It just wouldn't be fair to them. Besides, *I'm* not feeling too great. I think I got an appointment with a bath and room service."

Dan continued looking at me, conflicting emotions warring on his face. His brow creased, and smoothed again. The corners of his mouth lifted into a tentative smile then drooped once more. I prodded him gently in the side. "Come on, off you go. Have fun. I'm fine. *We're* fine. Just give us one more night to get over this jetlag and the Jones family will show you that we can party!"

I spoke with more confidence than I felt, not at all sure how I was going to manage the next few nights, and wishing Ellen were there to set me an example. Much as I longed to do the whole rock-star-family-on-tour-thing, I really had no idea how to play it, and, feeling bone weary to boot, I couldn't think straight either.

Dan stepped closer and pecked me on the cheek. "Are you sure?" he whispered tenderly. "I promised you...I said I'd look after you, and I don't want to let you down."

"You're not letting me down. If anything, I'm letting you down. I promised we'd be game, and yet, we conk out on this first night."

Dan put his arm around me awkwardly, trying not to dislodge Emily, then took in Josh's near-zombie appearance. He smiled.

"You're right. You're absolutely right. These kids need to go to bed. I'll have a limo take you back to the hotel. And you're sure you're okay if I...?" He gestured at the band, and I gave him a shove.

"Of course I am, you lovely eejit. Go and have fun and dissect the dress rehearsal, and I'll see you later."

The following night, we were back at The Arena, Emily, Josh, and I, watching the band for real. The early night had done wonders for our stamina, and even though we had had another busy day sightseeing, we were all wide awake and excited. The first support act would go on any second now, and the Jones family was ensconced in the green room with Tuscq, enjoying a buffet dinner, keeping a loose eye on the screens showing the crowd and the stage, and generally absorbing the pre-show atmosphere. I knew from days of old to hang back and be a little quiet, but of course the kids had no such qualms, and their incessant questions raised a few amused eyebrows.

"What are you doing?" Josh inquired when he saw Darren apply an ointment to his chest. "Can I have some?"

For a moment, the entire room fell silent, and I blushed. I recalled all too clearly that night when I had first bumped into the band again, just before the reunion tour that had kicked off my relationship with Dan. After that show, Dan had complained about a sore nipple owing to a persistent nipple erection chafing against his guitar strap, and I had proffered a cream to help him out.

Evidently, everyone else remembered that night, too, because all the band members started laughing. Darren shot me a look. "It's a special cream that your mummy recommended to us a long, long time ago, and it stops my skin from getting sore when I play the guitar."

I exhaled. Thank goodness Darren, too, had acquired the art of talking elegantly around the real issue for the sake of kids' ears.

Josh, however, wasn't done. "Really?" he gushed. "My mummy gave this to you?" He looked reverently at the little jar Darren was holding.

"Er, no, not this jar, exactly. But she gave me the *idea*," Darren clarified, and I decided to call my son away before he could cause further embarrassment.

Before we knew it, the second support act was on, a new band who had managed to gain a place on the charts of late, and the energy in the room notched up a few ramps. Dan started warming up and assumed that faraway look that heralded an impending performance. Emily giggled when she saw him shouting into a bunched-up towel, and I whispered to her to explain what he was doing. Darren and Mick were doing finger taps on their mugs, absentmindedly practicing riffs and chords. Joe was tapping at the table, preparing drum rolls and count-ins.

I shushed the children and quietly talked them through this final phase before the band went on stage, pointing out how each of the musicians seemed to have withdrawn into their own space, hardly talking to each other or aware of anyone else's presence.

"They're getting ready," I mumbled. "It's their routine for going on stage, a bit like when you have to put shoes and coats on to leave the house."

And then the moment arrived. The green room was eerily quiet these last few seconds before the on-stage signal, the cheering and chanting of the crowd relayed through the monitors being the only sound heard. The band lined up to go out, Dan first, followed by Joe, then Mick and Darren. The stage was in darkness until the first spotlight invited Dan to step out and the crowd went wild.

Josh, Emily, and I were watching from a little private family area to the side of the stage. We didn't have the best of views, but we *could* see everything, and of course we had watched the rehearsal the night before.

However. In all the excitement, I had completely lost track of time, and it was only a half hour or so into the show when Emily curled up on my lap with her thumb in. "I tired," she mumbled, twirling a lock of her hair around a finger while polishing her nose with the resulting strand.

Oh dear. I had hoped the kids would last through the gig, and Emily's exhausted state caught me off guard in a big way. We couldn't even go back to the hotel because we were due to travel through the night to get to San Francisco for the band's afternoon TV appearance. The children had been terribly excited about the prospect of sleeping on a bus, and had eagerly helped pack their little overnight bags, which were resting in a side room at The Arena right at that very moment. Perhaps I would get the children changed into their pajamas. That might be a good start.

I rose to my feet, hoisting Emily onto my hip, and went to investigate, pulling a surprisingly willing Josh behind me with my free hand. "I'm tired, too," he informed me.

Thus encumbered by my load and a very bad conscience, I bumped into a roadie in the deserted green room. I couldn't recall his name, but I had met him before. He flashed me a grin.

"Awright?"

I shook my head and sighed, hooking Emily up higher as I struggled to carry her weight. "I wish I'd thought to bring some kind of travel cot," I mused, suddenly realizing that would have been the most reasonable thing to do.

"The nippers are tired, are they?" The roadie showed surprising empathy with my plight. I nodded and shrugged at the same time, a most inelegant maneuver that resulted in Emily sliding out of my grip. The roadie caught her and gave her a quick cuddle.

"You don't need no travel cot," he informed me. "Why don't you do what Ellen used to do with Joe's li'l'uns?"

I met his expectant gaze and found myself at a loss. "What did Ellen used to do with her kids?"

The roadie grinned and flicked his head to one side. "Come on, I'll show ya." He set off, carrying Emily while I led Josh by the hand. He took us through the green room and out the other side, and the noise swelled as we crossed the passage that led up to the stage. Directly opposite the green room was the instrument room where the band kept the various guitars and basses they used for different parts of the show.

"Here," the roadie smiled.

I looked around, aghast. "Here, what?"

"Take your pick."

I still didn't know what he was talking about. He noticed my confusion and picked up a guitar case.

"This is one of Dan's. I'm sure he won't mind."

"Won't mind what?"

The roadie gave an infinitesimal roll of his eyes. "You really are new to this, aren't ya?"

I nodded, feeling incredibly stupid. He grinned again and stacked the guitar case inside a large, flat box on wheels. "Transport case," he explained. "Big enough for the bigger one."

"Ah." Rather than let on that I was still mystified, I followed him as he pushed the cases into the adjacent smaller and surprisingly quiet side room which already housed our overnight bags.

"Look, there's a pile of blankets and towels. They'll make a right comfy bed for the little nippers. Put the girl into the guitar case and the boy into the transport case. Piece of cake."

He delivered this information so matter-of-factly, there was no doubt he was serious, and yet, I was sure he had to be joking.

"You're kidding me, right?"

"Nah, look, it'll be all right, just for the show. Joe's kids used to sleep like this all the time when they were little, and Mick's, too. Trust me."

He handed Emily back to me while he laid out the guitar case, wide open, and cushioned it with blankets. It did look just big enough for my toddler, and, at his behest, I laid her gently inside the nest he had built and covered her with another blanket. She looked surprisingly snug and never woke, just turned on her side and continued sucking her thumb.

"You might want to bring their 'jamas next time," the roadie suggested, and it dawned on me that he really had seen this done many times before.

"Um...I have, they're right there." I pointed at our bags.

The roadie grinned. "Even better, but I'll leave you to sort that out for yourself. Now then, young man," he addressed Josh. "Reckon you'll be awright in here?" He padded the transport case with a stack of blankets and made an inviting-looking nest for Josh, too. Josh looked at me, and back at the roadie, then at his sleeping sister. He looked a little tearful.

"I...I don't want to be left alone here," he mumbled.

"Ah, but you won't be," the roadie answered. "See all them people out there? They're all helping to look after ya and if y'need anything, your mummy's just across that corridor, see? What d'ya reckon?"

I gave a small gasp. "Are you sure this is safe?" I whispered, lest Josh should overhear my concern and get even more worried.

"Safe as houses. Them instruments out there are worth thousands of pounds and the whole area is completely locked down. There's security guards on the doors, too. You can leave them kids here sleeping peacefully. They won't be comin' to any harm."

A pager went off on his belt and he consulted it. "I must be off. I'll see you later, and I'll keep an eye on the room whenever I can. Besides, you're only across the corridor, you can probably see the doorway from where you're sitting anyways." He rushed out before I could object.

I knelt down next to Josh. "Come on, sweetie, let's get you into your jimmy-jamas and give this a try," I coaxed. "It's a brilliant idea. It looks really comfy and…it's totally cool!" I fumbled in my handbag and withdrew my phone. "Look, I'll take a picture of the two of you sleeping like proper rock star kids!"

Josh liked the idea of that. I retrieved his pajamas and got him changed, and he quickly snuggled down. I changed Emily, too, before I took the photo. She slept through everything, and I sat with Josh and stroked his hair until he dropped off a bare five minutes later. Still feeling just a little uncertain, I rose to my feet and surveyed my sleeping children in their familiar sleepwear but most unusual bedsteads. Then I squared my shoulders and told myself to relax. The roadie was right; this area was in a complete lockdown zone, and if you didn't have a pass, you couldn't go anywhere.

Leaving the door ajar, I ventured back through the green room and into the family zone. I sat down, all alone now but with clear line of sight to the room where my offspring slept. Resolving to go check on them every few minutes, I finally gave myself up to the show again. It was exciting to get the best of both worlds, and I looked forward to a few short minutes of welcoming the band off stage on my own, just me, adult-Sophie-and-temporarily-not-Mummy-me.

Chapter Fifty-Five

"That was amazing! Congratulations!" I launched myself at Dan when the band spilled into the green room after the last encore. He swept me off my feet and whirled me around, glowing with energy and pride.

"Thank you, my sweet, it's so lovely to have you here," he roared and set me back down again to high-five the other band members." I grinned and for a moment neither of us said anything, letting the noise and chatter wash over us.

Surreptitiously, Dan pulled me close again and accepted a bottle of beer from a passing roadie. "Cheers."

I grabbed one, too, and we clinked bottles. "Cheers."

Dan put the bottle against his lips and tipped his head back, draining half the contents in three long swallows.

"That's better," he sighed when he came up for air. Suddenly, he looked around anxiously. "Where are the kids?"

"Asleep, next door," I informed him as nonchalant as possible.

Dan raised an eyebrow. "Really?"

"Uh-huh. A kind roadie suggested snuggling them into a sort of makeshift bed. He said you wouldn't mind..."

The other eyebrow shot into orbit, too. "They're sleeping in my guitar cases?"

"Well...um, Emily is. Josh was too big, so he's in a transport case."

Dan eyed me silently for a moment then gave a bellow of laughter. "Sophie Jones, I don't believe what I am hearing. Never in a million years would I have thought you'd be relaxed enough to succumb to the old touring tradition of sleeping the kids in the equipment cases. Good for you. Bloody brilliant."

He gave me a big hug and a quick kiss. "I must just go and see for myself," he muttered.

"Don't wake them," I shouted after him, resisting the urge to tag along. He should find out by himself that I really was relaxed enough.

"Good for you," Joe echoed. "I bet you were worried about this to begin with, but Ellen used to do this all the time."

"That's what the roadie said," I replied, but felt relief nonetheless at having this confirmed by Joe.

"Ah, Pete, he's a sweetheart. He's been with us from the start. I knew he'd sort you guys out."

"So cute," Dan butted into our conversation. "I'd love to take a photo, but it's too dark in there."

"Already done," I grinned, and showed Joe and Dan the picture I took earlier. "But what now? Won't the roadies need the cases?"

Joe shrugged. "Not for a half hour or so. They'll be taking down the stage first. And we're off on the bus soon anyway." He and Dan clinked bottles, and we joined the short but raucous after-party that had sprung up in the green room.

A short twenty minutes later, it was time for us to leave The Arena. Dan carefully lifted Josh, and I carried Emily out to the waiting tour bus. It was a little awkward, clambering on the bus with a sleeping child snuggled against my chest, but I managed and gratefully laid my daughter into the bottom bunk at the front of a row of beds running nearly the length of the bus.

"It's quietest here, and you and I will take the two top bunks above the kids," Dan explained after he had deposited Josh in the bed opposite to Emily.

"Cool." I giggled, unable to stop a tiny shiver of excitement myself. I had *been* on a tour bus just like this one, many years ago, but I had never tried the beds.

Dan heard my glee and nudged me. "Who knows…time to finish some unfinished business tonight?"

I slapped him on the chest. "Now, now, you got me blushing. We couldn't possibly…what with everyone else here!"

"Says who?" Dan was all innocence.

"Says me! And the kids are here…"

Dan belly laughed, but immediately cut his explosion short. "No longer a virgin, but now a prude?" He clicked his tongue. "Sophie, Sophie, what is the world coming to?"

"I am not a prude," I hissed. "But it *is* really cramped here and…"

"Welcome to the unglamorous side of rock star travel," Dan pronounced and changed the subject. "Let's join the others for a little bevvy at the back, shall we?"

And thus, in another uncanny replay of events from a lifetime ago, I found myself sitting in the lounge area at the back of the bus, wedged between Darren and Dan, drinking champagne and beer as the bus started up and rocked its way out of the parking lot toward the interstate. The roadies and equipment would be only a few hours behind us, and would head straight for the next stadium to set up the stage for sound check by early afternoon the day after tomorrow. It was an amazing feeling to be part of the logistical master plan of my favorite band on tour again.

Conversation flowed for a half-hour or so, fueled by bubbles and the knowledge of a gig well done. But quickly, the band members retired to their bunks, one by one. Dan, too, suggested we go to bed, and I agreed. I was still feeling the jetlag and was quite keen to try sleeping in one of the cute, swaying little bunks. Grabbing my overnight bag, I performed a quick change and clean in the little bathroom on the lower level of the bus, then padded my way along the now dark corridor toward the front. Dan was already in his bunk, and I half-climbed his ladder to give him a quick kiss goodnight.

"Is that it?" Dan whispered, his voice barely audible above the swooshing sound of the tires and the purring of the engine.

"Yes," I whispered back. "I think so."

My rock star reached out an arm and held onto my hand.

"Come on up for a quick cuddle, at least," he pleaded.

I cast a look down the length of the bus. All curtains were drawn, the bunks were in darkness, and the occasional snore further added to the white noise blanketing the coach.

"Okay," I conceded, suppressing a giggle. I climbed up the ladder and lay down beside Dan. The bed was extremely narrow and we had to lie sideways, facing each other. Dan's breath was hot on my face, warm and mint-scented. When on earth had he found the time to brush his teeth?

He caught me sniffing and tickled my ribs. "I got a lot more experience doing this than you. And oral hygiene is important." He sounded like my dentist, and I giggled some more, not least because he was still tickling me. Suddenly, I found myself lying on top of him, stretched out along the length of the bunk. In the pitch dark, I couldn't really see Dan's face, but I swear he grinned.

"Now, then, that's better," he murmured and stroked my face. He pulled me down onto him and kissed me, lips on lips, tongue on tongue. Despite the cramped environment and the immediate proximity of ten other people, two of whom were my own underage children, I felt myself responding with a long, low, almost desperate moan.

"Shh," Dan whispered. "The trick is to breathe deeply and slowly, and to barely move at all."

Breathe deeply and slowly. Barely move at all. I experimented with that while he resumed kissing me, and my head swam with lust. I had no idea Dan had perfected the art of tantric sex, but it was delicious.

Using barely perceptible movements, Dan very gently — and very slowly — tugged at my pajama bottoms until they slid down over my hips, then did the same for himself. I half-straddled him and our lower regions met up close, skin on skin, heat on heat. I felt electrified. A million butterflies tickled my tummy and my ladyship throbbed and danced in delicious anticipation. Dan moved, slowly, barely perceptively. He shifted his weight and slid his body down a little. Cold air touched my skin where his body broke contact with mine, and the sudden coolness only heightened the heat of the moment. I tried to keep my breathing slow and steady, but it was difficult as I grew dizzy with the effort of hovering above my lover. My arms trembled, and a thousand stars danced before my eyes.

Then Dan moved up again, gently, and he began to push up and inside me. The tip of his hardness opened my folds and I lowered my hips to speed his entry, but he pulled away.

"Steady on," he breathed. "Be patient. Hold still"

Dan placed his hands against my hips to support me, and I remained poised and unmoving while he entered me once more. Slowly and carefully, the movement progressed up inside me and I lost track of time, lost any perception of my own dimensions or his, so that he seemed to consume me whole. I was moist, I was *wet*, I was ready, and his hot, hard manhood brought my wetness to a boil. I had never felt anything as thrilling, as exciting, as challenging. We merged together, fusing into each other, and it took me a moment to realize that we were one. A delicious wave of release threatened to overwhelm me but I clenched my muscles to hold it back. Dan felt the contraction and moaned softly in response.

"You like that, do you?" I teased in a low, hoarse whisper and contracted again. Dan ground against me and the tension nearly drove me to the brink. I exhaled, finally allowing myself to sink farther still onto his hardness, until I was filled to the brim.

I laid my head on his chest and let myself melt into the moment. I dug my hands into his shoulders and savored the unfamiliar quietness of the sexual explosion, our tiny motions augmented a thousand-fold by the swaying of the bus. We lay like this for the longest time until I thought I would expire with desire. Languidly, I flicked my tongue against his nipple, producing a violent shudder and a barely suppressed groan. His groin rose and bucked, and he tangled his hands in my hair, burying his head in my neck to stifle his scream. Seconds later, he pushed me up, undoing the buttons of my pajama top so his mouth could find my nipples, sucking them in turn until he had to cover my mouth with hot, ferocious kisses to stop me from giving us away.

Melted together, breathing as one, swaying with the motion of the vehicle that carried us through the night, we finally came together, rocking and bucking and trembling. The climax crashed over us repeatedly like slow, persistent and unstoppable waves washing against the shore until the storm was spent and its force ebbed away.

The next week passed in a blur of traveling, rehearsals, shows, and — for the Jones family only — sightseeing. The last six hours on the bus to San Francisco seemed interminable, and everyone was questioning the wisdom of the decision to go by road, but nonetheless, after more than thirteen hours, we arrived at our destination on time and gratefully checked into our hotel.

The band disappeared for their TV appearance and a few other engagements that Jack had somehow organized *en route*, while the kids and I took some time to splash about in the hotel pool and postponed exploring the city until the following day. *Of course* we took in the Golden Gate Bridge, although the highlight for the children was a ride on the cable cars up and down the hills. The San Francisco show went off without a hitch, and I put the kids into their pajamas early on in the evening, ready to snuggle into their touring beds when they needed to.

Once they were asleep, I put my VIP pass around my neck and left the backstage area to join the sound engineers at the mixing desk for a spot of observation. Richard had talked me through the challenges of managing live sound during the last rehearsal, and I was curious to see this in action.

After the San Francisco gig, we once again climbed on the bus to have ourselves driven the much shorter distance to LA, where the schedule allotted the band two days after the gig for interviews and recording time. The record company threw a big after-party at the hotel, featuring glitterati and luminaries both from the music and film industries. While the kids slept safe and sound in our suite under the watchful eye of the hotel babysitting service, I mingled cheerfully alongside Dan, enjoying myself.

Dan steadfastly refused to comment on our situation, although we received many a curious question. He simply smiled and introduced me as his long-standing friend, Sophie Jones.

"Your picture will be all over the Internet within hours," he warned. "Are you okay with that?

"I am," I whispered back, having known from the moment I got on the plane with him what I was letting myself in for. "I...I feel like...I don't know, like this is right, after all this time."

"Good." Dan smiled. "There'll be speculation and rumors, and they'll dig up all the old history, every photo, every article. Well, you of all people know how it works. It'll be a storm, but it'll be a blast, and I'm fine with it as long as you are."

For a tiny moment, it appeared as though there was an opening for me to *ask*, in this most unlikely of places. For one second, we were alone among the hundreds of people around us, and I longed to confirm what "it" actually was that we were both okay with, to substantiate what we had been talking about these past few days without actually saying the words, to verify where we were going. "It" was between us almost every night. It was in his eyes right then, and I was certain it was in mine, too. But the music turned louder, the lights dimmed, and the place erupted into wild dancing. Three hours later, we fell into bed together, exhausted, exhilarated, hungry for each other, and far too busy to talk.

The next day, we linked up with Dan's sister, Jodie, and she showed Emily, Josh, and me around the city while the band was busy. She had organized tickets for us to take a tour of the film studios and of Beverly Hills, and the kids marveled at the sets, the 'real' King Kong and Jaws hanging about, and the big letters on the mountain.

We flew to Chicago from LA, complete with roadies and equipment, arriving in our hotel late on a Sunday night. The kids and I had been in the States for exactly one week, and we had become accustomed to the completely different lifestyle that Dan offered us there. Yet, after three shows and three sets of travel, not to mention three sets of intensive city-exploration for the children and me, we all crashed in Chicago and spent the day lounging about in the hotel, playing games, watching telly, and catching our breath.

I took the opportunity to ring Mum and Dad and even Rachel, just briefly. Naturally, she wanted to know what exactly was going on, but given the presence of the children, I played coy and promised to fill her in on my return.

"That tells me everything I need to know," Rachel guffawed. "I am having flashbacks here like you can't imagine. Be good. Or be bad, rather. Love ya!"

I had a huge smile on my face when I rang off. I hadn't bothered to correct her mistaken assumption about the flashbacks, yet I was getting them, too. In fact, it felt like I was living in an alternative universe where I was about to be offered — perhaps? maybe? pretty please? — a chance to take the route I didn't follow the first time around, in spite of, or possibly *because* of, everything else that had happened to me in the intervening years.

Even the stars were given a rare day off before the show, and Dan slept through most of it — as did the rest of the band, I assumed, for nobody surfaced until just before sound check. I felt like a pro during the Chicago gig when I expertly dispatched the kids to their touring beds and joined Richard at the sound desk again.

That night, he put me in charge of vocals. "You need to hear the vocals loud and clear," was his motto, so his job—or mine—was to make sure this happened. This also meant that effects, such as reverb on the guitars, had to be "killed" between songs when Tuscq would talk with the audience. Richard was running the effects for the guitars through a special sub-console, and I was to mute that loop whenever the band wanted to interact with the fans.

"Dan has a habit of speaking out of turn, without warning, and you need to be on the ball when he makes an unscheduled little speech," Richard advised.

It was a fantastic, if slightly nerve-wracking, experience being at the live mixing console, the best spot for listening to the show in the entire stadium, *and* being in charge of Dan's voice, but I relished every moment and dearly wished the show would never end. Who would have thought that I would get such kicks out of this task?

Yet end, the show did, and it was straight onto the bus for us all again, off to the last stop of the tour, the grand finale: New York.

Chapter Fifty-Six

"This is it," Dan told me on the morning of the last gig. "The biggest show of the tour. We'll finish with a bang and some fireworks." His eyes glowed with excitement while he helped himself to another croissant. We were in the hotel near the stadium, which was actually just outside of New York City, on the other side of the river in New Jersey. The kids had eaten their fill and were charging around the room, pretending to be airplanes while Dan and I finished up a late breakfast.

"How so? Are you doing something different tonight?" I poured more tea and sat back, pulling my legs up onto the sofa and reclining.

"You can say that again. For starters, we'll have three support acts. The two bands who've been touring with us, and another, completely new local artist. I've heard their demo, and they rock." He grinned. "I remember those days. This is our turn to give a new band the chance to play an arena. I'm telling you, those guys are a lot more nervous than we are right now."

"Cool." I had never really given much thought before about the reasoning behind the support line-up, but it made sense. A new, local artist, an up-and-coming band, perhaps slightly different in orientation—one of Tuscq's support bands was of the punk rock persuasion—and a rising star.

"And fireworks? What's that all about?"

Dan shrugged. "Jack's idea. He got special permission for an end-of-show, farewell-United-States fireworks display in this arena, and he got a camera crew to video the whole show for a promotional DVD or..." He took a sip of tea and smiled. "Or perhaps even a big-screen, Tuscq-on-the-road kind of movie. Who knows."

I spluttered. "My God, that would be *awesome*."

"Wouldn't it just? By the way..."

My cup of tea froze in mid-transit to my mouth. There was a mischievous, provocative glint in Dan's eyes. *Uh-oh.*

"What?"

Dan cleared his throat. "Do you remember that New Year's Eve gig?"

I laughed. "Of course I do. It was good to see you back on your feet."

"No, not *that* one. The other one." Dan shifted in his seat.

"Dan, I hate to remind you, but you do a New Year's Eve show every year. You'll have to be a bit more precise."

"The one where you sang. With me. On stage. Remember?"

My cup of tea was still in mid-transit, and I made an effort to set it down on the table. "Yes. I do."

Dan rose and came across to the sofa, lifting my legs and sitting down, then putting my legs on his lap and rubbing my feet. His eyes were soft and pleading. I knew that look. *Uh-oh* again.

"Would you? Again? Do me the honor of joining me tonight, on stage?"

A thousand emotions fought with each other in my head, the strongest being abject horror. I allowed myself a moment of contemplation before I spoke, not wanting to say the wrong thing. I could tell by the earnest look on Dan's face that he hadn't made this request lightly, or offhand.

"Why?" Eventually, I settled on a small diversionary tactic to investigate the cause of his plea.

He simply shrugged. "No reason. I haven't even discussed it with the band. It just...kind of occurred to me right now."

Emboldened by the fact that I wasn't actually in the official program, I dared to argue. "Do you really think it would be a good idea? I mean, come on, I'm not a trained singer. And I haven't practiced for years, not even in the choir."

"But you sing at home, all the time."

"I know." I *had* to stop singing in the shower, obviously. "But that's hardly the same. I...I don't want to let you down, but I'm really not sure it would be a good idea."

"You *have* done it before." Dan's voice sounded a little like Josh's when I wouldn't let him have a treat.

"That was a long time ago, and you ambushed me. Besides," I changed tack again. "How do you normally perform this song? You haven't played it all tour."

Dan sighed. "Exactly. When we do perform it, I have to get a female artist to come join me, and...it's never the same. This is your song, after all. It doesn't work with anyone else."

I came out in a rash of goosebumps. I recalled every line of that song so very clearly, even though I hadn't given it any thought for years and years.

"*I will get you back?*" I quoted one of his lines, turning the statement into a question.

"*But our future's bright,*" Dan responded, citing the very last line of the song, which happened to be 'my' line. Something shifted inside me and broke through the surface. We were still talking in riddles, but I had no doubt what he was suggesting.

Dan grabbed my hand. "It's the perfect song, isn't it? But don't worry, I won't do anything stupid like fall on my knees and propose to you in front of thousands of people."

"Oh good," I uttered weakly, not sure whether to be relieved or disappointed.

Dan massaged the back of my hand with his thumbs. "Look, I'll get Rich to give you plenty of reverb to make your voice nice and clear."

I laughed. "I know what he has to do, and I can jolly well ask him myself."

"Touché," Dan conceded. "I keep forgetting that you're becoming an ace sound engineer. So, will you do it?"

"You still haven't told me *why*. 'No reason' simply isn't good enough for me to go out and make a spectacle of myself in front of thousands of people." My heart was beating fast in my chest. Some weird, idiotic part of me actually *wanted* to do it. Besides, I knew he would talk me into it. I just needed a reason.

Dan let go of my hand and laced his fingers together. He exhaled sharply and looked me square in the eye.

"Because it would mean the world to me. Because I'd love to close this tour with you. Because I want to get to hold you on stage and plant a kiss on your cheek." He shrugged. "Just because it would be wonderful, that's all."

I shrugged, too. What the heck. "Okay," I whispered.

"Okay?" Dan asked.

"Okay, I'll do it," I said, louder than necessary.

Dan punched the air with glee and jumped to his feet. "You are the best. This will be perfect. And look, I can get you a voice coach to practice if that'll make you feel better."

And so it was that I spent the best part of that day ensconced in a studio with a voice coach who gave me a crash course in singing my lines, while Dan took the children to a radio interview, a photo shoot, and the sound check. When we met up just before the final rehearsal, Josh brandished several action hero figures while Emily had a gaggle of new Barbie dolls. I shot Dan a look and he chuckled.

"Unabashed bribery to keep them occupied for a half hour here or there," he confessed. "But it worked."

The rehearsal went well, much better than expected. The work with the voice coach had paid off—as long as I kept my nerve—and Richard was doing marvelous things at his desk to give me confidence. The other band members seemed excited about adding "Love Me Better" to the last encore, and Jack thought it was a stroke of genius.

The kids begged to stay up to see their mummy on stage and I promised to either keep them up or wake them just before it was my turn. All in all, this wasn't exactly the relaxing last show I had anticipated. I was full of nervous energy and little butterflies, yet I enjoyed the sensation.

Chapter Fifty-Seven

The crowd was wild. It was a mild, clear evening, and stars twinkled in the velvet blue sky above the stadium. My four rock stars were doing a fantastic job of shining on the stage, and the first set of encores was over and done with. The band rushed off the stage for a two-minute break before the final set of songs for the night, for the tour, the last one of which would be 'my' song.

"You ready?" Dan's body was drenched in sweat, and he hastily threw on a fresh shirt. I kissed his wet nose and dried his face with a towel.

"As ready as I ever will be."

"Are the kids up?"

"The kids are up and outside in the family area with Pete." Pete, the trusty roadie, had assumed quasi-babysitting duty that evening, and it appeared he didn't mind in the slightest. Dan had told me earlier that Pete had three kids of his own, which explained a lot.

"Good. We'll do it exactly as we rehearsed. Joe will count us in, and I'll start —"

"I know, I know," I interrupted, then backtracked. "Sorry. It's only that, if you explain it to me one more time, I might lose my mind, that's all."

"Ah." Dan grimaced. "It's like *that*. I get it." He hugged me briefly, then gulped down some water and lined up the band to go back out. This was it.

There were two songs to go before "Love Me Better", and I barely took them in while I waited in the wings for my cue. Excepting, perhaps, the one previous occasion where I had let myself be talked into an appearance on stage, this would have to class among the most surreal moments of my life. Time seemed to be simultaneously speeding up and slowing to a crawl. My ears felt as though they were full of water, and the echo of my own breathing inside them drowned out nearly all other sound.

The dark stadium was drained of all color, yet I saw bright white and pink sparks everywhere. I felt hot, but my hands were clammy, and my feet were cold. My lips were dry, and I resisted the urge to lick them. Right at that moment, I wasn't sure I could speak, let alone sing. And yet, there it was, my cue. The song had started and been interrupted, the stage was dark except for one spotlight, searching for me, and the crowd was chanting.

I fought the urge to cry as I took the first tentative step onto the stage. The last time I had done this, Steve had been watching, cheering, jollying me along. This time, I was on my own. Well, not quite. I was fairly sure the kids would be going mad with excitement in their seats right now. And of course, there was Dan, right in the center of the stage, and now also illuminated by a spotlight. He held out his hand, and I took another step.

The stage didn't look nearly as high when you were in the audience, but from up there, I seemed to be towering above the crowd. The auditorium was in darkness, and with the footlights glaring up at me, it was impossible to discern faces. The effect was not dissimilar to being alone in the stadium. I raised my eyes, letting my gaze follow the oval curve of the stands then out onto the night sky.

Swallowing hard, I kept walking with my eyes still trained on the sky. Dan followed my gaze, and when I finally reached him, he put his arm around me for a second and held me close.

I whispered very softly in my head. "I'll always love you, Steve. But I've got to move on. I—"

Before I could finish my mental goodbye, the stage lights came back on, and the crowd cheered. Dan held my hand aloft and introduced me, inadvertently yanking me out of my somber moment.

"Ladies and gentlemen, give it up for my good friend, Sophie Jones, who is here tonight for a very special, one-off appearance to close this tour with the biggest Tuscq hit ever..."

Joe tap-tapped away for the intro, the guitars came in, Dan sang, and my moment arrived. The last few seconds before I had to sing stretched to an eternity as every action, every moment slowed to a near-standstill. Blood roared in my ears and dulled the sound of the musicians around me. Once again, I experienced that familiar, strange sensation of hearing without hearing, of not knowing whether my voice would emerge when I opened my mouth, and what it would sound like if it did.

Dan squeezed my hand to heighten my cue. He looked at me and smiled, tilting his head in a small gesture of encouragement. I opened my mouth.

"You and me...were never meant to be..."

There. My voice. It emerged, loud and clear and in tune. I heard a cheer rising from the audience, but it seemed to come from a long way away as the dull sensation in my ears hadn't yet cleared. I ignored it and focused on my lines, my notes, and the words rolled off my tongue.

The first verse over, Dan and I joined our voices in the chorus and my heart soared. Inexplicably, tears pricked at the back of my eyes, but they were tears of purest joy. I was *doing* it, I was really doing it. Now that I had survived the initial moment, I would be all right. I wouldn't forget my words. I would stay in tune. I would totally carry this off!

Adrenaline whooshed through my body to cause a great wave of elation, and I could have happily broken into dance if the song had permitted it. As it was, I channeled all that energy into the tune, giving it my all, singing as though my life depended on it.

Dan and I held on to each other for the entire time. The crowd seemed to love it, and their cheers rose to a soaring crescendo when the final notes of the song had faded into the stadium. Dan hugged me tight for the world to see and gave me a big, fat, *very* official kiss right there on stage. When he broke off to look at me, pride and joy and something else shone from his eyes, and the look on his face gave me goosebumps.

Unbelievably, the crowd managed to cheer even louder, and Mick, Joe and Darren came to join Dan and me in the center of the stage, clapping their hands and patting our backs. It was a truly incredible moment, and I wished it would never end.

Right on cue, the fireworks went off over the stadium and the technicians dimmed the stage lights. The crowd *ooh*'d and *aah*'d over the spectacular display and once more broke into a rousing applause when it came to an end. The stadium lights came back on, the band took their bows, shouting thank-you's to their fans and waving goodbye. The elation, the joy, the pure delight, the excitement and the gratitude of the fans was palpable. Moreover, I could *feel* the pride, the exhilaration and the buzz among the musicians. It felt like a living thing, a physical presence with us on the stage that enveloped them — and me — in the richest reward of all, the knowledge of the love and admiration of thousands of happy fans. It was a truly potent drug, and I absorbed it greedily as I tried to burn every last sight, every feeling into my memory.

Naturally, there was the party of all parties at the hotel to celebrate the end of a highly successful tour. Celebrities and media folk, record company executives, TV and radio presenters, and other assorted industry dignitaries came by the dozens, and the hotel's ballroom was positively teeming. The kids were sleeping in our suite, and Dan and I had quickly changed into party gear. Fresh jeans and the trademark silky-blue shirt for Dan — top buttons duly undone — and a black sequined cocktail dress from the hotel's designer boutique for me.

"I hate these official parties," Dan mumbled under his breath while we exited the elevators. "Everybody who's anybody is here, and it's impossible to relax. But I suppose it's got to be done."

He fixed a smile on his face, and we started circulating. Dan worked the crowd with a vengeance, shaking hands, slapping backs, air-kissing models, posing for photographs, schmoozing and networking and oozing charm every which way. I noticed Darren, Mick, and Joe doing the same. In a corner of my mind, I was simultaneously amused the band still had to endure this publicity circus and impressed with their unfailing professionalism and goodwill in going along with the charade. It lasted for an hour and a half before things subtly changed.

One by one, the hangers-on left, no doubt off to the next glitzy event; the media teams were encouraged to depart; the record company executives said their goodbyes; and little by little, the atmosphere grew more relaxed, the lighting and music changed, and the real food appeared.

"Who can live off canapés anyway?" I overheard Joe as he ushered in a phalanx of waiters bearing platters of steak and chips, burgers, fried chicken, and Chicago-style, deep-dish extra-loaded pizzas. A collective whoop of appreciation rose, and the remaining party guests, me included, gratefully turned their attention to these more substantial culinary delights. People loaded their plates with food and carefully balanced them on coffee tables or knees. For a while, the sound of animated chatter was replaced by the contented clink of cutlery.

"Who on earth planned this?" I inquired of Dan when he joined me at a table with a plate laden with steak and chips.

"Joe and Jack, I suspect." He grinned. "We've got to say farewell to the good ole U.S. of A. in style, haven't we? And we're all hungry and exhausted. We deserve a bit of a feast, tuck in!" He cast an eye over my more modest plate and laughed. "You sure you got enough there?"

"Quite positive," I assured him. "Besides, there's only so much a lady can consume whilst squeezed into a tight-fitting cocktail dress."

Dan raised his eyebrows. "Is that so?"

I smoothed a hand along my unusually slim-looking tummy. "It's got stays sown inside," I explained. Dan joined his hand to mine, feeling the fabric carefully.

"My God, so it does. Well, I look forward to liberating you from those in due course."

I giggled. It was a heady sensation, this feeling of freedom to date my rock star, to retire to our room together without questions being asked, without a sense of guilt or the fear of discovery.

"I love it when you have that faraway dreamy smile on your face," Dan broke into my thoughts. "Penny for them?"

I shook my head. "They're not worth a penny, trust me." I leaned against him briefly to reassure him that all was well, then sat up again straight. "What's next?"

Dan looked at me blankly. "How do you mean?"

I waved my hands about. "Well, after all this is over and the tour's finished. So are we going home tomorrow, or what?" I scrunched up my forehead, trying to recall the exact travel date on our tickets. "I didn't think we were leaving the States for another few days. So what's next?"

Dan nudged me. "You and your ever-perceptive mind. It's impossible to sneak a surprise on you."

"A surprise?"

"Uh-huh." He clammed up and focused on his food.

"Care to elaborate?"

Dan shrugged and continued eating, chewing and rolling his eyes at me in a can't-speak-with-my-mouth-full way.

"Dan Hunter, you are the most terrible tease," I chided him with a laugh and took his plate out of his hands. "Tell me, *now*."

He swallowed and pretended to look contrite. "Okay. Right. Um."

He grabbed hold of a napkin and twiddled it around in his hands. For all intents and purposes, he looked nervous.

"What is it?" I persisted, partially out of desire to know and partially to put him out of his misery.

"Well, um, you see...I took the liberty of adding a little family holiday onto the tour, just for the kids, you, and me."

"A family holiday?" Unsure what to make of his announcement, I resorted to the old parroting technique.

"Well, yeah. We're already this side of the ocean, I thought we might as well take in…you know, a theme park."

"A theme park." If in doubt, continue with the parroting.

"Yes, a theme park, down Florida way."

I suppressed a belly laugh. "You've booked us into a theme park?"

Dan nodded.

"We've got those at home, you know." *Spoilsport*, my inner child overrode my killjoy observation, but Dan wasn't perturbed. He pointed a finger at me and pretended to cock a gun.

"Ah, but that's where you're wrong. The ones we have are *nothing* like these. I've done my research. *And* the weather is better." He pulled his imaginary trigger, blew the smoke off his finger gun, and put it away. "Got ya."

Now I let go of the belly laugh. "I suppose you're right. It's just so unexpected."

"And that's what makes it great. So, now that I've let the cat out of the bag, I might as well fill you in." He sat back and reclaimed his plate of food, speaking between bites.

"It's a big old theme park with rides and things, but there are several *fabulous* hotels, swimming pools and animals, it's like *everything* rolled into one. We can do things for the kids *and* adulty stuff, and everybody can have a great time. We might even get a little tan if we want to lounge by the pool." He paused for a drink before answering my unasked question. "We're flying out first thing, and we'll have almost three whole days before we have to go back. And yes," Dan grinned, "Josh will be back in school on Monday morning with the start of the new term. Don't you worry."

I shook my head, speechless for only a moment. "Of all the things you might have organized, this would have been the last thing I'd have guessed. You don't have to do this stuff just for us, you know."

Dan pretended to look hurt. "I'm *not* doing it just for you. I'm doing it for myself, because I've always wanted to. And—" he gave his fabulous rock star grin. "Because I can't wait to see the look on the children's faces when we get there. But now..." He rose to his feet and pulled me with him. "Now it's time to dance. And then I'll keep my promise of getting you out of that dress, woman."

And a couple of hours later—after we had partied hard, said our farewells to the rest of the band and promised to meet up for a 'post-mortem' of the tour when we were all back in the UK— he certainly did.

Chapter Fifty-Eight

"Wow!"

Josh's sound of adoration was genuine, excited, and very loud. We were being driven through the gates of Dan's chosen holiday theme park toward our hotel, and the scenery was imposing. Rides rose on either side of the well-tended, rose-lined boulevard, and a lake glinted in the sunlight under a deep blue sky. The air was balmy, and the kids seemed to enjoy the journey in this open-top limo as much as the adults.

"This is so totally awesome!" Josh enthused. "Dan, can we go on that ride over there with the waterfall? And that one over there, the space dome thing?"

Dan laughed and nodded. "Of course! We'll try and do a little of everything while we're here. But let's get to the hotel first. I think your mummy would like to freshen up."

"I certainly would," I agreed. Whilst I was happy and exhilarated to be there, in this divine place, with my kids and Dan, I was feeling gritty and grimy after a very late night and an extremely early start. A hot shower and a nice cup of tea would work miracles in restoring myself to a more normal me.

"Oh *man*, do we have to?"

The impatience of a five-year-old was hard to ignore, and I smiled at him reassuringly.

"I'll be as quick as I can, I promise. And maybe, just maybe, you guys might want to have a little splash in the bath, too."

"Never." Josh was adamant in his refusal.

Dan ruffled his hair. "Not so hasty, young man. Never turn down an opportunity until you have actually evaluated it properly."

"What does evaluated mean?" My son pronounced the unfamiliar word carefully.

"It means, take a look and see what's offered before you say 'no'," I enlightened him. Right at that moment, the driver pulled up in front of our hotel, and we all piled out of the limo.

Predictably, the children squealed in delight at the massive fountain-cum-exotic-fish-basin in the hotel's lobby, and even Dan looked impressed with the grandeur of the real, exotic plants trailing the central columns and providing an uncanny sense of being in the jungle even whilst we were walking toward the reception desk.

"This sure is some place," he muttered as he hooked his arm through mine. "I'm not entirely certain that three days will be nearly enough."

We checked in and were taken to our suite on the second floor—no high-rise buildings here—which boasted spectacular views over the whole park. Despite my desperate hurry to jump in the shower, I couldn't resist a little sit down on the balcony, and Dan joined me, proffering a glass of champagne.

"It's a bit early for that, isn't it?" I raised a token objection even while I accepted the glass.

"It's after lunch in the UK. Does that make it better?"

Dan had an answer at the ready and I clinked my glass to his.

"Maybe. Oh heck, definitely. Cheers."

We smiled at each other and had a sip. I let my eyes wander, taking in the varied scenery and the many attractions.

"I do believe I spot the Eiffel Tower," I mused in surprise, having set eyes on a structure that looked very much like the iconic landmark all the way back in Paris.

"I do believe you're right," Dan agreed, not sounding in the least surprised. "I think they have a little replica of some of the major European sights here." He held up a brochure. "Look — it's like a little bit of Europe."

I snorted but said nothing for a while. A little bit of Europe, indeed. Yet I felt an irresistible urge to go near this replica Eiffel Tower. It was like fate was calling to me. I simply *had* to go.

"Dan?"

Dan looked at me with his liquid eyes. "Yes?"

"I know it's a bit naff and silly, but…I feel weird." I laughed uncertainly. "Do you think…would you mind if we checked it out? The Eiffel Tower, I mean?"

"Not silly at all," Dan contradicted me. "And why not indeed? If we'd like to, who's to stop us?"

And so I jumped in the shower, making great haste in my impatience to get going. The kids, meanwhile, *were* merrily splashing in the bathtub, as I had known they would — especially when it turned out that it was an Olympic-size tub with a little slide going into it.

It was after lunch by the time a fresh-faced Jones family assembled in the hotel lobby with an equally freshly scrubbed Dan Hunter, and we decided that a meal would be a good idea.

"Why don't we check out what the European quarter has to offer, thereby killing two birds with one stone?" Dan suggested casually. Too casually, I thought, but I didn't pay much attention. My eyes were trained on a necklace he wore. A necklace he hadn't worn in a long time, a necklace I hadn't *seen* in a long time, one with half a ring on it. The other half of that same ring—Dan's erstwhile engagement ring for me—nestled in my trouser pocket.

How it came to be with me was a bit of a miracle, actually. I had found—rediscovered—the necklace whilst dusting a little while ago. It had fallen into my hands like a good omen, and I hadn't been able to put it back into the box under the bed. Instead, I had kept it on my bedside table and when I packed for our holiday, I had swept it into my bag. What I had planned to do with it, I didn't know.

Of course, I didn't go on holiday to my parents' house with the kids. We all came on tour with Dan, and the necklace had been calling to me ever since. As though directed by fate, I had meant to put it on earlier, but Emily had distracted me, and I had hastily stuffed the necklace in my jeans pocket. The fact that Dan wore his took my breath away. The implications were so powerful that I felt dizzy, but the spell was broken when my daughter's voice permeated my consciousness.

"Me not want to kill bird," Emily objected, looking tearful.

I snapped back into reality and hugged her. "It's just a saying," I explained. "Dan knows that I'd really like to see that amazing tower out there, and we need some lunch, so he thought we might combine the two by having lunch near the tower." I had to stop for breath after this long-winded dissection of our plans.

Josh jumped in right-away. "What tower?"

Dan took his hand. "Come on, young man, let me show you." He led the way out of the lobby and invited us into one of the little electric cars that people used to expedite their progress across the park. I hung back and retrieved the necklace from my pocket. I was driven by a weird compulsion, I simply couldn't stop myself, I knew, I just *knew*, this was right, and so I fastened it around my neck with trembling fingers. *There.*

"Your carriage awaits," Dan grinned, checking to see if I got his meaning. *Of course* I got it. Memories of the years gone by were coming back thick and fast, jostling for attention, consuming my mind, and I felt oddly out of touch with reality. Dan's eyes caught the glint of the ring on my necklace and his face lit up. He looked at me with eyes so full of emotion that I wanted to lean over and kiss him, but abruptly he broke our connection and started the car instead.

Dan chauffeured us himself, following a map he had obtained from the concierge, and within a few minutes we arrived in France. The replica tower loomed tall and gleaming into the blue sky, and there was a little boulevard of French-style restaurants leading up to it.

"Take your pick," Dan invited, and the kids ran toward the bistro.

"That'll have to do," I grinned.

Dan grinned back. "I'm sure it'll be fine."

We sat outside, under a little green umbrella shading a cast-iron table and chairs that looked like they had been plucked straight from the streets of Paris. The kids clamored for food and we turned our attention to ordering even though a million words needed to be said. *Later,* I promised myself.

The menu didn't disappoint, offering an array of authentic dishes, and for a moment, just a tiny moment, I could make myself believe that Dan and I were back in Paris—albeit not quite on our own. Predictably, Dan ordered steak frites, I had the mussels, and the kids both fell hungrily on a croque-monsieur each.

"You okay?" Dan's voice seemed to come from a long way away. He looked me straight in the eye, and his question was loaded with meaning.

I shook my head to clear the weird sensation. "This is totally surreal," I whispered. "It's like we've been here before, and I suppose that's the intended effect, but...I don't know, it's like I'm standing next to myself."

"I know what you mean," Dan replied. "I suppose it *is* the intended effect." He looked away for a moment but his hand lightly touched the ring on his necklace. He was telling me something. It was almost as if he were asking me something. My spine tingled. Was I ready for what I knew was about to come? Was I ready to let go and start again? With this man?

I supposed I was. I had been preparing to move on for months, had had innumerable late-night talks in my head with Steve, had cried and apologized and reasoned, and had somehow felt his response in my heart. *Make yourself happy. Make the kids happy.* It would be three years since his death soon. Not a terribly long time, but an eternity for the Jones family. Could I deny the children—or myself—the chance of becoming a real family if it were offered? Could I refuse another shot at love?

"Are you ready?" My rock star took my hand and I nearly jumped out of my skin.

"Gosh, you startled me," I burst out. "Sorry, I was miles away."

"I could see that," Dan said softly. "You okay?"

I nodded, not trusting myself to speak.

"You ready to move on?"

Oh my God, was he reading my mind?

I stared at him blankly, and he gestured at the children who were half-hovering over their chairs, evidently itching to explore the park.

"I think the kids want to get going," Dan supplied right on cue, and I let out an explosive laugh. *Silly me.*

"Of course, let's get going," I replied, snapping back into dutiful mummy-mode and grabbing my handbag. "What shall we do next?"

"Mummy! Mummy-mummy-mummy!" Emily's excited voice rang clearly through the thronged street. She had run ahead, leaving the bistro area and zooming up and down the boulevard like a carefree butterfly, and she had evidently seen something she wanted to do.

"Yes, sweetheart, what is it?"

"Mummy, me want to go on the round thing. With horsies!" Emily took my hand and tugged.

"The round thing with the horses?"

"Yes, yes, yes, the merry-go-round," Josh shouted. "Me too, me too, me too."

A merry-go-round. In the French quarter, right here in Florida.

I knew what it would look like before I could even see it, and I felt dizzy. Dan took my elbow and gently propelled me in the right direction. The touch of his skin against mine was warm and comforting, but it gave me goosebumps all the same. I shivered. Dan's voice seemed to come from a long, long way away.

"Why don't we *all* go on?" he suggested. "Look, you guys, you're a little small for the horses, why don't you sit in that carriage first, and maybe later we'll figure out a way to get you riding a horse each?"

It was a merry-go-round by the Eiffel Tower. Just like the one in Paris, eight years ago, if a little smaller. It even played the same music.

The ground shifted beneath my feet and I stumbled. Dan caught me and cast a worried look.

"Are you sure you're okay? You look like you've seen a ghost."

I shook my head and held on tighter to his arms. Meanwhile, we had caught up with Emily and Josh who were doing an excited little dance in front of the momentarily still ride.

"You can take the children on a horse if you sit with one each." The deep voice of the carousel operator sliced through my thoughts, and I tried to summon a response. These were my children. I had to say something, do something, do right by them. I opened my mouth, but Dan spoke first.

"D'you know," he said, using a confidential tone that had the operator take a step closer to hear. "D'you know, I think we might do that the second time 'round, if that's at all okay. I'd like to claim this first ride for me and the children's mother. Perhaps the children can ride with us in the carriage drawn by that horse?"

He pointed to a golden steed he evidently had his eyes on, and one that was hitched to a red fairy tale carriage. The operator shrugged and spread his hands wide. "Sure, if that's what you want."

"We do," Dan assured him, and jollied the kids into the carriage, whispering to them all the while.

Then he turned to me. "Milady?" He bowed and offered his arm again. I laughed and took it, already surrendering to the inevitability of what was to come.

Dan helped me up the steps onto the merry-go-round and onto our horse, settling himself snugly behind me with his arms around my waist. I crossed my arms in front of my chest so I could put my hands on his forearms, holding him just below the elbow, completing the circle of embrace. Dozens of children, some with adults and some without, occupied the other horses, and the whole place was heaving, yet we were alone.

"You ready?" Dan asked for the third time in ten minutes, and this time, I answered.

"As ready as I ever will be."

Dan tightened his hold on me in response and laid his chin on my shoulder, nuzzling his face lightly into my hair.

The carousel started moving, and all the children erupted into noisy cheers. I could hear Josh and Emily behind us whooping with joy as 'round and 'round we went. I closed my eyes and let the wind ruffle my hair, enjoying the moment, taking deep breaths, waiting, waiting for Dan to speak. Finally, his voice whispered in my ear.

"Sophie Jones, will you, at long last, marry me?"

I squeezed his arms and turned slightly so he would be able to see me speak. For a moment, I didn't respond, just smiled and smiled, feeling the joy shine out of my eyes and seeing him respond even before he heard my answer. The moment stretched and swelled and swallowed us whole, the certainty between us almost visible, iridescent in the bright sunlight, our joy heightened by the sounds of people laughing all around us. At length, I spoke.

"Yes, Dan Hunter. Yes, I will marry you."

Epilogue

Dan and I were married very quietly, and very privately, at the Wandsworth Register Office on the first Saturday after we returned from the States. I wore a blue dress, simple, elegant, and deliberately un-bridey, and Dan donned a suit. Rachel was my witness, and Joe was Dan's. Emily was my bridesmaid and Josh my pageboy. Mum and Dad came up from Newquay, and Jodie flew in from LA. Joe, Mick, and Darren attended with their families, as did Jack and Richard. Dan begged Jenny to come, and eventually, she relented when we persuaded her that she was practically part of the family. There was no press, no release having been issued.

After the ceremony, we had a small party at our favorite Italian restaurant, which we had hired out for the day, our only concession to making a little fuss for our nuptials. We ate pizza and pasta and seafood aplenty, and we played '80s music and favorite rock songs on the restaurant's ancient sound system. In the evening, we danced.

The following week, we moved the former Jones family's possessions into Dan's house in Clapham. I sold my little house in Barnes and put the proceeds into a trust fund for the children. Over the course of the next few months, Dan became a legal stepfather to the children, and we were a proper family.

Evidently, our marriage didn't remain a secret forever, but the media frenzy, when it happened, was short-lived, because essentially, we were 'old news', and we liked it that way.

Dan continues to be the lead singer of Tuscq, and the band is currently in the throes of making another album. Over the past three years, the kids and I have toured with Tuscq twice, school terms permitting. Since Emily started school properly, I have been officially working as a sound engineer, and I often engineer alongside Richard when Tuscq lays down new songs.

Increasingly, the band gathers in Dan's studio for rehearsals and demos because I am now able to mix and master independently. This setup works well for us, and the kids have started taking instrument lessons, too. Joe is taking great pleasure in initiating Josh in the skill of drumming, and Emily is learning classical guitar with Darren. Isn't that weird and wonderful?

So after all this time, I *have* become the rock star's wife. It is, and it isn't, how I planned my life, but I'm ludicrously happy.

Right now, I have to rush off to a doctor's appointment. I'm thirty-nine, and I didn't really expect to do this whole pregnancy thing again, but I'm kind of looking forward to it now that it has happened. I just want to make sure that everything's okay before I break the news to Dan. I'll probably tell him tonight. Or maybe I'll drop around to the studio as soon as I'm done at the doctor's.

I can't wait to see the look on his face.

Acknowledgements

As always, a great many Thank You's are in order to honor the many people who contributed to the writing of this book. I couldn't have done it without you.

Wonderful husband—Jon. Thank you for absolutely everything!

Fabulous publishers—A massive thanks to Amy Lichtenhan and Katie Henson of Sapphire Star Publishing for your patient guidance along my publication road and for dealing with my many queries and questions, and to Devyn Jensen for fabulous admin support. A special thanks to my editor, Nancy S. Thompson, for her great feedback and constructive comments!

Rocking supporters of my work and my promotional campaigns—A big thank you to THE HUSH Rock Band, iconic rock photographer Nick Elliott, radio host extraordinaire Alex Lewczuk, and everyone at Siren 107.3 FM.

Tireless and patient advisors on all things to do with the music industry, especially sound recording and touring—A *huge* thank you to Jane Risdon for all her wonderful anecdotes and her time, and also to her friend, Barry John Bayliss of Gospel Oak Studio, Warwickshire. Cameron Tilbury, CEO of MapleStar Music & Media, has been a constant source of support and advice, going well above and beyond! A special thanks to Alex Lewczuk again for test-reading relevant sections…and the whole thing! Any remaining mistakes or errors are entirely my own.

Fabulous Beta-readers and writing buddies—Enormous thanks to Sue Fortin, Deborah Smith and Katie Mettner. You know how much your input means!

Outstanding friends and supporters during the writing of this novel—I cannot thank you enough for all you do, and you all absolutely rock! Big hugs to Anneli Purchase, Evelyn Chong, Heidi Bartlett, Inga Kupp-Silberg, JB Johnson, Jean Fullerton, Kate Verrier, Kim Nash, Les Moriarty, Linn B. Halton, Mandy Baggot, Melanie Robertson-King, Nova Reylin, Rea Sinfield, Samantha Stroh Bailey, Sharon Goodwin, Sheryl Browne, and Tobi Helton.

Coming Soon
From Nicky Wells

New Story! New Characters! Introducing:

Fallen For Rock

Love, life, loyalties. Nothing stays the same when Emily gets drawn into the world of rock...

Glossy and sophisticated, professional high-flyer Emily has no time for nonsense such as the rock music her ex-boyfriend Nate adored so much. Yet when she unexpectedly comes into possession of VIP tickets—access all areas—for new rock band phenomenon, MonX, she can't resist the temptation.

The fateful gig turns into more than one night and Emily finds herself strangely drawn to this new and unfamiliar, glittery world. However, only weeks later, MonX and her own universe fall apart, with devastating consequences for all. When MonX lead-singer, Mike, appeals for her help, she reluctantly embraces a new opportunity. But she soon discovers that while she may be a rock chick after all, a *groupie* she is not... Or is she?

Just exactly where do her loyalties lie? And what direction will her life take now that she's left behind everything she treasured?

Fallen For Rock is coming your way in the summer of 2014!

And There's More...

Nicky has a little surprise planned for you in late 2013. Watch this space... you'll love it!

About the Author

Nicky Wells is your ultimate rock chick author. Signed to US Publisher, Sapphire Star Publishing, Nicky writes **Romance That Rocks Your World**, featuring the rock star and the girl next door.

Nicky's books offer **glitzy, glamorous contemporary romance with a rock theme** ~ imagine Bridget Jones *ROCKS* Notting Hill!

Born in Germany, Nicky moved to the United Kingdom in 1993 and currently lives in Lincoln. In a previous professional life, Nicky worked as a researcher and project manager for an international Human Resources research firm based in London and Washington, D.C. Like her leading lady, Sophie, Nicky loves listening to rock music, dancing, and eating lobsters. When she's not writing, she's a wife, mother, occasional knitter, and regular contributor to The Midweek Drive show on Lincoln's Siren 107.3 FM. Rock on!

Visit Nicky at http://nickywellsklippert.wordpress.com/ where you can find articles, interviews, radio interviews and, of course, an ongoing update on her work in progress. You can also follow Nicky on Twitter and find her on Facebook. Nicky is a member of the Romantic Novelists' Association.

Also by Nicky Wells

Sophie's Turn (Rock Star Romance Trilogy, Part 1)
Sophie's Run (Rock Star Romance Trilogy, Part 2)